The Visitors

Arthur C Clarke Award Entry

Owen W Knight

Content compiled for publication by Richard
Mayers of Burton Mayers Books.

Cover artwork designed by Martellia Design

Copyright © 2022 Owen W Knight

First published by Burton Mayers Books 2022.
All rights reserved.

ISBN: **978-1-7396309-2-8**

Typeset in Garamond

www.BurtonMayersBooks.com

The translation of the *Aretalogy of Isis* is from *Religions of Rome: Volume II*, A Scourcebook, Cambridge University Press 1998, by Mary Beard, John North and Simon Price reproduced by kind permission of Mary Beard and John North.

Other books by Owen W Knight:

Another Life

The Invisible College Trilogy:

Book 1 *They Do Things Differently Here*
Book 2 *Dust and Shadows*
Book 3 *A Perilous Journey*

~ CONTENTS ~

Praise For Another Life

'Another Life is a beautiful and thought-provoking meditation on the meaning and purpose of life, seen through the lens of a mystery story steeped in English folklore... The book's narrative voice and its depiction of details from the natural world are outstanding.'

British Fantasy Society

'Owen Knight blends a sense of mystery and ancient spirituality with profound questions about personal identity. The narrative interweaves dreams, memories and present reality, as the reader is led forward towards the book's revelatory conclusion.'

Dr Mel Thompson, best-selling philosophy author

'Intriguing metaphysical folk-thriller... A fusion of reality, dreams and time jumps - that shines a light on the classic folklore legends of the green man and mixes lost love with a mystery tale.'

Matt Adcock, writer and film/book critic.

1 - PETER

Fourteen years ago, I saved the world.

Not alone, of course. Many in our closed community helped me overcome the misguided intentions of the Sect. They, the Sect, believed that I would bring knowledge. Knowledge that would bring them to permanent power, as predicted in a centuries-old prophecy. I knew nothing of this. They lured my family here to finalise their plan. Every word I spoke, they analysed for clues to unlock the secret of changing the Earth's axis. I was young, yet the inferred wisdom empowered me and drove me to find the way to prevent them from triggering an apocalypse.

I had friends who lost their lives in the final battle. No-one in the outside world knew, then or now, how close we had come to disaster. Nothing like it would ever happen again, or so I believed.

Yet now, there is a much greater danger. Again, its epicentre is here in Templewood. Only the villagers and our global network of connections are aware. The implications reach far beyond and across the entire planet.

I thought I could handle this myself, as a matter of pride. After all, fourteen years ago, I had helped rid Templewood of the greatest threat to humankind in its history. I was in my mid-teens, the end of childhood and the beginning of the loss of my youth. I must warn the world. Not yet, not yet… The scale of the resulting panic and riots would accelerate the danger.

I have learned from the events of recent months that I cannot do this unaided. I need help. Though I have access to people, expertise and resources here and within our global network, no individual possesses all the qualities I am looking for. We need inspired thinkers with original ideas to find solutions to this new and unforeseen challenge. We need them now before we reach the point where all is lost.

But whom can I trust? I have many friends and colleagues: Richard, Alice, Carlos, Dr Hadfield and my closest ally, Amit, whose loyalty I cannot question. I cannot put them in a position where they could be forced to betray me. Yet without my knowledge and insights into what is happening, there will be no hope for humanity. Through my connections, I have identified three promising recruits. They live in the outside world: creative, left-field thinkers with the persistence and willpower to conquer adversity. Strong women who have no ties to others and are impervious to bribes, blackmail, or other pressures.

I will contact them, send them a sign, those in whom I will place my trust. None of the three knows each other. I will put them in touch. I know others who will help me to communicate my message. Then, with Amit, we will be five. Five is important. If we are five, we have the possibility of resistance. How we will achieve this, I do not know. There are no big ideas but, with five of us, we will find a way. I must take care not to let anyone here know, as much for their safety as mine.

2 - RACHEL

Sunday 7th June: Rachel Opens the Box

The taxi ground doggedly up the gravel slope towards the nursing home. The building stood proud and solid, high in the wooded hills, defying the drifting mid-morning spring mist. The harsh stone walls glowed in the clearing light, their sombre form suppressing the sound of birdsong.

Rachel paid the driver without a word, conceding a nod to acknowledge his profuse thanks for the tip, a gesture calculated to excuse her resolve to avoid conversation. No-one stepped out to greet her. Not a person was to be seen other than two residents seated looking out from the upstairs rooms, their wan faces, grey and ghosted, reflected behind the windows.

Discovering the left-hand door was locked, she leaned into the right-hand front door, countering its initial resistance. Why do they always assume everyone is right-handed? The sound from her leather heels, although unembellished with metal tips, echoed around the hallway from the marble floors, summoning two pairs of brisk footsteps from a room behind the tall reception desk that stretched opposite the entrance.

'Good afternoon, Ms Robinson. I'm so relieved that you

were able to come at such short notice.' Her colleague nodded, the thermostat of his expression resting midway between solemn and indifferent. Even had Rachel not met Jane Goodson on several previous visits, she would have been in no doubt that she was the director of the clinic. Rachel was ambivalent towards her, secretly admiring her well-tailored appearance and brisk, efficient demeanour, while resenting her apparent affluence, founded upon the illness and misery of others. She considered her overlarge diamond brooch was too extravagant, with its inappropriate flower design reminiscent of lilies. Rachel imagined her hearing the ring of an old-fashioned cash register each time a painkilling tablet, a bedpan, or a change of sheets was called for.

'I've been prepared for weeks. I arranged to work from home so that I could respond quickly to any change.' Rachel immediately regretted sharing her thoughts. She had learned the habit of disclosing her emotions only with those who shared them. She suppressed the thought that, to Jane, death represented little more than the loss of a customer.

'Come into my office.' Mrs Goodson turned and gestured to Rachel to lead the way. She adopted a practised, half-smile intended to convey efficient professionalism, no doubt selected automatically from a gallery of expressions appropriate to each occasion.

Rachel took a seat opposite Mrs Goodson at the tidy, oak desk, placing her handbag and coat on the other of the pair. She admired the desk with its leather inlay. It bore only a telephone, a large leather notebook with a carefully placed Mont Blanc pen and a banker's lamp lit, presumably, for effect, the room being amply illuminated by the sun through the window.

'Thank you for your message,' said Rachel. 'I knew I had to expect it eventually. I'm grateful in a way that it's taken so long.'

'We try to prepare our clients' families as best we can: to strike a balance between acknowledging the possibility of an early unwelcome outcome with the need to plan regular visits, to make the best of the time available. The end of life is always sad; a sense of unfinished business can, for some people, be worse than the loss, initially, and may lead to an extension of grief.'

'This woman is unreal,' thought Rachel. 'It's like being lectured to at a management best practice seminar.' Rachel had suggested to her husband that Mrs Goodson had an algorithm to calculate and monitor the expected profit from each client. And that was another thing: when her father had first arrived at the nursing home, he was a patient. Over time, he had become a client.

'How much longer do you think he has?'

'We don't know for certain. The doctors say it's a matter of days, if not hours. For that reason, I have to ask you to confirm the DNR instruction should remain in place. You are perfectly entitled, as next of kin, to revoke it. It would not be unusual to do so, and you need not worry about confidentiality if you do change your mind.'

'Thank you, but that would go against his expressed wishes. He made his decision when in good health; we must respect it now that he is nearing the end. This is his moment, not mine.'

'I wish all our clients' families were so pragmatic. I don't make judgements; I understand that it's not easy to let loved ones go. I am pleased you are taking his instructions into account.'

'All you care about is your bills being paid and not being sued,' thought Rachel.

'I'd like to see him now, as there's so little time left. We can discuss any other matters before I leave.'

Rachel stood up and picked up her coat and handbag.

'Of course. I'll take you up myself,' said Mrs Goodson, walking round to Rachel's side of the desk.

The corridors were quiet. They passed a few staff: nurses, porters, who stepped aside and nodded to the women in silent greeting, eyes lowered, as they walked towards the lift.

The lift doors closed behind them with a respectful, soft clunk, reminiscent of a limousine. Mrs Goodson touched a control screen with her pass key and selected from the list of floor numbers displayed. The lift rose with no sense of movement or distance travelled; its doors opened silently on arrival at the third floor. Rachel suppressed the thought that 'clients' might be moved upwards through the building according to their proximity to death, assisting them towards a promised heaven. She conceded, with reluctance, that the home had taken great care in designing the interior to ensure a serene ambience, down to the detail of the floor tiles, which dampened the sound of footsteps.

Mrs Goodson knocked gently on the door. A male nurse opened it, nodded to her and walked away down the corridor. 'I'll leave you alone together. You'll remember to use the large green button attached to the bed if you need assistance. Please use it to let us know when you are about to leave the room.'

'So you can check I haven't smothered him?' thought Rachel.

'Your daughter's here to see you, Mr Robinson.'

Rachel closed the door behind her and drew up a chair next to the bed.

'How are you feeling, Dad? You're looking well.'

'You can stop that nonsense straightaway. You know how I am. Nothing's changed, other than the amount of time left. I sometimes imagine a giant salami slicer whittling away at my life. Anyway, enough of that — I'm pleased to see you. I've something important to tell you. You must take me into the garden. Bring my wheelchair over here, please.'

Rachel drew the chair towards the bed. 'Stay still. I'll help you,' she said as he struggled to sit upright. Rachel took her time to lift his frail body, almost bereft of flesh beneath the skin, into the wheelchair.

'And don't let them know we're going outside. They'll send someone to follow us, to listen in to our conversation.

They probably are now. You know the rooms are all wired up. They say it's to monitor our welfare and safety. I can assure you that there's more to it than that.'

In a far corner of the garden, Rachel's father repeated the words he had so often said to her over the past few months: that he was unlikely to see her again. This time he confirmed that he had been told he was close to the end. It was time to say his goodbyes. They had prepared for this moment for a long time. Now that it had arrived, Rachel accepted the news with a sense of relief. The burden of her father's chronic, barely palliated suffering would soon be over, a blessing to both of them. They had already rehearsed this moment and worked through their life memories. Both had agreed that, when this time came, it would be treated without drama, emotion or prolongation.

Rachel listened to her father's instructions. She must visit his house and locate a box hidden under a plank in the cupboard beneath the staircase. The plank was marked with a blue stain. Inside the box, she would find two documents. One was his will; the other would contain details of an assignment he insisted she must undertake.

*

Rachel pulled the rug out from the stair cupboard and quickly identified and removed the marked plank. She lifted the box onto the kitchen table. With care, determination and perseverance, she struggled to lift one corner of the box to allow her to wedge the edge of the plank that had concealed it inside. The next step was to lever the lid and reach her hand into the box to locate the two items. She withdrew them slowly, taking care not to tear or otherwise damage them. She placed the box onto the floor to make more space on the table to inspect them.

The grey-yellow faded will was folded twice, top to bottom, its dozen or so pages stiff and dry. Paper flag markers, indicating the locations of signatures, drooped from the right-hand edge. The second item, an envelope, was thin and secured with a seal. Rachel inspected the heavy red wax. At the age of nearly thirty, it was the first she had seen.

Rachel procrastinated, anxious to confirm the provisions of the will and to uncover the mystery hidden inside the envelope, yet afraid of what both might contain. Too young; her father had died too young, barely into his fifties.

She was not a wealthy woman. She felt secure in her career as a teacher, with a modest income that exceeded her needs. She lived alone, in a simple flat. She felt secure knowing that her accumulated savings were sufficient to cover her mortgage payments for up to a year. Living alone did not trouble her: she enjoyed the freedom to spend her leisure time as she chose, without the need to compromise with others. She felt guilty that the expectation of a bequest from her father, shared equally with her sisters, would further consolidate her independence and security. It would render her free from future uncertainty for as long as she continued to be prudent.

A cup of tea would give her time to steady herself. She had brought some teabags and milk with her (she had emptied the house of all food several weeks ago when her father went into the hospice).

Reinvigorated by the tea, Rachel regained her decisiveness. She had come to her father's house to seek out these documents. Was she going to leave without opening them? No. The will, that must be the first thing. There was no point in worrying about the envelope, whose existence was presumably known only to her and her father. Reading the will was a normal consequence of death, a duty and a responsibility. Once she had read it, she could either act on it or destroy it.

She unfolded the will and opened it gently, wary that she could easily tear or crack the brittle paper. There were no surprises.

Thursday 11th June: Spies

He had not long passed fifty when illness descended swiftly to announce an impending and unavoidable end. It was only then that Rachel had become curious about the details of her father's occupation. He knew he was terminally ill, concealing his condition for as long as possible, including from her mother. When she had asked the question as a child, her mother had told her that he 'worked in security'. For years, she had an image of him in uniform deciding whether to let people enter premises, to refuse them, or to conduct a search of their person and belongings. As she passed through her teens into adulthood, she refined this view to imagine him as a sort of bodyguard, an assumption she had made from the amount of time spent away from home. She had not thought to ask him the question directly. Whenever she approached the subject, he gave vague answers and steered the conversation elsewhere. He was not the sort of man to harangue. He would frustrate questioners by his controlled evasiveness, wearying them into giving up.

She recalled an occasion in her early twenties when she believed he came close to opening up. It was after a family celebration. The guests had left. Her parents were relaxed and jolly from an unusual, but not excessive, amount of alcohol. He had suggested to her mother a final nightcap before going to bed. She replied that it was not a good idea, as they both had to go to work the next day and had had quite enough. Without thinking and for no real reason, Rachel had said, 'It wouldn't be good for a spy to be drunk on the job.'

As soon as she had spoken the word, she regretted her choice. It was not a word she had ever used in her parents' company, and she had never heard either of them use it. She sensed her father raise his guard. The smile remained on his face, though his body language changed. It was as if he had been caught out. She was surprised by his involuntary reaction and more so when he responded in a matter-of-fact tone of voice.

'It depends what you mean by a spy. There are different sorts — at least three. There are those who go out to observe people or gather information: infiltrators. Then there are those who monitor the activities of others, occasionally interacting with them, remotely.'

He looked her in the eye, still smiling.

'And the third?'

'There are those who stir up mischief by creating misleading scenarios, causing chaos.'

Rachel smiled back at him. She wanted him to keep talking; the best way would be to make light of it. She placed her hands on her hips, shaking her head from side to side. 'Which category do you fall into?'

She lowered one hand to lean on the back of a chair, to appear casual and to encourage him to respond. It may have been the effects of the modest accumulation of alcohol to which she was unaccustomed. Her hand missed the chair and she fell sideways onto the floor, banging her head on the table leg as she fell. Both parents fussed after her, asking whether she was alright and suggesting she lie down. No harm was done other than to end the conversation. It was time for bed.

The next day Rachel's mother suggested it was best not to ask about her father's occupation. She hinted — nothing specific — that it could put him, and them, at risk if other people were to know. It would be best to forget about it. Rachel's mother died shortly before her father's death, in a road accident on her way to visit him. He was left distraught. Rachel believed that it was his resolve to put his affairs in order that kept him alive for a few weeks longer.

*

Rachel had moved to the west of the country to take up her undergraduate place. Her A-level years had been stressful. The new city provided her with a cultural and emotional blanket to immerse herself in. After graduation, she was reluctant to leave its comforts. She applied and was accepted for a permanent position in the university library. She believed that this would help her to remain secure in familiar surroundings. She thrived on the company of each new generation of students. With each year, her self-assurance grew. She knew that she had a contribution to make towards their development. The few who annoyed her, or held incompatible or unacceptable values, she tolerated, reasoning that in three, at the most four, years they would no longer be a part of her life. Four full-time years in the library was enough to give her the confidence that she had more to offer. She decided to move into teaching, to share her enthusiasm for literature, to inspire new generations with purpose and pleasure.

Her altruism was not supported by the system and quickly led to frustration and disillusionment. It became clear, both to her and many she worked with, that the education system was flawed and inflexible. She tried on several occasions to make improvements, offering practical recommendations. Eventually, the lack of responsiveness and imagination (so she thought) and unwillingness to change things that were not mandated for change wore her down.

Her worst experiences were when she worked briefly in another part of the country at a selective state secondary school. So much energy was mischannelled into fundraising: to raise the 'odd half a million' or more from parents for a new science wing or sports hall — things the Government should be paying for.

There were two occasions she remembered well. The first was an evening when parents were invited to cheap wine and curly canapés, before being lectured by a blue-rinse speaker who told the parents to 'think how much you can afford to contribute monthly and then double it'. Rachel's annoyance was partly due to knowing that many of the gifted children who had passed the entrance examination were from low-income families.

On the second occasion, the parents were given a

presentation by someone she discovered to be a professional fund-raiser, paid the equivalent of eighty thousand pounds a year by the school. His line to parents was 'as stakeholders, think how much you should be investing in the school'. She had wished that a parent had stood up and asked how much it was recommended the staff, as stakeholders, should give. None did.

'There are no big ideas.'

Thursday 11th June: The Envelope

Rachel read the document, a printed note addressed to her personally, headed with her name in her father's handwriting:

Rachel, my dearest Rachel

I am nearing the end; it is imminent. And so, you must believe and attend to what I have to say. My body is weary, but my mind remains alert and fully functioning. I emphasise this to convince you that what I am about to say is factual and of the utmost importance, not just to you but to the entire world. I have never made demands upon you before, but it is essential that you follow this through, for the sake of humanity.

You must embark on a journey on which you will discover secret, life-changing knowledge. How will you know this to be true? I assure you that you will be in no doubt of its significance. You will require the assistance of four others. Two you will meet as a consequence of this message; the fourth and fifth you will meet in the company of your new companions.

How will you find them? You must reserve a table for three at the address on the enclosed note for the first Thursday following my death. Exactly two weeks later, the three of you will travel together to a specified destination where the real challenge will begin. Reserve the table in the name of Templewood. The others will be instructed to meet you there. You must memorise the contents of the note and destroy it. All will become clear.

Guard this information well. Do not share it with others. There will be dangers and there will be rewards. I wish you success.

Your loving father.

Could this be a joke? The final gesture of someone whose working life was centred on deceit. The urgency, almost desperation, of the message convinced her of its sincerity. It would do no harm to arrange the meeting, to compare notes with the other two. At worst, it would be an interesting, if not amusing, encounter. Supposing the other two did not turn up? The date and location might not be convenient for them. How was he able to specify such a precise date and time? Surely, he could not have predicted the exact date he would die (it would be a few days yet). There was no indication of when the note was written. He must have known how long he had to live and had written and hidden the document with this in mind. There would be no harm done; she would take the single opportunity to make contact and follow the instruction.

Rachel peered again into the envelope. Inside she found a small piece of paper she had missed on her first examination. Three pieces of information were listed. The name of what sounded to be a wine bar (she did not recognise the name — unsurprising as new bars were opening regularly), the time, but not the date, proposed for the rendezvous and a string of five numbers. She turned the slip over. Handwritten across the centre in a different, copperplate style — as if to represent a calling card — the words *L'art embellit la vie* provided her with no clue as to their meaning or significance.

3 - LISA

Thursday 11th June: Rumblings

'There must be more to life...'

Lisa gazed out of a window on the second floor of the office block.

'Which one will it be today,' she thought as she gazed in turn at three men and a woman in the street. Three were standing stationary, two in doorways, one in the centre of the precinct, the fourth sat on a street bench. Each appeared to be engaged in their own thoughts, studying their phones or a newspaper or, in the case of the seated man, eating from a paper carrier bag. Lisa instinctively identified them as a group — each one alone, yet the distance separating them was unnaturally uniform. Which one would follow her today?

Lisa returned to her desk and gazed across the rows of people staring at screens, some in conversation with colleagues, others making notes, in deep thought or leaning back. Some drank coffee. Those who were not sitting walked at a uniform pace. None exhibited any signs of joy, stress, or urgency. It was like being in an animal research laboratory, she thought. A controlled environment whose occupants had no sense of real purpose, or awareness of why they were here.

Lisa was not contemptuous of her fellow workers. She enjoyed their company outside of the office, usually on a Thursday evening at a nearby wine bar. Thursday was the evening of choice, with just Friday to get through before the weekend. On Fridays, everyone would leave for home, or whatever arrangement they had planned, as early as their work permitted.

No, the problem was that everyone appeared just to be 'getting on with it': grinding out each day, complying with the unspoken convention not to complain, other than to occasionally remark 'only one more day to get up early'.

Lisa worked as the internal IT customer service manager for the provincial office of a major international city insurance broker. She liked to do things properly; it was an obsession. She would list and tick off every possible task both in her mind and as a record in case questions were to be asked later, or a problem recurred.

She was employed on a rolling three-month contract which some of her friends regarded as lacking in security. Lisa saw it as liberating, an escape route. In the worst case, she would only have to endure a few weeks before becoming free. And the pay was good.

Her department's role was to provide an interface between the business users of the company's operational computer systems and the IT support staff. Reported problems were logged, prioritised, scheduled for correction, their progress monitored, and fixes implemented.

There was no doubt in anyone's mind of the usefulness of what she did. It was just that it was not possible to be seen as excelling, unlike computer system development, where a new system could make colleagues' working lives easier or more productive. She was dealing with errors, things that should not have happened and problems she had not created. The best she could do was to put things back to where they were before the problem occurred. She was the goalkeeper; she did not score goals.

She was frustrated that there was so much more that she could do to improve efficiency. If only someone in management with authority to take decisions would do so, and act upon her ideas and recommendations. Over the years, she had learned that, in large companies, the culture of the status quo prevailed. No-one would take decisions that would expose their careers to risk.

'There are no big ideas.'

It did not help that the company's systems were archaic, built on legacy technology. She was dependent on others to provide technical solutions. All she could do was to prioritise and monitor. What made life worse was that the director of the back office had confided in her that the business would collapse if the systems were out of operation for three days. Lisa was aware that some parts of the legacy systems were no longer supported by third-party suppliers. The programmers supporting these systems were equally outmoded — contract workers with scarce, outdated skills. People paid even more than she was to hold the systems together in an electronic spider's web. No doubt they were looking forward to the day when they had saved enough money to travel or buy a hotel or start some other business that they could control and enjoy. In moments of extreme pressure, she had considered whether it would be morally correct to report the dire state of the company's operations to the Financial Conduct Authority as posing a risk to customers. This would mean breaching the confidentiality terms of her contract (could she be sued?). There must surely be some form of protection for whistleblowers, but, at best, she would never be offered another position in the business sector. She would not be able to continue to contribute to her mother's care home fees. She had also discovered shortcomings in the IT backup and security procedures. Her specialist knowledge of computer security gave her an advantage over her colleagues. She duly reported her discoveries to protect herself and to enhance her acquired reputation of integrity.

Lisa was popular with her business user clients. She was regarded as open, transparent and 'a nice woman'. This alone was not good enough for her; something had to change. One day it did, when she received a direct message at work, on her personal mobile phone, in a private social media account. Usually, she would ignore such messages or, depending on the platform, delete them or consign them to junk. Before doing so, she made a point of looking at the sender. Her next step would be to block them or, in the case of unsolicited marketing messages, reporting them to the Information Commissioner. She considered this to be a public duty.

This message was different; it insisted on her attention by naming her, both by first and family names. It must be from someone she knew or who knew her — she had set up the account with an alias. It was non-threatening, polite… It addressed her as 'Dear Lisa', not to be expected in this medium.

She was invited — no, urged — to join two other female invitees at a wine bar, whose name and location were provided, at a set time and date. There she would learn something of life-changing interest. She was to ask, on arrival, to join a table booked in the name of Templewood. Not a common name, but not so unusual as to be curious. It hinted at a distant provenance from the Knights Templar, whose history she had read avidly in her teens, along with those of the Cathars and other groups linked with mystery and esotericism. The details were followed by a five-digit number (what on earth could that mean?) and a final line with the words *L'art embellit la vie*. Lisa's French was competent, although she would not claim to speak it *couramment*. Although the phrase was simple enough to translate, its significance was elusive. Perhaps she would be enlightened at the meeting, if she chose to attend.

Thursday 11th June: After Work

'Hi, Lisa. Fancy coming for a drink?'

'Hi, Jonathan. You know, I might just do that. I was thinking about working late on this new problem that came up today. It's a bit of a mystery, but it isn't affecting operations seriously and, who knows, if I sleep on it, I might come up with some ideas.'

'The usual place, round the corner?'

'Yes, let's do that. Do you mind if we keep it to the two of us? There's something I'd like to discuss with you. I'd like your opinion.'

'Sounds intriguing. How could I possibly refuse? How long will you be?'

'Can you give me fifteen minutes to tidy a few things up?'

'Great.'

It was unusual for Lisa to leave work as early as six o'clock. She had never felt constrained by the concept of a 'professional day'. She would joke with friends with less demanding jobs that it meant 'God sends the hours and I work them'. Today there was no pressing urgency to work late and, being a Thursday, it would be easier to find a quiet table at this time rather than later.

She and Jonathan found a spot away from people they knew. Lisa poured two glasses of wine. They spent a few minutes discussing their respective days in the office before moving on to other topics.

'Have you seen the national news today?' said Jonathan.

'No, I've been so busy that I haven't had a chance. So, what's happened now? Not more bad news?' said Lisa.

'It depends on how you look at it. The Government is introducing a raft of new restrictions in the hope of slowing climate change.'

'Not more, surely? They seem to add to them every month, not that we see much action, just more words,' said

Lisa. 'Don't get me wrong, I'm all in favour of anything, well, almost anything, that will protect our future. It's just that so many things increase costs and make it difficult for poorer families and individuals to cope. What's the latest, then?'

'It's mainly about new laws to drastically reduce fossil fuel usage and to get rid of them in certain cases.'

'No surprise there, then. Mind you, it wasn't that long ago that they brought forward the introduction of regulations in some areas. Cars mainly — getting rid of all diesels within ten years. It's still too long a wait. I don't see why they can't implement this sooner; all they have to do is offer the right incentives, like the ones they've introduced for electric vehicles.'

'The latest announcements are much more drastic,' said Jonathan, leaning across the table to top up both glasses.

'Well, come on then. Don't keep me in suspense.'

'All household heating and power to be electric within five years, with oil and gas eliminated.'

'Wow! The cost of conversion will be enormous. There probably aren't enough engineers to roll it out to every home. And the cost of electricity, over gas in particular, will hit a lot of people hard, as I was saying.'

'The argument is that by delivering power and heating by electricity, there is much more flexibility in providing the original power source. You can generate electricity from generators, water, solar, geothermal, wave power, as well as from gas and coal. If every home, business and factory were to run entirely on electricity, it would become easier to chip away at the use of fossil fuel sources, or to withdraw them at short notice.'

'I can see the logic of that,' said Lisa.

'Getting rid of coal was an obvious target but removing dependence on gas is a good thing for several reasons. As well as being a limited, non-renewable resource, there are the political implications and benefits.'

'Ah, yes. Producing countries cutting off supplies or

imposing massive price hikes,' said Lisa.

'Sabotage of pipelines is another risk. If any countries, or insurgents in the countries crossed by the pipeline, have a grievance, it's all too easy to destroy them. You can't continuously monitor and react to incidents covering thousands of miles of pipeline.'

'Are there any other changes?'

'You won't believe this — a one hundred per cent tax on red meat! And all single-use plastic is to be banned from food packaging within three years, with a few exceptions for health and hygiene purposes. Now, there's something close to your heart.'

'Really? That's good news on both counts. It's taken them long enough to do something about the plastic, although even more price increases for the less well-off who find it difficult to make the transition.'

Lisa had been vegetarian for several years, both for health reasons and to help reduce the emissions produced in the production chain. She had found it difficult at first and had been surprised by the foods she missed, even small things such as anchovies. It had been time-consuming, examining the labels of food products to check suitability for vegetarians. Once she had got into the routine, she took the trouble to check for other non-sustainable ingredients, such as palm oil. Her one regret was the likely future change in the landscape. If she were to be honest, she remained sceptical that cow farts could do so much damage. What would replace the green and pleasant fields of sheep, cattle and free-range pigs?'

'I forgot to mention, it's not just this country that's introducing these changes, there are ten others, ten out of the world's twenty largest countries by population.'

'That must represent what, about half the world's population?'

'It's just over a half and, as you would expect, includes most of the major economies.'

'It's about time they started working together. It's a

shame that it takes an imminent global catastrophe to trigger action. Let's hope something comes of it; there have been so many promises and false starts, not to mention the lack of detailed planning and costing to match the hype. It tires me to think about it.'

Lisa flopped back in her seat. Jonathan noticed that she was drifting into a reverie. He decided to change the subject to the topic that had prompted their meeting.

'I'm very keen to hear about this top secret matter you want to discuss,' said Jonathan.

'It's not really a secret; more of a mystery. I received an unusual message today: an invitation from someone I don't know or, if I do, didn't declare themselves. Normally I'd disregard such things — they could be from some weirdo who might turn out to be dangerous. This was different. The person knew my name and was almost imploring me to meet two other women in a wine bar I've not heard of. It said I would learn something 'life-changing' — not a phrase I warm to: too overdramatic and salesy, or hinting of serious injury. I've looked up the wine bar to check that it exists and its location. Here, let me show you on my phone. Do you know it?'

Jonathan paged through the website, his expression curious, with no hint of alarm.

'I've heard of it. I haven't been there, even though it's not far from the office. It's in an OK area. It's not as though it's in a no-go part of the city.'

'That's what I thought. However mysterious and enticing the invitation, personal safety is obviously an important factor. And it's arranged for early evening. I could leave at any time if it didn't go well. I can't imagine what it will be about.'

'Any idea who the other two women are? Do you know them?'

'It didn't say. I imagine it's as much a mystery to them as it is to me.'

4 - EMILY

Thursday 11th June: Memories

Every day, Emily set aside twenty minutes alone to talk to Peter. Fourteen years had passed since she had last seen him or had any form of contact. The conversation took place in her head, in the way that you would talk to a relative at their graveside. She would tell him her news, share her aspirations and her fears. Her brother, seventeen months younger than her, would be twenty-eight now. She wondered how he had changed. Whether he had met someone and had a family, whether he was too busy with the commitment he had made to the cause when he decided to remain in Templewood after that dramatic summer all those years ago, or whether...

Emily had remained single. She was regarded as outgoing and sociable by her friends and colleagues, who frequently tried to find her a match. She would go along with their good-natured attempts and would sometimes go on a date, or two, or three until she pulled back. She would explain the importance of her love for friends and companionship, yet she could not offer more. There was always the possibility that Peter might need her. It would be unfair to commit to others.

Her circle understood her need for independence. She shared little about her relationship with Peter, other than that he lived far away. They assumed she was in contact by phone or online. Explaining her daily meditative homage would seem weird. It was essential for Peter to remain a distant figure, to protect him.

*

'Why not choose a course away from London, Emily? I'm not trying to drive you away. On the contrary, I enjoy having you around the house. It's much better than being on my own. It's not too late to change your mind.' Catherine was delighted that her daughter had achieved — no, surpassed — the grades required to confirm the places on offer for university.

Her A-level time had been a period of recovery from the drama of the Templewood Summer. A time to absorb herself in work, not only the set tasks but to develop and extend her knowledge of her chosen subjects, to be able to demonstrate her capacity for thought.

'You should be applying for Oxford or Cambridge, with all the benefits that a degree from there would bring. Living away from home would be good for you: having a balance between work and study — the fun of the social life with fellow students, house-sharing and all that. Although you'd be living in for the first year.'

'That's precisely the point, Mum. Going to uni in London means I can live at home, save money and have fewer distractions.'

*

When she was halfway through her English course, Emily decided that journalism offered the promise of a career. Investigative journalism appealed to her sense of justice: to expose wrongdoing and bad situations and to help improve the world. She had not realised that the large conventional channels would not give her an interview. Regardless of however good a degree she might achieve, she would not be graduating from the 'right' university. Perhaps she should have taken her mother's advice and tried for Oxford.

She decided to take the long route, to work her way up through a local newspaper. If the quality of her work were recognised, she would attract the attention of the quality publications, who would surely make her offers. None arrived. Eventually, she acknowledged this truth and relocated to the West Country. Within a year, she had moved through three local and regional papers. Each time it became clear that her employers had no appetite for uncovering news of injustice and scandals. So often, in the momentum of a story, culpability would be attributed to a local business owner, whose advertising budget the paper could not or would not afford to lose.

'All they're interested in printing is accounts of petty crime, road accidents and council meetings. There are no big ideas.'

Her rolling contract was about to end. She had decided not to renew and had confirmed her decision to her employers. With a few days remaining, her editor, Jamie, arranged a final meeting to dissuade her.

'We're very pleased with the work you do for us. I thought that, given that you don't have another position to go do, we might be able to persuade you to stay on. I've had a word upstairs and I am delighted to be able to offer to increase your rate,' said Jamie.

'I'm grateful to you for that, and it's good to hear that my work is valued. It's not about the money, though. I don't believe the paper can offer the type of challenge I need. By that, I mean I want to be able to change things, to make the world a better place. I know that sounds glib and, you're right, I don't have another position lined up. I don't feel I can continue reporting the same old things in such a bland way.'

'I can understand how you feel. We've discussed the constraints the owners are under, especially given declining paper edition sales and the need to protect reducing advertising revenue. You really need to be on a national, to give you the opportunity to change the world and I do believe you have the talent for it.'

'Thank you. Maybe I should have read political science instead of English, to have honed my ideas and to have a piece of paper that validates my credentials. I realised too late that, regardless of whatever ability I might have, I'd made unfortunate choices of subject and which uni.'

Jamie looked at his watch.

'Look, it's nearly twelve-thirty, let's grab a spot of lunch. I'd like to hear more of your political views.'

'Now that sounds like a proper journalist talking. I thought the days of liquid lunches were over!' said Emily, laughing.

'Come on, this is my treat.'

*

'I guessed it would be quiet on a Thursday lunchtime. People are saving themselves for the evening,' said Jamie. 'Have you decided what you'd like to eat?'

'I'd be happy to share a bottle of wine and a couple of rounds of sandwiches, if that's OK.'

'Suits me fine. Let's do that. Excuse me while I go to the bar.'

Jamie returned with an opened bottle and two glasses.

'Great. Now, tell me how you'll go about changing the world, once you get the chance. I know you hold, how shall I put it, fairly radical views?'

'That could take more than a lunchtime, but I'll do my best. Yes, my views are radical, although they're not extreme or revolutionary, except in a figurative sense. I believe that what this country needs is a complete overhaul of Government. By that, I mean the way it's governed. We can't keep recycling the mantras of a ruling party of self-interested, xenophobic crowd-pleasers. There's no accountability, or even transparency, about most of what they do and, all the while, they're accumulating God knows how much information on every citizen to ensure they can prevent any possibility of revolt. Look how personal freedoms are being eroded, too. It infuriates me that they have the hypocrisy to criticise what the Chinese are doing in Hong Kong while this country is moving more and more in the same direction.'

Emily cocked her head and returned Jamie's smile. He had heard this much before.

'There's rather a lot to respond to, Emily. Where shall I start? Have you ever thought of leaving journalism to go into politics?'

'Often. The problem is that the task is so enormous. It requires a complete rethinking of the system. The possibility of getting any traction for radical ideas is remote. No-one will listen to a lone individual, standing as an independent. There's no chance of a novice politician forming a credible new party. You would have to start by working from within an existing party. That would mean either those in power effectively voting themselves out or aligning with factions in the others, people who are more concerned with destroying the system than replacing it with something better — the Robin Hood approach. There has to be a better way of doing things that makes the world a fairer place while keeping the trade structures that bind us in friendship to the rest of the world. Look how the present Government is trying to get out of providing aid. They seem to think of it as charity or something to be given in return for something back. Equality of nations and their populations is so universally important, and part of that is granting development aid to those less fortunate. What they fail to recognise is how aid is a force for peace. We have to stop trying to be insular and thinking that this country occupies a special place in the world. It's just new colonialism. It's so obvious that aid encourages trade, which in turn encourages friendship and brings peace.'

'If you had your own way, what would you do to change the system?'

'In an ideal world, we would dispense with political parties. People would vote for policies rather than parties.

The party system is like the Catholic church: you have to accept everything, rather than pick and choose the ideas you believe in.'

'How would your idea work then? Are you saying we'd abolish MPs?'

'No, we could keep the six hundred and fifty MPs. We'd vote for them in a different way, still along regional lines, but by Government department and policy. Let me explain. There are at present twenty-three ministerial departments: the Home Office, Ministry of Defence, Education, Treasury and so on. Let's call it twenty-six, to simplify the maths. The present constituencies would be replaced by twenty-five new regions and metropolitan areas. Within each of these, voters would each vote for a candidate for their area for each of the twenty-six departments, giving the same number, six hundred and fifty, MPs. The difference would be that each MP would be not only local but a specialist in a department, selected by their constituency as the best for the job and meeting the needs of their region. Each department's twenty-five elected MPs would then select the head of their department and the heads of each department would then elect the Prime Minister. To achieve a balance, everyone should vote for a first and second choice for each post.'

'This would create an enormous burden on the electorate to understand all of the candidates' policies and to differentiate them. Do you think many people would bother to do so?'

'You could argue that. On the other hand, at present, an individual candidate is canvassing on the basis of a predetermined set of policies, many of which could be irrelevant to their constituents. With my system, the choice would be between local candidates prioritising specific local policies, which should encourage more interest. With the current system, local issues sway the voting disproportionally. People might be voting, understandably, to stop a steelworks or car plant from being closed down.

This single issue might mean they vote for a candidate whose party holds objectionable views on race or immigration, but they are forced to take the package. Under the new system, they would be voting for separate business and Home Office candidates. They get the best fit for their views in each case.'

'There are certainly some advantages. And it doesn't get over the existing problems of the representation of minority groups. Mind you, I think that some of those will be solved as the older people with entrenched views die off.'

'I agree. There is a solution to that though: to give weight to votes according to life expectancy. We should respect the fact that the young are going to have to live with the consequences of long-term policies for longer than the old, and so weight their votes accordingly.'

'How would that work?'

'For the sake of argument, let's assume that average life expectancy for everyone is eighty years. A twenty-year-old would have to live with the consequences of a policy on climate change, for example, for up to sixty years, whereas a seventy-year-old would only have to for ten. The younger person's vote should therefore be weighted accordingly, for example counting as eighty, as opposed to the older person's ten.'

'Wow, you have thought this through. I'm impressed! I can't see the older electorate supporting the idea, though.'

'Who knows? In time, the collective, more humanistic views of the younger generations will gain momentum. I'm sure that, in time, this will eventually force such a change. For the time being, if I could find the ideal position on a national or international newspaper, I could arguably find myself in a better position to influence, rather than in politics.'

'How would the selection of local candidates work, with no political parties to decide? There has to be a limit on numbers, or the process would be unworkable.'

'That's a good question. I don't pretend to have all of

the answers. This is undoubtedly one of the challenges. You could set the candidate deposits at a high amount. Even financially disadvantaged candidates should find it possible to raise money from sponsorship if their policies are credible and have broad appeal. There has to be a vetting system to eliminate, for example, people with unspent criminal records. There's also an opportunity to bar people with a vested interest in businesses linked to the position. This would help to wipe out the sort of cronyism that goes on now. I'm sure that, with the will, it would be possible to create a fair and inclusive process to enable the selection of suitable candidates.'

Jamie glanced at his watch.

'Hey, time's moving on; we'd better get back to work. Interesting thoughts. I could continue this discussion all day. Well, Emily, I certainly wish you luck. You deserve to do well. Whether or not you decide to come back to our paper, do keep in touch. If I think of any friends of friends who could help you elsewhere, I'll let you know.'

Tuesday 16th June: The Message

Emily arrived at work early. Her sleep had been broken by the sirens of emergency vehicles attending what she would later discover to be a major incident about a mile from her flat. Her instinct, once it became clear that many vehicles were mobilised, was to get dressed and seek out a possible story. She was in the bathroom when a colleague from the newspaper rang to let her know that he and others were already on to the incident. It would be better if she would take over the continuity of the story later in the morning from the office. He would call her at nine to apprise her of the 'current situation', to 'pass the baton on'.

She arrived at the office well before nine to find several people were already working. She poured a coffee from the machine and took it to her booked hot desk for the day, ready to take out her laptop from its bag. A personally addressed stamped and franked envelope awaited her. Someone knew she was expected — and that she would be at that desk.

'Who could this be from? No-one writes letters to newspapers these days, other than to editors to comment or moan about an article printed in a previous edition. If someone wanted to give a tip-off for a story they would email or telephone, the latter in particular if they wished to remain anonymous for whatever reason: privacy, fear, malice...'

She waited until lunchtime to open the envelope. A walk around the city docks would allow her to read it away from curious eyes. It might contain something she would not want others to see. She sat at an empty bench and took a sip of coffee and a bite of her sandwich. A glance around confirmed that no-one else was nearby.

'Let's have a look at this.'

At the top of the page, in copperplate lettering, she immediately recognised the phrase, *'L'art embellit la vie'*. It could only be from Peter. He had said, on the day she left Templewood with her mother, that she should look out for a sign from him, however long it might take. Something they would both understand without being specific. She had given up hope of hearing from him. It had been fourteen years. Her joy at receiving the letter was tempered by the brevity of the message. It offered no greeting nor any news. Just an instruction to visit a church in a small village some twenty miles outside of the city, where she was to look at the stained-glass windows. She was to do this on the coming Saturday, between ten and eleven o'clock. What could it mean? Why not explain in the letter? At least he was still alive. She reasoned that, as it was addressed to her and sent by recorded delivery to the newspaper office, someone else might open it. He wanted to check that only she would recognise it as a message of significance.

Emily usually worked Monday to Friday unless covering

an exceptional weekend event. Her natural waking time paid no regard to Saturdays and Sundays. The church was easy enough to find; she was surprised that the door was not locked. There was no-one inside. The interior was clean, tidy and well-maintained. The smell of beeswax, oak and cool stone floors took her back to the last time she had visited a church, in the Templewood days.

When she was a child, Emily's mother would take her and Peter to visit churches on their infrequent days out. Whereas Peter found them boring, Emily took pleasure in recognising the variations of architectural and decorative features. And so it was here: she took her time to examine the embroidered hassocks set out on almost every pew. Some decorated simply with trees and flowers, others personalised to their owners, who presumably sat in the same seats every week, a recognition of their place in the accepted hierarchy. A few were dedicated to historical events, local or national, or commemorated those killed in battle or lost at sea. It would have been interesting to come here on a Sunday to see how many hassocks would be in use. But Peter wanted her to come here on a day when the church would be empty.

She walked around the nave, starting with the north wall (the unholy side), examining the stained glass and the statues and busts of saints and an occasional local historical figure. There was no hurry. She crossed in front of the altar to the south wall, where the window designs were larger and more prominent with the sun behind them. She had no idea of what it was she was supposed to be looking for. The windows were interesting enough, representing a range of styles and periods, including art deco. One image of a radiant setting sun reminded her of a nineteen-fifties domestic front door. She completed her circuit of the nave at the entrance before walking back along the south wall to her favourite: a Pre-Raphaelite design of three figures staring and pointing down into a pool of water, where a fourth figure was stepping in, about to be baptised or blessed. A shame there was no descriptive label. She gazed at it for a few minutes, admiring the good looks and implied purity of the figures and the bold clarity of the colours. The construction of the image drew her gaze from to the centre, in widening circles towards the outside, mirroring the ripples in the pool and ending at a signature inscribed in the bottom right-hand corner. Perhaps the artist was well known. She tried without success to read the painted handwriting. And then it clicked. It was not a signature; she read the words out aloud: *L'art embellit la vie.*

This was what she was intended to discover, but why? There was no other message in the window, not in word form. Having followed the instructions from the letter, she was so close. There was no way she could give up now.

Emily looked around her immediate surroundings. There was no clue to be seen. The only object close to the window was a low shelf of hymn and prayer books.

'The figures in the window are pointing downwards — there must be something hidden in one of these.'

She kneeled to face the uppermost of the three rows. It would take too long to go through each book if that's where the clue was to be found. Each was neatly positioned. Despite their age, they appeared in good condition, save one that had an upturned corner visible where someone must have accidentally creased the page. She would straighten it out.

She took the hymn book from the shelf and opened it. It was not a crease; a slip of paper dropped to the floor. She picked it up and turned it over…

L'art embellit la vie.

The phrase was followed by the name of what she would discover later that day to be a wine bar in the city, followed by a date and time. And the letters TL, written in capitals and double-underlined.

5 - THE MEETING

Thursday 25th June: At the Wine Bar

'Good evening, how are you today?' The young woman, dressed in a distinctive white shirt, black trousers and waistcoat and wearing an ID badge attached to a lanyard, greeted Rachel with a smile.

'Hi, I have a table booked in the name of Templewood.' Rachel had arrived at the wine bar ten minutes early. As the nominal 'host', it seemed the polite thing to do. The woman checked her terminal.

'Yes, here it is: three people. I've put you outside, as it's a sunny evening. Are you happy with that? Would you like to follow me?'

'That'll be fine. We might as well take advantage of the fine weather.'

Emily arrived a few minutes later. She spotted Rachel sitting alone. 'Excuse me, is this table booked in the name of Templewood?'

'Yes, I'm Rachel. Pleased to meet you.'

'I'm Emily.' They embraced and sat down.

'Are you OK out here, or would you rather sit inside?' said Emily.

'I'm fine, thanks.'

A few minutes later, Lisa bustled through the tables, glancing firstly at their occupants and then over each shoulder, looking worried, as if seeking a companion lost on the journey.

'Templewood,' said Rachel, pitching her voice loudly enough for Lisa alone to hear.'

'Oh, hi. I'm Lisa.'

'I'm Rachel, and this is Emily. Good to meet you. What can I get you both to drink?'

'White wine for me, please,' said Lisa.

'That sounds good to me,' said Emily.

"I'll order a bottle. We can get to know each other a little before we move on to the serious stuff,' said Rachel.

They continued their small talk for several minutes, putting each other at ease with their introductions until the discussion reached the point where they became unsure how much more personal information they should share on a first meeting, opening a silence that prompted the hovering question.

'Does anyone know what this is all about?' asked Lisa.

"I've no idea,' said Rachel, 'It sounded like a bit of an adventure, so I thought there was no harm in meeting up. How about you Emily?'

'I'm not sure… well, I have an idea. I received a letter at work, out of the blue, with a coded phrase I recognised. I was told to go to a church on a particular Saturday and to look at the stained-glass windows. A weird instruction, I'm sure you'll agree. I was quite happy to visit a church — I'm not religious, by the way; I just like the architecture. After a while I began to wonder what the hell I was doing there — what was I looking for? It wasn't obvious. And then I looked again at a particular window I'd found attractive. In the bottom right-hand corner, I noticed the words. It was the same French phrase as in the letter, that I recognised from the past, one that not many people would be familiar with. *L'art embellit la vie*.'

'Those words were in my message too,' said Lisa. 'How

about you, Rachel?'

'I've not heard of the phrase before.' Rachel hesitated. 'I suppose I should mention that I was given the instruction to book the table here in a note left with my father's will. I was to arrange it for the first Thursday following his death.'

'How could he possibly know when — sorry to put it so bluntly — when he was going to die?' said Lisa. 'Surely, he wasn't…'

'No, he wasn't murdered. He died after a long illness. The note also said that the others, presumably you two, would be instructed similarly. I was to reserve the table in the name of Templewood. As we now know, this was the common feature to all our messages, a sign by which we could recognise each other. It confirmed we were talking with the right people.'

'So that's why we're here, although I'm not sure it helps us understand the reason,' said Lisa. 'There was no real clue in the message I received. I was just told I had to come here today at the specified time and given a few numbers. Was there anything else in your message, Rachel? Any clues as to the purpose?'

'Not really,' said Rachel. 'Except I was told that exactly two weeks after today's meeting the three of us must travel to a specified destination where we will have to undergo some sort of assignment. It also said that I would discover life-changing knowledge. It made me laugh at first — the words could have come from a Victorian séance. I would have treated it as a joke if it weren't for the fact that I found it while I was looking for my father's hidden will. I was also directed to some numbers, on a separate piece of paper. Presumably, he didn't want the solicitor to have all of the details. Another odd thing, as you've recognised, Lisa, was that the piece of paper said we were to meet today, the Thursday following his death. Someone must be aware of all of our movements and what's going on in our lives. They must have known when my father would die to be able to set up this meeting. And they couldn't have given you two a date and time before contacting me. Emily, you say the French phrase was inscribed on the window. How were you told about the arrangements?'

'I found a note in a hymn book,' said Emily. 'It contained the details. Unlike yours, there were no numbers, although there were two letters, underlined emphatically. The note can't have been there long. I realised afterwards that I must have been directed there on a Saturday as it was the least likely day anyone would look at the hymn books. They would have been in use the next day and the note could have been lost. Of course, it might have been placed there by someone who tends to the church, who tidies it up before the Sunday services.'

'I wonder why yours has letters and ours have numbers,' said Rachel.

'No idea,' said Emily. 'Are the numbers the same on both of yours?'

'I don't know,' said Lisa. 'Although mine's five digits.'

'So was mine. I was instructed to destroy it,' said Rachel. 'But I do remember the sequence. Let's write down what we know.'

Rachel produced a notebook and tore out a sheet of paper. She scribbled the sequence and passed it to Lisa, who added hers, before passing it to Emily to add the two letters from her message.

'Well, there's a little puzzle to solve,' said Lisa. 'Clearly, we've been given three parts of something we have to put together to find an answer.'

Each looked to the other two. They nodded in agreement.

'Looks like we're going to need another bottle of wine,' said Emily.

'Some bar snacks even,' said Lisa.

They laughed and agreed they would share the bill. Emily called one of the bar staff over.

'I don't see any obvious connection. Do either of you?'

'Well, we know we have a task to perform, to uncover

some important knowledge. What we don't know is where to go to find it,' said Rachel.

'I've got an idea of where we have to go to,' said Emily. 'I just don't know where exactly it is and how to get there.'

'Then perhaps the letters and numbers are telling us where to go,' said Lisa.

'I think you're right,' said Rachel. 'The message I received said that we must travel together to a "specified destination".'

'And this is the only information we have to go on,' said Emily.

'Perhaps the numbers represent letters, and we have to put them together to spell a name. The two letters that Emily has could be some sort of key,' said Lisa.

'How do you mean?' said Rachel.

'Well, just as an example, if we took each of the numbers and counted forward from each of the letters given, it might spell a word, or two words, or an anagram,' said Lisa.

The women tried combinations of this idea, without success. They stared at each other with frowns and pursed lips, looking for inspiration.

'I have an idea,' said Emily, taking out her phone from her bag.

'What are you looking up?' said Rachel.

'Maps. I think it could be a map reference. If you put the letters together with the two sets of numbers…'

'Yes, a grid reference,' said Lisa. 'One number for eastings and the other for northings. The letters represent the square on the map. I know this from my walking trips many years ago.'

'Sorry, I don't follow. You'll have to explain,' said Rachel.'

'It's quite simple, once you know,' said Emily. 'On a map, the whole of the country is divided into squares, uniquely identified by a pair of letters. Once you've found the square, the numbers are used to count the distance to the right or downwards to find the exact spot, or at least within a few metres. Normally it's two letters follow by two three-digit numbers.'

'That sounds promising. So where is it, this mysterious place?'

'Hang on, I'm trying to find the website. Here it is. Yes, a grid reference of two letters and six numbers, which we have, will get you within a hundred metres of a location. Hmm, I suppose it could be a very accurate one, with the additional numbers. Oh look, you can key in a reference to locate a place.' Emily continued to frown as she keyed in the coordinates. 'No that doesn't work. The square with those letters is in the sea.'

'Perhaps they've been written deliberately the wrong way round, to make it less obvious,' said Lisa.

'Good idea, I'll try that.'

'How will you know which way round the numbers go, the north and east whatever,' said Rachel.

'Let's see what we come up with. We can try both combinations.'

Emily keyed in the two letters, followed by the sets of numbers. The query returned a map location in the middle of a lake a hundred miles to the north.

'Not impossible,' said Lisa, 'If we were to meet on a boat, for example, although unlikely.'

'OK, I'll try reversing the numbers.'

''This looks promising,' said Emily. 'It's by the side of a minor road through woodland. Some sort of clearing. Let's pan out to see where it is. Oh no…'

'What's wrong?' said Rachel.

'Is it somewhere you know?' said Lisa.

'Well, sort of. I'm aware of the general area. My Mum would recognise it, I think.'

'Does that mean there is a connection between you and the sender of the messages?' said Rachel.

'Well, yes, I'm pretty sure my message was from my brother, Peter. I haven't seen him for well over ten years. He said at that time that if he needed me, he would give me a sign that I would recognise. The sign was in the message — the French phrase — he needs us to come to him.'

'He must have sent all of the messages then. I don't understand. Why is he being so secretive? Why doesn't he ask you just to go to wherever he lives? And why has he asked the three of us, when none of us has ever met? How does he even know Lisa and I exist?'

'From what you say, Emily, it sounds as though he knew Rachel's father,' said Lisa.

'I think that's likely. As for the secrecy, he's in a very high-powered role. I would imagine he's concerned about security and the danger of the messages being intercepted.'

Emily knew she had to take care not to give too much information and to avoid mentioning the possibility of danger. Not that she knew much, other than of the existence of Templewood, the hidden community of five villages, and what had happened there all those years ago. She needed to carry Lisa and Rachel with her, to ensure the journey and the meeting took place.

'I wouldn't be able to find it. I've only been in and out when asleep or in darkness. It's very remote and doesn't appear on maps as there's a military and research facility there. We lived there for a while, one summer. We were originally driven there at night by my father. Access was strictly controlled, although my Mum drove out and back in once. Because it's a classified area, there were no signposts, so she had to remember the route she'd taken.'

Emily said she would ask whether her mother would be willing to take the three of them to the rendezvous location. It would be good if Catherine could drive them there. They could take the train to meet her at her home in London.

'Perfect! That way we can be sure of all being in the right place at the right time.' said Lisa.

'You're both up for it then?' said Emily.

'No way I'd miss this,' said Rachel. 'Aren't we rushing ahead a bit, though? We've been instructed to meet there exactly two weeks after today's meet-up. We don't know how long whatever it is we're supposed to do will take. Are we all free to spend however long it takes away from here?'

The women looked at each other. Emily spoke first.

'Well, I'm freelance, so I can more or less do as I please. I've given in my notice, and I have enough savings to live off for now. How about you two?'

'I've given up my job too,' said Rachel. 'Technically I'm employed until the end of August, although they won't be expecting me to do any work. The pupils are all off doing exams. Most have already completed them. It's not as though I have to prepare for next year. I should be looking for a new teaching position, but that can wait. What about you, Lisa?'

'I've decided not to renew my contract. Next week is my final week. I had been planning a year abroad, but a few things fell through. I haven't booked anything yet. The trip can wait. I own my flat, so I can arrange for all the bills to be paid and for a friend to look in from time to time to check everything's OK.'

'Do you think your Mum would agree to this?' said Rachel. 'It seems to be the best option, even though we have a map reference, or think we do. It's a bit of an imposition. Perhaps we should manage on our own.'

'I'll ask her. I'm sure she'll agree, given her knowledge of the history of Templewood. Especially as the messages have come from Peter — she'll know it must be something important. If we go up to London the night before, we can make an early start the next morning.'

'Just one thing,' said Lisa. 'I'd prefer to travel to London alone. I know it sounds silly but I'm claustrophobic. I need my own space to be able to cope.'

'I'm sure that won't be a problem,' said Emily. 'Whatever makes you feel comfortable.'

'That's sorted then, well…almost,' said Rachel. 'It's a bit of a coincidence all three of us being free.'

'Not necessarily,' said Lisa. 'My contracts typically run for six months. They wanted me to stay on but it's so frustrating when you know you could be doing more for a business if only someone with authority on the permanent team would stick their head over the parapet and champion new ways of doing things. At least with contract work you know when the frustrations are going to come to an end. It's easier to stick it out than it is in a full-time job.'

'I can imagine so,' said Rachel. 'I'm absolutely fed up with curriculum changes that seem to have no real benefit or purpose other than to introduce change for the sake of change. I'm not happy at all with the direction education is going. I'll be pleased to get out, for a while at least.'

'What will we need to bring with us?' asked Lisa. 'We don't know how long this will take.'

'Best to just plan as though for a long holiday and take a single case, just casual clothes and shoes,' said Emily. 'We'll have to take it as it comes. Oh, by the way, mobile phones don't work in Templewood. It's all part of the security.'

'I suppose that's a blessing in a way, having to do without them. I'm sure we'll manage,' said Lisa.

'Are you sure you want to do this?' said Emily. 'Once we're there it could be difficult if you wanted to leave, owing to Templewood's remoteness and seclusion. We don't really know what we're letting ourselves in for.'

'I'm sure it won't be a problem, especially if your brother is in an important position.' said Rachel. 'This is just too exciting to pass up!'

'I agree,' said Lisa. "If I didn't go, I'd regret it for the rest of my life.'

'Yay! We're under way,' said Rachel.

The women clinked their glasses together.

'To us, and our big adventure!'

'OK, let's exchange numbers and then we can enjoy the rest of the evening.'

6 - TO TEMPLEWOOD

Wednesday 8th July: To London

The women arranged to take the train to London to meet Emily's mother. Catherine would drive them to the specified location. They agreed to travel separately. Emily suggested to Rachel that, as well as this being Lisa's preference, it might 'suit her convenience' if they all did so. The truth was that she was worried that some unknown person or persons could be watching one or all of them. She knew there was no justification for her fears. Her thoughts were dictated by the history of deceit and misinformation that had taken place during the Templewood Summer.

They arrived early evening within an hour of each other at Catherine's flat to discover she had prepared a feast worthy of a midsummer Christmas.

'Just help yourselves,' said Catherine. 'I think I've catered for most tastes — there are vegetarian and vegan options. Please say if you can't find anything to your taste. There's wine, beer, soft drinks… Just make yourselves at home.'

'Oh Mum, this must have taken you ages to put together.'

'Well, if there's anything left over, I won't need to cook

again for a few days. Look, if you don't mind, I've been called out at short notice to meet someone to discuss a work issue. I'll be back late, so don't wait up for me. Help yourselves to anything else you can find. Emily knows where everything is. We'll set off about ten in the morning. That should give us plenty of time.'

"I was hoping Dad might be joining us.'

'I'm afraid not, unless he turns up unexpectedly. You remember how it is with us, both working on different things. We see little enough of each other, whether it's because of work or for security reasons. I'm looking forward to the day when we can give all of this up and lead normal lives.'

'That's a shame. I was hoping we'd eat together so that my new friends could get to know you both.'

'Yes, I'd have liked that too. Don't worry, there'll be plenty of time for us to introduce ourselves on the journey. You just enjoy your evening. Now, if you'll excuse me, I must get ready to go out.'

'Of course,' said Rachel. 'Thanks for laying this on for us.'

Emily, Lisa and Rachel passed the evening grazing through the freshly prepared food and wines.

'I doubt we'll see a spread of this quality for a while,' said Emily, 'But we'll be well looked after in Templewood.'

'It's a shame your Mum couldn't be here to share it with us,' said Lisa.

'Yes, I suppose I'm used to her disappearing at short notice on work matters,' said Emily. 'I must say, I'm impressed with your willingness to undertake this journey at short notice. What motivates you to do it? What are you both hoping to get out of it?'

'I'm frustrated with what I'm doing. I want to feel I'm doing something worthwhile with my life,' said Rachel. 'I feel flattered that someone has singled me out to help with something. It sounds as though whatever it is will be important in some way and should be fulfilling. For years

I've gone to work each day, and worked many of my weekends, with little sense that I'm achieving anything. I'm surrounded by colleagues who are all very pleasant and dedicated in their own way but who are just ticking boxes: keeping their heads down to protect their jobs and get a good performance evaluation. No-one will risk thinking outside of the box. That's not enough for me. I don't just want a job or a career, I need recognition for my abilities. It sounds as though this could be an opportunity to add value to something. It's always good to be headhunted!'

'Very true,' said Emily. 'How about you, Lisa?'

'Pretty much the same, really. I'm easily bored and constantly need new challenges. I want to be stretched to the limit, to be growing all the time. It's like an itch that has to be scratched. If I'm offered something new and interesting, I accept straight away. I don't stop to think whether there will be a problem, there are always problems. I prefer to get on with things and work out how to solve them as I go. I sometimes wonder what made me this way. My parents weren't pushy. They were always full of praise for my achievements and were positive in their criticism — encouraging me to look at different ways of doing things if I made a mistake, rather than pointing out I was wrong. This could be at the root of it. The ongoing desire to please others, my parents in particular, by performing above their level of expectations. It's ridiculous, as I'm confident in my abilities and don't consciously go out of my way to please, only to do a good job. What are your reasons, Emily, apart from the message apparently coming from your brother?'

'The family connection is the main thing. There's a past connection, too. When we lived in Templewood, it was like another world. A strange mixture of a community set in a nineteen-fifties time warp but with access to all kinds of modern technologies developed as by-products to scientific research. It's best if you wait until we arrive and then I can show you. So, yes, I'd like to see how things have moved on in the years since I've been away.'

'Have you had any more thoughts on why your brother wants us in Templewood?' said Lisa. 'I wonder how he thinks we can help. I can see there is a vague connection to be made between the three of us, but I can't see that we have unique skills that could make it worth all this trouble. Sorry, that sounds rude. I know you both have your own specialisms; I just don't see what we all bring that he couldn't source locally.'

'We'll find out soon enough,' said Emily. 'I expect it's a matter of trust as much as anything else. He needs people he can rely on, for whatever reason.'

'Still, it must be pretty important,' said Lisa. 'I must say I'm really excited about it.'

'So am I,' said Rachel. 'My God, look at the time. I was hoping your Mum would be back by now. Would you mind if I call it a day? Let's tidy up first.'

'Yes let's,' said Lisa. 'It's going to be a long day tomorrow.'

'There'll be many longer ones to come,' thought Emily, smiling.

Thursday 9th July: The Journey to Templewood

Catherine helped the women load their bags into the car. Each had brought a single suitcase and hand luggage. They looked as if they were about to be taking a short-haul flight. Rachel and Lisa had expressed concern that it was difficult to plan how much to bring for an unknown period away, a worry Emily had waved away as being part of the adventure.

'How long will the journey take, Mum?' asked Emily, shortly after they set off.

'It depends on the traffic. Once we get out of the city and all this stop-start I'll have a better idea.'

Emily, Rachel and Lisa exchanged small talk. Once the roads opened out, Catherine joined in, able at last to relax her concentration on the traffic.

'Right, tell me again about these mysterious messages.

Emily's given me her account, but I'm keen to hear your versions, directly,' said Catherine.

Rachel and Lisa told their tales in turn.

'If it weren't for Emily — well, Emily and Lisa — I'd have had no idea what was going on — the map reference I mean.'

'It helped knowing that the messages, at least my message, was from my brother,' said Emily.

'So, you know exactly where we're going then, Emily,' said Rachel. 'You've been there before.'

'I know where we're going but not how to get there. Mum knows the way — well, roughly — from many years ago. I told you we spent a couple of months at Templewood.'

'I don't actually know the way. I'm relying on the satnav directions. It's odd. It says it's an invalid location and is not showing a map of the route, but, as you can hear, it's giving me voice directions. It must be down to the security and the hidden location.'

'We've no idea why we've been chosen for this, Catherine,' said Lisa. 'Do you know?'

'Not really,' said Catherine.

'Catherine, I've been thinking,' said Rachel. 'If, as Emily says, you've lived there, in Templewood, and Emily has lived there too, and Peter still does…'

'Carry on,' said Catherine. 'Don't be afraid, say what you want to say.'

'A place which doesn't appear on maps and has a military base… Does that mean that you are somehow involved, or have been involved, either with the military or some sort of secret service work? Is that right? Are you in on this too, Emily? It sounds as though the whole family is.'

'You certainly have been thinking it through, haven't you Rachel?' Catherine smiled into the driving mirror. 'Tell me, what do your parents do?'

Rachel gazed at each of her travelling companions in turn as she considered her response.

'It's always been drummed into me that I should never tell anyone about my father's work. I suppose it doesn't matter now that he's dead. He was a spy of some sort. Quite high up, I believe. I don't have any proof, it's just something understood within the family.'

'I'm sorry to hear that he's passed away. Was it from natural causes, if you don't mind my asking?' said Catherine.

'Yes, he died recently after a long illness. He wasn't even fifty.'

Rachel noticed the expression of Catherine's reflected eyes transition from the social smile to the neutral gaze of a dispassionate observer. Exactly as her father would have done.

'That's such a shame. What was his name, your father?'

'Caradoc.'

'His surname?'

'I'm sorry?'

'What was his surname: your family name?'

'Caradoc. His name was Lancelot Caradoc. After the Arthurian knights.'

'Interesting. I knew him well, many years ago. We didn't actually work together. Our paths crossed from time to time — both mine and my husband Michael's. We were always switching between colleagues. The work could be, well, let's just say interesting: there were risks.'

Lisa laughed. 'Oh great. I'm on my way to a secret location with three strangers, all of them are connected, two of them through espionage. It's for a purpose I don't know, and it could be dangerous. What the hell am I doing here?'

She flopped back in the seat, affecting an expression of shock and exasperation. Why hadn't this possibility, or the like, occurred to her before? There had to be something behind the secrecy of the mission.

'Don't worry Lisa,' said Catherine. 'We're all here together for a reason, including you. None of us is a threat to each other. You say you have no idea why you've been chosen. The connection is most likely through your parents.

What do they do?'

'I don't know exactly. They worked together, or did until my mother went into a care home. They had done for years. That's how they met. Research work: astronomy, astrophysics, something like that. My father still does. I don't often see him as he works abroad.'

Catherine and Emily's eyes met in the driving mirror. Each knew what the other was thinking.

'Where did you go to school, Lisa?' asked Catherine.

Emily pursed her lips and nodded to herself.

'Various places,' said Lisa. 'My parents moved around every few years, as they took up positions in universities in different countries. Why?'

'I suppose you've answered my question in a way. Often, children of research scientists are sent to a boarding school for that reason, that their parents are moving around. To give the children a semblance of stability, a sense of home. Was it ever discussed, boarding I mean?'

Catherine's calm tone put Lisa at ease.

'Yes, it was, actually. When I was about eleven, they said they wanted me to go to a school dedicated to the needs of children whose parents who had international connections through their work. It was quite exclusive, apparently. You had to sit an entrance exam. The problem was that I instinctively hated the idea of being away from my parents and being stuck with strangers for three terms a year. You could go home for the holidays, but it wasn't for me. I suppose I threw a sort of tantrum, and they gave in.'

'No connection with spying then,' said Rachel. 'I wonder why you've been contacted.'

Emily noticed Catherine glance at her in the mirror. Neither said anything. Both had recognised the connection, or the potential: her mother's and Rachel's father's work, the exclusive Templewood school that fitted Lisa's description. Had things been different, Emily and Lisa could have been classmates. Emily could see the past returning in a reinvented form: a new threat. Peter was aware of this and needed help. She would do whatever she could to assist. Rachel and Lisa were unaware of the strange world they would encounter. It was probably for the best.

Catherine had been driving for three hours. They were now in open countryside; the road began to rise into woodland. From the front passenger seat, Emily noticed a black car with tinted windows pull up to the junction with a side road a couple of hundred metres ahead. The car had plenty of time to emerge in front of Catherine. Emily noticed her mother flash her headlights, inviting it to do so. She had been driving at a steady pace, presumably aware of how long the journey would take. Approaching the junction, Catherine slowed. The car turned onto the main road and accelerated to Catherine's former speed.

The road rose deeper into the woodland. A road sign announced a long tunnel ahead. Both cars slowed as they approached the unlit entrance.

Midway through the tunnel, the leading car braked sharply. Catherine stopped within a couple of metres of its boot. Two men jumped out of the front seats and ran towards Catherine's car.

'Oh my God, we're going to be robbed.'

Rachel and Lisa took a sharp intake of breath. Emily had guessed that the appearance of the black car was no accident.

'It's OK,' said Catherine. 'Get out quickly and jump in that car. Go! Go!'

Rachel and Lisa glanced at each other, opened their doors and dashed with Emily and Catherine to the other car. As they did, the men rushed past them, opened the boot of Catherine's car, grabbed the luggage and threw it in theirs. Catherine and one of the men snatched each other's keys and completed the switch of vehicles. Both resumed their journey at the same speed and distance as before.

'That was cool, Mum. Totally unexpected.'

'Why have we changed cars?' asked Rachel.

'Just a precaution,' said Catherine. 'In case we're being

followed or tracked.' She glanced in her mirror.

'There: they're turning off now.'

'Are we nearly there?' asked Lisa.

'Not long now. Another forty minutes,' said Catherine.

*

The empty road continued to weave uphill through woodland, with glimpses of fields below. They saw no other vehicles nor any side roads.

'What's that noise?' said Lisa, alarmed by an intermittent bleeping.

'I hope we're not running out of fuel,' said Emily.

'It's a signal that we're nearly there,' said Catherine. 'Just around this next bend, I expect. I'll be dropping you off here.'

'You're not coming with us then?' said Emily.

'No, I can't. I'm sorry in a way but I have work to do on the outside.'

The bleeping changed to a continuous tone, then stopped.

'OK, here we are. The Templewood road is on the inside of the next bend, hidden by that pile of logs. You must walk down the track. Make sure you are quickly out of sight of the main road. A CCTV camera will spot you. Walk on past it until you come to a large metal gate.'

Catherine pulled off the road. She urged the women to take their bags and get out of the car as quickly as possible.

'Good luck! I wish I could come with you. I hope to see you all soon. Give my love to Peter. Tell him I miss him so much.'

Catherine waited until they had disappeared from sight down the track. She turned the car one hundred and eighty degrees and sped away.

*

Anyone driving on the remote and deserted road who had seen the pile of logs would have had no idea that it marked the location of the hidden track. The metal gate and the adjoining fence were too tall to climb and were topped with

50

spikes and razor wire. Beyond it, two more gated fences blocked the route; the middle one of the three was marked 'DANGER OF DEATH — ELECTRIC FENCE: KEEP CLEAR'.

They heard the vehicle before it appeared at the furthest gate, which opened to let it through, then closed. Once inside, the vehicle turned to face the direction from which it had appeared.

'It looks like a prison van. There are no windows in the back,' said Lisa.

'Security I expect — to hide the view of the route from the occupants,' said Emily. 'Or the occupants from the outside world.'

The gate in front of them opened, allowing them to pass through, then closed immediately. The gate in the electrified fence opened. The rear doors of the van opened automatically. It was empty. No-one got out to greet them. There was no need: it was clear they were to climb inside. Emily walked round to the driver's cab, hoping to see Peter or someone from the past she would recognise.

'It's empty.'

'What do you mean, empty?' said Rachel.

'There's no driver; It's a driverless vehicle. Oh well, there's no other option — we'd better climb in the back.'

The women stepped inside; the doors closed. They looked around the sparse interior, lit by obscure glass windows in the roof. A centre aisle separated four rows of leather-upholstered seats. Emily, Rachel and Lisa each chose a place marked with a cool bag. An illuminated sign instructed them to fasten their seat belts. A recorded announcement: 'vehicle departing', sounded. The final part of the journey was under way.

'It's quite comfortable really, despite the lack of a view,' said Rachel.

'Well, we have been invited here. You'd expect them to look after us,' said Emily, adding, 'It feels strange to be coming back.'

'Let's see what's in here,' said Rachel. She opened the cool bag to discover hand-labelled, wrapped sandwiches, fruit, a bottle of water and a linen napkin.

'Just what I need.'

Thursday 9th July: The Templewood Summer

Almost an hour after they had stepped into the van, it glid to a silent halt.

'What's happening? Why have we stopped?', said Rachel.

'We must be here, in Templewood. I wonder where exactly we are,' said Emily. She tried the handles of the rear doors. They would not open. A minute passed before they heard footsteps approaching. Both doors opened wide.

'Peter! It's so lovely to see you after all these years.'

Peter held both doors open, as wide as his arms allowed, as though inviting an embrace. The women climbed out, carrying their bags, blinking and shielding their eyes from the sunlight.

'Lisa, Rachel… meet my brother Peter. Oh, Peter, I've missed you so much!' She hugged him, rocking from side to side. From mid-embrace he waved towards Lisa and Rachel.

'Pleased to meet you both. Come inside the house. We've lots to talk about.'

'The Abbot's House. You're still living here? Is Dad here too?'

'No. He visits Templewood from time to time. Sometimes he spends a few days here; other times he stays somewhere else — I'm not sure where. Come in, come in! I'll put the kettle on.'

'You two talk to Peter for a minute. I just want to look at my bedroom.'

Emily ran up the stairs and into the room that had been hers for the Templewood Summer. It was as she remembered it. She opened the familiar sash window and leaned out to take in the view of the large garden, which she recalled extended to over an acre. When the family had first arrived, it was overgrown. It was well-tended now. The pond had been restored — still bordered with bulrushes but now filled with clear water, waterlilies in flower and goldfish. The horse chestnut tree seemed taller and broader, its seeds in their spiked cases. The pear tree was shorn of its ivy fleece and bore young fruit. The wall surrounding the garden, no longer obscured by blackberries, both absorbed and reflected the heat of the summer sun onto espaliers supporting young fruit. Emily smiled as she looked at the familiar shed, behind which lay the well, as it was originally believed to be. Its locked metal cover concealing the underground passage leading to…

'Are you going to join us Em?'

Emily woke from her nostalgic reverie and returned to the group downstairs.

'It's a lovely house. Is this where we'll be staying?' said Rachel.

'I'm afraid not. There's not enough room for all of us. I need to keep the main bedroom free for my father's unexpected visits. I've arranged for you and Lisa to stay with our friends Richard and Alice. They're a little way out of the village, down by the canal. You'll like them and they'll look after you.'

'I'm surprised Richard's still alive, given how much he smokes,' said Emily.

'Oh, he gave up, a long while ago. I expect it was Alice nagging him.'

'I assume they're a couple, Alice and Richard,' said Lisa.

'No, Alice is Richard's niece. We made that mistake originally,' said Peter. 'I'll pour the tea.'

*

'I'm so pleased to see you again, Peter. I've been so worried for you. I think about you every day and was beginning to wonder whether something dreadful had happened to you. I know you said you would find a way of making contact, but I had no idea it would take this long.'

'I'm sorry, I didn't want to worry you. I thought it was

best not to, given how things are here. There are people on the outside who keep me in touch with how you are. I prefer to keep it one way — them contacting me when it's safe for them to do so, rather than me contacting them. I couldn't risk being suspected of betraying or undermining what's going on here. Still, we're here now, and we can all get on with the task in hand. So, I need your help, as people I can trust.'

'How can you be sure we can help, when you've never met us?' asked Lisa. 'Especially as we've no idea why we're here.'

'And how do you know you can trust us with whatever you're going to share with us?' said Rachel.

'There are connections,' said Peter. 'Things that bring us together and unite us.'

'Rachel told us that she believes her father was involved in some sort of secret work,' said Emily. 'She told us during the drive here. Mum knows, or rather knew him when he was alive. And from what Lisa has told us, it sounds as though her parents, too, are linked to Templewood through their career specialisms.'

'I'm not sure about that,' said Lisa. 'I'd never heard of Templewood before. I'm sure I would have remembered the name if they'd mentioned it.'

'Emily's right,' said Peter. 'There is a link. It's only right that you should be aware of the connections.'

'I still don't see what Rachel and I bring to the party — apologies again, Rachel, no offence intended — it's just that there doesn't appear to be anything special about us, other than these links,' said Lisa.

'I need people I can trust, new people from outside, with fresh and original ideas. I'm sure Emily has explained to you, that Templewood is a secret location: a community of five villages where no-one is allowed in or out except under special circumstances. Temple Walden is the largest of the five, the hub, as it were. Then there's Little Walden, Lower Walden, Woddesleigh and Hexton.'

'If no-one's allowed in or out, how are you able to explain our presence here?' said Lisa.

'That's where your family connections to Templewood count.' Peter nodded his head from side to side, pursing his lips. 'Actually, I took a bit of a liberty. I said that you could advise on IT matters, Lisa, and that Rachel would be able to provide some valuable input on teaching methods and the way the school curriculum is organised.'

'You mean we've come here to work? To think that I believed I had been recruited for an exciting adventure!' Rachel smiled.

'To be honest, Rachel, I wouldn't worry about a lack of excitement,' said Peter. 'Believe me, what you'll find here will be more than enough, but I'll come to that another day. Oh, and it's your linguistic skills that are likely to be of most interest.'

'How on earth do you know about that? I admit that it's an area of special interest to me. I've never had the opportunity to use them, although I'd love to. Peter, you still haven't told us the real purpose of bringing us here. What exactly is expected of us?'

'There's a lot to take in. Things that will surprise and even shock you. I'm not entirely sure what's going on myself, only that there is danger, not just to us but to the whole world. What I'd prefer to do is to tell you about what happened here in the past, fourteen years ago. Things happened here that the outside world was totally oblivious to yet could have destroyed the planet.'

'Nothing serious then,' said Rachel, laughing. 'Come on then, tell us all about it.'

'OK. Make yourselves comfortable. This could take a while.'

*

Peter described what he and Emily knew as the Templewood Summer. It had begun when their father announced to the family that they would be moving from the city to Templewood, where they would move into The

Abbot's House. He claimed to have inherited it from a distant relation who had died, leaving no other family. Emily and Peter had not wanted to move away but, as teenagers still in their school years, they had no choice other than to be with their parents. They would attend the local school as day pupils, in the company predominantly of boarders from countries around the world.

After their arrival, they learned that Templewood, with its five villages, comprised a secret location that did not appear on maps and was home to a military and research centre. This was possible due to the authority of a global organisation known as The Sect, whose contacts in governments worldwide ensured the cooperation of all entities necessary to maintain the secret conspiracy. They discovered one of the Sect members, Hugo Payne, a resident farmer and landowner, to be the head of Military Mapping, the organisation responsible for controlling and maintaining the national mapping system. In this role, he was able to dictate the contents and omissions from maps. The Sect's contacts in overseas governments colluded in ensuring that air traffic control systems and airlines avoided the area and were unaware of its existence.

The Sect had existed for centuries. Its influence on nations and governments was covert. They slipped in and out of power according to the political temperature and the prospect of permanent influence. Their goal of world domination had been limited only by science and technology, although they were able to keep ahead of many advances in both fields. The Sect was guided by a prophecy whose origin was lost in history. A stranger would arrive, who would provide the key to unlock the knowledge that would grant them the means to assume permanent global power. Peter had been identified as the person who, unbeknown to him, would fulfil this prophecy.

The Sect was made up of two factions: the Pros and the Cons. The Pros represented the radical, progressive arm, focussed on forcing change to achieve their goals. The Cons adopted a measured approach, preferring to let natural events and destiny take their course. Ultimately, the local branch of the Sect was controlled by a group located outside of Templewood, known as the Masters, a secretive group that visited Templewood from time to time, each disguised to protect their anonymity.

During the Templewood Summer, the Sect was on the cusp of implementing a plan to steer an approaching asteroid to collide with the Earth and alter its axis. This would change the climate in almost every country and allow the Sect to take control of the planet through their global representatives. Survivors would be provided with genetically modified food capable of being produced in unnatural climatic conditions. The Sect was oblivious to the impossibility of their plan and the certainty that the impact would destroy almost all life. Peter, aided by his friends and supporters, devised a plan to raid and destroy the Sect's Templewood control centre at the military base. After gaining access through a network of underground tunnels, they prevented them from remotely launching the rocket that had been prepared to create the collision with the asteroid.

Through this intervention, many villagers' lives were sacrificed to save the world. In the aftermath, the Pros and Cons were reunited in their determination to rebuild Templewood. Peter was embarrassed, yet proud, to be hailed as a hero. He stayed on in the village to assist with the rebuilding of the community. Emily and Catherine returned to the city. Michael continued to come and go, remaining a shadowy figure as he always had been.

Peter looked at each of his audience in turn as if asking a question or assessing their response. Almost two hours had passed since he began his account, frequently interrupted by their many questions. Each new piece of information opened new lines of interrogation. Hardly surprising, given the dramatic story of catastrophe averted and the threat of another.

*

'This is incredible! How come I haven't heard about this before? It must have been all over the press and television,' said Rachel.

'There was no publicity, none whatever,' said Peter. 'Remember, this all happened within Temple Walden and its satellite villages. It was easy for the Sect, with its network, to keep it quiet.'

'It's a bit scary to be somewhere with a military base,' said Rachel. 'What's that here for? Are they planning some sort of coup?'

'Not at all,' said Peter. 'Their purpose is to protect both the research centre and the inhabitants in the unlikely event of some form of outside attack or intrusion.'

'Why didn't you go back to the city with your family, Peter?' said Lisa.

'At the beginning, I genuinely wanted to help the villagers — I still do. I was regarded as a saviour — a bit over the top, really. All I'd done was to help make the local people aware of the dangers and assisted in organising the response. Any rational person would have done the same. I was also a large fish in the small pond of Templewood. Call it ego, perhaps... It all went fine for a while, then I gradually noticed things starting to change. The Masters began to visit Templewood more frequently, to take more direct control. For some while, there had been rumours of a 'Third Force', a new group or entity with a different agenda. Emily, you remember that I told you that Dad said that there were other forces at work, apart from the Sect and the maquis — the local resistance group. That there was this Third Force, becoming disruptive. At the time, I was told they were a dissenting faction within the Sect who had come in from outside, to replace those Sect members who left after the villagers' revolt, and that, as well as frequent visits from the Masters, these Third Force people were now here permanently, telling everyone else what to do although no-one seemed to admit to seeing them. This seemed to pose a threat, although I couldn't work out what it was. I remember that there was something very odd about the way Dad explained it to me. I'm sure he was telling the truth, but he seemed to be hinting that things weren't quite as he described them to me. It was as though there was a subtext he wanted to communicate, without being explicit, in the way you would if you knew someone was listening in. It took me a long while to finally get to the bottom of it. When I did, I discovered a threat as bad as, if not worse than, the Sect's ridiculous asteroid idea.'

'Well, are you going to tell us about this new threat?' asked Rachel. 'You can't leave us in suspense like this.'

'And you haven't told us about all of the people we knew here in the past,' said Emily.

'It's getting late. You've had a long journey and it's almost dark. I suggest you spend tonight here, as Dad's away. Actually, I haven't seen him for months. We'll take you down to Richard and Alice's house tomorrow. There's a lot to take in from what I've told you this evening. It's probably best to have a decent night's sleep before I fill you in with what's happening here now.'

Friday 10th July: Those Who Remain

Emily heard Peter downstairs in the kitchen. She threw on yesterday's clothes and tiptoed down, taking care not to wake Lisa and Rachel.

'Morning. I hope I didn't disturb you; I'm usually up early. Did you sleep well?' said Peter. 'I'll make some coffee,'

'I was straight out, surprisingly. I did have some strange dreams though.'

'Do you want to tell me about them?'

'Not really. I'm more interested in talking to you. We've a lot of catching up to do.' Emily sat down at the kitchen table. 'Who's still here in Templewood, of the people we used to know?'

'It's mostly the same people as when you and Mum left.

The four farms are still intact. Hugo Payne at Whytecliffe Farm with its microclimate. It's still being used to experiment with new plant cultivars. Solomons Farm is still run by Roland Nightingale. He's scaling up the new ones that show promise, in conjunction with Alexander Martel's seed farm. The one change in the farming community is Saracens Farm. You'll remember that it was previously experimenting with genetically modified animals and insects. After Thomas Fitzjohn was killed in the raid on the control centre no-one seemed interested or qualified enough to take the farm over. Eventually our friend Sarah — Sarah Montfort — agreed to, on condition that she be allowed to change direction.'

'Ah, Sarah, the last child to be born in the village,' said Emily.

'Indeed, nothing's changed there. Even today, no-one really knows what the Sect was working on that caused the infertility. As for Sarah, she's a different person from the shy and nervous girl we used to know. And Saracens, well, in practice, it's no longer a farm — more of an experimental scientific unit. After Sarah finished at the school, she was sent overseas by the Sect and given a first-class scientific and technological higher education and training.'

'I did wonder whether she might still be living with Richard and Alice,' said Emily.

'She stayed with them until she finished at the school. It was fortunate that they were there to take care of her after the discovery that she had covered up the death of her mother, albeit from natural causes.'

'Yes, I remember that well. She was afraid of being made to live at the Sect's control centre, more or less as a prisoner.'

'Well, the Templewood Summer put paid to that concern. Since then, the village, or rather the native residents, have been working much more cooperatively. The divisions between the Pros and Cons have mostly disappeared, thank goodness. Arthur Welles is still the figurehead, token mayor. That's less of an issue now that the villagers work together on the whole, "guided", if I might put it that way, by the Masters.'

'Does this mean that the Sect, both the Pros and the Cons, no longer have world domination at the top of their agenda? Or do they have some other new goal? Or is that where this Third Force fits in?'

'I knew it wouldn't take long for you to ask that. It's fair to say that they are working together. In the old days, the Pros' method was to adopt a radical approach to achieving power, whereas the Cons' policy was gradual, organic change. Both are now focussed on introducing new technologies and scientific developments to gain power as a single unit. They believe that by delivering and being the sole controllers of inventions and discoveries that change the planet for the better, they will gain power almost seamlessly and with little or no resistance.'

'Does this mean that these new discoveries in some way originate with this Third Force? Who exactly are they?' said Emily.

'I'll explain all of that in due course. As you know, the Sect has a history going back centuries of being privy to "new knowledge" of scientific advances, ahead of the rest of the world. This is what has historically provided them with their power base. The sources of their knowledge have always been kept secret until now, but, yes, the presence of the Third Force has given them an enormous leap forward towards being able to achieve their aims. The first thing I want to do is to show you all around so you can see for yourselves what Templewood is working on and what's been accomplished to date. There's been some excellent work that will benefit everyone.'

'OK, I'll have to trust that there's a good reason for the order in which you want to do things. Lisa and Rachel will have a lot to come to terms with, given that no-one from the wider world could possibly believe what happened during the Templewood Summer. Tell me Peter, are any of our old school friends from the village still here, apart from Sarah?'

'Yes, a few. Most ended up going back to their own countries to continue the Sect's secret work locally. Carlos, Amit and Françoise stayed on and are still here, as is Eric Betterby. In fact, Françoise is living and working with Sarah at Saracens. Dr Jay's still alive and practising as is Gygges, the lawyer, who still acts as clerk to the Council meetings. Gygges has mellowed a lot. He claims to have been freed from the former tyranny of the Pros.'

'Yes, I remember that well.'

'What about you, Peter? I assume you don't have a long-term partner?'

'No, it's partly down to the nature of life here. Ours was the last generation of people who grew up in Templewood. We have people from other countries visiting and on work assignments. I've had a few short-term relationships, as have most of our friends. It's difficult to take things to the next stage when you both know you're not going to be together in the same place forever.'

Peter looked up towards the ceiling.

'Someone's getting up.'

The upstairs floorboards creaked. A door opened. Rachel stood at the top of the stairs, smiling, then ran down, sliding her hands along both bannisters.

'Hi, Rachel. You look lively. Did you sleep well?' said Emily.

'Yes, thanks. I'm really looking forward to our big adventure here.'

'That's good to hear. Ah, here's Lisa, too. Let's have some breakfast, then we'll go down to Mill Cottage.'

Friday 10th July: The Third Force

Lisa and Rachel helped themselves to more breakfast, all the while talking excitedly. Emily was not hungry. She drew Peter to one side. 'Peter, can I have a chat with you?'

'Of course you can. There's no need to look so serious. What's the matter?'

'It's about the past, what's happened in the years since Mum and I left Templewood while you stayed behind,' said Emily.

'Let's talk outside,' said Peter. He made a silent gesture, pointing to his ears. Emily understood.

'No, not the garden. Let's walk over to the field… Keep away from the trees.'

'Surely they don't bug the trees,' said Emily.

'Best to just do as I say. It's important. I'll explain another time. It'll all become clear, trust me.'

He turned to Rachel and Lisa, who were carrying coffee and toast to the table. 'We won't be long.'

Emily and Peter left the front door open behind them and crossed the road, stepping across the dry shallow ditch into the field.

'We can talk here,' said Peter.

Emily walked a few steps before turning to face Peter.

'Why has it taken so long for you to get in touch again? It's been the best part of fourteen years.'

'Not quite that long. I did get a message to you a while after you left, giving you a clue to what was happening. I know that you met the messenger. What did he tell you?'

'I know, I know. You're probably not aware of this. Not long after Mum and I left Templewood, I had some sort of breakdown. It was probably a late reaction to everything that happened that summer. I ended up spending a few months in a clinic. Mum was very good to me during that period and helped me through. Yes, I got the message. The person who came to see me gave me the secret code phrase we agreed, so I knew I could trust him. There was a lot of good news, mostly about how everyone in Templewood was pulling together. The rebuilding of the community was going well; there had been changes. He mentioned the Third Force. He was a bit evasive about who exactly they were. I had the impression that they were a dissenting faction within the Sect who had come in from outside to replace those Sect members who left after the villagers' revolt and that they were becoming disruptive. They had introduced their own agenda and were now telling Arthur, the farmers and everyone else what to do. He said no-one knew what their plans were, although he hinted that they presented a new threat. He said something about them "understanding the unique features of Templewood and the opportunities the location provided". He also said that the Masters now visited regularly, whereas before they visited Templewood infrequently, only when an important message was delivered.'

'That's about right.'

'Oh, Peter, please try to help. I want to know what's going on. I was so grateful to hear that you were OK and that I shouldn't worry about you. He couldn't tell me anything about Dad, though, which was a concern for months until he resumed his occasional, unannounced visits. He told me that you would make contact as soon as you were able. That was probably the single most important thing that helped with my recovery. And then nothing! For all those years. Why didn't you get in touch again?'

'I was concerned for your safety. I didn't want to allow the Third Force to make a connection between us, in case something... well, in case something happened.'

'That's precisely what worried me. Mum had her suspicions. She was aware of Dad's concerns about dark forces in Templewood that presented a new challenge. She said he'd used the very words: Third Force. At the time, she took this to be a description. Now that she understood that it was the name by which they were known, the term carried more weight, more menace. She thought that what I'd been told sounded like the sort of message designed to keep us happy and at the same time stop us from investigating or taking other action. She talked about speaking to her former secret service colleagues to see what they knew and whether they were able to assess the threat.'

'Did she say whether she was able to find out anything?'

'No, you know what Mum's like. She keeps this sort of thing to herself. Even now, it's difficult to tell whether she's still engaged in secret work. Then there was me. She didn't want to jeopardise my recovery. Going back to the messenger, Mum asked what made me so sure you were not a prisoner, being forced to work on the Sect's latest big idea. I told her what you had told me on our last day in The Abbot's House.'

'What was that?'

'You said that the Sect had made mistakes, but they were sincere in their objectives for change and that you could use your influence to work from within. You also said that it helped that they still believed that you had prophetic powers. No-one else in this world would ever be in such a position to hold their attention and influence them.'

'Precisely. In that case, surely you can understand why I felt I needed to protect you. Any further attempts at contact would have increased the risk. There was a job to be done — there still is — and, as you say, I was in a unique position of trust and perceived value.'

'You know, one very sad thing she said at the time was that she recognised that, once the message I was so certain would arrive from you did so, I would answer whatever call you made on me. She thought that you and I would forever be linked in a never-ending quest that would govern our actions for the rest of our lives. There was another odd thing…'

'What was that?'

'She said to me, "Humanity depends upon you. You have a destiny to fulfil. Let me help you in whatever way I can.'"'

'So, she did know more than she was letting on,' said Peter.

'What about Dad? Do you see much of him? I assume he spends most of his time here. Mum said she doesn't see him very often and I rarely do.'

'Not a lot. He drifts in and out. He's pleasant to me and, we get on well, but there's still that underlying sense of distance between us.'

'Is that to do with finding out you were adopted?'

Peter had learned that he had been adopted during the Templewood Summer. He had suffered an accident on a remote section of the canal and was bleeding profusely. He had travelled several miles, by kayak, to explore a hidden tunnel on the canal bank, close to a torrential weir. He had suspected the tunnel was used by the Sect to transfer goods and equipment from barges to the military base. The canalised river was flooded from recent torrential rain, causing the kayak to overturn, leaving him injured and losing blood from a gash in his leg. He eventually struggled to get out from the water and discovered Eric Betterby, stranded in the whirlpool beneath the weir, unable to escape the current. Eric had met the barge by arrangement and had assisted with unloading. After it had left, he had fallen into the swollen waters and was carried over the weir. Peter rescued Eric, using a lifebelt attached to a rope. Eric hailed a tractor driver, working in the adjacent fields, to assist and take Peter to the cottage hospital. He received treatment for his wound, including a blood transfusion. His blood group revealed that he could not possibly be related to Catherine and Michael. They explained that he was the orphan of two colleagues, unknown to them, who had been killed in a secret Government operation. Peter needed protection. He had been identified as the child who would eventually unlock an ancient mystery, revealing information that was believed would enable the Sect to assert world power. Catherine and Michael had brought Peter up with the same love and devotion they had bestowed on Emily, their natural child.

'No, I'm over that now. Whenever I do see him, he does his best to act like a real father. I do believe he cares. I'm still wary of what side he's on though. You can understand that it's best not to ask too much. The one thing he did tell me was that he suspected that the Third Force was planning a complete takeover and that the Masters had their own plans for me. He tried to send me away — for my own good, he said — but I was having none of it. Things have moved on a lot since then.'

'In what way?'

'I'll tell you more later, over the coming days and weeks.'

'Why not now? What's the great mystery?'

'I want to put things into context first, to show you, Lisa and Rachel what's going on without prejudicing your views. You know what this place is all about, but it's going to be new and strange to them. They need a gentle introduction. Thank you for your help in persuading them to come here, by the way.'

'No problem. It wasn't difficult; they regard it as a big adventure.'

Peter glanced across the road towards The Abbot's House. 'We'd better be getting back. They'll be wondering why we're so long.'

*

'It takes about half an hour to walk to Mill Cottage, but it's only a five-minute drive,' said Peter. 'Richard and Alice have a car these days, one of the few private vehicles in the village. Richard will be here shortly to take us over us and collect your bags. It might be a bit of a squeeze; I'm sure we'll manage. Now, I have something for you both. It's a sort of, well, a cross between an induction and a welcome pack, a guide to Templewood that I've had put together for the infrequent new arrivals. You'll find a lot of useful information — nothing too secret, for obvious reasons. Let me know if there's anything you don't understand or that needs clarification. I'm also going to give you each a mobile phone. The setup instructions are included in the pack.'

'I thought mobile phones didn't work here,' said Rachel.

'Only those that are authorised, where we can control the devices, the apps and their use. Don't worry, they're pretty much state-of-the-art, but you won't be able to contact anyone outside of Templewood, whether by messaging, social media or through websites. It's all part of the essential security.'

'I don't care,' said Rachel. 'I could do with a break from all that.'

'Doesn't bother me either,' said Lisa.

A car drew up outside. Emily answered the door to let Richard in.

'Emily! It's so good to see you again. How are you?' Richard stretched out his arms to greet and embrace her.

'And you must be Lisa and Rachel. I'm Richard — delighted to welcome you here to Templewood. It'll be good to have some new company, especially from the outside world.'

'Come in, Richard. Come and meet our new friends properly,' said Emily.

'If it's all right by you, I'd sooner make a move. It'll give them more time to settle in and get to know Alice.' Richard turned to Rachel and Lisa. 'Peter has told us a little about you both. We're looking forward to hearing your own stories. I see your bags are packed and ready. Let me carry them to the car.'

'I'll give you a hand,' said Emily. Would you two like to check you have everything?'

'I'll grab my handbag,' said Rachel.

Richard placed the bags into the boot. 'Emily, would you like to sit in the front with me? Rachel, Lisa — make yourselves comfortable in the back.'

'Are you coming, Peter?' said Emily.

'No, there'll be more room without me. I've just remembered I have a meeting to go to. I'll catch up with you later.'

Richard pulled away, taking what seemed unnecessary care to check for any traffic coming up from behind. His was the only car to be seen.

'How come there are so few cars here?' said Lisa.

'Most people don't need one,' said Richard. 'Everyone walks or cycles or, if people need to go to one of the other villages, they ask someone who has. There's also an hourly shuttle service between the five villages, six days a week. Most of the little motorised traffic is commercial vehicles or from the base. You're welcome to use our car whenever you like, as long as you keep within Templewood. It'll be automatically disabled if you get within a few kilometres of the boundary. Otherwise, you can borrow our bikes and cycle to wherever you want to go. We have a dinghy and a canoe you're welcome to use on the canal, too. Oh, and on weekdays, the school bus passes Mill Cottage once a day in each direction. The driver will be happy for you to flag him down. And it's totally safe to walk — there's no crime here.'

The car pulled into the drive of Mill Cottage. Alice opened the front door and shook her long white hair over her shoulders before kissing each of the women on both cheeks.

'I thought Peter would be coming with you.'

'He said he'd join us later,' said Emily.

'Come in, come in. I'll make us all some coffee, assuming you drink coffee.'

'Coffee would be great,' said Lisa. 'What a lovely house; have you lived here long?' Rachel nodded, smiling.

'About fifteen years. It was a wreck when we moved in; we both believed it deserved to be saved, and we wanted to live outside of the villages, away from daily contact with others. You'll have guessed from the name that it's a former mill, and it's located on the site of a medieval monastery. It represents an important part of Templewood's heritage. It's much too big for the two of us; you are welcome to stay for as long as you're here.'

'That's very kind. We'll be careful not to get in your way. I expect you know that Peter's going to introduce us to people who want us to work with them on education and IT matters, so we'll be out a lot of the time,' said Rachel.

'Well, if there's anything you need or anything we can help you with, just let us know,' said Alice.

Richard came into the kitchen, carrying the bags from the car.

'There is one thing,' said Rachel. 'Peter mentioned the Third Force, but he seemed reluctant to tell us anything about them. What can you tell us, assuming you know who they are?'

'Yes, we do know. Everyone does,' said Alice.

Richard and Alice exchanged glances.

'It's a long story,' said Richard.

'Well, we're here, and we have plenty of time,' said Rachel. She smiled at each person in turn, then sat at the kitchen table, her hands folded in front of her as if waiting for one of a group of miscreant pupils to confess.

'I'm not sure how to put this,' said Richard. 'It's a big subject, bigger and more far-reaching than you can imagine. We knew you would ask us — we've discussed it with Peter. I don't wish to be evasive; it's best if Peter explains when the time is right.'

'I don't understand why the timing is important,' said Lisa. 'If it's such a big issue, we ought to know how it will affect us. Surely nothing's going to change by leaving it for another time.'

'No indeed,' said Richard. 'Let me explain Peter's reasoning. The situation is complex. Here in Templewood, you will encounter things you will never have dreamed of. Peter's plan is to introduce you to everything that's going on here — the objectives of our community, the research, the role we'd like you to play…'

'How intriguing! Is it something illegal or subversive? Are we in any danger? I don't wish to sound rude, particularly as you are being so kind in putting us up,' said

Lisa. 'I'm sure you can understand how strange the whole situation is for us.'

'You're not at all rude,' said Alice. 'I don't blame you for being concerned. I don't believe you are in any more danger than we are, and there's nothing illegal going on. Ultimately, the work of Templewood will provide enormous benefits to the vast majority of the human race.'

Emily folded her arms. 'Please, Alice. Don't say too much. No surprises for us. Not yet.'

'I'm sure it won't be long before Peter explains everything — I know he will. In the meantime, please trust us.'

'You're right,' said Rachel. 'Let's lighten up. We've only just arrived. There'll be plenty of time for all the other stuff.'

'I'll show you your rooms,' said Alice. 'I suggest we spend the day relaxing and quietly getting to know each other. Everything is new to you and, as you say, it's all a little strange. Do feel free to ask us for anything you need or want explaining. I'll leave you to look around the house and garden, while I prepare some lunch. Will something light be all right? We'll have a proper meal this evening with Peter.'

'Yes, that sounds good,' said Lisa. 'We'll give you a hand.'

'Emily, why don't you go and talk to Richard while I get to know our guests better?' said Alice, gesturing with her head towards the garden. Emily took the hint.

*

Alice spent the afternoon chatting to Lisa and Rachel about their backgrounds, their views and aspirations and their likes and dislikes. Nothing of importance was discussed; Alice allowed the girls to drive the conversation.

'Look at the time, I hadn't realised it was getting late,' said Rachel. 'Come on Lisa, let's wash up.'

'I'll tidy things away and show you where to find everything, then I'll get started on preparing dinner,' said Alice. 'It's Richard's turn to cook, but he's still deep in conversation with Emily. I hope you'll both be comfortable here. I know it's not grand; we prefer comfort to style.'

'Yes, thanks. It feels very comfortable and homely. Thank you for making us so welcome. Before we forget, we need to sort out how to pay you,' said Lisa.

'What do you mean? What do you need to pay us for?' said Alice.

'For our accommodation, for letting us stay with you,' said Lisa. 'We'll buy our own food, of course.'

'Nonsense,' said Alice. 'There's enough room for you both, and it's a pleasure having you here.'

'We should still make a contribution to your household expenses,' said Rachel. 'It's only right.'

'What expenses? There are no expenses,' said Alice.

'Presumably, you pay Council Tax; then there are the utilities: water, electricity…'

'There are no such expenses in Templewood,' said Alice. 'There are no taxes of any kind, and water and electricity are provided free of charge. I'm sure Peter will explain. Here he is now.'

I hope you don't mind me coming in without knocking,' said Peter. 'The door was open.'

'Of course not,' said Alice. 'We were just explaining to your friends were that there are no taxes or utility charges in Templewood.'

'It's one of the perks of living here,' said Peter. 'Everyone is working, in some way or another, on supporting the Sect's work or providing services to the community. In return, the villagers live comfortable lives at little or no personal cost. Healthcare and pensions are provided free of charge. Loyalty is rewarded by keeping everyone happy and free of day-to-day worries.'

'Supposing someone is really ill and needs specialist healthcare. Do they have to go outside?' said Rachel. 'I don't imagine a place of this size would have a proper hospital.'

'In general, no. It would be most unusual,' said Peter. 'Residents benefit from the pioneering work undertaken at the military base, including medical research. There is a cottage hospital, as it's known, although it's a little larger than the name suggests. In the unlikely event that someone needs any other form of treatment or care, it can be provided by other centres run by the Sect worldwide.'

'I'm having trouble coming to terms with the idea that there's a military base here. It feels a bit sinister,' said Lisa.

'As I said yesterday, it's nothing to worry about; it's purely for security purposes,' said Peter. 'In the unlikely event that Templewood were to be located and attacked by an outside party, it's there to provide a defence. Its other role is to house elements of the Sect's global research in a secure environment. You certainly won't see troops in uniform on the streets.'

'I still don't understand how, if Templewood is unknown to the outside world, it can afford to provide these benefits,' said Rachel. 'Especially as it has no commerce with the surrounding area.'

'The Sect has secret connections and adherents worldwide,' said Peter. 'They control more or less unlimited funds. As for the people living here, they, we, could probably manage without any form of currency. It's just a token trading mechanism. Nobody has any desire for wealth — everyone has access to everything they need.'

*

'A splendid dinner. Thank you both so much,' said Rachel.

'It was a pleasure. Peter, Emily… Are you sure you wouldn't like to stay here tonight? There's plenty of room, as you know,' said Alice.

'Thanks, we'd better be getting back. There are a few things I'd like to chat to Peter about.'

'What's happening tomorrow?' said Rachel.

'We'll let you settle in over the weekend and get your bearings,' said Peter. 'Emily can show you around Temple Walden. That won't take long. As outsiders, you'll find it a little strange. In some ways, it seems as if it's caught in a time warp, stuck in the nineteen-fifties, like a village in an Agatha Christie novel. Then on Monday, things start to get interesting — the start of your proper introduction to Templewood. I've arranged an outing, a visit to one of the farms. Emily and I will meet you in the morning at Flour Mill Lock. Will ten o'clock be OK?'

'Sound interesting. I'm sure we can manage that. How will we find it?' said Lisa.

'It's about a mile downstream. You can't miss it — just follow the canal towpath. Richard and Alice will set you off in the right direction,' said Emily.

'I'll drive you back to The Abbot's House,' said Richard. 'Let's make a move. It's getting late.'

'Sleep well, you two,' said Alice.

7 - THE FARMS

Monday 13th July: To Solomons Farm

Peter and Emily had sat waiting at Flour Mill Lock for half an hour.

'Where on earth are they?' said Emily. 'Thank goodness for the tea room.'

'It's only a twenty-minute walk. They can't possibly have got lost if they followed the canal,' said Peter.

'Unless they walked along the north side. There's no through footpath and the bank's overgrown.'

'Ah, here they come now.'

'Sorry we're late,' said Rachel. 'It's such a lovely change to be able to walk in the countryside. There's so much new to see. We kept stopping to look at things.'

'No problem,' said Peter. 'We should have offered to meet you at Mill Cottage. On the other hand, it's a good idea to start learning your way around. Right... where we are now is directly north of Temple Walden — you just follow the road up the hill for a mile. Solomons Farm is part-way up and off to the left, towards the east. That's where we're going today.'

'Why are you taking us to a farm? What are you going to show us?' said Lisa.

'That's a surprise.'

*

'Well, if it isn't Emily Walden. I never expected to see you back here. You've hardly changed.'

'Good morning, Mr Nightingale. You're looking very well,' said Emily, smiling broadly, uncertain whether 'looking very well' would be taken as a polite greeting. Her enduring memory of him was the bright red face and the bulging eyes that looked about to explode.

'Call me Roland. We've no need for formalities. You'll find things are different here in Templewood these days. Everything's much more open. We have your brother here to thank for that. I understand that you and your friends have come to help us. I'm not sure how, or even why we need help, but the more people we have the better. Of course, they have to be people we can be sure we can trust.'

'Which is why they've been selected,' said Peter.

'I'm sure,' said Roland. 'Introduce me to your friends'

Introductions and pleasantries exchanged, Roland invited the group to follow him through a network of footpaths across the farm.

'All the fields seem to be growing the same crop. I don't recognise the plants. What are they?' said Lisa.

The plants grew to shoulder-height and covered the deep red earth from close to the top of the hill to where the canal lay below. Grey-yellow leaves, their edges, some tinged, some coloured, with black grime, speckled, mottled, encrusted, which, at its thickest, dripped an oily liquid. Flowers grew from the upper branches, their colour indefinable, close to purple yet not purple. It was not a known and recognisable colour that could be named.

'*Purgatem arem*. They were brought here, given to us as a gift,' said Peter. 'They clean the air of pollution. Of course, all plants do that to some extent. The interesting thing is that these use the extracted pollutants as a growth agent. The more they absorb, the more they grow and multiply. The amazing thing is how tolerant they are of temperature variations. Most plants will grow only in, say, temperate, tropical, alpine or desert climates... These will grow anywhere, from zero to fifty degrees centigrade. We've performed selective trials in a number of locations — all secret of course. Soon we'll be in a position to roll them out across the world.'

'That's weird. It's like something out of science fiction. Won't that give the game away?' said Rachel. 'That something's going on that's out of the ordinary? There must be a genetic feature that identifies them as being so different from anything else recorded,' said Rachel. 'It's as though they've come from another planet.'

'What about the issue of introducing them to other countries: places like Australia and New Zealand, and others, presumably, where there are strict laws regulating alien species?' said Lisa.

'To answer your point, Rachel, it depends on what you mean by unnatural. It all depends on what you are familiar with,' said Roland. 'Whilst it's true that they are unrelated to any species anywhere in the world, they have a similar life cycle to the plants we know and grow. By applying our expertise of the phytotomy and phytomorphology of existing species...'

'Stop there, please — you've lost me already,' said Lisa.

'I'm sorry. By studying the internal and external structures, we can demonstrate that they are unique, that is to say, not part of any known species or genus of plants. In fact, they cannot strictly be classed as members of the kingdom of plants. To complicate matters more, they are in fact two life forms, with a symbiotic relationship. It's easier to understand if you think of one of the pair as being a vegetable, but not quite, and the other as a fungus, but also not quite. The fungal element absorbs what we regard as pollutants and produces nutrients that benefit the vegetable.'

'Peter, you say they were brought here as a gift. Who brought them, and where did they get them from? Were they bred, if that's the right word, in a laboratory, by some secret genetic process?' said Rachel. 'And to pick up on Lisa's point, are they legal... and safe?'

'I'll tell you more in a few days' time. Please bear with me, I'll explain everything when the time is right. The important thing is to give you a general idea of the work we're doing here, then I'll put it all into context.'

'Let's go back to the farmhouse,' said Roland. 'There's something else you might like to see and then we'll offer you some tea.'

Roland led the women along a path through the trees surrounding the farmhouse to a low-level building, half sunk into the ground, its roof covered with grass and wildflowers.

'This is new,' said Emily. 'I remember the telephone exchange used to be here, just two rooms in a dreadful nineteen-sixties building. This camouflage is interesting and quite attractive.'

'Oh, the planting. It's not camouflage. When we decided to get rid of that dreadful old building, we were determined to replace it with one that blended more naturally into the surroundings. We wanted it to complement the classic design of the farmhouse,' said Roland. 'Its function is still telecommunications. The actual exchange is now fully automated and relocated at the research centre, where it's better protected. We use this building for monitoring. It's more convenient than bussing the staff out to the base. I believe you'll be spending some time here, Lisa.'

'So, this is where I'll be. I've no idea what's expected of me, but I'm pleased to have a new challenge,' said Lisa.

'I'll quickly show you around inside and then we'll have that tea.'

Tuesday 14th July: To Whytecliffe Farm

'Where are you taking us today then, Peter?' said Rachel. 'I hope it will be as interesting as yesterday's visit to Solomons Farm.'

'On a boat trip, initially. We'll be hitching a lift on a barge to Temple Mills Lock, a few miles on from Flour Mill Lock where we went yesterday, and then I've arranged for us to borrow some bikes for the rest of the journey. It's a six-mile ride to Whytecliffe Farm. There's something there I'd like you to see. You won't be disappointed.'

'Six miles! On our second day? I can't remember the last time I rode a bicycle,' said Lisa.

'It'll soon come back to you. The roads aren't exactly busy, so you'll be quite safe,' said Peter.

'I'm more worried about being out of condition,' said Rachel. 'It's all right for you rural types!'

They took the short walk from Mill Cottage to the canal. The engine on one of the barges came to life. The bargee, a young woman dressed in blue dungarees, her long hair tied back, placed a wooden ramp to span the small gap between the boat and the towpath. Hardly necessary, thought Rachel; there was little difference in height.

'That must be ours,' said Peter. 'Come on, climb aboard. It's probably slower than walking, but you'll need to save your energy for the bike ride.'

The women crossed the ramp and climbed a short ladder to sit on the roof of the barge, where they could enjoy the sun and the views. The bargee remained silent, occasionally smiling in response to eye contact with her passengers.

'I'm surprised how quiet it is,' said Rachel. 'I would have expected it to start with a loud chugging and clouds of diesel smoke.'

'It's electric,' said Peter. 'We don't use fossil fuels here. The nearest we have is biofuels — they're used mainly for agricultural vehicles and the few hybrid cars left.'

After twenty minutes, they arrived at Temple Mills Lock.

Rachel and Lisa enjoyed watching the water level drop as one pair of lock gates closed behind the barge and another pair opened. The barge passed through and drew alongside the bank. The bargee threw ropes over two cast iron bollards to secure it fore and aft. Peter led the party to a brick shed where he and Emily helped Lisa and Rachel adjust the saddles of their bicycles before they set off. It took Lisa and Rachel only a few minutes to regain their youthful confidence and control. An hour later, they arrived at Whytecliffe Farm.

*

'I remember this place well,' said Emily. 'It looks so different now. The first time we came here, there were so many different kinds of fruits and vegetables: olives, bananas, apricots — things you wouldn't expect to grow in this country.'

The fields, divided by hedges and fences, stretched from the edge of the canal to the foot of a cliff face, some miles away, and beyond to the eastern horizon.'

'How could that be? As you say, none of those grow here, in this country,' said Rachel. 'Presumably, they're grown under glass, or in some ultra-protected environment.'

'Not at all,' said Peter. 'They grow out in the open, as they would in Europe, Africa and elsewhere. The plants and trees were genetically modified to tolerate an extreme range of temperature and water conditions. They also benefit from the microclimate that exists in the shadow of that cliff face to the north creates a unique environment for testing. Hugo Payne, whose land this is, has been developing genetically improved versions for years. The Masters are waiting for the right time to announce them to the world. The intention is to distribute them freely, to developing nations in particular, to alleviate hunger and poverty.'

A pickup truck pulled out from behind a hedge, with no warning. It glid to a halt, silently, other than the sound of the tyres in the ruts of the dry mud track.

'That made me jump! I expect I'll get used to these quiet

electric vehicles eventually, just like I did when they introduced the trams in the city,' said Emily.

Two men jumped down from the truck and walked towards the group, each with a hand outstretched.

'Emily! I'm surprised I recognised you after all these years. Welcome back.'

'Hello, Hugo. How are you? And you, Eric? Rachel, Lisa… meet Hugo Payne and his nephew, Eric Betterby. Peter and I go back a long while with them.'

'Pleased to meet you,' said Hugo. 'You do indeed. Peter saved Eric's life many years ago. It was the beginning of a complete change in the dynamics of relationships in the village. In fact, if it weren't for Peter, we may none of us be here.'

Peter turned away, pretending to admire the view while they completed their introductions.

'Jump on the back of the truck. You can leave the bikes here — no-one will steal them. We'll take you to see our exciting new crop.'

They drove along parched tracks through fields of grasses, fruit trees and fruiting crops, some of which they could not recognise, until they reached a tall, thick hedge, running from the canal bank towards the distant northern cliff face.

'That cliff was created by a giant landslip caused by an earthquake, centuries ago,' explained Emily. 'It's what's given the area an extraordinary microclimate, allowing the cultivation of fruit, vegetables and trees you wouldn't normally find in this country.'

Hugo drove alongside the hedge to a gap midway in its length. He and Eric stepped out of the truck and held the rear doors open while the women climbed down from the high interior.

'What's this crop?' said Emily. 'It looks similar to bamboo in the way it's growing. I can see that it's not, from the differences in the stalks and leaves.'

'We call it *lignum petrum* — stone wood. You're right in

that bamboo is the closest comparable plant. You probably know that bamboo is a type of grass — this crop is unrelated. It shares many characteristics of bamboo: it's strong, fast-growing, malleable. It has a high strength-to-weight ratio, yet it can be worked in many ways: cut, split, shaped and so on. The leaves can be spun, or woven into cloth, without the use of the harmful chemicals used to produce material from bamboo. Unlike bamboo, it doesn't require treatment to resist insects and rot and is not damaged by contact with water. This makes it particularly useful to replace or supplement the use of bamboo in construction, which you may or may not know is a common use in the parts of the world where it grows. Not only is it virtually indestructible, it offers protection against earthquakes and cyclones. Its strength helps to protect the buildings, while in the event of a collapse, or damage, the light weight means that there is less risk to human life. And of course rebuilding, particularly of simple buildings, is inexpensive.'

'It sounds wonderful,' said Emily. 'Almost too good to be true.'

'One of the things I like about it is that it provides benefits to all sections of society, from the sophisticated buildings of developed countries to the simple dwellings of those in the third world,' said Eric.

The benefits to the environment are enormous,' said Hugo. 'It's organic, does not require processing with harmful agents… And it will virtually eliminate the need for concrete and all the water that concrete requires.'

Hugo and Eric enthusiastically described the work they undertook with other crops. They answered the women's queries with clear explanations, unencumbered with scientific jargon. Peter remained quiet; there was nothing more he could add, either by description or further explanation. Eventually, he drew attention to the time.

'We should be getting back now. I need a shower before the Council meeting this evening. Will you be there, Hugo?'

'I certainly will.'

'You're on the Council, Peter?' said Lisa.

'Yes, I was elected on when Michael, my father, resigned. He thought it wasn't right to continue as he was away for long periods and hardly ever able to attend. I didn't exactly put myself forward.'

'You were a popular choice, Peter, given your contribution to the community. You deserved to be press-ganged,' said Hugo. 'I'll give you all a lift back to the village.'

'Perhaps you could drop Lisa and me off at Flour Mill Lock. We can walk on to Mill Cottage from there,' said Rachel.

'Nonsense, I'll take you all the way. In fact, I'll drop you off first. It's no trouble.'

'What's the plan for tomorrow, Peter?' said Lisa.

'We'll be going to Saracens Farm. Lots of interesting research going on there. You'll enjoy it.'

Wednesday 15th July: To Saracens Farm

'Emily! I was beginning to wonder when you'd get round to coming to see me,' said Sarah. 'Françoise! Françoise! Emily's here, with her new friends from the city. Welcome to Saracens Farm. Well, are you going to introduce us, Emily?'

Sarah hugged Emily so hard that she took her breath away.

'This is Lisa, and this is Rachel.' Each hugged Sarah, more gently.

'Here comes Françoise now.' Françoise smiled and stretched out a hand in greeting.

'Peter told me you were working with Sarah,' said Emily. 'That's so good after all she's been through in the past.'

'We work well together,' said Françoise. 'It all started shortly after Thomas Fitzjohn was killed in the collapse of the Sect's control centre. I'm sure Sarah won't mind me saying that she was apprehensive, lacking in confidence when she was asked to stay on here and manage the farm.

Hardly surprising, given some of the animal genetics research the Sect had insisted Fitzjohn do as part of the terms of him continuing to live here.'

'I was more interested in science and technology,' said Sarah. 'Fortunately, I was offered fast-track education and training overseas. Françoise and some of the villagers looked after the farm while I was away. By the time I came back, all of the animal projects I had objected to had been discontinued. What animal and insect research that continues here is benign and conforms to normal — more than normal: enhanced, welfare standards. Françoise looks after that side of things. I concentrate on the technology.'

'You do have the genetics sideline with Dr Jay, though,' said Françoise.

'True. That's because I have the benefit of having worked with Thomas and learning from his experience. I've no qualifications, only the informal learning that I've maintained out of interest. While I was at uni, I'd attend some life sciences lectures — nothing to do with my course. It was a good way to study really: informally and selectively, taking an interest only in those topics that were of interest or use, with no obligation or pressure to take exams. As for the farm, since I've been back here, I've built a team of almost thirty people. A long way from when Thomas ran it on his own with occasional assistance from me and some casual labour. Come along, let me show you around, and then I'll try to answer your questions.'

*

'Some of the work we do here is tactical, such as looking at ways in which we can extend the life of batteries. It's ridiculous that in this day and age that we still need them. We can't wait for a replacement technology to become operational, so it makes sense to make more efficient use of the technologies we know and understand. We're so dependent upon batteries; think how dependent we are on mobile phones, for example. The real goal is to replace the phone with new methods of communication. If we can achieve that, it would deliver a real win-win result. It would eliminate the need to mine many of the rare minerals used in their manufacture, as well as dependence on the batteries.'

'How can you possibly replace them?' said Rachel. 'There are more mobile phones on the planet than people. What could you put in their place?'

'It's an enormous challenge, and one that personally interests me. To find the answer, you have to look at how communications work in general.'

'I don't see how you can find anything new to explore,' said Rachel. 'We're limited by our senses, both to send and to receive messages. Whether it be by written or oral language, or visually — electronically — through screens or some other visual interface, leaving aside tactile communications, such as braille.'

'I agree, we are limited, and that's the challenge — to overcome the limitations, to think in new ways. Perhaps to communicate without using our senses.'

'How would we do that?' said Emily. 'The only thing I can think of is telepathy or some other form of thought transfer.'

'You're on the right track,' said Sarah. 'What we have to do is to look at how all living things communicate: the ways birds flock and fishes move intuitively in shoals. We call it intuition without having any true idea of how the group acts as a single entity. Even then, once a possible solution is identified, there are other considerations to be taken into account. It's not as simple as saying "right, this is how we're going to do it from now on".'

'I know I'm being remarkably dim,' said Lisa. 'I don't understand. What are these considerations?'

'There are several strands. Obviously, there are the channels… Who are the parties communicating? Are they one-to-one, many-to-many, etcetera? We manage those things now, by passwords, encryption, permissions and so on. Where real value can be added is by analysing the purpose and intent of the messages. Information filtering, if you like, or truth validation and probability. And then there are the thought processes themselves. If we could speed up the way people think... That's already been identified as a key route for speeding up athletic performance, in footballers, for example, and it has much wider applications. Just think how valuable all these things could be in political diplomacy and avoiding conflict.'

'That implies monitoring communications,' said Lisa. 'I know it's common enough in the present world, we all know that. What you're saying suggests it will happen in a more widespread way and in much greater depth.'

'I agree,' said Sarah. 'Somehow, we have to balance controls and personal freedom with the benefits. The potential for tackling crime by predicting it has been widely discussed and speculated upon. If you could prevent crime and terrorism by the use of predictive algorithms, the social and financial cost of combatting and dealing with them could be reduced enormously. It could be taken a lot further too, introducing information filtering as a method of truth selection.'

'How do you put controls in place that are reasonable and not subject to abuse? It must be virtually impossible,' said Emily.

'Surely, to minimise the possibility of abuse of surveillance, you'd have to put even more monitoring in place. For example, you'd need to capture a lot of information about who is doing the monitoring,' said Lisa. 'It smacks of the Stasi, with everyone spying and informing on everyone else.'

'I'm not pretending it will be easy. That's one of the reasons it's so important to be ahead of the rest of the world in this area. The Sect is a force for good. It's far better that a single trusted party should control the content and flow worldwide, rather than numerous bodies, some highly disreputable, or even malicious.'

'Hmm,' said Rachel, exchanging glances with Lisa while

pretending not to.

'Let's move on. Tell us about some of the other work you're doing,' said Emily.

'Another key area is climate solutions,' said Sarah. 'We all know that the planet is at a tipping point and that nations and individuals are doing nowhere enough to facilitate changes in lifestyle. A priority area is the generation of cheap, clean and efficient energy.'

'Hardly surprising, it's a topical subject and in the news almost every week,' said Emily. 'I assume the focus is on extracting energy from natural resources — geophysical and the like.'

'Not entirely,' said Sarah. 'We believe that there are potentially a lot of free energy sources. Some of the work is directed at developing the ideas of Nikola Tesla.'

'I thought that had been debunked a long while ago and that his ideas were followed mainly by conspiracy theorists these days,' said Lisa.

'Indeed, the conspiracy theories go back a long way,' said Sarah. 'Let's not forget that Tesla's ideas attracted a lot of attention at the beginning of the twentieth century, to the extent that he was offered finance by J P Morgan.'

'I think you'll find that it was quite a small amount, around a quarter of a million dollars, if I remember rightly,' said Emily.

'Nevertheless, it attracted a lot of interest from the US Government and major business enterprises,' said Sarah. 'So much so, that one of the theories was that the oil industry regarded Tesla as such a serious threat to their revenues that they conspired to shut his enterprise down. I ought to correct myself here: we are picking up on Tesla's goals, rather than the specific ideas he was developing.'

'What else are you doing to combat climate change,' said Rachel, leaning backwards to avoid a bee. 'I thought bee numbers were in decline — there's no shortage here.'

Sarah grabbed at the air and caught one of the insects.

'Is that wise? Surely, it'll sting you,' said Lisa.

'There's no danger of that. It doesn't have a sting.' Sarah opened her hand. 'It's a drone. Our focus here has moved from genetically modified insects to replacing them with drones. There are numerous challenges, many of which we've now overcome. It will soon be a major success story and one that will benefit every country in the world.'

'Wow, that's impressive,' said Rachel. 'Does this mean that it will be possible to programme them to work crops and orchards more thoroughly and efficiently?'

'Exactly,' said Sarah. 'The drones will work the target crops with close to one hundred per cent efficiency, replacing or supplementing the work done by not only bees but also butterflies and other insects, as well as other creatures such as birds and bats. About thirty-five per cent of plants grown for human consumption require pollination. Most people are not aware that cereals don't, but thirty-five per cent is still a significant proportion.'

'Françoise mentioned your "genetics sideline" with Dr Jay. Tell us more about that,' said Emily.

'That's a big subject. It would take too long to go into the detail. Essentially, we are developing anti-ageing solutions in conjunction with the hospital. These come in a wide range, from slowing down the ageing process to replacing bodily organs and parts with artificial or cloned materials.'

'It sounds laudable,' said Rachel, 'How do you deal with the quality of life aspect?'

'That's one of the biggest challenges. As with any machine, there is only so far you can go with repair and maintenance to keep it performing effectively. Obviously, there is no point in prolonging the life of a client, as we like to call them, if their future life quality cannot be improved, or if the demands of care and sustenance become unduly onerous. There has to be a net gain to society, and we need the safety net of the client's agreement. Only the client can make that judgement.'

'Surely there comes a point where your "client" is

incapable of making that judgement or is too afraid of the consequences to decline further treatment,' said Rachel. 'That's where medical ethics committees and shared decision-making come in.'

'I leave that to others. I'm not involved; it's a specialist field,' said Sarah.

*

The tour of the farm and its research facilities had been interesting, with a hint of disappointment. The women agreed later that there is only so much to get excited about: visiting a series of research laboratories and production lines, which could be doing or making anything, for all they knew.

'We should be getting back now,' said Emily. 'Thank you so much for everything. You must be very proud of what you do.'

Lisa and Rachel nodded and smiled in agreement.

'It's been a pleasure. Come back whenever you like.'

'I'm sure we'll be seeing each other fairly regularly from now on.'

'Oh, Lisa, Rachel. Let me give you a little souvenir. Come with me.' Sarah led them to one of the farm buildings, leaving Emily alone with Françoise.

Françoise looked over her shoulder to check the Sarah was out of sight.

'Emily, I'd like to have a chat with you sometime. There's something I need to discuss with you, in confidence.'

'What can I say? Yes, of course. Can you give me an idea what it's about?'

'Not now, not here. It's something that's worrying me.'

'In that case, just let me know when it's convenient.'

'Please don't mention this to anyone.'

'Don't worry, I won't.' Emily nodded in the direction of the returning women. 'Here they come now.'

Lisa and Rachel were each carrying one of the drone bees. 'It's only the casing,' said Sarah. I thought they'd be interested. Here's one for you, too, Emily.'

'Thanks,' said Emily. 'We really must be off now. I hope to see you both soon.'

The women embraced each other in turn. As they left, Emily turned to see Françoise and Sarah walking towards the farmhouse, each with an arm around the other's back.

Monday 20th July: Interviews

'Today's the big day,' said Peter. He had walked to Mill Cottage to meet Rachel. Together they would take the school bus, due to pass in fifteen minutes, where he would introduce her to the Head of School, Sally Marlowe.

In the days when Emily and Peter were pupils, Sally's position was that of history teacher, with the additional responsibility of fulfilling a backup role for other subjects in the humanities. At that time, she was married to Stephen Marlowe, the parish priest. Stephen died in the collapse of the Sect's control centre, not as a consequence of the bringing down of the roof: he was shot, shortly before the collapse, by James Gillie, the gamekeeper, who had secretly brought the weapon into the cave. James had identified Stephen as unstable and a traitor to the villagers. He had discovered that Stephen was about to scupper the villagers' plan to destroy the centre, in his belief that the Sect's plan to destabilise the Earth's axis would bring about the Second Coming. Sally was initially under suspicion of colluding with Stephen. She was soon exonerated; Stephen was found to have acted alone. Perhaps out of guilt, or a wish to atone for her husband's act of betrayal, from that day on she applied herself exclusively to her career and was eventually appointed Head Teacher upon the retirement of her predecessor.

Peter and Rachel took the short walk to the bridge over the canal. There were no formal stopping points for the bus; all that was required was to wave it to a halt. The school and its pupils may have changed over the years, the bus had not.

It looked as though it had been built in the nineteen-fifties, with its curved lines, its cream bodywork and bright green mudguards and radiator. The bus served each of the five villages, starting from Lower Walden, travelling on to Temple Walden, Woddesleigh and Hexton, before arriving at St George's School on the outskirts of Little Walden.

'I didn't expect the bus to look like that,' said Rachel. 'It must throw out a hell of a load of pollution.'

'Not at all,' said Peter. 'Remember, I told you we don't use fossil fuels in Templewood. As for the appearance of the bus, the shell and interior are the refurbished original; the engine has been replaced — it's electric.'

'That's an incredible achievement. How are you able to do that here, when the rest of the world lags behind?'

'Well, for a start, we have the research capability. And the will. One of the most important factors is that the Sect, led by the Masters, is in control of the resources and the decision-making process. You could say that they are a benign dictatorship.'

'You mean there are no elections?'

'There's no need. Everyone is looked after, and everyone plays their part. It's win-win all the way.'

'I'm not sure what to say,' said Rachel. 'The idea is so foreign to what I'm used to. Oh well, I'm new here. It'll probably take a while to adapt.'

'Just go with the flow, and you'll have no problems,' said Peter.

Aboard the bus, the conversation was subdued. Most pupils spent the journey in silence, some making final additions or changes to their homework. The exception was a group in the rear seats who engaged in good-natured horseplay. Rachel kept her questions to the journey, its route and the surrounding countryside. She would discover soon enough what was expected of her at the school.

On arrival, Rachel and Peter were led from the bus to Sally's office by one of the teaching assistants.

'Just knock,' said Peter. 'I'll leave you here. You can

catch the return bus at the end of the day. Good luck!'

'Thanks. I'm looking forward to this, although I have to say I'm a little nervous.'

'You don't need to be. You'll be fine.'

Sally opened her office door. She greeted Rachel with a handshake, followed by an embrace and a kiss on the cheek. Rachel returned Sally's smile, taking in her appearance. The long curls marked her out as a woman of the turn of the century. Sally had never been concerned with fashion. She had always regarded it as a mark of vanity and a potential distraction from the work of her husband, likely to set her apart from him and his work. She did not regard this as a problem; she had her own career in which Stephen had supported her without interference. She believed that it was essential for the spouse of a priest not to stand out from the parishioners — she should be someone with whom all of them could identify. In the years following Stephen's death, she had continued in her habitual ways, although she no longer maintained a connection with the church.

'I've heard good things about you,' said Sally.

'I'm delighted to hear it,' said Rachel. 'How on earth can she know anything about me?'

'It appears that your true potential has not been realised, or even recognised, up until now. I believe that we can provide you with challenges and opportunities that have eluded you in the outside world.'

Rachel took a slow, deep breath and adopted her best pose of appearing at the same time professional and relaxed. 'That sounds intriguing. I'd like to learn more about your objectives and plans. What are you looking to achieve, and how may I help?'

Sally smiled. 'That's what I like to hear, a positive attitude. Let me pour you some tea. Our main goal is to produce a generation of thinkers. Young people with the potential of becoming world leaders in whatever field they choose to enter. I believe that the purpose of education should be to encourage students to extend the boundaries of human knowledge and experience, rather than to be repositories of facts. I see one way of achieving this is to deliver a method of accelerated learning and development, using whatever techniques and resources that may require. As for your role in this, we would like you to undertake a brief analysis of our curriculum and working methods. Feel free to speak your mind and give us all of the bad news, together with your recommendations. Once we've reviewed your findings, we'd like to discuss with you your proposed changes and to develop and agree a road map for implementation. Subject to mutual agreement, you would then lead this next phase. You will have unlimited freedom to make whatever radical changes are necessary to deliver the desired outcome. Budget will not be a problem.'

'I can't believe this. Am I dreaming?' said Rachel.

'Not at all, it's why you were invited here, or part of the reason. It's very important to us. Now, I'd like you to give me a summary, in terms of your skills, expertise and ideas, of your initial thoughts on the main areas of focus? Take your time.'

Rachel took a deep breath, crossed her legs and placed her hands, one on top of the other in her lap, looking upwards as she considered her response.

'I would be looking to introduce a programme of self-directed learning, assuming you don't have that in place already. It's been proven that learning things by rote and practising them by repetition just does not work. There are critics who are always keen to remind people that you never forget multiplication tables, but that's down to early learning. There are, of course, several such essential building blocks that we use in our everyday lives that need to be accomplished as quickly as possible — you will be aware of that. The key thing, as students mature, is that they need a methodology that motivates and sustains interest. I've tried to impress this upon my former employers without success. There just isn't the freedom within the national curriculum to innovate or to veer from the norm.'

'Why do you think this is?'

'It's all down to resources. For reasons of cost, the educational system can only provide a standard, vanilla, range of services, with little or no opportunity for specialisation below degree level. Students are offered a limited range of courses, of which several are compulsory, regardless of the usefulness of the amount of detail necessary to meet the objectives of the student.'

'Can you give me some examples?' said Sally.

'Take mathematics, for example. Everyone needs to achieve a basic level of education to cope with daily needs. We need arithmetic to be able to deal with money, to understand timetables, weights and measures and so on, but teaching the application of much of the knowledge is limited. As a simple example, students are rarely taught how to construct a cash flow forecast for their finances, yet many are forced to learn advanced geometry, which may be of little relevance to their lives or their main subjects of study. In some schools, pupils are forced to study three sciences, when a combined science course would often suffice. I believe the intentions are good — to ensure equality of opportunities — it's just that, well, what use are valencies and atomic weights if you want to be a barrister? I can understand why this should be the case: to offer a wider range of choices, there would need to be more teachers, trained in more subjects, at greater levels of detail. There just isn't the money and will available. I firmly believe we should be working towards a system where students have a bigger say in their education to be able to make informed choices. By being given control, they can make informed decisions, guided and supported by their teachers.'

'What about the teachers? What changes would you propose to their methods?'

'Teachers should be trained to identify the pupils' strengths and weaknesses in a wide range of skills. They should then match these attributes with the requirements of a wide range of professions, trades and vocations to determine the best fit. A specific curriculum should then be developed for each pupil to allow rapid further development of those skills.'

'You mentioned the limited resources available to most institutions, which contributes to the necessity to provide a "vanilla" education, as you put it. How would you address the requirement for an increase in those resources, in addition to the additional budgets required?'

'By a combination of directed self-study and smaller, more focussed teaching modules. Instead of class lessons for thirty pupils, all studying the same topic or topics for forty-minute periods, topics should be broken down into ten-to-fifteen-minute sessions, each with defined preparation and follow-up tasks. The class sizes would vary according to the level of interest, demands and relevance.'

'I like what I hear,' said Sally. 'What do you think would be the main implementation challenges?'

'Definition of the skill-matching process, module definition, planning the curriculum outline, teacher training... You've already mentioned budgets. There are quite a few.'

'How do you think success would be measured?'

'It depends whether you mean the success of the system or the benefits to the pupils. Arguably, many modules could be constructed on a pass/non-pass basis. Other, more creative modules would need to be assessed on a granular basis, with the more advanced ones subject to expert sector assessment, outside of the educational system.'

'I like that idea — extending the learning process beyond the educational sphere.'

'At the high end, more rigorous controls and standards would have to be designed. There are numerous dangers of involving commercial enterprises. For example, they could, if not monitored, devise programmes that limit the student's expertise to that required by a single specialist company, leading to a lack of freedom in future employment. It's also important to balance the benefit to potential employers of identifying the best candidates for their own vacancies with the wider needs of society.'

'What you seem to be saying is that there is a debate over where exactly the specialism you are advocating ends.'

'Precisely. One possibility is to provide expert peer-level evaluation of the modules, to define and agree those limits. All of this is obviously my ideal world view of the direction education should take. I can't ever see much of it being adopted.'

'Unlike wherever you have worked before, here there are no restrictions to change. There are no external examinations or qualification goals, no political influence and no artificial budget restrictions. In Templewood we seek the best. We are goal-oriented, in control of our own destiny. Tell me, Rachel, if we can offer you the resources you require, are you happy to take on the role?'

Sally looked Rachel directly in the eye, waiting for her to absorb the scale and importance of the offer. 'What do you think? Will you accept the challenge?'

'I don't know what to say. It really is like a dream. I've so many ideas that I thought would never be listened to... Yes! Yes! When do I start?'

'You already have. That's why you are here. Let's take a break for five minutes, then I'll introduce you to some of the other members of the team.' Sally stood up and gestured towards the door. 'Oh, and by the way, I understand you have other hidden skills. I believe you've done some research into a new form of linguistics: examining alternative methods of communication.'

'You certainly have done your background preparation. Yes, it's a personal project in that there are few people involved in the research. Unlike other fields, those who are interested are unusually reluctant to share their findings.'

'You may have hit the jackpot here then, Rachel. You could find your research is of interest to a wider audience tan you could imagine.'

*

Lisa, meanwhile, was at Solomons Farm with Roland Nightingale. As expected, Roland had given her a tour of the telecommunications centre. In her experience, Heads of IT and Telecommunications were always keen to offer tours of their physical empires. There was never anything new or interesting to see: it was all a matter of scale. One row of cabinets, flashing lights and wires looked much the same as any other. The only differences were the size of the installation, the neatness of the wiring and the physical security arrangements of multiple doors and cages.

Roland led Lisa back to the farmhouse. He introduced her to 'my wife' (it occurred to Lisa later that he had not mentioned her by name) and asked her, in an endearing, yet formal, manner to kindly bring them some tea.

'Tell me, Lisa, have you found it satisfying, working for large corporations as an anonymous, dispensable employee, despite your skills, competence and dedication?'

'Well, you certainly get to the point quickly. That just about sums it up. If I hadn't had been a contractor, confident of my ability to being taken on in a variety of enterprises, I would have found it very frustrating. There is so much I have to offer, but no-one in management ever wants to risk disrupting the status quo. True, people listen to what I have to say, yet no-one is prepared to take action. Like most employees, I've found it best to be competent, polite and cooperative, to occasionally put forward recommendations and suggestions for change but not to press or repeat them. In that way, I've been able to renew, or be offered, rolling contracts or, at the very least, I've been given good references. In answer to your question, no, it has not been satisfying. It's not all negative — I've been able to buy my own flat, the bills are paid, and I have enough disposable income to enjoy my personal life. I'd just like to feel more fulfilled in my career.'

'I thought as much,' said Roland, sitting back in his armchair, crossing his legs and interlocking his fingers. 'I think we can offer you something far more interesting.

Something that will use many of your skills, both formal and, well, how can I put it… unofficial.'

'All very cryptic. I'd be interested to learn how you know so much about me.'

'We've been aware of your abilities for quite some time. You first came to our attention when you were at university.'

'I don't understand. My time at uni turned out to be completely unremarkable. Quite disappointing, in fact. I worked very hard and was predicted to get a first. Unfortunately, I was quite ill in my final year with some undiagnosed condition that resulted in extreme lethargy. I found it difficult to concentrate and remember things. Eventually, it cleared up on its own and I managed to get a 2.1. I thought of resitting and was encouraged to do so. I decided, in the end, that it was better to get into the job market rather than spend another year with no money. After all, a 2.1 is still pretty good.'

Lisa had never attended a job interview held in such informal surroundings. Normally, during a final interview, there would be a second employer representative present. Typically, it would take place in a sterile meeting room with floor to ceiling glass walls, exposing the interviewee to the silent, curious gaze of others walking by. Bright lighting across a large table would illuminate every expression, tic and gesture. Lisa acknowledged the benefits of the present approach. She felt relaxed, willing to open up to a stranger who could allegedly be irascible.

'Allow me to interrupt you there. It was not your academic potential and achievements that brought you to our notice. Of course, once we were aware of what you were capable of, we began to pay detailed attention. No, your name first came up after you received a visit…' Roland hesitated, in anticipation of Lisa's reaction.

She could not disguise her shocked expression.

'…from the authorities. I'm sure you will remember well the discussion they had with you.'

Lisa had believed that the incident had been forgotten. At the time, she had been let off with a warning. No further action had followed. Roland continued, beaming with triumph.

'I'm surprised that, if you were going to hack a website, you would choose to select a particularly sensitive government organisation. Surely, you must have expected to get caught.'

'I don't know what to say. It was curiosity. It was at a time that my course was focussed on computer security. I wanted to see how secure the site was. There was no malice or criminal intent. I just wanted to see if I could do it — it was an intellectual exercise.'

'You were very fortunate that no further action was taken. You could have gone to prison, even though it was a first offence. Why do you think you were let off with a very discreet caution? I'll tell you. We recognised your skill in getting as far as you did. It allowed us to identify a security flaw, which we quickly closed. Although you didn't try it again, we had to continually monitor you. That's why you were subsequently offered the position with GCHQ, to convert you from a poacher to a gamekeeper.'

'I only stayed there for six months, and I paid the price. I know I'm still being followed today, all these years later. Believe me, I've given all that up.'

'On the positive side, you are here today.'

'Are you intending to blackmail me?' said Lisa. 'You know I can't afford this to get out. I'll never get another job in IT.'

'Not at all. We have no interest in that.'

'Then what do you have in mind for me?'

'An opportunity to relive your youthful mischievousness. We want you to apply your utmost efforts to break into our network. Your role will be to test our systems to the limit and report any weakness or vulnerability. The difference will be that, instead of being an overgrown teenage hacker, sitting in your bedroom late at night causing mischief, you'll have full access, local and remote, to our Templewood sites as well as those we control overseas.'

'Wow, that's much more exciting than what I've been doing for the past few years!'

'And, when you eventually return to the outside world, we will provide you with first-class references.'

'How's that? I thought everything here was hidden, top secret.'

'We have contacts all over the world. The references could be from government agencies in many countries, endorsing your work at the highest level. Do you have any questions?'

'When do I start?'

Monday 20th July: Drinks after Work

Lisa and Rachel arrived at the New Inn, opposite the Temple Walden village green. The forecast was for a fine evening; Peter had proposed that the four meet for an early evening drink at seven to celebrate the new arrivals' first day at work. Rachel had arranged to meet Lisa half an hour earlier. She had suggested that it would be interesting to compare their day's experiences before Emily and Peter joined them.

They chose a table at the foot of the sloping garden, overlooking the green, away from potential listeners. Both were wary of Peter's advice to be discreet when discussing Templewood and its residents within earshot of others. Advice they agreed was sensible as they were newcomers to the area. Not that it would be a problem today; both were keen to share the excitement of the start to their new lives. They now felt they could justify the wisdom of their decision to come to Templewood.

'That's excellent news, Rachel. I'm so pleased you'll be doing something creative, where you can use your skills and ideas.'

'Once I get properly started yes. I'll need to spend a week or two looking at their current methods and then draw up a plan for change and a road map. It'll then have to be agreed and any new resources put in place… It could be a few months before we see any real change, but, yes, it's exciting. Your new role sounds exciting, too. All the fun of being a cybercriminal, or a spy, with none of the risks or consequences!'

'Well, they know I have a history, one I've tried to keep quiet over the years. It's explained how I've ended up here.'

'What do you mean?' said Rachel. 'What did they know about you, and how?'

'In my teens, I hacked into a Government system — not for any political reason, just because I could. I was caught and let off provided I went to work for GCHQ. I had no choice, really.'

'You didn't tell us that. How exciting! What was your role at GCHQ? Were you there long?' said Rachel.

'I've never talked about this before. It's not the sort of thing you can discuss, for both state and personal security reasons. I don't suppose it matters here. I wasn't there long — I left after six months. I learned a lot about how the Government monitors people and what they use the intelligence for. I won't go into details; it was too shocking. I thought that sort of thing only happened in films. I was so disappointed. I thought I'd found the ideal job, where I could use my talents. What I hadn't realised at the time was that I'd never be able to shake it off — the hacking and leaving GCHQ. I'm convinced I'm still being followed today. That's why I wanted to travel up to London alone, so I could shake off my "minders". Rather ironic, given that they steered me in this direction.'

'So, what did you do next, after leaving GCHQ?' said Rachel.

'I had to earn a living. Fortunately, no-one stood in the way of me getting another position. It's not as though I'd been convicted, and it wasn't in their interest to publicise it.

And so, I ended up in boring old insurance.'

'It looks like things are about to change for us all now.'

'Yes, and the best thing of all,' said Lisa, 'is that we didn't have to apply for the positions. They found us! Oh, and there's another thing I learned today. Roland told me that when I was young, I was offered a place at the school here. It's all beginning to fall into place now.'

'That explains why you weren't prosecuted for the hacking,' said Emily. 'They knew your parents' connection and marked you down as a future recruit.'

'I knew my parents were part of a worldwide scientific network, but I had no idea it ran so deep,' said Lisa. 'It's odd, I feel safer now. All these years I've felt threatened when, in reality, I've been protected.'

'I glad we came here now,' said Rachel. It's good to know we can be working on something where we'll make a difference. We've both taken a bit of a chance, and it was potentially risky.'

'Yes,' said Lisa. 'Like you, I'll have to spend some time familiarising with the existing systems and protocols, before any rigorous testing for weaknesses. I'd like to know more about this Third Force though, and why it's such a big secret. Peter said it took him years to find out what it was. If it is, as he says, a bigger threat than an asteroid striking the planet, it must be serious.'

'I'm not sure it is a secret. I get the impression everyone knows, except us. Richard won't tell us, because he's agreed that Peter will. Peter said he'll tell us in due course, once we've gained an understanding of how Templewood works… I assume it must be some sort of terrorist threat, sabotage probably — people trying to destroy the work that's being done here, for whatever reason. I'm not really worried about it; that sort of thing's a danger anywhere in the world these days, and we must be safer here, with the military presence.'

'Well, Richard did say we were safe and that there's no crime here. Perhaps Peter was referring to a global terrorist organisation, a threat from outside, although if the location is kept so secret, how did outsiders discover it?'

'I've no idea. I agree that's a possibility. It may be that they want to get hold of the benefits of the research being undertaken, although that doesn't sound likely,' said Rachel.

'Alice said that she didn't believe we are in any danger. She also said there's nothing illegal going on. I'm sure they wouldn't let us put ourselves at risk, especially so soon after arriving.'

'Mind you, she didn't respond to me asking whether there was anything subversive happening.'

'I think we could be looking for a problem that doesn't exist. After all, here we are, in a secret location with new people. No-one outside knows where we are apart from Catherine. It's only natural to have the occasional doubt. The important thing to remember is that everyone seems to be working together on the same side, on research that is claimed will provide enormous benefits to the majority of the world,' said Lisa.

'True,' said Rachel. 'Let me tell you about another odd thing. During my interview at the school, Sally talked of its main goal being to produce a generation of thinkers. They aim to produce young people with the potential of becoming world leaders in the career of their choosing. It reminded me of a public-school prospectus, ratcheted up a few notches.'

'She may just be talking things up, encouraging ambition in young people.'

'Maybe, although in most schools they express it differently, talking about "maximising students' potential", to be more inclusive of pupils with less natural ability. It was the way she said it. I had the sudden image of a community with a dystopian view of world domination. I was sceptical of how Peter described the Sect and its ambitions when we arrived. Now, it looks as though everyone's in on the plan. Which means that we're part of it too. What do you think is going on?'

'I'm sure we'll find out sooner or later. At the moment, I'm more interested in the excitement of it all,' said Lisa.

'Agreed,' said Rachel. 'Look, here come Emily and Peter.' She stood up and waved.

'Hi, how are you both. Let me get you another drink, and then you can tell us about your day,' said Peter. 'What can I get you?

'I'll get these,' said Emily. 'What would you like?

'Red wine for me,' said Lisa.

'I'd prefer white if that's OK?' said Rachel.

'I'll get a bottle of each.'

*

'So, tell me about your day, both of you,' said Peter. 'How are you finding things here?'

Rachel and Lisa took turns to describe their first impressions with enthusiasm and excitement, despite having spent the day being inducted into the workings and expectations of their positions, as well as the usual health and safety briefings.

'I forgot to mention,' said Peter. 'Your salaries will be paid into accounts at the Templewood Bank. I hope that's not a problem. It's all part of the security. Did they mention that at work?'

'No, they didn't,' said Lisa. 'I'll need some of the money to pay for my mother's care home fees.'

'Don't worry, that won't be a problem. We've arranged to pay those for you,' said Peter. 'When you eventually leave Templewood we'll transfer the balances to your outside accounts — all very discreetly, of course.'

'That very generous of you. The fees don't come cheap, though,' said Lisa.

'We couldn't possibly expect you to come here and be out of pocket. In fact, all of your regular bills and expenses will be paid. We'll be taking care of your homes — everything will be as you left it. You have nothing to worry about.'

Lisa and Rachel looked at each other in amazed silence.

'You really do want us here, don't you? I don't know what to say, other than thank you,' said Lisa.

'I don't understand. How can you do that? I mean, how can you know so much about us that you can step in and, well, run our lives for us?' said Rachel.

'Everyone leaves a digital footprint,' said Peter. 'The data is everywhere, in varying quantities. The granularity depends on the online activity of the individual. Some data is easily accessible; other information is more difficult to get hold of. Although many other individuals and organisations have access to vast quantities of personal information. Gathering the data is, in some ways, the easy part. The trick is to use and refine it, either at an individual level or a related group or groups. To make judgements and predictions of behaviour, using AI and machine-learning software.'

'Is that right, Lisa? Can IT really be used in this way,' said Rachel.

'It's becoming more and more common,' said Lisa. 'That's why a lot of people are deciding to go off-grid, as far as is possible with the Internet. The problem is that so much of our daily lives demands use of the web. As for using the data, it's becoming much easier to build a complete picture of an individual from their data. Take something as mundane as car or house insurance. Until recently, insurers made judgments largely based upon postcodes, even though two ends of a street could be completely different in character, house size and occupancy. Nowadays, they can assess you as an individual, taking into account all aspects of your lifestyle to assess you as a risk.'

'It's misuse though — doing it without consent, using my information to take over parts of my life. Even if I would have agreed,' said Rachel, looking towards Peter.

'Yes, it is, but it's for your benefit, and there was no way we could have asked you before you arrived. Believe me, your information is safe with us. And no-one will know it's not you paying your bills,' said Peter.

'Don't worry about it, Rachel — there are probably far

more sinister bodies using your data right now.' Rachel and Peter laughed.

'That's no comfort to me at all! OK, I'll drop the subject, but there's something else I want to ask. Peter, how is it that Templewood, or the Sect, gets their knowledge of all these new discoveries and inventions ahead of the rest of the world?' said Rachel.

'Well, there's a big question!' said Peter, smiling. 'All in good time. Don't worry, you'll soon find out. It won't be long.'

'I suppose we can trust you on that subject, especially as you are doing a lot for us. You haven't yet told us what your role is in Templewood, Peter,' said Lisa. 'You do have a job, as such, I assume?'

'I have a role; whether or not it can be called a job is another matter. I suppose I'm a coordinator, of sorts. I liaise between the various sections of the community — the mayor, the Council, the farms and other businesses, and the base — a sort of facilitator. I talk to people, find out if they have any problems, both personally and with their work here. If there are ways in which I can help, by getting people together, negotiating and commissioning resources, then I do my best. Given the divisions in the village in the past, it's so important to ensure people keep working together.'

'What about you, Emily? What will you be doing while we're here? Is there a local newspaper, or online news service?' asked Rachel.

'I need to speak to Emily about that,' said Peter. 'We have the Templewood Gazette, which has a print news run, but no web-based feed. It's for security reasons, to avoid the unlikely event of people outside hacking in. To answer your question, I'd very much like to arrange for Emily to assist them, working closely with me.'

'I assume the Gazette is still owned by Martel?' said Emily.

'Yes, and still edited by Simon Barrington,' said Peter.

'I don't really know Barrington. I think I only met him

the once. I'm sure I can work with anyone — yes, I'm happy with that,' said Emily. 'It'll keep me close to what's going on.'

'Excellent!' said Peter, leaning forward, his hands on his knees. 'Everything's beginning to come together.'

'Peter,' said Rachel, 'Can I say something? I know I keep repeating myself, but I have the feeling that there's something really big that you're keeping from us; something important that you're holding back.'

Rachel and Peter made eye contact in silence. Peter looked away first.

'Yes, that's true, and for good reasons. It was essential that you should get settled in and to see how Templewood works, so that you could put everything into context. You'll be interested to know that soon I'm going to show you something that will astound you, something that will help you make sense of what's going on here.'

'Sounds intriguing,' said Rachel. 'I do like a mystery. And I like solutions even better.'

*

They had not noticed dusk descending until one of the bar staff carried a tray of covered tea lights into the garden and placed one on each occupied table.

'We ought to go soon,' said Rachel. 'I don't really want to walk back to Mill Cottage in the dark, and there's work tomorrow.'

'You're right. It's been a lovely evening; it's passed so quickly. Let's meet here again on Friday, shall we? It'll be a good start to the weekend,' said Lisa.

'Can we make it Saturday — Fridays can be a bit hectic, and I like to plan for how much work I'll need to do over the weekend,' said Rachel.

'Let's do that then,' said Lisa. 'Same time?'

'How about a little later, say, half seven,' said Emily.

'Is that OK with you, Peter?' said Lisa.

'How about this for an idea?' said Peter. 'Why don't Emily and I come over to Mill Cottage on Saturday afternoon. I'd like you to prepare yourselves for the important information that you've been so patiently waiting for.'

'About time too!' said Lisa.

'And then I'll take you somewhere later, to show you something that will blow your minds.'

'Sounds intriguing,' said Rachel. 'How could we possibly refuse?'

'Sounds like a good plan,' said Emily. 'OK, let's go home.'

They stood up, brushed a few small insects from their clothing and looked around to check they had all of their belongings.

'What's the matter, Rachel?' said Emily. 'What are you staring at? What have you seen?'

'What's that over there, the bright glow behind the trees?' said Rachel.

'Not a fire, I hope,' said Lisa.

'I don't think so. It's in the east; it's probably the moon rising.' said Peter.

The group exchanged final goodnights, hugs and kisses.

'Thanks for the wine, Emily,' said Lisa. 'My turn next time.'

'Oh, and about Saturday,' said Peter. 'Dress casually, for our little walk in the evening. Make sure you wear shoes suitable for walking.'

'Wouldn't it be best to do the walk first, before going for a drink?' said Lisa.

'That's what I have in mind. It'll take us a while to reach where we're going. We should be back around sunset,' said Peter. 'Believe me, you won't be disappointed.'

'I can't wait. I'm excited already!' said Rachel.

Wednesday 22nd July: The Council Meeting

Dr Eleanor Hadfield leaned forward to gaze through the window of her office, upstairs in the east wing of St Georges

School. Her arms rested upon across her antique yew pedestal desk. Her hands stroked the deep green leather inlay. It amused her to think of the contrast between its aged solid frame and her chosen career as Head of Science, a position requiring her to keep up to date with progress and evolving schools of thought. The desk provided her with continuity and dependability, an anchor to things unchanging, detached from whatever value it might realise at auction. Her one concession to status was her title. She preferred to be addressed as Doctor. After all, she had earned the distinction. It spared her from having to draw attention to her abilities by other means.

Dr Hadfield had enjoyed a long career at St Georges. She was valued as a scholar, a teacher of science and a member of the community. The assistance she had provided to Emily and Peter fourteen years ago had been crucial in helping them to thwart the Sect's plan. In the aftermath, her contribution was recognised when the Templewood Council appointed her as its first female member. On the occasions that she was reminded of this, she applied her acquired discipline to ignore the comments and suppressed her irritation. Things were different now: the community had moved on from the patriarchal society of earlier years. It was now only the farmers' wives who were near-invisible. She had met them at infrequent social events and had decided that they must be too busy managing farm business to socialise more or to become actively involved in village affairs. The younger women of Templewood were not burdened by the conventions of the older generation; mortality would bring a gradual, silent revolution. Dr Hadfield would lead by example and would restrict her lectures to the academic studies of her students.

It was almost time to leave for the Council meeting. She would, as always, participate in the debate as an equal, happy to let Sarah take credit for new ideas that she, Eleanor, may have seeded. Sarah was young; she was the future. She must use her time well.

*

The scheduled meeting of the Templewood Council began in the customary way, opened by Ronald Gygges. Gygges acted as Clerk to the Council and custodian of its agenda and protocols. Peter was convinced that Gygges had been born middle-aged: short, balding, his thin hair greased back to his scalp. He was always dressed in an old-fashioned three-piece suit that must once have been smart — 'dapper' came to mind — now faded, with shiny patches of wear on both jacket and trousers. After declaring the meeting open, Gygges reminded all present of the one subject that was not to be discussed or even named. He then rushed the full complement of eleven council members through the action points of the previous meeting before moving on to the main business of the second item. The Templewood Council was more than an inward-looking body concerned with the local affairs of the five villages. Its primary function was to control the community and report the progress and problems of its operations to the Sect through its nominated representatives, the Masters.

During the Templewood Summer, the Council had been divided between the Pros and Cons. Three of the four landowning farmers, Alexander Martel, Hugo Payne and Roland Nightingale, together with Dr Jay and Simon Barrington, had comprised the leading members of the Pros. The Cons had been represented by Richard Blanchflower, Andrew Blund (the estate agent, whose role was to control and, where necessary, subvert the sale of properties) and three others, now deceased. Thomas Canville, the bookseller, had drowned in mysterious circumstances, shortly after allowing Peter and Emily sight of one of the two copies of the Book of Mysteries, which recorded clues and information associated with the ancient prophecy. Thomas Fitzjohn, the rebellious farmer, who was opposed to the Pros' genetic experiments on wildlife and insects, died in the collapse of the Sect's control centre, as did the music teacher Piers Corman. Piers had helped inspire Peter to coordinate the means of creating the collapse, by orchestrating the rhythmic chants of assembled villagers to set up echoes and reverberations that brought down the roof, preventing the Sect from launching their missile.

Today, new members served in their places: Dr Hadfield, Sarah Montfort and Peter. Peter's father, Michael, had been a member. Michael was one of the few people allowed the freedom of movement to come and go to and from Templewood. It was accepted that his secret Government work benefitted the Sect's cause. Michael had resigned from the Council several years ago, owing to his frequent absences from the village. Peter was unanimously elected in his place.

Sarah had been a good friend to both Emily and Peter at the time they attended St Georges. Sarah and Peter remained friends to this day. Orphaned and bullied in her teens, she was resilient and astute in her assessment of events and relationships in Templewood. She had passed through the Sect's graduate programme, specialising in material sciences and technology and now managed Saracens Farm. Thomas Fitzjohn's family had historically owned the farm until a devastating fire destroyed the farmhouse. He was forced to sell to a consortium of the other three farmers, although he was allowed to continue as a tenant on condition that he continued the work of the Sect, researching genetically improved (they preferred the word to 'modified') species of animals and insects. Thomas was unhappy in this work and confided his dissatisfaction to Sarah when she helped out during weekends and holidays. Her interest in the principles and ethics of genetics was noted by the Sect. After graduation, she willingly accepted their offer to continue working in research, albeit not with animals. Over several years, she developed an interest in technological solutions to the challenges posed by the ambitions of the Sect, guided by the Third Force. The importance of her work earned her a place on the Council, where she was respected for her measured and rational approach.

The eleventh member of the Council was Arthur Welles, the mayor, who had held the role of Council Leader and neutral adjudicator in the event of tied votes for over thirty years.

'Item two, progress on strategic projects. Mr Nightingale, please present your report for item two point one, Consolidation of Crops,' said Gygges.

'Mr Gygges, members of the Council. We have now worked through two complete reproductive cycles of the *Purgatem arem* crop. The individual plants reproduce vegetatively, that is to say asexually, with no need for pollination or human intervention and with great vigour. They are hardy and tolerant of a wide range of temperatures and resistant to all known pests. Their main function and benefit, as you are aware, is to extract pollutants from the atmosphere, thus improving the quality of the air we breathe and reducing the effects of global warming. We estimate that under average conditions the crop will extract eighty-four per cent of detected pollutants. A valuable by-product of the crop is the conversion of the extracted material to a fertiliser that expedites growth of the crop, with a surplus that can be used for other purposes.'

'Thank you, Mr Nightingale. Does anyone have any questions or comments?' said Gygges.

'This sounds very promising,' said Hugo Payne. 'Have you detected any negative features during your trials?'

'None that will be a problem at the present time,' said Nightingale.

'That sounds more like a yes,' said Richard Blanchflower. 'Would you please provide us with a little more detail?'

'I mentioned the speed with which the plants reproduce,' said Nightingale. 'This is, of course, beneficial. Once we start to roll them out to the outside world, we can create a dramatic and rapid impact on air quality worldwide. I also mentioned their hardiness. This is an understatement. They are resistant not only to physical damage but also to fire, frost and herbicides. They are virtually impossible to kill. Indeed, they have the ability to sense a threat and will respond by division. It is therefore essential that they are grown in a contained and restricted area, to avoid undesirable spreading.'

'Are you confident that can be managed?' said Gygges.

'As with all science and technology, responsible management and controls are essential. Yes, in answer to your question.'

'Good. Let's move on,' said Gygges. 'Mr Payne, please update us with progress on your programme.'

Hugo Payne shuffled his papers and leaned forward, his hands placed on top of one another in front of him.

'We're continuing our work on genetic improvement to combat stress factors in plants. This is essentially a logical continuation of the work we've been doing for years: modifying plants to adapt to unusual or unaccustomed exposure to heat, cold, drought, flooding, heavy metals, salt, excessive light and pests. The development work, as you know, is undertaken by Mr Martel at the seed farm, where the gene chipping and modification takes place. Basically, we at Whytecliffe nurture and grow the modified crops in a test environment. With the additional assistance we've received from the Third Force, it's no exaggeration to say that we now have the making of a new plant kingdom for which these hazards are not an issue. Within two years, at the very most, we will have established a range of food and materials products that can be delivered out to, and will thrive in, any country in the world.'

'Excellent news,' said Arthur, his enthusiasm echoed by the nodding of heads and exchange of glances around the table. Hugo offered to describe his work in more detail. Gygges suggested that the meeting remain focussed on the key points of its agenda. Separate meetings could be arranged, if requested, to explore the detail of individual projects.

'Mr Martel, do you have anything to add to what Mr Payne has reported?' said Gygges

'Nothing that needs concern the meeting. We have well-established protocols for the physical processes of genetic engineering, using the benefit of Sarah's knowledge and wisdom. We engineer the modifications, Mr Payne trials them and feeds back any issues.'

'Good. Thank you. Sarah, please tell us where you have reached with the work you've been doing,' said Gygges.

'As you all know, I've always been keen on ecology and the importance of maintaining the balance of plants and wildlife species. Unfortunately, with the decline of the bee population for various well-documented reasons, my work in developing alternative solutions to replicate pollination by artificial means has become increasingly significant. I am pleased to report that I am making excellent progress and have produced a small range of prototypes of drones to replace the work undertaken by insects. Some of you will be aware that the basic idea is not new and that trials have taken place in the outside world. Unfortunately, these have not got far beyond the conceptual stage, with only crude prototypes having been developed. These are typically manual-controlled drones measuring four centimetres wide and weighing around fifteen grams. I don't need to tell you that these are impractical, both in terms of size and method of operation. For example, an almond tree will produce in the region of fifty thousand flowers. You can imagine the difficulties to be faced. In fact, I have been working on numerous challenges. Clearly, the size of the drone is a major constraining factor. If we are to replace or complement bees, we must develop something that embodies the key characteristics of bees, both in terms of size and behaviour. Something that has the manoeuvrability of a bee, which can collect pollen from one flower and transfer it to another, programmed to perform its work independently, without the need for significant human intervention. One of the biggest challenges has been to develop a means of pollen transfer. We need a form of weak glue, rather like a Post-it note, or something resembling Velcro, which can collect or pick up the pollen from the source flower and then release it to the target. We now believe we have the answers, and we will be conducting volume trials. Once these prove successful, we will be in a position to go into mass production.'

More nodding and pursed lips of approval spread around the table.

'Good. Now for your report please, Dr Jay,' said Gygges.

'Certainly. Mr Gygges, members of the Council, I am delighted to announce dramatic progress with our programme of anti-ageing trials. These have been conducted with volunteer outpatients and are intended to slow down and, in some cases, halt the human ageing process. Essentially, we have been working on combining knowledge, some of which is available from the outside world, on two fronts. I will keep my report brief, given that the results are based upon cutting-edge science, which is not necessarily easy to explain in layperson's terms. Firstly, we discovered that certain people with a mutation on a single copy of the SERPINE1 gene appeared to have a longer average lifespan and ten per cent longer telomeres, the small protective cap of nucleotides at the ends of chromosomes. These caps shorten and unravel over the lifetime of an organism's lifetime and are linked with the biology of ageing. Secondly, we are able to use advances in the use of CRISPR gene-editing techniques to slow, halt or eliminate age-related diseases, notably Alzheimer's. At this point I must acknowledge with gratitude the assistance I have had from Sarah, to build on the knowledge passed to us by the Third Force. The only other thing I wish to add at this stage is that I am confident we are on the brink of a major leap forward in extending normal human lifespan by a significant percentage.'

Dr Jay smiled and looked around the room, inviting

comments and praise. Peter fidgeted in his seat, taking care how best to frame his response.

'I have to say, Dr Jay, I have some concerns over the issue of extending people's lives by unnatural means.'

'Why should that be?' said Sarah.

'It's down to the quality of life. Ageing is a natural process. If we take away some of the factors in the normal process, we surely run the risk of bringing other, hidden problems to the fore. Instead of dying of old age, there could be worse fates in store. I don't know — I can't really justify it, it's just a feeling.'

'I can't think of many worse fates than Alzheimer's,' said Dr Jay. 'And with genetic editing and other means at our disposal, we can whittle away at many of the causes of death and discomfort, not only extending but improving the quality of life.'

'Peter, as you know, I was the last child to be born in the village,' said Sarah. 'Our population is falling here, as it is in our locations worldwide. As you also know, we have believed for many years that the unprecedented presence of infertility is linked to some aspect of our work, which we have been unable to pinpoint. We have to take action.'

'I agree with you, Sarah,' said Dr Jay. 'As regards our falling population, there are just three things we can do: solve the problem, bring more people in, or extend the lives of those here. Fortunately, the Third Force is providing assistance.'

'Yes, yes,' said Gygges. 'But for now, we must move on with the meeting. Item three on the agenda, if you please: proposed future projects. Mr Nightingale…'

'Thank you, Mr Gygges. We are in the process of producing a proposal to address issues associated with telecommunications. There are two strands to this: mobile phones and telecommunications generally. With mobile phones, there are many well-documented problems, including battery life and the shortage of rare minerals used in the construction of the physical devices. Batteries have been a problem for many years. We want to be able to take a giant step forward in battery technology so that we can either reduce the amount of charging required or make it more efficient. Potential methods include wireless power transfer and far-field wireless energy harvesting. This research is relevant not only to mobile phones but to wider industrial and commercial operations. If we could produce reliable batteries with extended periods of use, then fossil fuels to, for example, propel aircraft, could become a thing of the past. There are, nevertheless, numerous problems to be solved with far-field technologies, not least the potential health risks.'

'This strikes me as a tactical, rather than a strategic project,' said Gygges. 'Batteries are such archaic devices. I can't imagine them being in use in a hundred, or even fifty, years' time.'

'I agree, for several reasons. We won't be using mobile phones as such in the future; there will be alternative methods of communication. As for batteries…' Nightingale took a deep breath. 'We believe that the Third Force has knowledge of a previously unknown source of energy — clean, cheap and efficient….'

'How do you know this, and why aren't we pursuing that line of investigation?' said Gygges.

'From observation and deduction. They haven't yet shared it with us. Once they do, we'll be onto it straight away.'

'You mentioned two strands to your work in these areas. What is the other?'

'The Third Force is assisting us to locate new sources of trace minerals as well as identifying previously undiscovered ones.'

'This all sounds promising. We look forward to hearing more. Who's next? Any other future project proposals? Mr Payne? Sarah? Mr Martel?'

Sarah and Martel shook their heads. Sarah added that she might have something to offer at the next meeting, once her idea was properly formulated. She did not wish to take up the Council's time today. Hugo Payne hesitated, tapping the base of his pen on the table before deciding to speak.

'I, too, hope to have something to offer next time. You are aware that the Visitors have introduced us to a new raw material that is capable of replacing the need for many other of our traditional construction materials. It's strong, durable, rigid... but it can also be worked. It's almost indestructible. It grows organically and eliminates the need to take other resources from the planet. I believe it is capable of providing a replacement for concrete, wood and steel, thus also saving substantial quantities of water used in the production of those items. It appears to have some characteristics in common with organic matter. On the other hand, it is not classifiable — it is not animal, vegetable, or mineral, according to the accepted definitions of those categories.'

'This sounds promising,' said Gygges. 'Tell us, what is the source of this material?'

'I think you can guess that,' said Hugo. 'Rather than speculate now, I hope to be in a position to give a more detailed update at the next meeting.'

'Good. Let's move on to item four, security. Your report please, Mr Martel.'

'There's nothing significant to report, I'm pleased to say,' said Martel. 'The regular checks of physical security have revealed nothing untoward. We have completed the quarterly review with our international colleagues to validate the invisibility of Templewood to the outside world. There have been no instances of intrusion, whether deliberate or by accident.'

'Has anything been reported from Market Cranford?' said Gygges.

'I'll let Blund respond to that, if I may,' said Martel.

'Very well. Mr Blund, if you will...'

Blund sat up straight, his elbows on the table and his hands clasped together.

'Thank you, Mr Gygges. As you all know, my wife and I run an estate agency business with premises in two locations, Temple Walden and Market Cranford, that is to say, one office in Templewood and the other in the outside world.'

'Yes, yes. We know all that. You've been asked by Mr Martel to report on security, from the perspective of Market Cranford,' said Gygges.

'I'm coming to that,' said Blund. 'We, or rather my wife, has had a busy time in the past month with many new enquiries and several potential sales and purchases progressing towards completion. As you would expect, the enquiries are mainly from local people, within a fifteen- to twenty-mile radius of Market Cranford, most looking to upgrade, with a few downsizing. A small minority come from further afield, ostensibly looking for a new home to complement a career move. These are the ones we observe most carefully, as they are more likely to take an interest in the surrounding area.'

'Have there been any signs of an awareness of the existence of Templewood?' said Gygges.

'None at all. Occasionally there will be questions as to what lies in this direction, although they all seem to easily accept the existence of the natural barrier of the hills. We do, of course, have the relevant maps in the office from which they can verify this to be the case. They may well check again using their own maps but all of the country's maps are based on the national Military Mapping standard, on which, as you know, Templewood does not appear.'

'Does anyone ever ask whether you have other branches, with more properties on offer,' said Arthur.

'No, as far as customers in Market Cranford are concerned that is the sole office,' said Blund. 'The Temple Walden office continues to only offer properties in Templewood, catering specifically for those few legitimate Sect members who may be moving in or out of the area, where approved.'

'What about advertising in Market Cranford? How is that handled?' said Gygges.

'Our only advertising is through the local edition of the Templewood Gazette. Occasionally, larger, prestigious properties may be networked with national press advertising. The only other publicity we use is our shop window. We have deliberately avoided creating our own website, although we sometimes use the sites of third-party aggregation services.'

'Good. The next item on the agenda is community matters,' said Gygges.

This part of the agenda was designed to allow residents to put forward concerns and proposals arising from the day-to-day life in the five villages. These were invariably minor. Villagers were content in their lifestyle (most knew no other) and the Council responded quickly to any reported concerns to ensure this continued to be so. Gygges listed the topics; actions were assigned to address them and recorded. No items were raised under the heading Any Other Business. It remained to Arthur to summarise and bring the meeting to a close.

'I have one item of business to raise. We've heard a lot of good news today. Almost everything has been positive. With this in mind, I have decided to retire from the Council at the end of the year, by which time we should be rolling out of many of the developments we have heard about today. I would like to go out on a high note, and this should provide the best opportunity. I believe that we are in a position to recommend to the Masters on their next visit that they should put the mechanisms in place to trigger their plan for global control. I therefore propose a motion that we put this to the vote. Will anyone second the motion?'

Gygges raised his hand.

'All those in favour.'

All present raised a hand, except for Peter and Richard.

'Against?'

No hands were shown.

'I assume that you two gentlemen are abstaining,' said Arthur.

'Yes, I'm not sure we are quite ready,' said Peter, calmly looking towards Richard.

'I agree,' said Richard. 'We must take care — it all went horribly wrong last time.'

'Yes, but we are working cooperatively now. No-one is excluded,' said Arthur.

'Motion carried,' said Gygges. 'So, one last time — any other business?'

A few members shook their heads.

'Next meeting,' said Gygges. 'We need to set the date for the next meeting.'

'Yes, of course,' said Arthur. 'Given where we are, I propose we should set fortnightly rather than monthly meetings from now on. We need to keep on top of things.'

'I'll see to that,' said Gygges.

'Good, thank you. This meeting is closed.'

The entire group moved to an anteroom, where two tables bore drinks and canapés. With the formal business complete, the Council members took advantage of being together to hold informal discussions and catch up with news, without having to make advance appointments for meetings.

'Well, Peter, I must say you've done well. Young Lisa looks promising. As you know, I was wary of bringing in outsiders, but she's got off to a good start. Very personable, too,' said Roland.

'I've heard good things about Rachel, from Sally,' said Dr Hadfield. 'She's a much-needed breath of fresh air. It's good for the pupils to deal with new people. They will be stimulated, not only by her ideas and methods but by her enthusiasm and her exposure to a different world.'

'And we're all pleased to welcome Emily back. I never thought we'd see her again,' said Hugo. 'She'll be a valuable asset to Templewood — someone we can rely on to do the right thing.'

'She'll do an excellent job on modernising the Gazette,' said Roland.

'I hope so,' said Barrington. 'It's long overdue. We need a person like Lisa to guarantee the security necessary to bring us into the twenty-first century. She will also assist us to produce an online edition.'

'Let's not get too excited. We're off to a promising start. There's a long way to go,' said Peter.

8 - THE THIRD FORCE

Friday 24th July: Amit

'Amit. It's good to see you after all these years. How are you?'

Emily had arranged to meet Amit for a coffee in Temple Walden. She was curious to discover why he, like Peter, had chosen to remain in Templewood after the events of the Templewood Summer. Amit had been a trusted, loyal friend to Emily and Peter at St Georges School. He was one of three school-friends (along with Françoise and Carlos) assigned to create a diversion from the raid on the Sect's control centre by entering a tunnel on the canal. Eric had recognised the possibility that they could be captured or killed, once discovered. He had untied their boat, denying them the means to cross the canal, close to the weir.

'I'm fine, thanks. You haven't changed a bit. Let me get the coffees and then you can tell me what this is all about.'

Emily looked around the coffee shop. It could have been anywhere, except there was an old-fashionedness about the customers and staff, or perhaps just a lack of fashion and style. The sense that time had stood still here; there was no sense of awareness of the trends or fashion accepted as the norm elsewhere.

'Here, I've bought you a croissant too. You always liked them.'

'Thank you. That's very thoughtful, I'm surprised you remembered. So, tell me, what do you get up to here. Are you with someone, I mean, do you have a partner?'

'Not really. I travel a lot, to and from the other global sites. I'm not often long enough in one place to meet anyone. It would be nice to share things with somebody else, especially as we all have the same purpose. Perhaps it'll happen one day; you can't force these things.'

'What do you do in your work, with all this travel?'

'It's liaison work mainly. I expect Peter told you. My job specification says I am a global programme manager. That sounds too grand for something that's really ticking boxes for the things that are going to plan and resolving the problems with those that are not.'

'Peter described his position similarly: liaison and coordination. What's the difference between your role and his?'

'Mine is more like hands-on operations management, a sort of COO. Peter is more like a CEO, keeping everyone on mission and happy. We work well together; I enjoy helping wherever I can, and it gives me pleasure to see things moving forward. How about you? I hear you're going to be working with the Templewood Gazette.'

'Yes, I've been asked to assist them. I've been a journalist for several years, although that makes it sound more glamorous than it is. Working on a provincial newspaper is all formula stuff. You can't afford to offend anyone and so there are no opportunities for "the big scoop", unless someone important is arrested. At least the Gazette is not dependent on advertising and, given that the audience is captive, in more senses than one, and appears to be working towards the same goals, there should be lots of positive news. Obviously, I'll have to use discretion and be clear in my mind of what's confidential and what's not, and to avoid controversy. Still, my glass is half full. I'm sure it'll be more fulfilling than what I've been working on up until now. And that's where you come in.'

'What can I do to help?'

'Oh dear, I didn't mean to jump in with this so quickly. I'd really like to do a proper catch-up with you, we've so much to talk about. I'll tell you what. Let me explain how I think we could work together and then we'll do the social stuff, if that's all right with you.'

'Yes, let's do that. So, what changes do you plan to make to the paper?'

'It's too early to say yet, in detail. I bought a copy yesterday and, in many ways, it seems unchanged from when I was here in my teens — mainly traffic accidents and social events, although there's more reporting of events in the outside world than there used to be. It seems far less heavily censored. I forgot to ask Peter whether there's still a Market Cranford edition. I don't suppose you would know?'

Market Cranford was the closest town to Templewood, although no-one in Market Cranford would recognise the name of Templewood.

'Yes, both are still owned by Alexander Martel,' said Amit.

Emily laughed. 'I remember the time, years ago, when Mum escaped for a couple of days. She didn't realise she was not supposed to go outside. She just hailed down Dad's official car with the smoked glass windows and persuaded the driver to let her borrow it. She brought back a copy of the Market Cranford paper. That's how we discovered that the calendar in Templewood was set to one day behind the actual date so that news could be censored and manipulated here.

'That's changed now, as part of the new openness,' said Amit. 'We're now on normal time. We held a celebration to mark the change. It was a bit like setting the clocks forward in Spring, except it was twenty-four hours, instead of one hour. A few of the older people objected; they thought they were losing a day of their lives, that they were going to die a day earlier.'

'Ha, I can believe that! It must make publication of the two newspapers easier though, having the same date now. Are they still different? Why does Martel continue to publish a Market Cranford edition? It's not as though he needs the revenue — he doesn't even bother with advertising in the local edition.'

'It's a security measure. To control the news in Market Cranford and to monitor and check that there is no awareness of the existence of Templewood.'

'I can't believe that they have still no idea there that Templewood exists, how no-one has stumbled upon it by accident. How does the Sect manage it?'

'As you know, Templewood doesn't appear on any maps; there is only one road in and out, which is hidden from view, as you saw when you arrived. There's the physical barrier of the hills and the cliff, and the whole area is classified as a military zone. There are air traffic controls — no planes are allowed to fly overhead — all movement in the area is monitored by the Sect's global operation. No normal person is going break into a military base, especially as they wouldn't know its exact location and size.'

'And of course, people here are provided with all of their needs here. Which brings me back to what I was going to say. I think the Sect is missing a big opportunity, to reinforce the spirit of the community and the fact that everyone is working together for the common good. There needs to be more positive news on the achievements coming out of the work here, what they mean for local people and how they will benefit the human race as a whole. What are you frowning at, Amit?'

'Oh, nothing. It was just your choice of words.'

'Which words?

'Human race. It sounded a bit odd. Never mind.'

Emily and Amit eyed each other awkwardly, both unsure how to continue.

'You haven't yet told me how you think we could work

together,' said Amit.

'I'll be in touch with a lot of what's happening. I've spoken to each of the farmers and I'm sure they will talk to me on a regular basis. Peter can keep me up to date on what he's allowed to mention from the Council meetings. It's the more general news and feedback from the villagers that I need. You must pick up a lot of information from your programme management and liaison role that would be very useful. Perhaps I could use you as a sounding board for anything else I might want to write about, before publication? That could save me from a lot of embarrassment if I were to say the wrong thing. There has to be a balance; they will be my articles and I'll have to stand by them and be responsible for whatever I print. How would you feel about that?'

'It sounds OK, in principle. Why don't we give it a try?' said Amit.

'I hoped you would say that.' Emily leaned over and gave Amit a hug. 'That's great. Thank you so much. And you never know, I might be able to get you a discount on a lonely-hearts ad. And now you must tell me all about life in Templewood for the last fourteen years.'

'I'd love to. Look, time's flown by — it's almost lunchtime. Shall we get a bite to eat? If you have the time.'

'I'm fine, let's do that.'

*

'Thanks, Emily, that was a lovely meal. If you'll excuse me, I must be getting back to work now. Good to see you again. I'll pay next time.' Both stood up and walked towards the door.

'Yes, I must be getting back, too. We'll have to make this a regular event. Oh, and just one more thing — would you be able to provide me with a contact, or any information about what goes on at the base these days?'

'That's easily done. You could do worse than to start with Carlos. He heads up a key global programme there, with a large multidisciplinary team, addressing "all matters astronomical", as he describes it.'

'Why would they have such a large team in such a specialist area?'

Amit hesitated, unsure of whether he should have mentioned this.

'If you think back to the time of the asteroid, it makes sense. I don't know the details of what they do. You'll have to ask Peter, or Carlos. I'll ask Carlos to give you a call? He'd love to see you.'

Saturday 25th July: We Have Visitors

The week passed quickly. Rachel and Lisa immersed themselves in their new positions with commitment and energy, both keen to demonstrate their ability and gratitude for the offer of meaningful and worthwhile roles. They hardly noticed the fine weather, which held through the week and into Saturday. In the city, it would have been a distraction, encouraging lunchtime walks and picnics in the parks. Here it was different.

'Come in, Peter; you too, Emily. Have you eaten? We've saved you some lunch,' said Richard, holding open the door and leading them into the kitchen.'

'We're fine, thanks,' said Emily. 'Hi Rachel, Lisa. How's your week been?'

'It's amazing. We've seen so many interesting things in such a short time, and we've been made to feel welcome. Peter, you must be so proud of what you do here,' said Lisa.

'Especially as the villagers owe so much to him, bringing everyone together, to cooperate,' said Emily.

Alice came downstairs to greet the arrivals. 'Good afternoon. I understand that Peter has something important to say to the three of you.'

'Indeed, I have,' said Peter.

'And so you should, Peter. I think it's about time that you told us what's going on and more about why we've been brought here,' said Rachel.

'Yes, I'd like to know more. It's not as though outsiders are generally invited or made welcome,' said Emily.

'At least you must have had some idea of what to expect, Emily, as you've spent time here in the past. Peter, I'm curious why you've left it until now to tell us. And why here, at Mill Cottage?' said Lisa.

'Those are good questions, Lisa. I'll do my best to explain. I wanted you all to have a period of getting used to your new surroundings. To let you gain your own impressions of how things work here and the widespread goodwill and spirit of cooperation,' said Peter. 'That includes you, Emily. There have been some massive changes since you went back to the city all those years ago. It's good that you all seem to be acclimatising well, and I'm pleased you're enjoying working in a new, satisfying environment. As for coming here today, there is no way that you could guess what I'm about to share with you. It's private here, and away from the village. I thought it important that Richard and Alice should be present to confirm what I have to say and to reassure you.'

'Uh oh. This sounds as though the bubble is about to burst,' said Rachel. 'What have we let ourselves in for?'

'Let's go outside,' said Richard, tapping his nose.

'Good idea,' said Alice. 'You go ahead; I'll bring out some homemade lemonade with ice.'

'Sounds as though we could do with something stronger,' said Rachel.

'All in good time,' said Alice.

They strolled to a long table at a corner of the garden. Richard raised the sunshade.

'You can't be too careful. We sweep the house regularly in case of bugs,' said Richard.

'I would have thought there would be more bugs in the garden.'

'Not that sort, Rachel. We check there is no-one listening in to our conversations. It's safer outside.'

Alice poured the drinks. 'Here you are. I've brought

some nibbles out too. We're fortunate with the weather. It's been so changeable this year. Well, let's not keep our guests in suspense, Peter. Would you like to get started?'

'OK. Make yourselves comfortable. This could take a while. You need to be prepared for the unexpected, things you could not possibly imagine to be true from your own experience,' said Peter.

'Great. I said from the outset that I was looking forward to an adventure,' said Rachel.

'This is deadly serious,' said Peter. 'I mean that quite literally.'

Rachel's smile melted away. Lisa stared at Peter, apprehensive of what was to come.

'It can't be any worse than the Templewood Summer,' said Emily. 'Come on, tell us.'

'You'll definitely all be surprised; even you, Emily,' said Richard, snorting. Alice remained silent, staring at the grass, her hands clasped together, her white knuckles prominent.

'We have Visitors,' said Peter. 'That's what we call them: The Visitors. They've been with us for a while now. They are the Third Force. They are one and the same thing.'

'You mean the Masters, the new people here who control the Sect and its activities?' said Emily.

'No.' Peter looked up and around him. Emily knew her brother well enough to recognise that he was collecting his thoughts, to organise how he would best deliver the information.

'Let me go back a while, to the time when the Sect was working on its plan to divert the asteroid. Emily, you'll remember that they deployed a technology to render it invisible, so that it couldn't be detected easily. In this way, they were able to hide their intentions from anyone unconnected with their plan. They were also keen to avoid the panic that would result from a general awareness of what was happening. While they were working on the invisibility aspects, they were sending signals into space, both from here and from their other centre in North Korea. Those signals were picked up by the inhabitants of another, distant planet.'

'Is this a joke? Some form of hoax?' said Lisa.

'I only wish it were,' said Alice.

"Carry on, Peter,' said Richard.

'The signals were interpreted as evidence of intelligent life on our planet. They, the Visitors, locked onto them and chose their moment to send two vessels, one to each location. They remain here today.'

Peter paused. The garden fell silent, save for the rustle of the breeze through the trees and bushes.

'That's impossible! There are no known alternative life forms anywhere near Earth. If anyone or anything wanted to come here it would have to travel from somewhere light-years away,' said Lisa.

'A minimum of fourteen light-years away, given how long ago the Templewood Summer was. That's assuming they could travel at the speed of light,' said Emily. 'So how did they manage it?'

'I don't have the answer to that,' said Peter. 'One possibility is that they were using the same invisibility technology as the Sect, possibly a more advanced development. Another theory is that they are capable of relaying messages at speeds faster than light. Yet another idea is that they have mastered time travel, in which case distance would not be an issue. It's also possible that they already had vessels in the vicinity of the asteroid, which just happened to pick up the signal by accident. These things are not important. All that matters is that they, the Visitors, are here.'

'If that were the case, how come they weren't detected at the time?' said Lisa.

'They were,' said Peter. 'No-one realised until later. At the time the Sect detected the asteroid, they also picked up a signal from the vessel. In fact, there were two. It, or rather they, slipped in and out of visibility, rather like the way a prism hides colours. The Sect wasn't interested in them at the time. Why should they be, they had their minds set on diverting the asteroid? It was only years later, when they examined the historical footage, that they noticed something odd. They checked it out and discovered the two ships, both in more or less the same place. Eventually, we detected movement and they disappeared briefly. The next thing was that both landed, one in Templewood, the other in North Korea, presumably because they, the Visitors, had detected the Sect's signals from both locations.'

'Hang on, let's step back a bit. We're assuming they've been here for fourteen years. When exactly did they arrive? When were you first aware that they were here, in Templewood?' said Lisa.

'Seven years ago,' said Peter. 'We weren't aware they were coming until they arrived, which is presumably why no-one outside of Templewood detected them either.'

'Where are they now? Where is this spaceship? How large is it?' said Emily.

'It's out to the east of Temple Walden, towards the estuary, hidden in woodland close to the canal,' said Peter. 'It's about a couple of hundred metres across. It's not always completely visible. Sometimes it almost disappears; you can just make out a faint outline in the depression in the ground where it sits. I'd imagine it's some sort of exploratory vessel, relatively small and designed for research purposes.'

'What about the Visitors themselves — do they come out? What do they look like?' said Emily.

'No, nobody's seen them, as far as we are aware. You won't bump into them walking down the street,' said Peter.

'Mind you, if they're as advanced and intelligent as we believe they are, they could probably disguise their appearance, so as to pass unnoticed and not startle anyone,' said Alice.

'Strangers would soon be spotted here, though, being as Templewood is closed to the outside world,' said Rachel.

'Not if they impersonated local people, or were invisible,' said Richard.

'Why should they want to come here, to a planet whose population is in close to self-destruct mode? What do they want?' said Rachel.

'Again, I don't know. We haven't entirely decided whether they are benign or hostile. It's still early days, in terms of communication, even after seven years. The Masters are quite enthusiastic about them. They see the arrival of the Visitors as their latest vehicle for establishing overt global power. In fact, they're not far from making a new attempt. The problem they have is how to do it in a way that doesn't cause panic or revolution.'

'There's always a price to pay with these things,' said Richard. 'There's something the Visitors will be wanting from us, believe me.'

'I agree that's a possibility,' said Peter. 'You and I have had this discussion several times, Richard, and I can understand your scepticism. There's been no indication, so far, that they have an aggressive agenda. They have brought a lot of benefits, though. I'd like to believe that they simply want to help us. We have to keep our minds open, and we need to ensure the villagers do the same, while being alert to all possibilities.'

'I have to agree with Richard. Why would they come all this way if there wasn't something they wanted?' said Emily.

'It could just be curiosity,' said Lisa. 'We send satellites and probes to distant planets and beyond, so that we might understand our universe better, and to seek out other life forms. Clearly, the Visitors are more advanced, scientifically at least, and have achieved things that have so far eluded us.'

Peter turned to Emily, Rachel and Lisa.

'Part of the challenge we face is to ensure no rash decisions are taken. I don't like to use the word superior, but we have to recognise their advanced intelligence and, given what we have seen they are capable of, any form of confrontation would not go well for us.'

'I can't believe all this is happening,' said Lisa.

'Well, I can assure you it is, and you'll see the proof soon enough,' said Richard.

'Who else knows they're here — the Visitors,' said Lisa.

'Everyone,' said Peter. 'Everybody in Templewood knows, and in North Korea, as well as key Sect members worldwide. The first reaction of some of the villagers was to attack. We had to persuade them this was not a good idea, that if the Visitors were so advanced and capable of travelling across the universe to get here, they would certainly be more than capable of protecting and defending themselves and may well respond with aggression.'

'This is exciting, much more so than I thought it would be. I'm really looking forward to it,' said Rachel.

Peter shook his head.

'What about the benefits you mentioned? Tell us about them,' said Lisa.

'You've seen some of them already, at the farms,' said Peter. 'The pollution-eating plants, the new, organic building material, the things that Sarah showed you at Saracens Farm. These are just some of the gifts they have brought. Ever since they arrived, we've been working on them, developing them.'

'What about the spaceship; what does it look like?' said Lisa.

'I'd prefer to show you,' said Peter. 'I've arranged for a barge to take us part of the way, as far as Flour Mill Lock. We'll walk from there.'

'What, now? Today?' said Lisa.

'As soon as you're ready. You'll need something to keep you warm in case it turns chilly later. I'm pleased to see that you're both wearing sensible walking shoes as I suggested — the path is rough in places. Oh, and I'll bring a rucksack with some water. You'll have lots more questions, I'm sure. I'll try to answer them as best I can.'

'Are you going to join us, Richard, Alice?'

'No,' said Alice. 'We'll be here when you get back. It will be late; we'll wait up for you. Peter and Emily can stay here tonight. I'll see you on your way.'

Alice led Emily, Peter, Rachel and Lisa to the gate. Richard cleared the table and carried the tray inside.

'Good luck! We'll see you later,' he called as she disappeared indoors.

'Bye, now,' said Alice, waving them off. 'Take care.'

Emily turned briefly to speak to Alice.

'I must say, Richard seems to have mellowed from his old self.'

'I don't know about that. You're seeing him on a good day. He's going along with everything, while keeping his own counsel. It's a good thing to have someone around who questions things, though.'

*

Emily, Peter, Rachel and Lisa walked to the bridge, where the barge was waiting, the same vessel that had carried them on their previous trip. The bargee said nothing, as before, occasionally smiling.

The bargee started the engine and unmoored; the barge drifted silently towards the centre of the canal before setting off on its course. They passed quickly downstream, through Flour Mill Lock and another, a mile further on. There was no moving traffic on the canal and few walkers on the towpath. By the time they reached Temple Mills Lock, all work had stopped for the day. They disembarked and thanked the bargee.

'She's deaf,' said Peter. 'I should have mentioned it earlier.'

'I did wonder,' said Rachel.

'It's about an hour's walk from here,' said Peter. 'No-one comes this way, other than those barges trading with Longhaven.'

The canal passed through farmland, stretching out towards woodland to the south. Towards the north, in the distance, the late afternoon sun illuminated the cliff face.

'Is that Whytecliffe Farm, over there?' said Lisa.

'Well spotted,' said Peter. 'I'm pleased to see you're getting familiar with your surroundings already. All of this land, on both sides, belongs to Hugo Payne's family. It's all traditional crops here; it's only beneath the cliff face that the microclimate supports the more exotic crops: the trees, fruit and vegetables that would not normally grow in this country.'

As the evening approached the temperature dropped a couple of degrees to a pleasant level of warmth.

'What's that noise up ahead?' said Rachel.

'It's a weir. Much larger than the two we passed at the locks when we were on the barge.'

'Is that the one where Eric rescued you, all those years ago? I've never seen it before,' said Emily.

'Yes, you can see how dangerous it is now. Imagine what it's like when the canal is flooded after rains.'

'I haven't seen the tunnel either, the one that leads from here to the base,' said Emily.

'That's concealed behind the rock face on the opposite bank, close to the weir. It's cordoned off by a chain, which was originally put in place to discourage boats from landing next to it. Here we are now — it's over there.'

'I can't see anything, there's just a blank wall of rock.'

That's the whole idea, to disguise it. It can only be opened from the inside.'

'Do many people know the spaceship is out here?' said Rachel.

'It's common knowledge. We actively discourage them from coming anywhere near. There's surveillance in force. If anyone decides to approach it, we send a party out to stop them. There's an underground railway in the tunnel that gives fast access from the military base.'

The group walked on, beyond the weir to a footbridge carrying an overgrown track.

'It doesn't go anywhere, it just crosses the canal,' said Rachel.

'It dates back to when the canal boats were horse-drawn,' said Peter. 'It allows the horses to cross to the other side of the canal, while the boat passes underneath.'

They crossed the bridge. As soon as they set foot on the opposite bank, a group of twenty men and women, some armed with semi-automatic carbines, emerged from the bushes and blocked their path.

'Oh my God, why are they here?' said Rachel.

'To prevent others from taking the route we're about to,' said Peter. He walked ahead and showed a document to the woman who appeared to be leading the group. After a brief discussion, the woman and some of her colleagues saluted Peter and stepped aside.

'Now, follow me, there's a path.'

Peter held back the low branches between two bushes to reveal a narrow track not visible from the canal. It curved abruptly to the right, then to the left and then straightened out. Peter picked up a thick stick, concealed in the undergrowth, to beat back the overgrown vegetation, which frequently obstructed their way.

'Keep close together. It starts to go uphill shortly — it's quite tricky in places but not dangerous.'

As the incline steepened, the path began to zigzag up the contours, occasionally revealing a view of the distant escarpment and the canal below. Progress was slow; the stops for breath became more frequent.

'I didn't realise how unfit I am,' said Lisa. 'How much further is there to go?'

'Not far now,' said Peter. 'We'll soon be at the top. Let's press on, we want to be there and back down before it gets dark.'

At last, the trees thinned out, and they could see daylight between them. The incline levelled out; they found themselves facing the opposite side of a hollow, some two hundred metres away.

'Be careful, there are a few steep drops,' said Peter.

They spread out into a line as they approached the edge. The hollow was so deep it appeared dark, even in daylight.

'I can't see the bottom, only darkness. Where is this spacecraft, Peter?'

'Shh,' whispered Peter. 'Wait a few minutes. Keep looking down.'

At first, they thought they were imagining it. A faint pulsating glow, hardly detectable. As the seconds and minutes passed, an eerie light became visible, similar to that they had seen in darkness from the pub.

'What on earth is it?' said Lisa.

'I'm not sure I like this,' said Rachel.

'They know we are here,' said Peter gesturing to the women to keep their voices down.

The glow began to change form from an almost imperceptible light to a mist, translucent, with a colour of dirty mustard. Slowly, the mist mutated, its shape coalescing to a flattened sphere, then further, almost to a disc resembling a floppy yellow frisbee with a nub at its upper centre, like the top of an old-fashioned biscuit barrel. Its form allowed light to pass through, but the detailed shapes of objects within or beyond could not be made out.

'It looks like something from a 1950s B film,' said Rachel. 'A bit of a cliché, the stereotype image of a spaceship.'

'Are you sure this isn't just an illusion, Peter?' said Lisa. 'A trick of the atmosphere, some sort of gas rising from a buried source?'

The shape rose a few metres within its pit.

'It's starting to spin; it's turning slightly. It seems to be tilting, as though it's aligning itself… stabilising,' said Emily.

'Well, there's your answer,' said Peter.

'It's starting to give off heat. Can you feel it? Are we safe here? Especially if they are aware of us,' said Lisa.

'You're right. I think they want us to leave. It could be dangerous,' said Peter. 'We've seen what I brought you here for; let's make a move before it starts to get dark.'

*

Little was said on the walk back to Temple Mills Lock. Peter sensed the women's unease, their nervousness that something unseen and threatening might appear while they were vulnerable, away from human help. Their mood eased once they arrived at the lock and climbed back on board the barge. Yet still, they held back from talking about what they had seen and its implications. Their lives would be forever changed by the awareness of another life form among them.

'Let's talk about it when we get back to Richard and Alice's,' said Lisa.

Darkness enveloped Mill Cottage, silhouetted against the faint summer night's light, still glowing behind the hills on the western horizon. Richard and Alice welcomed them back with offers of tea and coffee.

'Just water for me, please,' said Rachel. 'I'll have enough difficulty sleeping without stimulants.'

'In that case, we'll head off for an early night,' said Alice. 'I expect you have lots of questions for Peter. Why don't you go and sit outside and chat?'

'I think our guests are unsettled by what they've seen,' said Peter. 'It might help reassure them if you and Richard joined us, at least for a little while.'

'I suppose you're right,' said Alice. 'Not for long though.'

'I'm OK,' said Rachel. 'I feel more comfortable now that we're all back together. I don't expect it makes much difference whether we're in or out and it's a warm evening.'

'I could do with something a little stronger,' said Lisa. 'I bought some wine earlier; it's in the fridge.'

'You sit down, I'll fetch it,' said Peter. He returned a few minutes later with a jug of water, a bottle of wine and six glasses and carried them outside to the garden, where everyone was now sitting.

For the second time that day, they grouped around the garden table. In contrast to their earlier, relaxed discussion, now they were assembled as if at a formal project meeting. All were sitting upright, with their hands or arms resting on the table, as if there were a need to consider their words carefully. Peter was the exception, leaning back, his hands behind his head, an ankle over his knee. Peter began to pour the wine.

'Not for me thanks,' said Rachel. 'I'll have nightmares. It's all just starting to hit me — the enormity of what's going on. I can't believe I'm here.'

'That's one of the reasons I left it for a while,' said Peter. 'It was important that you should see Templewood in a normal light, well, as normal as it gets here, so as not to colour your judgement.'

'Well, this has blown all that out of the water,' said Lisa. 'It's difficult to see now how everyone carries on normally.'

'There isn't a choice,' said Emily. 'What can you do, other than to carry on? Faced with such an overbearing presence, there's no alternative.'

'Yes, that's true,' said Peter. 'That's why I want to offer you the option to leave if you choose. I can arrange for you to be taken back home whenever you like. You would be paid in full, and I could arrange some financial compensation for the disruption to your lives. How do you feel about that? We would, of course, expect you to abide by an oath of secrecy. I don't imagine that would be a problem for any of you.'

Lisa and Rachel looked at each other, expressionless, and then to Emily, as though silently asking confirmation.

'I'd like to stay,' said Lisa. 'I'm enjoying the work and the change of environment. I feel that I'm doing something worthwhile at last.'

'Same here,' said Rachel. 'Leaving wouldn't achieve anything. The Visitors would still be here. If there is a danger, it will exist equally in the outside world. If we're here, we'll be in touch with what's happening and in a better position to react.'

'There doesn't seem to be any immediate danger,' said Emily. 'You can count me in.'

Emily turned to Peter. 'Peter, I've just realised something. When we first came here, fourteen years ago, I was taken, blindfolded, to meet someone described as very important. When I arrived at the meeting location, I was still not allowed to take the blindfold off. His voice was electronically distorted, so I had no way of telling who it was. This made me wonder whether it was because I might recognise him. Anyway, the point I'm coming to is that he told me that there are times during history when knowledge is imparted to a chosen individual or group. This happens after the passing of a time interval of every seven years. It's starting to make sense: we first came here fourteen years ago. Seven years ago, the Visitors arrived and brought their gifts. Here we are, another seven years on, and something big is going to happen. You knew that when you invited us here, didn't you?'

Peter smiled. As the wine began to flow, they all began to relax.

'One thing I don't understand,' said Rachel, 'is how the Visitors pass on this knowledge. Take the gifts they've given you: the crops, for example. Presumably, they come from the spaceship, yet there's nothing to be seen inside it, it's a gaseous blob, with nothing that looks solid about it.'

'I hate to keep saying this,' said Peter. 'I don't know the answer. No-one's seen it happen. There must be some sort of material transition process as things travel from inside to outside of the craft. Or it may be part of their invisibility capability. Or perhaps it's only an illusion of translucence. Solid objects may be located in the centre, including the Visitors themselves. Who knows?'

'So how do they actually convey these gifts to you? Do they speak a language that we can understand?' said Lisa.

'The gifts are bought by drones. That's probably the best way to describe them. They are very small. So small that it's difficult to understand how they are capable of carrying such loads. There's no visible power source. All you can see is this small disc, attached to whatever they are delivering, that appears to be the power source and means of control. Everything arrives inside what looks like a large rubber ball. On the outside are instructions embossed in a form of hieroglyphics, describing what's inside, what it's for and how to use it. At first, the graphics were difficult to interpret, but we've largely cracked the code and find it relatively straightforward, other than where there are new concepts involved.'

'It sounds a bit like buying flatpacks from IKEA,' said Rachel.

'I have to admit that it's quite exciting,' said Peter. 'At first, the gifts were simple things. I imagine they may have been testing us, trying to discover what was useful to us and how well and wisely we used things.'

'They could have been observing human intelligence, to see how much we were capable of understanding,' said Emily.

'That's spooky,' said Rachel. 'It's like they're using us as laboratory rats.'

'I can understand that they need to know they are not wasting their time on us,' said Peter, 'It all points to a much superior intelligence.'

'You can see now why Peter decided to delay telling you about the Visitors. There's a lot to take in,' said Richard.

'Everyone agreed you need to be settled in first, as far as is possible in somewhere like Templewood,' said Alice.

'You did a good job, Peter, in persuading the people we've come into contact with to keep it quiet from us, not to let on,' said Lisa. 'You clearly hold some influence here.'

'Do the villagers still regard you as a prophet, someone who can unlock mysteries for them?' said Emily.

'That sounds a bit ominous. Where did you get that from?' said Rachel.

'Oh, it's a long story,' said Peter. The villagers have a Book of Mysteries, a sort of bible, a repository of information built up over the centuries about a prophecy that would enable them to gain world power. Do you remember I told you about the two factions of the Sect: the Pros and Cons? Well, each had their own version, varying according to the information they had collated and, in some cases, wanted to conceal from each other. You have to bear in mind that Templewood has been cut off from the outside world for centuries, firstly by geological factors, then later by choice.

'The key elements of the prophecy were that, at three different times, various people, or groups, would arrive in Templewood. The first would come from the east — bringing wisdom. The second would arrive, bringing knowledge of other lands. Finally, and this is where I was supposed to come in, a child would arrive, bringing the key to their understanding of how to create a world-changing event. How to change the world order and how to bring them to power.

'Apparently, generations of people in Templewood had been given advance knowledge of science and technology, delivered through the medium of a sage, or savant, appointed by some undocumented process. I had the misfortune to have been identified as the person they had been waiting for, who would deliver the third stage.'

'Do you think the historical acquisition of knowledge through a sage could be related to what's happening now? That there has been previous alien communication, perhaps centuries ago?' said Lisa.

'That's a good question,' said Peter. 'It's a possibility, but we've no way of knowing. It could be that it's taken centuries for the Visitors to pass on enough information to accelerate our civilisation to the level it's at now and that we've finally reached the level where they can take things to the next stage, whatever that is. After all, human civilisation has taken millennia to progress from caves to where it is now. It's only in the last century or two that human knowledge and scientific capability have taken off exponentially.'

'We have no idea what the next stage is, what they have planned for us,' said Richard.

'Richard has a good point,' said Emily. 'As he said earlier this afternoon, there's always a price to pay. Look at all the so-called gifts they have brought: pollution-eating plants, organic building materials, technological ideas… These are all things that will make our lives better. Why would they want to do that?'

'Perhaps they just want to help, to be kind to another life form and not be seen as a threat,' said Lisa.

'There's another possible reason,' said Emily, looking around the room, as if expecting someone to volunteer an answer that was not offered.

'What's that?' said Rachel.

'They want to take over the planet,' said Emily. 'They are testing us out to see how much knowledge and innovation we can cope with and how we use it.'

'Surely, if they're so clever, they could have done this at any time,' said Lisa. 'Why didn't they invade fourteen years ago, as soon as they discovered Earth, especially if they've mastered time travel?'

'Perhaps they didn't need to then. It could be that their own planet is dying and that they were seeking out alternatives to migrate to, and it's only now that they have to decide.'

'Well, they've made a pretty dumb decision to come here, in that case,' said Richard. 'Look at how we've messed up our planet, almost to the tipping point! We'll probably be extinct in a hundred years.'

'Don't you see?' said Emily. 'That's all the more reason to bring us their gifts, so that we can reverse the damage. By giving the Sect the means to gain global power, they will have allies to do the work they don't want to do or are incapable of.'

'I don't understand,' said Rachel. 'What would they be incapable or unwilling to do?'

'If they were to try to take over the planet directly, they would be regarded as oppressors, a conquering race,' said Emily. 'This way, they will be seen as saviours. Just saying.'

'What do you think, Peter?' said Lisa. 'Are they good 'uns' or bad 'uns'?'

'I'm keeping an open mind. I have to be careful as,

whether it's a good or a bad thing, my opinions are listened to. If I were to be seen as opposing something, especially an idea backed by the Sect, I have to be on strong ground. It's all very well being in a position of influence; just as in any political system, you are only as good as your last decision. The important thing is to be prepared for all eventualities. To be able to react quickly if and when the time comes for a change in direction. That's where you all come in.'

Emily yawned.

'Yes, I'm tired too,' said Lisa. 'It's been a long and strange day. I'm off to bed.'

'Me too,' said Rachel. 'I'm so glad I'm staying in a house with other human occupants.'

Thursday 30th July: Carlos

'Hi, Carlos. I'm glad you could make it,' said Emily. 'How are things?'

Carlos and Emily embraced, both unsure which cheek to kiss first. Not that it mattered with someone you knew well from many years ago.

'Pretty good, on the whole. The work is interesting and challenging. I believe that what I do is recognised and valued, both by colleagues and the Sect. I'm happy to be working with like-minded and dedicated people.'

'Amit told me about what you do — well, your role rather than what it comprises. You clearly took Dr Hadfield's science lessons seriously!'

'Not just the lessons, I can truthfully say that the help she gave us in working out the real purpose of the Sect's plan with the asteroid had a profound effect on me. It made the science real — too real in some ways.'

'She must be very proud of you and what you've achieved.'

'I like to think that I'm repaying the debt to her and to my parents for the encouragement they gave me. It's glib to say that that's the aim of education and upbringing — to be able to build upon and surpass the achievements of one's parents and teachers. Isn't that the whole purpose? If no child were able to improve upon the knowledge of their parents, we'd all still be living in caves.'

'Too true! What you're doing now, though, well, it sounds like a key position. You must tell me more about it. Let me get you a drink.'

'Just mineral water, please. It's collected locally from a spring in the woods.'

'In that case, I'll have the same.'

They talked about the old days, their time at the school and the friendships that grew to the point where they would have been willing to lay down their lives to defeat the Sect's plan. It could have ended so badly, had Eric not scuppered the rowing boat which was to have carried Amit, Françoise and Carlos to the tunnel entrance on the canal, where they had intended to distract attention from a larger group of villagers who were about to invade the military base using another tunnel from Mill Cottage.

'So here we are, fourteen years on. You haven't changed much. I always knew you'd go far.'

'There's going far and staying still. I do believe it's better to excel at something worthwhile in a defined environment than to be mediocre or average in a larger pool.'

'That's exactly what I want to hear about. Tell me all about your role and what you are doing. I ought to warn you, though, that I'm going be working with the Templewood Gazette. So don't give too many secrets away, or at least make sure I know what's confidential.'

'I will, and I know I can trust you, Emily. I expect Amit told you I am now the Global Programme Manager, Astronomy and Astrophysics Research and Monitoring. Rather a grand title, although it sums it up quite well. The group's mission is two-fold: observational and theoretical. On one level, we observe what has happened in the past, what's happening right now, or rather is being observed right now — taking into account the enormous time lapses between occurrence and observation — and what the possibilities and likely outcomes are.'

'Quite a small task then,' said Emily.

Carlos laughed.

'We could probably employ a hundred times as many people and still be wanting for resources. That's not a complaint; I get most of what I ask for. We have to identify and focus upon what we regard as key areas for research. It's not only research and observation, there's a security and defence aspect that has to be addressed. We've plenty of experience of that, of course, it's only recently that... Oh, never mind.'

'Don't worry. Peter has told us about the Visitors, and he's taken us to see their spacecraft. I imagine they present you with a unique challenge.'

'We've certainly learned a lot, thanks to the benevolence of the Visitors. We've discovered so many new concepts and issues that have made us rethink the laws of physics. We also have a lot of new information, which has allowed us to fill in many gaps in our understanding of long-established theories. It's so exciting! We are acquiring ideas that we could never have dreamed of.'

'It's good that you're so enthusiastic,' said Emily. 'But don't you ever wonder what it would be like to live and work in the outside world? With your skills, you could do really well in so many fields, working with experts.'

'I'm doing that already, here. I'm working on a global assignment where nationality, gender, religion and physical ability are irrelevant. It's an inclusive environment where people are valued according to what they can contribute. Status is not important; there is a role for everyone here, each according to their talent, and not only on this programme. It's a bit of an odd question, really; you've come here to help us when you could have chosen to remain outside.'

'What about job security, though? Isn't there the possibility that something could go wrong, something that's not your fault, and that everything could collapse around you? After all, if much of the work revolves around new ideas, there must be scope for errors, however much research and planning you do and however good your team is.'

'With any new venture, especially at the cutting edge, there's always going to be an element of failure at some point. You have to work to the old mantra: "Try again. Fail again. Fail better". At present, I believe I am the best person for the job. That doesn't stop me from identifying potentially better candidates and encouraging them. If I felt someone else could do better, I'd happily stand aside.'

'One of the things I don't understand — and there are many — is what you call the observational work. There are so many amateur astronomers worldwide, often with powerful telescopes and a network of contacts. Surely some of these must have detected the Visitors' arrival, or at least some unusual events that they would have videoed and shared.'

'Yes, that's always a danger and a concern. Here, in Templewood, and at our other sites, we have the most advanced technology to be found anywhere in the world. This gives us the advantage that we should be able to spot things before anyone else, and, of course, we have our own network of observers. We still have to be aware of enthusiastic amateurs who are unconnected to our work.'

'Even if you do spot something of significance first... I don't understand what you can do about it. If something exists, it's there for others to discover too. It must only be a matter of time.'

'We have many tools at our disposal. You are forgetting how such incidents were managed at the time of the asteroid. Do you remember when I was asked by our group at school about how the Sect could be concealing things? I was asked to contact my father, who is a communications expert, about ways in which this could be done. I pretended I was doing research for a school project, so as not to raise his suspicions or, worse still, put him in danger for revealing secrets. He confirmed that it is possible to conceal large objects, to make them undetectable. It's all to do with bending light around the object you want to be invisible. This is how the Sect was able to conceal the asteroid until quite late.'

'Ah yes, I remember now.'

'We've refined that capability considerably, so that it works with objects that are much further away. We also have alternative methods, which I can best describe as placing a visual filter around the globe to distort what can be seen and make certain things undetectable.'

'That's amazing. It must have so many applications on Earth, as well as in space.'

'Yes, although there are different challenges to be addressed on ground-based applications. Mainly to do with how people deal with altered perception, particularly of near- and middle-field objects. I'm sorry, I'm probably boring you by now.'

'Not at all. I'm looking forward to learning more over the coming weeks and months.'

'I'm happy to help you with copy. Amit told me you'll be working with the Templewood Gazette. It will be good to be liaising with someone I know and can trust.'

'OK, that's enough about work for now. I'd like to catch up on village gossip. Tell me everything you know.'

Emily had hoped she would learn more than she did about the workings of the village. Carlos was so involved in his work that his relationships with others rarely went beyond the boundaries of his prestigious position. Perhaps this was one of the reasons he had been appointed. He would occasionally socialise with his colleagues, out of duty and respect and to demonstrate his humanity and normality. He was usually the last to arrive and the first to leave, the latter to ensure he did not witness anything embarrassing or which might compromise working relationships.

Surely, he must notice things, everyday events, in the

village. He had to shop, attend medical appointments and cycle to work. There must be things he recognised as unusual, worthy of comment and retelling. Emily's personal experience of people with similar traits was that they were often the first to be made redundant when staff cuts were required. It was always the competent workers, the ones who did 'real' work, rather than boasting about their achievements or playing political games who were 'let go'. These were often seen as the ones least likely to make a fuss or to sue. Perhaps things worked differently here, with the shared goals in a closed community. She hoped that any future threat from the Visitors would not destroy this harmony.

Emily rebuked herself for her negative thoughts. She recognised that she was imposing her own values on Carlos and decided to think of the positives. Carlos was a straightforward, honest person, an old friend who would be her new friend too. He would be valuable, not as someone she could use — that would be deceitful — more as a trusted source of information and someone she hoped would come to her for help if the need arose.

Sunday 2nd August: Trust

Richard leaned back in his chair, enjoying his wine at the end of the Sunday evening meal in the garden of Mill Cottage. Emily and Peter had joined them and had helped Alice with the preparation.

'I'm so enjoying this,' said Emily. 'It's like having a second family.'

'I'm pleased you offered,' Alice had said. 'I prefer Richard to be out of the way when cooking for more than the two of us. It's not that we argue — he has his own way of doing things. He thinks that a sign of a good meal is to have used every implement in the kitchen. I prefer to be economical with the workload and tidy up as I go. If only it were possible to wash up before the meal instead of after.'

'Lisa, Rachel,' said Richard. 'You've been here three weeks. Now that you've had time to settle in, what are your impressions of Templewood?

'I'm enjoying myself,' said Rachel. 'One of the good things about being somewhere different is that you take stock of things. You worry less about trivia and focus on what's important. It helps not having much stuff here too, other than clothes. I don't really like owning more than I need. I'm finding the whole experience liberating. What about you Lisa?'

'I don't know where to start, really. If someone had told me I would be going to live and work in a place that was invisible to the outside world and was home to alien visitors, I might have had second thoughts about coming. It was a good idea of Peter's not to tell us straight away; we could get a feel for what passed as normal village life before jumping to conclusions. They, the Visitors, don't appear to pose a threat — quite the opposite. And what with the interesting work and the chance to be part of a bigger venture, something I would never ahem imagined would happen to me, well… It's all good.'

'A bit of a change from when Emily was last here,' said Richard. 'Let's hope it continues that way.'

'How do you mean,' said Emily.

'The real test will come when the new discoveries are rolled out to the rest of the world. It should be good news for everyone, as long as the benefits are shared equally and the Masters ensure all countries, groups, religions and so on are treated the same. That sounds a bit condescending — I'm sure you get my meaning.'

'So many lessons have been learned from last time,' said Peter. 'I still find it difficult to believe, after all these years, that the Sect thought it possible to divert an asteroid to collide with the Earth and change its tilt, while they and a chosen few hid underground waiting, literally, for the dust to settle and then to resurface and take charge of a world where every country's climate had changed.'

'At least we still have the benefits of the modified crops and trees, developed to adapt to new climates,' said Emily. 'The Sect always described themselves as a "benign dictatorship". It's probably what we need to stop the rest of humanity from destroying the planet, whether by climate change or aggression.'

'That's the expression Peter used when we first arrived,' said Rachel. 'It's difficult to imagine any form of dictatorship as being a good thing.'

'Yes, the concept of what the Sect intends to achieve is good,' said Alice. 'By levelling out inequalities between nations, there will be fewer reasons for greed or envy. If every country has access to similar levels of resources, or a balance between resources that enables fair trade, there will be no need to feel threatened by other powers.'

'The nature of the gifts from the Visitors will make the process easier,' said Rachel. 'In the past, we've had to allow developing countries to catch up using technologies and materials that the developed world is trying to shed. Taking excessive amounts of water to make concrete, using fossil fuels, and so on. With the new organic building materials and crops that eat pollution, it should be possible to decelerate climate change.'

'And by helping other nations by sharing these gifts, we gain their trust. Trade and aid are so important in helping to avoid conflict.'

'I need to stretch my legs,' said Emily. She stood up and walked across the garden towards the statue of the stone devil standing on top of the wall. She remembered Peter, on their first visit to Mill Cottage, insisting he had seen it face in a different direction when he looked at it a second time. Whether or not this happened, the statue helped Peter and Richard to locate the nearby concealed tunnel, housing a simple rail track with handcarts that led to the Sect's control centre.

'Isn't the moon lovely?'

'Oh, you startled me, Alice,' said Emily. 'I didn't hear

you coming.'

'Are you OK? You look worried. Would you like to talk about it, Emily?'

'I just feel a little uneasy. Nothing, really. It's something I've noticed since I've been here. Everyone keeps talking about trust. I can understand Peter. He's had to take a risk in bringing us here, but the farmers — especially Roland — Carlos, Richard... it's surprising how frequently they use the word. I don't know; it's probably me.'

'Do you know why that makes you feel uncomfortable?'

'Not exactly. Something doesn't feel right. I don't know whether they're trying to convince themselves that things are how they'd like them to be, rather than how they are. I know I've not been back here long; they need to get to know me again. It feels different here, sometimes a little too perfect. Everything seems to be going to plan. There is an almost symbiotic relationship with the Visitors: we sort of make them welcome in Templewood, and they bring us gifts. No-one's involved in disputes. It's all too harmonious. It sounds ridiculous, but I can feel an undercurrent of unease, an elephant in the room.'

'I know what you mean,' said Alice. 'I feel it myself and so does Richard. It's strange, he's always been so outspoken. To see him so... so accepting, it's not the Richard I know. We all had such a difficult time when you were at school here; I suppose everyone is glad those days are long gone. Too grateful in some ways. It makes people wary of making critical judgements.'

Alice put an arm around Emily's shoulder and stroked her arm as they both looked up at the moon.' Emily leaned her head towards Alice's shoulder in silence.

'I'm glad we're having this discussion, Emily. It's helping me to face the truth that there is something beneath the surface. Shall I tell you what I think it is?'

'Yes, please do.'

The sky was a mist of stars, punctuated by the occasional planet, appearing as pins attaching a flag or an illustration to a backcloth. Emily wondered why Alice did not answer immediately. She remained silent, glancing discreetly sideways, pretending to look at another part of the garden. Tears rolled down Alice's cheeks.

'Fear. We're all living in fear.'

9 - ARRIVAL

Monday 3rd August: Arthur

'Come in, Emily. I'll put the kettle on. No, please don't bother taking your shoes off. Have you eaten?'

Emily followed Arthur into the kitchen. She bent down to stroke the two cats, one of which stood, arched its back and shook the tip of its raised tail.

'They love visitors. A shame I don't have more. It's been like that since my wife died.'

'Oh, I'm so sorry, I had no idea. How long ago was this?'

'Six months, although in some ways she'd passed away much longer ago. Dementia: a cruel, drawn-out death.'

'That's very sad. Do you have any other family?'

'No. Angela and I were not able to have children. Probably the usual village curse. What makes it worse is that my role demands that I am seen to be impartial. That makes it difficult to build close friendships, apart from the cricket club. I'm sorry, I sound like a sad old man, which I'm not really. I've plenty of interests to fill my spare time — not that there's ever been much of it with everything that's gone on here for the past fifteen years or so — things to keep me from becoming morose. You know, I often feel Angela is still here. I find myself talking to her, and it's as though I hear her reply. This must sound strange to you.'

'Not at all. If you've been with someone for so long, it makes sense. Think of the positives — you have fond memories of her, and you miss her. So many couples drift into indifference, or worse, and have no alternative than to put up with a poor relationship, whether it's because they can't afford to split up or to put on a face for their families. No-one can take away your memories. I'm sorry, that sounds ironic given that she suffered from dementia.'

'I know what you mean. I appreciate your kind words. Let's pour the tea. I don't imagine you take sugar, do you?'

'Just a dash of milk, please. I like it strong.'

'Come and sit down and tell me what it is I can help you with. We'll sit in the front parlour as you're a special guest.' Arthur poured the tea and led Emily out of the kitchen. 'Would you open the door for me, please? It's awkward with the tray.'

Emily had never heard the word 'parlour' spoken. To her, it was a term from the early- to mid-twentieth century, like 'antimacassar', redolent of upper-middle-class gentry who had the means to reserve an otherwise unused domestic room for privileged visitors. The room was a shrine to Angela. This could have been a room in a National Trust or English Heritage house, arranged to recreate the setting in which a famous author or other historical figure had lived. Emily regretted not removing her shoes on entering the house. She walked slowly over to the sideboard, taking the trouble to look at the photographs, each displayed in a unique silver frame, marking memories from several decades of marriage. She was unfamiliar with the etiquette of respecting the dead. She could not think of an appropriate gesture, the equivalent of a curtsey, a discreet bow or hands joined in prayer. There was not a trace of dust; everything was clean and tidy, with a faint smell of flowers she recognised but could not name. A familiar smell, as if remembered from the house of an elderly relation.

This was, in a way, how she regarded Arthur, a dignified,

older man, resigned to his circumstances, his only companions two cats, one long-haired, white and brown, the other a tortoiseshell. Yet with his flowing mane of long, silver hair and stubble, he had something of an ageing rock star about him: dignity, a presence, the air of a life lived fully.

'Let's take the window seats. We can look out over the garden while we chat.'

Emily sat in one of an identical pair of old-fashioned high-backed chairs, decorated with a William Morris print that she recognised: 'Strawberry Thief'. The chair was firm and comfortable. She could imagine Arthur dozing off, gin and tonic in hand, to his memories, while staring at the perennial-filled garden.

'I thought it was about time for us to get together,' said Emily. 'We've always got on well, and I know I can trust you completely.' She picked up her tea and took a sip. It was hot; she replaced it on the tray.

'That's very kind of you,' said Arthur. 'What is it that you'd like to talk about?'

'It's not kind at all, it's good to know that I can talk openly with you, about anything. I'm worried about how things are here, the way everyone accepts such a bizarre situation as normal, without question or complaint.'

'It's a product of how we in the village came to where we are today. The days of conflict, of slavishly following the directions of the Masters, without complaint, while knowing that their plan would lead to disaster. We are still led by them, of course — there can be no other way — but we can see a bright and promising future. No-one wants to go back to the old days. I'm sure many of the villagers worry about the direction in which their lives are going. Sometimes it's better to live a life of illusion — to hide painful realities, things you can't change or control.'

'Alice told me that people are afraid, and that's why they won't confront the truth, that not everything is as rosy as it seems. Do you worry too, Arthur?'

Arthur gazed out of the window, tilting his head from

side to side, his lips formed in a pout.

'Yes, I do. After the events of the Templewood Summer, I thought that I could deal with anything that came along. I've never let problems hang around. It's not in my nature. I'll tell you what really worries me. We know we have to deal with people — creatures, beings, whatever they are — that may well have no feelings for us. Their lives are so different from ours. With their superior intelligence and development, they might regard us the same way we think of animals or even insects. It reminds me of reading King Lear at school. "As flies to wanton boys are we to the gods."'

'You think they will kill us for their sport?' said Emily.

'I don't know. Not yet. It depends on their agenda. We don't know the real reason why they are here. It could be friendship, a form of charitable procession going from planet to planet to improve the universe. That's the commonly held view. Or it could be that they need something from us, or need us for ourselves.'

'Why would that be?'

'There may be some attribute or capability humans possess that we don't recognise, but they do.'

'I'm sure Peter feels the same way. Do you ever discuss it with him?'

'We haven't had an in-depth discussion. The nearest we get is when I make suggestions for him to consider. He's polite and gracious, and I'm sure he takes note. I must be seen to be impartial in all matters. It wouldn't be right for Peter to be swayed. He has to draw his own conclusions. He's probably the most important individual in the village.'

'All the more reason to do something about it.'

Wednesday 5th August: Françoise and Emily

Emily carried her coffee to the far corner of the café, where she would be out of earshot of the few other customers. The intermittent noise from the coffee machine would insulate her conversation with Françoise from the rest of the room. Thank goodness a remote place like this has cafés, she thought. There were probably as many here as in the city, in proportion to the population size. Unsurprising, given that the villagers' lives were heavily supported and subsidised by the Sect. There was no commercial entertainment: no cinema or theatre although, occasionally, plays and concerts would be staged in the village hall. This encouraged close personal and family relationships. It was almost like the nineteen-fifties when, as Catherine would say, people would 'make their own entertainment'.

Emily looked at her watch. She was early, not that it mattered if Françoise were late. Time ran at a different pace here, expanding and contracting according to need and urgency, or lack of it. She had no idea why Françoise wanted to speak with her, other than the hushed comment at Saracens Farm, whispered away from Sarah and Emily's friends. Why did she feel unable to express whatever it was that was worrying her in front of others? The thought had been worrying Emily since the trip to the farm. Was it that Françoise did not wish to alarm Sarah or the others? Did she want to repeat something that she had been told in confidence? Or was it information about something or someone else that could be interpreted as a betrayal? Soon Emily would have the answer. Nobody in the café had paid her any attention, which was a surprise and a relief. She considered herself new to the area (the Templewood Summer did not count, being so far in the past) and had expected to be regarded with curiosity or suspicion. This indifference gave her added confidence that her conversation with Françoise would remain private.

The bell over the door rang. Françoise walked in slowly, as if pretending to be invisible.

'Sorry if I've kept you waiting. I wanted to be sure I wasn't followed. I don't know why. There's no reason why I should feel guilty about meeting a friend from the past.'

'No problem — I haven't been here long myself. What

can I get you?'

'Just a coffee, please. Black.'

'Sure. I'll get a refill, too. I'm sure we'll have lots to catch up on.'

*

'How long have you two been together, if you don't mind my asking?' said Emily.

'Three or four years now. I started out helping Sarah at the farm. She was finding it difficult managing on her own. We found we worked well together and shared similar views on the important things in life… Things just moved on from there. It was a natural process. Organic, you might say.' Françoise laughed. 'We get on well together. I suppose I'm more sociable than she is. Hardly surprising given how she was brought up, looking after a sick mother. She does talk about you and how you and Peter saved her from being taken into care when her mother, well, you know.'

'Yes, that must have been a stressful period. She must have been terrified of what could have happened, being in her teens and still at school when her mother died. It was fortunate that Richard and Alice were around to adopt her. Imagine being bullied at school and feeling you have no alternative than to cover up your mother's death, keeping her body in a sealed room for weeks.'

'It was fortunate that you and Peter arrived in Templewood when you did. It helped put paid to the bullying too. Most of us at the school were aware of it. We should have done more to stand up for her and to protect her. It's easy to look back and say that now. At the time, no-one understood the pressures she was under at home. You and Peter were probably the first real friends she made.'

'She helped us a lot, explaining village alliances and the history, the legends and the prophecy. If we hadn't had her help, it could have been too late to respond to the threat from the Sect. It's good to know you two are together and that you get on so well.'

'That's what I want to talk to you about,' said Françoise.

'Sarah's starting to behave oddly over the past few months. Not all of the time, but every now and then, she has prolonged periods of introversion and avoids eye contact.'

'I think we all do that from time to time,' said Emily.

'Not to this extent. It's as though she's in a different world. I'm tempted to say she seems possessed — that would be an exaggeration. It's more like… like she's being controlled in some way. She becomes oblivious to me and tries to avoid me. Not in a hostile way; it's as if she's torn between resisting something and giving in to it. And then suddenly she'll be back to normal, as though nothing had happened. I've tried to talk to her about it, but she refuses to discuss it. She'll be very apologetic and say it's not my fault and that it's something she has to deal with on her own. I believe she's trying to protect me by keeping me at a distance from both her and whatever it is that's troubling her. I don't know what to do for the best.'

'That's worrying. What exactly happens when she has these phases?'

'Usually, she goes off and spends a lot of time outside. I caught her talking to the trees once. Well, not just the trees, the whole landscape, as though she was addressing mother nature. It was so weird. I mean, she didn't seem unbalanced or ill in any way. It all sounded quite normal. The nearest comparison I can make is when you walk down the street and overhear someone talking on their phone with an earpiece in. You hear one side of a conversation with an invisible audience.'

'You don't think it could be some form of meditation or talking aloud to help her to focus on her thoughts — some form of mindfulness? What does she talk about?'

'No, I haven't often managed to get close enough to hear the detail. When I have, it's in the form of a dialogue, well, one side of a dialogue. Sometimes she asks lots of questions about what she should do, things like that. I've never really heard enough to understand what her imaginary conversation is about.'

'It doesn't sound as though there's necessarily anything wrong,' said Emily. 'It may be that she finds it helps her to think, to focus — to work out the answer to a problem. There could be other explanations, too. She could be praying, for example.'

'I could accept that, if that's all there were to it, but it's not. The lack of eye contact is strange; she looks downwards or away from me, like a guilty child. She's also become secretive about her work, some aspects of it at least. She used to share everything with me, but now there are things, certain topics, that she keeps to herself. She only works on them when she believes no-one is watching.'

Emily thought about Françoise's comments. Could she be imagining things, or was there another reason?

'Excuse me asking this,' said Emily. 'I'm not being rude or prying into your personal life. Is it possible that there is another cause? Is your relationship going well?'

'I don't mind you asking. There's no real problem there, except when she has these phases. It's as though she's a different person, secretive. I sense there's something she doesn't want me to know, that she's protecting me from something.'

'It does all sound odd. I'd like to help, but I'm not sure how I can. Do you have any ideas?'

'Not really. I'm grateful to have someone to talk to, to share the problem with.'

'I agree. I'm pleased you've told me and that I'm now aware of it. It doesn't sound like she's ill or unstable. Perhaps she really is trying to adopt a new approach to focussing on her work. You'd think she would discuss it with you, though. Let's keep in touch on this. Promise me you'll let me know if there's any further change.'

'I will. Emily, I am grateful to you for listening to me. I do realise it sounds as though I'm going behind Sarah's back, and I suppose I am. I'd like to ask a favour. I know I can't impose an obligation on you, but I'd be grateful if you would keep this conversation between the two of us. As you know, Sarah's on the Council. She's doing an excellent job in her work, as far as I can tell, and I wouldn't like people to start doubting her capabilities or commitment.'

'Don't worry, that's taken as understood. We both care for her, and we want the best for her. Just make sure you keep me in the loop. One more thing... Do you ever regret not leaving Templewood?'

'Not really. I'm happy here. Or would be if I wasn't concerned about the Visitors. Once things settle down, become clearer, we're looking to take a break outside, for a short while, if we can get permission. As regards the longer term, I wouldn't want to live anywhere else.'

'Is this for a holiday of some sort?'

'No. We, Sarah especially, would like to adopt a child. As you know, that's not possible here, as there are no children. I'm sure the Sect will help us to overcome whatever physical problem prevents her from doing so when the time comes. There remains the problem of selecting a father — I'm sure you'll understand what I'm saying.'

Emily nodded.

'A child would make our life complete. If only we had one now...'

Françoise gazed upward wistfully. Emily knew it was time to leave.

Friday 7th August: The Masters

Top Secret – Memorise and Destroy.
International Committee for Change – Notice of
Extraordinary Meeting.
To be Held 8 p.m. First Friday in August, Archangel
Hall, Temple Walden.
Agenda: Global Change Programme — Progress
Report and Action.

*

Peter knew that the meeting would be called. He had not expected it to be so soon. He and the other members of the

Council had each received their summons, as he preferred to call them — they were hardly invitations, there was no question of declinature, refusal or excuses not to attend. The documents, printed in copperplate handwriting on a small sliver of rice paper, were passed to them personally, discreetly and anonymously, usually in the street, by an unidentifiable passer-by, disguised, yet identifiable as a legitimate messenger. They would hastily show a token, before handing over the message and disappearing down the nearest side street. No-one ever challenged or followed them; there would be no point. The message was duly memorised and swallowed.

Archangel Hall lay hidden in a maze of alleyways in the centre of Temple Walden. A small archway marked the opening in the terrace of stone houses, to an alleyway, which was the only route into the maze. The infrequent visits of the Masters marked the few occasions when a security presence was visible on the streets. Armed and uniformed men and women from the military base blocked all streets within a quarter of a mile radius, despite the single point of access, to all except the Council members, directing those few individuals who tried to explain that they were returning home, or had other legitimate business there, away from the area.

The farmers, Payne, Nightingale, Martel and Sarah, stood waiting for Peter and the other Council members to arrive. When all were present, a dozen soldiers escorted them to the hall, six to the front and six to the rear, to the door and knocked in the prescribed way. The door was answered, as always, by a figure in a long grey cloak and a tall conical cap.

The guards stood aside and faced back down the lane, their weapons at the ready for an unlikely, unexpected attack. The councillors stepped inside onto the marble floor of the ornate interior, with its gilded carvings of mythical figures and tormented souls embellishing the wood panelling at ceiling level. They walked slowly along the corridor to the junction with another passage running from left to right. Ahead of them was a screen that could be passed to either side. They walked around it to where the space beyond lit up to reveal a square area with a fountain at its centre. The dish, into which no water flowed, was supported by figures looking upwards, cowering in fear of those above: four horses, bearing their apocalyptic riders.

'Good evening, ladies and gentlemen.'

Another tall figure, dressed in a long grey cloak with the hood cast back appeared. He, too, wore a conical hat covering his entire head, with a slit at eye level. The absence of an opening to speak through had the effect of muffling and disguising his voice.

'Please follow me.'

He led the party along a series of winding passages, each ornately decorated with carvings and paintings of hellish scenes. The building smelt musty, suggesting infrequent use and that it had been opened up solely for this meeting.

The guide stopped to open a door and gestured to the group to enter. They were led around another screen. At a curved table on a low platform at the far end of the room, sat eleven figures, cloaked in white and similar conical hats. They were indistinguishable, save for the one at the centre, whose hat was taller. It was he who would conduct the meeting. presumably the leader of the meeting, if not of the whole group. The councillors were invited to take their high-backed, carved wooden seats at an identical, facing table. Arthur took the central seat. The room had no windows. The only light came from concealed lamps at floor level, behind the far table, serving further to disguise the identities of the group. The escort bowed towards his masters and left the room, closing the door behind him. A key turned in the lock. Two more hooded figures, dressed in grey, stood between the two tables at either side. Their role was to convey papers and other articles between the two groups when requested. Councillors were forbidden to approach the Masters' platform.

In earlier times it would have been unknown for all of the members of the Council to attend a meeting with the Masters. The Pros had historically been the dominant group and insisted that only the farmers (this was before Sarah took control of Saracens Farm) and Arthur, whom they tolerated, rather than welcomed, were invited. Peter had met the Masters on more than one occasion during the Templewood Summer, when they attempted to prise from him the knowledge he was believed to possess, which would assist with the fulfilment of the prophecy.

The identities of the Masters were unknown. They were never seen without their hoods or other disguising headgear, which they wore between landing and taking off from the airstrip at the military base. Peter had wondered whether they had special silk hats to sleep in; he kept the thought to himself. As for their identities and their roles outside of Templewood, he suspected that they were members of Governments of major nations. Not the leaders — it would be unthinkable to allow eleven world leaders to travel together or to be in the same location unless there was an enormous security presence. Even then, the small risk of an accident wiping them all out would be unacceptable. No, they were more likely to be senior ministers, or the equivalent, or trusted special advisers with extraordinary power and influence and a hotline to their leaders. Their personal security arrangements in Templewood appeared to be minimal although, as Peter was not privy to the details, who knows how many covert armed guards and cameras were watching over them. To Dr Hadfield, Sarah and Peter, it grated that the Masters were just that: all men. Peter had reminded them that progress had been made in Templewood and that, when he had first arrived, the female partners of those in authority had remained, or had been kept, more or less invisible. To him, it was ridiculous that he should consider this as worthy of comment. He, together with Sarah and Emily, represented a new generation, unencumbered by the gender limitations of the past.

*

The leader of the meeting raised a gavel and struck three raps on the table to signify it was to begin. Gygges responded with a call of 'Order, order, order,' before the leader delivered the ritual opening speech. His true voice was modified by an electronic voice box to disguise his identity.

'We are here today to perform our duty as the proper representatives of the Sect, whose Articles of Faith decree the following:

The Sect is God's Authority on Earth and the defender of the true faith.

It is empowered by the divine will of God to be ever vigilant to protect humanity against the evil of God's fallen twin.

It is the destiny of the Sect to govern nations for the benefit of mankind.

It is the responsibility of the Sect to respect and manage the forces of nature and the universe. The Sect has divine authority to employ all means at its disposal to ensure the execution of God's will.

Through good works, adherents of the Sect will achieve enlightenment and eternal life through reincarnation, progressing through seven stages of initiation until they are at one with God.

May we perform our obligations with diligence, compassion and humility. Let the session begin.'

Gygges passed copies of the agenda to the nearest grey-hooded figure, who dealt them to the Masters and then to the other councillors. The agenda followed that of the Council meeting. The difference here was that less time would be spent on security and community matters. These were considered by the Masters to be local issues, the management of which was considered to be within the remit and capabilities of the Council. It would be an admission of failure, should the Masters be asked for guidance, other than for the agreement to significant changes, or issues impacting on the outside world. The Masters noted with interest and approval the arrival in Templewood of Peter's sister. They agreed that Emily's experience of the wider world would complement her knowledge of Templewood and bring benefits. They were told of the work commissioned from Lisa and Rachel, which they had approved following Peter's recommendation many months ago.

Martel, Nightingale, Payne and Sarah presented their reports of technical progress, including updates since the Council meeting. The Masters scrutinised each report, asking questions, seeking weaknesses and inconsistencies; their occasional nods signalled cautious satisfaction with the responses. This was the main business, the primary reason for their visit, upon which a major decision hung. Once the debate of the reports was complete, the Masters' leader struck his gavel once more and spoke.

'Councillors. We thank you for your detailed and comprehensive reports. We now wish to debate these matters in private. Will you please adjourn to the adjacent room while we do so? We will resume once we have made our decision on what action to take. In the meantime, you will be required to remain in this building, and you are not to communicate with anyone outside, by any means.'

Few words were spoken while the councillors awaited their recall. There was little to add to the detail they had provided the Masters and no evidence of dissent. They were aware, too, that whatever words they exchanged would not be private. An hour and a half passed before the chamber doors opened, and they were invited to re-enter. Silently, they rejoined the Masters.

'We have considered the progress made and are satisfied. We believe that we are now ready and, in a position, to move ahead with our plan for a coordinated, peaceful push for power across all of the nations we control. The moment is right. Across the world, the tide has swung in overwhelming favour of global action on climate change. The tipping point was the announcement of the order to be enacted simultaneously in many countries, to enforce the rapid reduction or elimination of fossil fuels. The doubters' opinions and influence have been overtaken. There is a grass-roots desire for change. Those Governments in denial, or who have delivered nothing in the way of effective action, are about to be elected, or forced, out of office, including those of some of the leading nations in which we and our people are embedded. We believe, too, that we have created an environment where pernicious, corporate self-interest will be rejected in favour of the greater good, as a consequence of the sacrifices made by our devoted adherents, sometimes with their lives. Armed with the gifts from the Visitors and the discoveries and advances you have developed here, we are confident that we can make the transition towards a better world. Our common aims in multiple countries will lead to improved, harmonious international relations, leading to a world with a long-term future, a world where the planet will be protected, and peace will rule. It remains for me to seek your assurance, Arthur. Do you and your colleagues agree that there is no reason why we should not proceed?'

Arthur looked around at his fellow councillors. None signified an objection; most averted their gaze or shuffled their papers or their feet.

'I can see no objection,' said Arthur. 'Unlike the previous bid to take power, fourteen years ago, there is no risk to the planet. I can foresee nothing that can go wrong.'

'Very well. So be it. Is there anything else you need to do in Templewood as a result of this decision?'

'We must prepare the local population to be aware of the importance of their role,' said Arthur. 'Mr Barrington, in his capacity as the editor of the Templewood Gazette, guided by its owner Mr Martel, will be key to managing the PR and generating a sense of pride and unity.'

'That sounds straightforward enough. Does anyone else have anything to add?'

Peter raised his hand. 'With respect, before taking the

final decision, we should do a formal risk analysis to confirm that there is no reason not to proceed. I would be willing to coordinate this personally.'

'Why do we need to do that,' said Gygges, 'when all of the benefits are obvious?'

'It's not a question of the benefits; we conduct an in-depth examination of whether there are any factors previously unconsidered, that will jeopardise the plan or introduce unforeseen danger.'

'We have already performed our own risk analysis and have found no significant adverse indicators,' said the leader of the Masters.

'I'm referring to the work done here, that you are relying on us to deliver,' said Peter.

'How long will this take?' said the leader.

'It should only take a couple of weeks to identify the major topics of potential risk. Once those have been documented, we can then, if necessary, investigate them in more detail and evaluate them, and define the steps necessary to mitigate. I suggest that a few weeks' delay to validate how we change the world's future is a worthwhile investment. I can quickly put a team together.'

The Masters looked from side to side at their fellows. It made sense. The answer to hundreds of years of wars, food shortages and planetary abuse could surely wait a few weeks more. Several nodded in agreement.

'Very well. We will reconvene in two weeks for an extraordinary meeting.'

Sunday 9th August: Risk Analysis

Sunday arrived. Peter had arranged to meet Emily, Lisa and Rachel at Mill Cottage. He summarised the debate at the Council meeting, cautioning that some business was confidential, and another matter was barred from discussion. This prompted curiosity and questions, which only stopped when Peter asked whether they wanted to listen to what he had planned to say. Did they want him to continue or not?

'I need your help. I can't go into detail, but I would like you to ask questions and seriously consider the risks associated with the new developments you've seen. It's something I've offered to do on behalf of the Council. They've agreed it's a good idea.'

Peter explained his thoughts on the risk analysis and his reasons for enlisting their assistance.

'It's over the top to describe it as risk analysis — that's too formal. What I am asking is for you to help me to identify anything, everything, that could possibly go wrong if the Sect introduces the new discoveries to the rest of the world.'

'I'm not sure we're qualified to do this,' said Rachel. 'So much is outside our particular skill sets. Are you sure we can add any value?'

'Surely, there are others here who are better qualified. Don't get me wrong, I'm happy to help,' said Lisa.

'It's not about qualifications. The danger is that people here are too close to the situation. I need fresh minds, uncluttered with the baggage of living in Templewood. Talk to the farmers; they were at the meeting. They'll be expecting you to contact them to put your questions. Talk to whoever else you think will have a useful opinion to offer. I'll have additional input from local people, including Amit and Richard. We need an intuitive, commonsense approach towards identifying anything that could go wrong.'

'That sounds sensible to me,' said Emily. 'We need to understand what they think individually. You can count us in. How long do we have?'

'No more than a week. We'll get together on Friday evening to discuss your findings. And then I'll work all night, if necessary, to put a report together.'

'That's not long to investigate such complex matters,' said Emily.

'That's all the time I've been given,' said Peter. 'Treat it

171

as an intuitive exercise, and you'll be fine. Whatever you come up with will be better than nothing. I'm sorry I wasn't able to give you more notice,' said Peter.

Monday 10th August: The Sect

'It's been a long day. I need a cup of tea. Will you join me, Rachel? We can have a catch-up on how things are going.'

Dr Hadfield sighed as she and Rachel walked along the first-floor corridor of St George's School.

'That sounds like a good idea,' said Rachel.

'Great. We'll take it in my study. You probably think it odd that I refer to it as a study, rather than an office. "Office" sounds too business-like — we are a place of learning, after all. Come in and sit down over here.'

Dr Hadfield's study was arranged with her desk at the window and a pair of sofas set facing each other in the interior part of the room, an area where she could receive guests in comfort and set them at ease.

Rachel had been assigned by Sally to work closely with Dr Hadfield on the first draft of the new programme design for the curriculum. Dr Hadfield acted as the Deputy Head and was familiar with the day-to-day operation. In the short time that the two had been working together, Rachel had adapted quickly to Dr Hadfield's standards and methods of working. She was direct and friendly while maintaining a professional distance from other staff members and pupils. She insisted on being addressed as 'Doctor'. And why not? Rachel understood that her level of academic achievement should be recognised and respected, setting an example and a goal for the pupils. Her desk was tidy, almost bare, contrasting with the overflow of books from the shelves lining the wall opposite the door and onto several tables. The books were organised into piles with handwritten notes dividing and cataloguing their organisation.

They spent a quarter of an hour reviewing Rachel's progress, her queries and thoughts on change. These were discussed objectively and without judgement. Rachel enjoyed working with Dr Hadfield and had begun to feel more confident that her own abilities and ideas were recognised and listened to.

'Another cup?' said Dr Hadfield, walking over to the kettle placed by the sink, concealed by a screen in the corner of the room.

'Not for me, thanks.'

Rachel knew that Dr Hadfield was on the Council and was therefore in a position of knowledge and, presumably, some influence. The meeting presented an opportunity to learn more about what was going on.

'Would you mind if I asked you a question? Not about work, more about the history and organisation of Templewood.'

'Not at all,' said Dr Hadfield. 'Ask away.' She sat down at her desk with her fresh tea.

'Peter has told us, Lisa and me that is, about the Sect and how it plans to use its knowledge to establish "global power", if I may put it that way. Will this change things here? I mean, will they open up and, well, will Templewood and its location no longer be secret?'

'No, I wouldn't think so. Our ancestors — and you must remember we are an extended international family — have always been in and out of power, or at least significant influence, over the centuries. I expect that Peter will have told you that some of the earliest detailed history is recorded in connection with the Knights Templar. The real story goes back a long way, to the Ancient Greeks and Egyptians. Much later, the Sect enjoyed one of its longest periods of prominence, during the Italian Renaissance. They were the real power behind the Medici. After the Medici, the next major phase was through the Freemasons and the Invisible College. The name tells you how they like to work: an invisible, controlling elite, exercising power through the offices of another body.'

'Why is that? Why don't they take power directly?'

'They are a force for change and improvement. Empires come and go. Some maintain their position for longer and over a wide geographical area, like the Romans. Eventually, they run out of steam, their focus wavers and declines. This is another of the reasons for control by proxy. They glide into power and then disappear, waiting for another window of progress and influence, although there is continuity of the Sect in every major country and society. It's part of the reason why they have several secret locations worldwide.'

'They must have infinite patience to work in that way.'

'It's not a short-term project.'

'So, what's the endgame?'

'You mean you haven't worked that out yet? The Visitors have been preparing us, not just the Sect but the whole human race. To reach the point where we have developed to the stage where the Sect can at last directly govern the whole planet. They claim to want to create a harmonious world, prosperous and equal, with no wars, poverty or famine. The Visitors' work will then be complete; they will move on to another civilisation.'

'Is that how they are regarded? As an intergalactic police force?'

'I'd say not so much a police force as a moral arbiter. Putting right the wrongs firmly and fairly.'

'Does it worry you, or the Sect, that this is at the expense of free will? That we humans have no choice in the matter?'

'How can I best answer that? Let's say that they, the Visitors, effect change by showing a better way. I'm sure that you can see that their objectives match those of right-thinking people. They're giving us a helping hand. Without their gifts, the knowledge they bring, our free will would be useless. We wouldn't be able to make the necessary changes in an acceptable timescale. So, to answer your question, no, I'm not worried, I'm grateful.'

*

That evening, Rachel related her conversation with Dr Hadfield to Emily and Peter.

'Let me ask you something, Rachel. It's interesting, the way you quote her. Did she really use the word "we" so frequently?' said Emily.

Rachel thought about the question, trying to remember Dr Hadfield's exact words.

'Yes, I believe she did. Why do you ask?'

'Because back in the Templewood Summer, she was one of our key allies in our search to find out what was going on. I wouldn't say she was rebellious against the Sect exactly, but she was open to debate — sharing information and helping us understand various scientific possibilities of how their plan could work out. It seems she's gone all establishment now. She's one of them.'

'That's understandable,' said Peter. 'She is a member of the Council, privy to most of the information that I am and a part of the decision-making process. It's another example of how the villagers are working together.'

'OK... Perhaps I'm mistaken,' said Emily. 'Something is making me uneasy here. Perhaps it's because she's a scientist. I don't get a feeling that critical analysis is at the top of her, or anyone else's, agenda.'

'What draws you to that conclusion?' said Peter.

'It's just a feeling. I can't justify it as I wasn't there. I sense the same attitude from a lot of the people I meet. They all seem to be going along with everything, thinking it will all turn out well. Can you see, Peter, this is how the Sect managed to get so far with their ill-founded plans last time?'

'I hear what you say, Emily,' said Peter. 'I'm not sure that there is anything we can do at present, especially based on feelings and instinct. I agree that we should all be aware of developments and that we, you and me, Rachel and Lisa, together with our trusted friends must share information openly between us, in complete confidence. I'll speak to Dr Hadfield when I get a chance. The presence of you newcomers is very important to me for reasons which will become clear. I can protect you as long as you don't draw attention to yourselves unnecessarily. Do you understand what I'm saying?'

'I think so,' said Rachel. 'I'd like to understand more when the right time comes. As for right now, I'm happy to promise not to be disruptive. You can rely on me.'

10 - DISAPPEARANCES

Monday 10th August: Abduction of Five

'Peter, something's been nagging at me for a while,' said Emily. She had held back from raising the issue in front of others. She knew she would be more likely to get a response if she broached the subject in private. They were home alone in The Abbot's House. Now seemed a good time.

'That usually means I'm in for a hard time,' said Peter, smiling as he turned to face Emily. She ignored the comment.

'You mentioned that at the Council meetings there is a subject that's closed to discussion. Something that nobody is allowed to mention. Can you tell me more about that? In strictest confidence, of course.'

'I wondered when you would bring that up,' said Peter. His attempt to maintain the smile was not enough to completely disguise the change in the tone of his voice to that of resignation or mild irritation (she could not tell). 'Why do you want to know?'

'I'm surprised you ask,' said Emily 'Here we are, helping with village business in an environment where, unbeknown to the outside world, there is an alien invasion under way, albeit localised at the present time, and you ask why I want to know anything that might shed light on revealing the complete truth.'

'You didn't mention "the complete truth",' said Peter.

'Oh, stop being picky, Peter. You know what I'm asking. Why won't you just tell me!' Emily could be irritable too. After all the years apart, she knew him well enough to recognise when he was being evasive, or prevaricating, or blatantly procrastinating. 'If you want my cooperation and assistance, you have to be open with me and trust me. After all we've been through together, it's not as though I'm likely to breach your confidence.'

'I'm sorry, I know that; that's not the problem.'

'So, what is the problem? You know that I know that something's up, so just get on and tell me.'

'Let's go over the road. It's stopped raining.'

Emily stood up quickly and put her shoes on. Peter dallied over the same task. He ambled over the road towards her, taking an unnecessary amount of time to check that no vehicles were coming. It was unlikely that there would be, at this time of the morning.

Emily stood face to face with Peter, raising her eyebrows and gently tilting her head from shoulder to shoulder. Further words were unnecessary.

'Some people have gone missing. Five in all. There's no trace of them.'

'When did this happen?'

'At the weekend, on Saturday. There are no clues as to what might have happened to them; they just vanished.'

'Was there any connection between them? Were they members of the same family or did they work together?'

'There was no family relationship. Of course, everyone here's connected in some way, whether by work or friendship. It's a small place. But no, no obvious connection. They were all ordinary people, remarkable in their ordinariness.'

'Is it possible they've just decided to leave Templewood? It must happen from time to time, however idyllic normal life is here, if idyllic is the right term in the present circumstances.'

'We would have known. You know how tight security is here. It may be unobtrusive on the whole, but the boundaries are well-monitored, as is the area immediately beyond Templewood. We've checked, and there have been no unusual communications between them or with anyone outside. There are no reports of accidents or crime that would explain things. There was nothing strange about their work or social activities. They just suddenly disappeared within the space of a few hours. In each case, their families reported them as missing. They couldn't offer any logical reason either.'

'So why is this such a big secret? You would expect there to be news reporting, police enquiries, posters... The families must be up in arms about this policy of silence. Oh, I think I understand.'

'I think you may well. We believe the Visitors have taken them.'

'Oh no! Why do you think that?'

'It's happened once before, a few weeks earlier. An elderly man found his way up to the spacecraft. He somehow avoided the guards you saw on the way there. They were alerted when they saw an increased glow in the sky. They rushed up to the crater, just in time to see him slowly vanishing, as though dematerialising. Later, they found his wallet on the track, which is how he was identified. We don't really know what he was doing up there. His family said that he suffered from dementia. He'd been missing for a couple of days, and they were worried he might have drowned in the canal as there had been no sightings. It's a long way to wander, though.'

'So, there are not five disappearances but six,' said Emily.

'Six from here. There are more, actually. The same pattern occurred at the Sect's other main location, in North Korea, where the other spacecraft is. First one person, then five taken in a similar way.'

'My God, this I awful. Why keep it quiet? What good will that do? Surely someone should be asking questions and negotiating with them!'

'It's been decided, ordered, decreed whatever, that we can't risk any form of upset with the Visitors. It could undo all of the good work that's taken place. The view is that they are here with good intent. That's why we've received all of the benefits that we're working on.'

'You can't possibly believe that, Peter. Are you saying that to ensure the Sect can continue to reap these benefits, the Visitors can do as they please, including kidnapping people? You have to stand up and make sure steps are taken to negotiate the return of those missing. It's unacceptable that there's a ban on talking about the problem.'

'I can't do that.'

'What do you mean, you can't do that? The Council and the Sect respect you. Many of them hold you in awe for what you did in the past. Why can't you do the right thing and overturn this ban on talking about the disappearances?'

'Because I recommended it. It was my idea.'

'Peter, what the hell has got into you? How can you possibly justify such a course of action?'

'I looked at the options and decided this was the safest option. We can't exactly make a raid on their spaceship and recapture them. We don't even know that's where they are.'

"How can you justify sacrificing six people? That's what it is, a sacrifice, a trade-off between people's lives and the knowledge the Visitors bring. It's totally immoral. You and your bloody analysis. You've completely disregarded the biggest single factor: what the Visitors want from us!'

'Not at all. That's the very reason I'm confident that to bide our time is the best and only option. The six will be returned in due course. I'm sure it's the right course.'

You could be talking to them, finding out whether the prisoners — there's no other word for it — are all right and negotiating their return. You could at least try to find out what they want them for, the reason they've been taken.'

'Look, I don't believe they will come to any harm,' said Peter, his voice now calm, his tone controlled. 'Think about it. The Visitors are continuing to provide us with innovations that will benefit everyone on the planet. There is no reason they should be doing this on the one hand and harming us on the other. If they wanted to kill those taken, they could do so easily. Why bother taking them? I'll tell you what I think is happening.'

'This had better be good. You let us risk our lives to come here. You've been economical with the truth regarding what's going on. It's only when we question things that a little more comes out, and then a little more. You give us the minimum possible information until pressed. Peter, how many more things are you hiding from us?'

'Would you like me to tell you what I think, or not?'

Emily and Peter stood staring at each other in silence. Emily knew that Peter was in control of the situation. He was a good brother and a good man and was both rational and imaginative in his decision-making. She craved the reassurance that he could justify his actions. Yes, if she put her mind to it, she could leave Templewood and take Lisa and Rachel with her, or could she? They knew too much to be allowed to leave. Even if it were possible, what was happening here would still be the case. She was now fully embedded in the crisis. Yes, it was a crisis, the second global crisis of her short life — she was a conspirator, a willing one. 'You can only change things from the inside,' she remembered her mother saying.

Emily closed her eyes and nodded.

'I do believe they are here to help us. To do so, they need to fully understand us, our nature, our anatomy, our thought processes,' said Peter. 'I believe they have "borrowed" the six to analyse and understand what makes us human so that they can best tailor their gifts to our needs. And so, I persuaded the Council to do nothing, to maintain radio silence on the issue and await their return.'

'You say they've been gone a few weeks. How can you

remain confident they will be returned?'

'In other ways, life continues as before — before they were taken. We continue to receive new knowledge. It's important to remember that the Visitors come from a distant galaxy. We are a new species to them. They need time to make their analysis and to draw conclusions as to the best way forward.'

'Peter, it seems to me as though you've lost the plot. You come across as totally uncritical. Surely you recognise the possibility that you could be wrong, that we could all be at risk. The entire planet could be taken over and the human race wiped out.'

'Believe me, I do acknowledge that as being a worst-case scenario. If it turns out to be true, then I don't have an idea of how to resist. I don't believe that will be the outcome. Why would the Visitors be providing us with so much assistance, only to destroy us? They could have done that as soon as they arrived. Emily, you know me well. I have thought through every possibility and its consequences. As we stand now, I believe I am doing the right thing. I am, however, on guard and am prepared to change direction if needs must. Let's see what the coming days bring. Trust me.'

'Why do you think they've taken six people: the same number from two locations? Why not just the one, or more than six? Do you think the number has any significance?' said Emily.

'Yes, it's strange. I don't understand why they didn't take all of them the first time. It could be that once the Visitors realised him not to be a good specimen — sorry, I know that sounds callous, I'm trying to look at it from the Visitors' point of view.'

'Has there been any sign of them? People don't simply disappear.'

'Not a trace. At least there are no bodies, so there is hope. There's another reason we believe the disappearances are connected. In each case, the people's friends or family found a similar object. I've seen one. It was a heavy, solid piece of metal with five corners. It was like a three-dimensional pentagon in the form of a solid pincushion that fitted neatly into the palm of a large hand. Every now and then, its appearance would change, and it would become vaguely misty and translucent, like the spacecraft, with a similar dirty mustard colour. It was as if the Visitors had left a sign that they had done it, a sort of placeholder.'

'Was one found when the first person, the old man, disappeared?'

The conversation was interrupted by an urgent knocking at the front door. Peter opened it to discover Amit, out of breath from running.

'Good news, Peter. The missing man's been found. He's been returned,'

Emily joined them at the door.

'Excellent news,' said Peter. 'Come in and tell us about it.'

Amit collapsed onto the sofa, still trying to regain his breath.

'He was found wandering close to one of the locks. He was recognised from the posters and taken to the cottage hospital. He's there now, with his family.'

'We ought to get over there to see if we can find out what happened.'

*

At the hospital, they were taken immediately to Dr Jay. He explained that the whole family, together with the rescuers, had been transferred to the military base to be quarantined while they awaited the completion of a series of tests. These needed to be performed diligently, given that this was the first time a human being had been exposed to an alien life form. The full range of tests could take up to a week. Dr Jay had received an interim report that confirmed no signs of radiation or any other physical harm had been detected. He had given instructions that he should be updated immediately with any news. He would let Peter know immediately he heard anything.

'I'm pleased to hear he's no worse than when he disappeared,' said Peter.

'That's not entirely the case,' said Dr Jay. 'The family members said that his mental condition had deteriorated. It may be the shock of the experience — hardly surprising — and he may make a full recovery. It's too early to say.'

'Has he been able to describe what happened?' said Peter.

'He doesn't remember anything. Not even the spaceship. Again, it could be the shock of the experience. He's in no fit state to be questioned at present. Once he's recovered a little, we might find out more, under hypnosis, possibly. I can assure you, Peter, we won't waste a moment. It's a major opportunity to learn more about the Visitors.'

Tuesday 11th August: The Asteroid

Emily was confused by her discussion with Peter. She wanted to believe him, to be confident that he was making the right decisions for the right reasons. There was no precedent for Peter behaving in other than a proper way on matters of importance. She resolved to think positively. Was it reasonable for the Visitors, with no detailed knowledge of the inhabitants of a distant planet, to be capable of understanding their behaviour, based on remote observation? Supposing this were not the case, that somehow, they did have what they considered to be a comprehensive view, one which required only fine-tuning at close quarters. Emily had an idea, or the seed of an idea. She needed to discuss it with someone. Immediately, the name of the best person came to her.

*

'Dr Hadfield, I've been wondering,' said Emily, staring out of the window of Dr Hadfield's study.

'That's an ominous sign. It usually means that you've had an idea that will cause some sort of disruption, with the best of intentions, of course, and demanding time and effort from those around you. I'm joking, Emily! Tell me about it.'

'I was thinking back to our discussion, years ago, when we were discussing the asteroid that the Sect was planning to divert to collide with the earth. We speculated that the Sect was aware of its trajectory and its imminent arrival and had been for a long while. In which case they could have spent years, possibly centuries, planning for their ultimate bid to take power by initiating a huge catastrophe.'

'Yes, how could any of us forget. To think that the rest of the world was unaware of how close we came to catastrophe.'

'Well, at the time, we speculated that they had developed technology to make it invisible so as not to alert and alarm the population.'

'I remember that well, too. Carlos confirmed that his father had told him that it was possible to conceal large objects. To make them undetectable, by bending light around the thing you want to be invisible.'

'Just supposing that the asteroid was not what we thought it was, but some sort of artificial satellite designed to pass close to the Earth, for surveillance purposes.'

'I'm not sure about that. I believe it was all part of the prophecy. It's referred to in the Book of Mysteries.'

'I've thought about that too. Why would our ancestors, the villagers' ancestors I mean, have included the appearance of the asteroid in the prophecy? They may have had a good reason to do so. I wonder whether it's possible the Visitors may have been here before. That's why they predicted that it would return. If that were the case, it would explain why the prophecy didn't predict an exact date for its return.'

'It could be a coincidence. A significant event occurred which coincided with the appearance of an asteroid. They wouldn't have had the scientific knowledge to be able to predict when, exactly, it would reappear.'

'It depends how long ago but probably not the exact

date, I agree.'

'We know that the Book of Mysteries documents several discoveries that were communicated in some mysterious way to our ancestors in Templewood. Advances, mainly scientific and technological, that were made known to them before the rest of the world had access to the knowledge.'

'Yes, it's the basis of the Sect's power. The advance knowledge provided them with the means of influence on Governments throughout history, at pivotal periods of change. It's probably true to say that the changes were the result of the information they had received. Knowledge begets power, as you might say.'

Emily was familiar with the history of the Book of Mysteries. Years ago, she and Peter had uncovered the first two volumes hidden at the back of the village antique shop. The then owner, Thomas Canville, had described to her and Peter the secret origins and history of the books and how differing, annotated versions were held by the Pros and Cons.

'I've never really thought about it in detail, the mention of the asteroid,' said Dr Hadfield. 'You could be on to something. Our ancestors may have been signalling an earlier arrival, or arrivals, of the Visitors that coincided with the asteroid.'

'I believe it could be more significant than that,' said Emily. 'They could have been documenting the appearance of what initially appeared to be an asteroid, which proved to be the Visitors' spacecraft.'

'I hadn't thought of that, either. It's a possibility,' said Dr Hadfield. 'This could be the latest of a series of appearances, over many centuries, at landmark stages in human history.'

'It would make sense of a lot of the events in the Book of Mysteries,' said Emily.

'Tell me more. You're more familiar with the book.'

'I would need to think about it. It's been a long time since I've seen a copy. I would need to refresh my memory.

I have to go now. Leave it with me. I'll check out the references and get back to you.'

'It's all beginning to fit together.'

Friday 14th August: The Risk Analysis Is Complete

'So, how did it go? I imagine you've all had a busy week,' said Peter.

Peter had suggested that the four meet at the New Inn, a convenient central point for them to meet after work. They had carried their drinks and some bar snacks across the lane to the sports field, where they would not be overheard. Peter had thought to bring a picnic blanket. They took a few minutes to relax from the stress of their day and exchange personal news before turning to the subject they were there to discuss. All were agreed that their discussions with the farmers and others had been valuable. They had found everyone they spoke to helpful.

'Rachel,' said Peter. 'You were going to talk to Hugo Payne and to Dr Hadfield. How did it go?'

'Hugo was very enthusiastic. You can tell he takes pride in his work. He made it clear that he'd considered the possible downsides of the *lignum petrum* crop. Briefly, there are none that are not manageable.'

'So, there are some?' said Peter.

'I'm coming to that. The roots are deep, dense and compact. If left unmanaged, it could spread wildly and quickly. The roots, like the main plant, are virtually indestructible. I suppose the closest comparison is to Japanese Knotweed. Hugo estimates it would take centuries for all parts of the plant to break down. The time taken for the tissues to degrade is, of course, one of its major qualities. He says this should be easy to control. You can place vertical barriers into the soil to stop the roots from spreading. He isn't aware of any other dangers. It's not poisonous; there are no threats to indigenous species or to wildlife. I think we can take it that there are no serious negative aspects to its use. Hugo said that Sarah is working on a genetic modification to help control the spreading, while retaining the other benefits.'

'Good,' said Peter. 'How did you get on with Dr Hadfield?'

'I know this sounds unbelievable. It just wasn't possible to get a meeting with her. She's been so busy and sent her apologies.'

'I must ask you to follow her up. She was a key player in defeating the Sect's ambitions during the Templewood Summer. If anyone has anything to offer, it will be her. Will you please try to contact her over the weekend?'

'I will. I have some important questions for her.'

'Lisa, how did you get on with your discussions? You've been talking to a few people, I believe.'

'Yes, I went back to Solomons Farm and had a long talk with Roland Nightingale. He showed me the *purgatem arem* crop again. It really is impressive the way it takes so much pollution out of the atmosphere and uses the carbon to fertilise the other half of itself, as it were. It's only when you see how much is produced that you realise how bad the air quality is becoming. Even here, where so many green policies have been adopted. I explored every avenue I could think of, to try to identify anything that could go wrong. Roland was very cooperative. The only thing I could come up with is if the crop were to cross with or threaten another indigenous species in some way. Sarah maintains it's impossible; I have no way of proving it one way or another.'

'While you were with Nightingale, did you discuss the telecommunications developments?' said Peter.

'Yes,' said Lisa. 'Again, it all sounds good news, this wireless power transfer and far-field wireless energy harvesting. My only concerns are those that people have worried about for years: the danger of radiation interfering with brain function. There's no way of telling before it happens. All we can do is continually monitor those people exposed to the sources and react if something untoward is spotted. I'm sorry if that sounds woolly but, as with most things we're discussing, the benefits are clear, even if the hazards are not.'

'You've also been talking to Sarah and Dr Jay, I believe?' said Peter.

'Yes. Sarah's drones are a wonderful thing, especially with the decline in the bee population. Essentially, they are miniature robots with limited, programmed intelligence, working in a narrow field, if you'll excuse the pun. The only problem I foresee is some sort of operational or control failure, the sort you can get with any drone, where the device collides with another object. Given that they are so small, and if a large number were to escape, they could cause damage to machinery, in particular aircraft, if they were to fly into the engines. Individually, they pose little risk. It's the fact that there will be so many of them.'

'Did you speak to them about the ageing solutions?'

'Yes, I did. I'd like to thank you for the pointers you gave me from the Council meeting reports. Of course, I agree with Sarah's worries about prolonging poor quality lives or overrepairing badly diseased or damaged bodies and brains. What we need is, firstly, discussion and definition of rigorous controls and, secondly, the establishment of a moral philosophy and operational code by which these controls can be measured and tested.'

'That sounds an excellent idea,' said Peter, 'And one that should gain general acceptance. Anything else?'

'Yes, the one other concern I have is the possibility of introducing alien genetic material into human bodies, creating, well, a mutation of some sort.'

'What do you mean by "alien", Lisa?' said Peter.

'We probably all know that it is possible to introduce animal parts into human bodies. How far can this be allowed to go? At what point do people cease to be human and become a new species? If certain modifications became accepted and standard, would the boundaries be pushed further? Would this allow new diseases to enter the canon?

Could those diseases create epidemics that would be capable of wiping out the human race? These are the alarm bells that rang for me. I'm just a lay person; we need to appoint expert scientists to reassure us, or otherwise.'

'Emily, you were going to speak with Martel and Arthur to get their views. Did you have any joy?' said Peter.

'Martel was OK, as cooperative as you could ask. He didn't have much to add to what we know already. He's comfortable with the genetic editing work he undertakes at the seed farm, based on feedback from Hugo Payne and advice from Sarah. It's almost a mechanical exercise. That's a little worrying, as he didn't show any real concern about mutations. Perhaps he didn't want to discuss that aspect. He's very focussed on putting a positive spin on developments in the Templewood Gazette. He speaks to Simon Barrington almost daily. He does make a point of including me in their meetings and he asks my opinion. I can see how important it is, not only to keep the villagers on message but onside, too. It heads off criticism and dissent. I'm constantly working on them both to allow me to provide more content. I know it would be subject to further editing and possible censorship. That comes with the job. If I'm to be trusted, as I am, with confidential information, I need to demonstrate a responsible approach. Because Martel is also the overall head of security here, I also spoke with Andrew Blund. I don't know why. His only real responsibility is to ensure that no outsiders can move into Templewood, essentially by monitoring general enquiries through his Market Cranford office. I don't really understand why he's on the Council. I wonder why I bothered, actually. I didn't learn anything.'

'No surprise there. I've never understood why he's on the Council either,' said Peter. 'What about Arthur? How did you get on with him?'

'We had an enjoyable talk. We spent a while reminiscing about the old days, as you would expect. That's probably where his problem lies. He doesn't seem to have the inclination or energy to disagree with anyone.' Emily turned to address her words towards Rachel and Lisa. 'He's never had any real power. He was never anything more than a figurehead as mayor. Nowadays, he has little will to say anything controversial or to stand in the way of anything. He's looking forward to being out of it. Who could blame him?'

'No concerns raised there, then?' said Peter.

'No, not really. There was just one moment when I thought he was going to open up.' Emily frowned.

'Well?' said Rachel. 'Don't keep us in suspense.'

'Despite his waning interest in the Council and its workings, he wanted to know more about why I was asking him so many questions. I thought it was safe to admit that I was generally analysing the possibilities of what could go wrong from a journalistic point of view. I didn't mention that it was part of the input to this discussion. He said that there was one question that nobody ever seemed to ask.'

'What was that?' said Peter.

'The reason why the Visitors are here and why they are providing us with these so-called gifts. The biggest risk is not knowing what they want from us.'

'There must be a few questions over the Sect's agenda when they begin to take power, too.'

Saturday 15th August: Visitors from the Past

Emily asked Lisa and Rachel to join her and Peter at the weekend at The Abbot's House, to discuss her thoughts on the Book of Mysteries and whether it held clues to previous encounters with the Visitors. She wanted to share her thoughts and findings and to validate them. This was a matter of such importance that she felt it essential to check that her imagination was not overstimulated, that she was being critical of the evidence and not just seeing what she wanted or feared to believe. Emily told the three that the meeting was to discuss a matter of 'great importance and possible significance'. She did not go into detail, except with Peter, whose assistance she enlisted to arrange access to the Book of Mysteries. Peter organised a secret session to allow Emily to spend a whole day going through the two versions of each of volumes one and two and the single extant version of volume three. The two copies of volumes one and two were historically held by the Pros and the Cons, who had appended their own annotations and notes of interpretation to their respective copies. The third volume had been missing for many years, until Peter had discovered it in St John's Church, hidden beneath the fallen bust of a crusader in chain mail, smashed by intruders who had been searching for the book. The books continued to be stored in secret, secure locations, under guard, separately for what were originally the Pros' and the Cons' copies, that differed in their historical annotations. The single, known copy of volume three was kept at a third location. As decreed in the agreed protocol, three members of each branch of the Sect were obliged to be present whenever the books were accessed or moved.

Today, Emily, Peter, Lisa and Rachel could hold their discussion indoors and not have to cross the road to the field to avoid possible, albeit unlikely, monitoring of their conversations. Besides, it was raining, the sort of persistent summer drizzle on a still day that demanded activity to avert feeling low in spirits. No harm would be done from the overhearing of what they had to say. Indeed, it could be beneficial and add credibility to whatever conclusions they might come to.

'Thanks for coming,' said Emily. 'It was prompted by something Lisa said about possible historical sightings of the Visitors. Before the Templewood Summer, I mean. I've been doing some research to determine whether the Visitors might have been here, on Earth, at various times in the past. My preliminary thoughts are that, although there is no certain proof, the indications are that it is highly probable.'

'I've been looking forward to this,' said Lisa.

'There are quite a few pointers to previous visits,' said Emily. 'I'll stick to the four that I think are most promising. I'd like this to be an open discussion, so please jump in whenever you wish. I'll deal with them in historical sequence, starting with the earliest'

'This is incredible, so exciting,' said Rachel.

'So, the first is embedded in the Aretalogy of Isis, the Egyptian goddess who, together with her husband Osiris, were the most widely worshipped of deities.'

'Excuse me asking, what's an aretalogy?' said Rachel.

'It's a form of sacred biography, in the form of a text or poem,' said Peter. 'This one provided us with clues of how the Sect was planning to change the tilt of the Earth's axis. It sounds like you've discovered other things in it, Emily.'

'Yes, I have, but let me read you the text first.' She laid a copy of it on the table in front of her and read, slowly and clearly.

I am Isis the tyrant of the whole land. I was educated by Hermes and with the help of Hermes devised both sacred and secular scripts, so that everything should not be written in the same script.

I established laws for humans and created legislation which no-one has the power to change.

I am the eldest daughter of Kronos.
I am the wife and sister of King Osiris.
I am she who invented crops for humans.
I am the mother of King Horus.
I am she who rises in the Dog Star.
I am she who is called God by women.
By me was the city of Boubastos built.
I divided earth from heaven.
I appointed the paths of the stars.
I regulated the passage of sun and moon.
I invented fishing and seafaring.
I made justice strong.
I coupled woman and man.
I arranged that women should bring babies to the light after nine

months.

I legislated that parents should be loved by their child.

I inflicted punishments on those who are not affectionately disposed towards their parents.

I, with my brother Osiris, ended cannibalism.

I showed initiations to humans.

I taught them to honour images of the gods.

I founded sanctuaries of the gods.

I ended the rule of tyrants.

I ended murders.

I forced women to be loved by men.

I made justice stronger than gold and silver.

I legislated that truth be considered a fine thing.

I invented marriage contracts.

I assigned languages for Greeks and barbarians.

I made good and evil be distinguished by nature. I made nothing more respected than the oath.

I delivered the person plotting unjustly against another into the hands of the person plotted against.

I inflict punishment on those acting unjustly.

I legislated mercy for the suppliant.

I honour those who avenge themselves with justice.

By me justice is mighty.

I am mistress of rivers, winds, and sea.

No-one is held in honour without my assent.

I am mistress of war.

I am mistress of the thunderbolt.

I calm and agitate the sea.

I am in the rays of the sun.

I accompany the passage of the sun.

Whatever I decide is actually accomplished.

To me everything yields.

I free those in chains.

I am mistress of seamanship.

I make the navigable unnavigable whenever I decide.

I built the walls of cities.

I am she who is called Thesmophoros.

I raised islands from the deep into the light.
I am mistress of rainstorms.
I conquered fate.
To me fate listens.
Hail Egypt who nourished me.

'The first thing worth noting is why Isis is held in such veneration: why she becomes the most widely worshipped deity in the world of the Egyptians and beyond. Let's take a look at the text. There's a long list of benefits to society that are attributed to her: she makes laws, she "invents crops" for humans. This I take to mean that she has introduced crops and the practice of farming, as opposed to hunter-gathering. She teaches the people of the time other new skills: how to read the stars, so that they might learn to navigate the oceans to fish. She has "built the walls of cities" — this may refer to introducing construction techniques.'

'An interesting theory,' said Peter. 'She is bringing skills, teaching people how to respect and harness nature. I'm aware that in other Egyptian writings adherents of Isis are not allowed to destroy a living tree or block a spring.'

'How old is this poem?' said Lisa.

'No-one knows exactly,' said Emily. 'A version was found on a stele at Cyme, which is believed to be a copy of one from the temple of Hephaestus, where construction is believed to have started in 449 BCE, although the first evidence of the powers of Isis dates from 2686-2181 BCE. I'll continue. Isis is also a civilising influence. At the most basic level, she eliminates cannibalism. At a more sophisticated level she introduces a system of justice that cannot be bought with gold and silver, that is to say has embedded controls to protect against corruption and political influence, a system that recognises the values of truth and humility. She separates religion from the secular and teaches rites of initiation, presumably into the realms of the arcane knowledge reserved for those deemed worthy of receiving it. The poem also includes a statement emphasising her ultimate power.'

'I can see that it could be read in that way, although others could read it differently,' said Lisa.

'I don't dispute that,' said Emily. 'I don't, and could not, claim it provides proof, but the poem does provide us with a lot of evidence.'

'I don't see any real evidence of extra-terrestrials,' said Rachel. 'What I do see is a lot of major achievements for one individual, some taking society from a primitive to a sophisticated level.'

'I hear what you're saying. I'm not so sure. I'm beginning to think that the name Isis doesn't refer to a single individual. It's a concept to define the unknown power that is bringing these gifts. As for extra-terrestrials, the clue is in the wording. Why does she say, "I establish laws for humans", unless she is not one? It's not the way we talk.'

'I must have read that poem a hundred times or more and I hadn't spotted that,' said Peter, 'There again, I wouldn't have been looking for it at the time.'

'Let's move on,' said Emily. 'The next thing I looked at was how new knowledge was communicated to the Sect and how key individuals who might be useful to the Sect were identified and recruited. The Ancient Egyptians believed that arcane knowledge was revealed in dreams. It's referred to in the Egyptian Book of the Dead, which we discovered at the time was first written down around 1600 BCE. Peter, you'll remember that time in the Templewood Summer that I woke you in the night to tell you that I'd uncovered the Sect's plan.'

'How could I possibly forget?'

'Well, I went back to the sections in the Book of Mysteries, to the passages I discovered then. As with the aretalogy, I realised that they could have a different meaning from what I'd inferred at the time. I'll go through my thoughts and findings. Apologies in advance, Peter, a lot of this will be familiar to you, but it's essential that Lisa and Rachel know.'

'That's fine, go ahead,' said Peter.

'I'd discovered that acceptance into the Sect was by a process of mystic rites, a tradition going back to the ancient Greeks and Egyptians. The Masters identified those they regarded as the chosen ones, individuals with special powers or who would serve a particular function, who would be made to pass through certain rites. The rites took the form of three stages. The first was purification, followed by familiarisation with sacred objects and finally the imparting of secret knowledge. Music and drama played a significant part, and it was all placed in some context of death and rebirth: the connection with nature and the seasons, the immortality of the soul. I went back to the account of such a ceremony that I'd read in the past. I wrote down some notes, which I'll refer to.'

Emily shuffled her papers, trying to find the section she was looking for. Rachel began to fidget with impatience.

'Ah, here we are... Purification. "The aspiring Sect member is given a date for the initiation by some sort of direct sign. It may be way off in the future, and much patience is needed to ensure the candidate is prepared and ready. But not in too much of a hurry. The second stage is the imparting of secret knowledge. The initiate is briefed on how to prepare for the imparting of knowledge and how to provide evidence that they have received it, to prove to the Sect that they are a genuine candidate and are not bluffing, or otherwise deceiving them, or that the Sect has made a mistake in choosing them. The aspirant attends a ceremony with incantations and singing and the revelation of sacred objects and documents, accompanied by a play or ritual to bring the knowledge to life. This includes being shown sacred books containing the details of the next stages of the initiation."

'The Book of Mysteries represents the modern equivalent. The account refers to parts being written in unknown characters. The contents are encoded within designs and drawings to prevent any unauthorised person who gets hold of them from interpreting the message. At the ceremony, the initiate is instructed on how to prepare for the final stage, including details of how to interpret the secrets of the Sect. The final stage is in two parts: receiving instructions on how the secrets of the Sect will be revealed, together with the responsibilities and duties of the initiate. At this point, the initiate assumes the capability for receiving or interpreting the secrets and arcane knowledge, often in a dream. This is the second part.

'There are other writings from the Ancient Mysteries that hint at visitors from space. This passage was written by the Naassene Gnostics about how the universe is timeless:

> *Bearing seals, I shall descend;*
> *Through ages whole I'll sweep,*
> *All mysteries I'll unravel,*
> *And forms of Gods I'll show;*
> *And secrets of the saintly path, Styled "Gnosis," I'll impart.*

'There's so much there, in a few lines: "descending", from what, a spacecraft? Travelling through the ages, unravelling mysteries, that is to say, revealing secrets. And forms of Gods may refer to a superior intelligence. And this one, describing the search for knowledge and enlightenment and the promise of secret knowledge.

> *Know what is in front of your face. And all that is hidden will be disclosed. There is nothing secret that will not be revealed. And nothing buried that will not be uncovered.*

'And this passage shows how you will recognise it:

> *Seek and do not cease to seek until you find.*
> *When you find you will be troubled.*
> *When you are troubled,*
> *You will wonder and rule over all.*

'There's more, making connections between chosen individuals, reincarnation and eternal life. This is from one of so-called Gnostic Gospels, the Gospel of Thomas:

Whoever finds the interpretation of these words will not know death.

'There is so much evidence,' said Emily. 'Not proof, I agree, but evidence. Let's move on, to the Book of Revelation.'

'I haven't read the Bible since I was at school,' said Lisa. 'All I know about the Book of Revelation is that it's full of plagues, death, hell, fire and brimstone, and the Four Horses of the Apocalypse.'

'And the number of the Beast: six hundred and sixty-six,' said Rachel.

'There's lots more to it, especially in terms of predictions, including the Rapture, the time when true believers will meet their maker,' said Emily. 'I looked up the Rapture in the Bible. Mum's got a copy of the Dake Annotated Reference Bible, King James version. This is what Thessalonians, chapter four, verses sixteen and seventeen says:

For the Lord himself shall descend from heaven with a shout, with the voice of the archangel, and with the trump of God: and the dead in Christ shall rise first:

Then we which are alive and remain shall be caught up together with them in the clouds, to meet the Lord in the air: and so shall we ever be with the Lord.

'This could refer to the Visitors taking people up into their spacecraft. At the time we, Peter and I, took the Book of Revelation to refer to changing the axis of the Earth's tilt so as to change the climate, giving the Sect the opportunity to take power using their knowledge. That's still the case, but now we can see that the Visitors are the driving force, that it is not the Sect in control. The Sect is just the means of gaining control over the Earth's population.

'Peter and I were treated to an explanation of the Sect's understanding of the prophecy, as identified in the Book of Revelation, written in about 95 AD. Although it was presented by Stephen, the village priest, it was not the conventional theory you would hear from a man of the church.

'He explained that the Book of Revelation is an apocalyptic, or arcane, book, which describes events causing and leading up to Armageddon, when Babylon, the present political and economic world, will come to an end. This will be preceded by a series of prophecies, trials, warnings and plagues, culminating in a series of cataclysmic events, collectively known as the Tribulation. Following the destruction of the present world, the Day of Judgement would follow. Thereafter, the world would be a better place, free from corruption and the tyranny of nations. A place where all the peoples of the world will live in harmony.

'He said that there is a school of thought that demands that readers require esoteric knowledge to be able to grasp its layers of meaning, which was something that the Pros and Cons subscribe to. He explained that "apocalyptic" implies that the knowledge will be imparted in a dream or vision and that the predicted events are related in this way, the same way in which its author, John, was overcome by a state of ecstasy, when commanded to write down the Revelation in the form of a book. He was instructed neither to add nor to take away anything he was told or saw, under pain of death, or the plagues he would hear described. He was instructed to broadcast the Revelation to the seven churches.

'Stephen described the contents of Revelation in sequence. Again, I've brought some notes. I made these immediately after the meeting. I'm glad I thought to bring them here.'

Emily began to read aloud from the notes.

'A door is opened in heaven and the trumpet-like voice summons John up to be shown the shape of things to come. He goes into a trance-like state, in which he sees a God-like figure on a throne bathed in an emerald-shaped rainbow light, encircled by twenty-four seated elders. Thunder and lightning pour from the throne, symbols of the source of power within. It is surrounded by seven lamps and four many-eyed beasts, in the form of a lion, a calf, a man and an eagle. The enthroned figure holds a book, or scroll, sealed with seven seals, which no man can open. One of the elders proclaims that the Lion of Judah has prevailed to open the book and loosen the seals. A slain and resurrected lamb, with seven horns and seven eyes, takes the book from the right hand of the figure on the throne and proceeds to open the seven seals.'

'What makes you think this describes the Visitors?' said Lisa.

'The whole of Revelation is an allegory, which was convenient for the early Church to appropriate, to reinforce their beliefs and power over worshippers. The first clue is the word 'heaven': things are revealed from above. John is invited up to see and hear the future from a figure seated on a throne, with twenty-four elders at his side and beasts with many eyes. The book appears to correspond to an early version of the Book of Mysteries: a recorded body of knowledge, a definitive statement that combines statement and belief. The terms of reference for an organisation, if you like. What is written in it cannot be changed. It is the book of destiny, a prophecy of what will come to pass. There's much more to come.

'We learn of the seven seals. The first four seals introduce the Four Horsemen of the Apocalypse, including, Death, who rides a pale, yellow-green horse and is followed by Hell, who has the power to kill a quarter of the population of the Earth by the sword and by famine. The horsemen respectively represent conquering or crusading, warring, justice and death, with attendant famine. The chaos described is caused by the current and past world leaders, who inflict war and eventually famine, through their abuse and neglect of natural resources. The opening of the fifth seal provides a temporary respite, calling upon the souls of the martyrs, who must wait a while longer to be vindicated for their cause.

'I believe this refers to the ones chosen to lead – the leaders of Templewood, who must be patient and await the right moment for the event that will lead to them taking their rightful place as responsible stewards of the planet, using their accumulated knowledge and wisdom, acquired over the centuries.

'The opening of the sixth seal presages a great earthquake. The sun becomes black; the moon turns the colour of blood. We are told the stars of heaven will fall to the Earth. The sky splits asunder and rolls up as would a scroll. Mountains and islands are moved from their places. It is almost but not quite the end of the world; there is more to come. This fits with the Norse myths and the Ancient Mysteries. Next, we are told of four angels, who may be the horsemen in another guise.

'They stand on the four corners of the Earth, preventing the four winds from blowing. Another angel appears to command them not to hurt the Earth, seas and trees until the chosen ones, dressed in white robes and carrying palms, who will be spared, are marked, that they should be recognised.

'So here we have the chosen ones, the faithful who will be spared, about to be marked in some way as such. The seventh seal is opened and is greeted by silence, before a new series of seven begins. Seven angels, each with a trumpet, are greeted by another angel, who fills a censer with the fire from an altar before casting it to the Earth, creating thunder, lightning and an earthquake. Each of the seven angels, in turn, sounds their trumpet, to give warning of coming judgements.

'The first summons up a rain of hail, fire and blood that

destroys a third of all trees and all the green grass. The second brings a volcano, whose lava turns the sea to blood, destroying a third of all sea life and a third of all ships. The third announces a comet, Wormwood, which falls from the sky and poisons the waters, killing a third of all people. The fourth tells of an eclipse, or darkening of the skies, dimming the light of the sun and moon by a third and extinguishing a third of the stars.

'We are presented with a comet or an asteroid, whatever, which will wipe out large numbers, before the Earth is plunged into darkness. Rather than a comet, we could read this to be the Visitors' spacecraft. Next, we are told of the torments about to be inflicted upon those other than the chosen ones.

'The fifth to seventh trumpets announce torments to befall those who will not be spared. The fifth begins with a star falling and opening a bottomless pit, from which giant armoured locusts emerge to torment the unchosen for five months. This is the first woe. The sixth angel's trumpet heralds the loosing of four angels of death, who will kill a third of mankind with their army of armoured horsemen. We are then told of another angel descending, holding a book, or scroll. When he reads from the book, seven thunders utter in their voices a message, which John is instructed not to write down, but to eat. He is told it will be sweet to the mouth, but bitter to the belly.

'We may take this to mean that the angel is sharing with John a message he is to convey to the nations of the world. It is shocking in its content but for the greater good. He must use this message for the benefit of all those worthy members of the human race. The message remains secret. Here we have the secret knowledge that will be passed on to the Sect to enable them to gain power.

'An angel endows two witnesses with the ability to prophesy. They will be protected while their work is in progress, after which they are killed by the enemies of the good. They ascend to heaven on a white cloud.

'We believe that this section forms a part of the background to the Sect believing that Peter had the power to interpret the prophecy. Again, people ascend into the sky, possibly into a spacecraft.

'The trumpet of the seventh angel sounds and a pregnant woman appears, clothed with the sun, the moon at her feet and wearing a crown of twelve stars. A beast, in the form of a seven-headed, horned dragon casts a third of the stars to Earth while waiting to devour her offspring. The woman gives birth to a male child and war breaks out between the forces of good and evil, with good triumphing. The devil pursues the woman, in the knowledge that he has but a short time left to prevail. A second beast rises out of the sea with a mortal wound that is healed. The beast is destined to make war on the good; it has the power to rule the nations. A third beast comes up out of the earth and marks his own with "the mark of the beast".

'The forces of evil realise they have only a short time in which to recover their power and engage in a final war, in desperation.

'Four more angels appear in turn, to proclaim the hour of judgement, the fall of Babylon, to condemn the followers of the beast and, finally, to call upon a figure sat upon a white cloud, bearing a sickle, to "reap the harvest of the earth", which he does. Yet another angel urges a comrade to gather the harvested vine of the earth and cast these grapes of wrath into a winepress, producing a torrent of blood.

'I take this to mean that the Visitors, their spacecraft appearing as a white cloud, together with the powers that rule Templewood would sit in judgement, once they had put in place a world Government of consensus, regardless of former international boundaries and cultures.

'Next, seven angels pour the vials of wrath upon the Earth, in the forms of plagues: grievous sores upon those bearing the mark of the beast; the sea is turned to blood, killing every living soul on the sea; rivers and fountains are turned to blood. Another is poured upon the sun, scorching men with fire. The world is plunged into darkness, leaving the victims to think only of the pain of their earlier plagues. The river Euphrates is dried up, permitting a conquering army to cross. The rulers of the old kingdoms are gathered together at Armageddon. At last, when the seventh angel pours his vial, a great voice announces that it is done. Again, there follows thunder, lightning, hail and a great earthquake, the like of which has not been seen before, that splits the great city into three. Islands are sunk, mountains are flattened. The old world has fallen. The rulers have lost their power, both in matters of state and in commerce. A mighty angel tosses a stone, like a great millstone, into the sea, to symbolise the destruction.

'The essence of this is that having wiped out all opposition, the Sect, aided by the Visitors, will rule the Earth. Note also the reference to the millstone, which is echoed by the Norse legends.

'For the old order, there will an end to wealth, the city's lights will dim. There will be no more brides and bridegrooms.

'This could refer to no children being born in Templewood. A more worrying aspect is whether the Visitors plan to wipe out the rest of the world's population, once they no longer serve the Visitors' needs, whatever they may be.'

'It could be referring to eliminating just the old powers and not the Sect's followers, the chosen ones,' said Lisa.

'I agree that's a possibility,' said Emily. 'We're approaching the end now.'

'A white horse bears a rider leading the heavenly army of the faithful and true, urging them towards battle, wherein the beast is destroyed and cast into the bottomless pit, where he shall remain for a thousand years until the final battle.

'You might ask why for only a thousand years? Remember, when Revelation was written, a thousand years represented infinity. As far into the future as could be imagined. The fact that we are reading these words two millennia on should not deflect us from the message. And finally…

'In the new world, there is no more sorrow, death or pain. The tree of life bears fruits each month and its leaves are for the healing of nations.

'I expect you'll need some time to digest all of that,' said Emily. 'We have unusual events happening in the sky, prophecies, catastrophes, judgement and retribution, all leading to a world changed, arguably for the better, with the perpetrators of evil having been eliminated.'

'As you say, there is no proof, but I can see the possibilities,' said Lisa.

'I'll move on to Fenja and Menja,' said Emily. 'Their tale originates in the Poetic Edda, first written down in Iceland during the 13th century, although thought to date back to the Icelandic Viking Age, between 793 and 1066 AD. Fenja and Menja appear in the legend of the lesser Grotte-mill, built with stones from the lower world and working in the depths of the sea. In later life, the giantesses were sold as slaves to King Frode and made to turn the mill, to grind out gold, peace and goodwill. This they did until they were forbidden to rest by the King, who was greedy for yet more gold. They exacted a terrible revenge by turning the mill with such speed that the millstone broke into pieces, and the foundation was crushed under its weight. After this, it ground only salt and dust. This triggered an earthquake of such magnitude that it was felt in heaven, and the Earth was put out of alignment with the stars. The earthquake changed the climate and caused a terrible winter, the fimbul winter that lasted for years, prompting mass migration to warmer climates. In a later version of the myth, the Grotte-mill and the giantesses were captured by a sea-king who made them grind salt in the mill on board his ship until it sank. This explained how the mill came to stand on the bottom of the sea. It was said that "there was produced a whirlpool in the sea, caused by the waters running through the hole in the millstone, and from that time the sea is salt". Over time, the tales of the two mills merged into one.

'Here we have several points of connection between the Norse myth and Revelation: heaven, a millstone dropped into the sea, an earthquake, climate change. I feel there's another connection I'm missing somewhere.'

'That's an incredible amount of material,' said Rachel.

'Yes, collated over several centuries,' said Peter. 'You'll see from the two copies of books one and two that there are variations of interpretation expressed in the annotations by the Pros and the Cons. No doubt these differences were material in widening the attitudes of each group on how to take their cause forward — the Pros by forcing change and the Cons by adopting an evolutionary approach, allowing events to take their natural course.'

'The question I have,' said Emily, 'is, why now? Why have they decided to return now?'

'Because the time is right. The Earth is in a mess, ecologically, with its conventional rulers unwilling or unable to implement change at the necessary pace,' said Peter. 'The Visitors' own planet, as you've pointed out previously, could be dying, and there are willing allies, in the form of the Sect with a shared agenda. The thing is, the Visitors have brought lots of good things over the centuries, but this time they are starting to take. Right now, it's people they are taking. You're right, Emily. We have to do something. We need to get the Sect to put their plan on hold while we try to work out what's going on. Thank goodness this risk assessment has come at the right time.'

Sunday 16th August: Deposits on the Canal Bank

'Peter, thank you for coming over, especially on a Sunday,' said Amit. 'It might not be anything significant, but I thought you ought to know.'

'No problem. It's always best to share information as

quickly as possible. It gives more time to address any issues that might arise. How may I help?'

'I heard something odd this morning,' said Amit. 'One of the canal boats that bring goods in from the coast spotted a large mound on the shore, close to the estuary. It was on the wrong side of the estuary, the uninhabited side, inland from Longhaven, close to where the river meets the canal, which was why they thought it peculiar and decided to investigate. It's all open marshland there — nothing will grow in the brackish water apart from grasses and reeds and the odd bush. The bargee stopped to take a closer look. It was an enormous heap of granules, possibly some chemicals, right on the riverbank, next to the water. They brought back a sample.'

The marshland opposite Longhaven extended for miles along the coast and its hinterland and stretched inland for a few miles to the sea lock, where it joined the canal. Many lives had been lost in the treacherous mud of the marshes that in a few steps could change from being firm, to squelchy, to a deadly bog. No-one, not even the hunters from Templewood, who in the winter months might take an expedition along the canal towards the sea, would dare risk their lives to engage in their wildfowling sport here.'

'Perhaps they were dumped there by another boat, waiting for someone to collect them,' said Peter.

'I think he'd have known if that were the case. There are so few barges that travel that way. And they only sail towards the estuary at night to avoid being seen from Longhaven. As you know, it's in the radar blackout area, so detection isn't a problem at night-time.'

'It does sound peculiar. A bit risky, too, bringing some of the material back to Templewood without knowing what it was. There could be a chemical or radioactive hazard.'

'They said they took sensible precautions, handling it with the barge's grab and wrapping it multiple times. There was no flesh contact.'

'We both know that that isn't necessarily good enough.

However, that's where we are. Where is the sample now?'

'I told them to take it to Sarah at Saracens Farm for analysis. It seemed best to keep it low-key. I explained to them that it was only a precaution and that they should keep it to themselves to avoid spreading any alarm. They seemed happy to do that.'

'Very wise. Thank you for the information. I'll go and see Sarah now. Hopefully, she will have had time to examine it.'

*

Sarah welcomed Peter cautiously. Her analysis of the material had produced a surprising result, which she shared with Peter. The identification was straightforward; there was no immediate cause for alarm. The reason for the deposit of such a large quantity of a common material remained a mystery.

'I have an idea,' said Peter. It's a bit far-fetched. I'd like to discuss it with Dr Hadfield. Do you mind if I take a sample to show her?'

'Not at all, I'll bag some up. After all, it's quite safe. Will this be enough?'

'Yes, fine, thank you. I'd like her to see for herself.'

'Tell me what your thoughts are. Why do you think it was left there?'

'Oh, it sounds so ridiculous. I'd prefer to discuss it with her first. It's more in her line of expertise.'

'As you wish. I think I see where you're coming from.'

'I'll let you know when I've spoken with her.'

*

'Thank you for agreeing to see me at such short notice, Dr Hadfield,' said Peter.

'You're welcome, Peter. I'm sure it must be important if it's that urgent. Take a seat and tell me how I may help. Tea will be arriving shortly.'

'I've come to ask your opinion on a scientific topic.'

'I hope it's not too technical. I'm only a mere teacher of science,' she smiled. 'You might do better to find an expert.'

'There's no mere about it. You're a respected scholar with an in-depth knowledge of your subject across a wide range of disciplines. There's another reason I want to discuss it with you. I can ask theoretical questions in confidence, without alarming anyone else.'

'I thought there must be more to it. By all means, you have my full attention.'

'Thank you. Well, to begin with, Amit was approached by some bargees this morning. They had found a large, flattened area on the canal bank, close to the sea lock at the estuary, on the Templewood side. It was covered with this. They said it looked as though a large pile of the material had been deposited and subsequently removed. I've brought a sample with me.'

Peter dropped the drawstring bag onto Dr Hadfield's desk. She examined the contents, then smelled them. Her smile turned to a puzzled frown.

'Is it what I think it is?'

'It's salt. Sarah confirmed it. The stains are evidence of intense heat around the pile — not burn marks. Salt and heat seem an unusual combination. There seems to be no reason for it to be there. It's not as though it's a valuable commodity.'

'When you say a large area, how large?'

'It was circular, about a hundred metres in diameter.'

'The only use I can think of is for road gritting. I know there are no roads that far out. If it had been intended for use in Templewood or the military base, it would have been taken straight in, not left on the bank.'

'Exactly!'

'Clearly, you've thought this through and have an idea. I assume this is what you would like my opinion on. Tell me what you think.'

A knock at the door announced the arrival of tea. Peter and Dr Hadfield waited for the tray to be placed on the desk and the young man who delivered it to leave the room before continuing. Peter took a sip and placed the cup and saucer on the desk.

'The place where it was found is close to where the Visitors' spacecraft is located. I wonder if they were responsible,' said Peter.

'That hadn't occurred to me.'

Peter thought for a moment.

'The bargees said that there was another area close by, similar in shape, which was covered in some sort of mud or silt. And there was a third area with a circular mark, a flattening of the vegetation. They said it was as if a rocket had taken off or landed. I can't explain what caused the heat. It's difficult to imagine that such an advanced civilisation would depend on flammable fuel to power their vessels, but it looks as if it's been made by some powerful heat source.'

'What do you think they're up to, Peter?'

'One possibility is that they could be surveying, testing and analysing elements of the landscape to analyse its composition. My concern is that it might be something more sinister.'

'This sounds intriguing.'

'It could be something even more worrying. Supposing that's the reason they're here: to take salt from the planet. Perhaps they need salt in the same way that we do, and their reserves are running out. This could be the missing connection that Emily was talking about yesterday when we were discussing the likelihood of earlier landings by the Visitors. She reminded us that there are references in the Book of Mysteries to the Grotte-Mill, and the sinking of the millstone, and how that caused the sea to become salty.'

Peter related the evidence of the Visitors' previous arrivals to Dr Hadfield. It was starting to make sense. The connections Emily had identified were logically sound. He acknowledged the importance of stepping back and evaluating the 'facts' and not accepting them unquestioningly. Yes, she may have identified significant connections; on the other hand, they could be coincidental, imagined. Yet, so much of what had happened in the past few years would be unbelievable to most people. It was by confronting the evidence, however far-fetched it might seem, that the truth could be distilled.

'It's amazing,' said Dr Hadfield. 'I'm fairly familiar with the Book of Mysteries and had wondered over the years since the Visitors' arrival whether some of the contents were evidence of previous journeys here.'

'All the same, if they need salt, why come all the way here for it?' said Peter. 'Surely, if it doesn't occur naturally in their landscape, or if they are running out of it, they could make it using a chemical process.'

'If they have the raw materials, the chemicals, that is,' said Dr Hadfield. 'They'd need huge quantities, which may well not be available to them. It wouldn't be practical, whereas here there are almost unlimited supplies. Some of the salt mines are enormous, and then there's the sea. Two-thirds of the Earth's surface is covered by oceans, and the technology for salt extraction has existed for decades, with hot countries desalinating water where it's scarce. I suppose that if that's all they want, then it shouldn't be a problem.'

'I don't think we should take that for granted. We don't know how large their planet, or empire, is. If the Visitors believe it's worth travelling so far to identify and confirm the source, they must have both a desperate need and a requirement for enormous quantities. You wouldn't come all this way to collect a pile of the size found on the canal bank. They could be looking to wipe out most or all of the salt on the planet. I've no idea how much that could be. There's also the possibility of trace minerals. Where you find salt, you often find other elements, such as boron and lithium.'

'The environmental cost would be catastrophic, especially if they intended to desalinate the oceans, whether totally or changing the salinity. Why don't we do some quick research to get an idea of the scale we could be talking about? Come over to the other desk. Let's look a few things up online.'

Peter and Dr Hadfield each suggested queries to key into the search engine. They quickly confirmed that salt is the main mineral constituent of seawater with about thirty-five grams per litre, or 3.5%. They discovered that ocean salinity had been stable for billions of years, owing to a process that removes as much salt as is deposited. Estimates of the combined size of the oceans ranged from three hundred and twenty-one to three hundred and thirty-three million cubic miles — figures they both agreed were beyond imagination. They found estimates stating that if all of the salt in the ocean were removed and spread evenly over the Earth's land surface, it would form a layer more than 500 feet thick, about the height of a 40-storey building.

'It's the low percentage of salinity in the oceans that I find most worrying,' said Dr Hadfield. 'It means that the amount they would have to take to make a significant difference in the balance would be lower than if the percentage were high. So many sea creatures are dependent on saltwater to survive. And so many economies, particularly in third-world countries, are dependent upon fishing. If the fish were to die out, it would plunge millions of people into poverty and starvation.'

'If they also went after the salt mines, a shortage could affect the entire world population,' said Peter. 'Look up salt mines.'

Dr Hadfield and Peter were amazed to discover the sizes and locations of the world's largest salt mines. The largest, the Sifto Salt Mines, located in Ontario, Canada, was located 1800 feet under Lake Huron. It is large enough to incorporate a small town, where four hundred people work.

'It says here that, at its current rate of production, it has sufficient reserves to last until the end of the century,' said Dr Hadfield. 'The Khewra mines in Pakistan are the second largest in the world, producing 325,000 tons of salt a year. The output over its lifetime is estimated to be two million tons. Amazingly, this isn't even a dent in the salt that's stored here, which is estimated to be about 6.687 billion tons. Interestingly, fifty per cent of the amount mined is used to build support columns in the mine.'

'There's another potential issue. If the Visitors know that we are dependent on salt to survive, that provides them with information that could encourage them to enslave us.'

'We're in danger of racing ahead of ourselves. This is all speculation with very little evidence.'

'That's in hand. I've arranged for cameras to be put in place at the site, as well as other monitoring equipment. Let's hope they soon return.'

'I'm glad you came to see me and entrusted me with this information,' said Dr Hadfield. 'I agree that it's best to keep it to ourselves for now, particularly with the Council meeting coming up.'

Friday 21st August: The Council Reviews the Risk Analysis

Two weeks had passed since the meeting with the Masters. The day had arrived for the Extraordinary Council Meeting called to review Peter's risk analysis report. Gygges opened the meeting. In his opening address, he urged the members, all of whom were in attendance, to adhere to the single agenda item, to review the report. Confidential copies had been distributed in advance of the meeting. Gygges asked Peter to present his findings in the sequence in which they appeared in the report. All would be invited to debate the major topics before forming agreed recommendations for further action. At the end of the meeting, any additional summary actions would be proposed, discussed, modified and agreed upon.

'Does anyone disagree?' Gygges looked around the room for possible objections. There were none. 'Good. Peter, over to you.'

'Thank you, Mr Gygges. Members of the Council, this assignment was put together quickly to comply with the instruction to report back within two weeks. To complete it in a timely fashion, I enlisted the help of Emily, Lisa and Rachel.'

'A very succinct, clear and comprehensive summary, especially given the short time you had available to you for the investigation and analysis. We thank you for your excellent work,' said Gygges. The Council members nodded in agreement. 'Have you had time to prepare recommendations for how we should address the risks?'

'I have. Would you like me to present them?' said Peter.

'We certainly would. Ideally, I would like us to be able to agree to them,' said Gygges.

'And to put in place a plan of action, with an appropriate budget and time scale,' said Arthur.

'I trust that they will not introduce any delays to the Sect's plans,' said Gygges. 'Please take us through each of your recommendations. We will then vote on which to adopt and whether to request further investigation. Who will second this?'

Arthur raised his hand, as did others. This was the response Peter had hoped for. Indecisiveness by the Council had caused problems in the past.

'In that case, I will try to be as brief and clear as possible,' said Peter. 'First of all, the *lignum petrum*. I have two recommendations. We must ensure that once the crop is made available outside of Templewood, it is subject to specified conditions that they allow us to monitor. We will insist that the crop is contained within demarcated areas, away from other crops. It must be surrounded by vertical barriers into the soil to a depth of five metres to prevent the roots from spreading. If the crop is discontinued, for any reason, all traces must be fully removed by excavation and destroyed by burning in an enclosed furnace at a specified temperature. Sarah is also working on a genetic modification to help control the spreading. We should ask her to prioritise the delivery of this.

'Next, there is the issue of the *purgatem arem* crop. This has been a success story from the start. It offers a real breakthrough in removing pollution from the atmosphere, with the bonus of using the extracted carbon to self-fertilise. Our discussions with Roland did not identify any definite risks, other than the possibility of it crossing with or endangering other native species, which Sarah says is not possible; Nevertheless, to err on the safe side, we should impose similar conditions as for the *lignum petrum*.

'We also looked at the telecommunications developments: the wireless power transfer and far-field wireless energy harvesting. Although potential risks from telecommunications and electrical power sources have been debated widely for a long while, there is no proof of any danger from radiation interfering with brain function. This does not mean that danger is non-existent, only that it is not proven. What I recommend here is that all those exposed to the sources are continuously monitored for health issues.

'Moving on to the drones... These pose no more than a minimal risk at an individual, day-to-day level, other than operational or control failure or collision, which is a risk with any type of drone. These are, of course, very small. There is a risk that programming failure could result in swarming, causing damage to machinery and aircraft engines. Proper regulation will help regulate their ownership and usage, although there will always be a residual, minimal risk.

'The work on ageing solutions presents ethical as well as humane issues. Sarah has flagged her concerns about prolonging poor quality lives or applying excessive procedures to diseased and damaged organs and minds. I recommend that we draw up a moral code designed to define what is ethical. From that, we can develop a legislative framework within which rigorous controls are specified, with appropriate monitoring and enforcement.'

'Forgive me interrupting, Peter. This does sound like a recipe for procrastination, prevarication and delay,' said Gygges.

'I disagree,' said Peter. 'The work and its implementation

can continue uninterrupted. The risks we seek to avoid are medium- to long-term concerns. We can decide on the remedies as we continue to go forward, although there is one area that I recommend must remain sacrosanct.'

'What's that?' said Arthur.

'There is a line that must not be crossed. We must ensure that, under no circumstances, do we allow non-human genetic material to be integrated into human bodies. I am sure that many of you will be aware of rogue research into introducing animal parts into human subjects. Taken to its logical conclusion, if this were to be permitted or tolerated, we would face the risk of creating diseases — epidemics even — capable of wiping out the human race. It's one thing to integrate technology into human bodies and brains, although I have reservations there, too.'

Sarah nodded.

'That brings us to Mr Martel's work with genetic editing,' said Peter. 'Mr Martel was very helpful, as were all of the farmers. OK, he's very relaxed about his work and doesn't have any worries about undue consequences arising from it. Although I'm not an expert, I agree with his and Sarah's assessment that it's almost a mechanical exercise. The one concern that I had was the possibility of mutations. Sarah has done her best to put my mind at rest on that subject. Well, she has almost succeeded. She's the expert, so I shouldn't really comment.'

'You just have, Peter,' said Arthur. 'Tell us about your concern.'

'It's nothing, really. I shouldn't have said anything. It's just that… Intuitively, I can't help worrying that there is an opportunity for someone, either through personal ambition or malice, to experiment and possibly succeed in creating a hybrid species. A chimera, that will unleash all sorts of unforeseen problems. It's for that reason that all I can recommend is that Sarah monitors the situation for any untoward signs.'

'Peter, I've explained to you that there is absolutely no

risk,' said Sarah. 'However, I have no problem with agreeing to your suggestion if it makes you more comfortable.'

Peter thanked Sarah. His sheepish expression betrayed his embarrassment at having gone beyond the brief he had set himself by emphasising a personal, unobjective concern. Having mentioned Sarah's assurance, he should not have commented further. The best tactic to overcome the glitch in his presentation was to move on as quickly as possible.

'As regards more general risks, I believe I can provide positive reassurance. Mr Martel is, as you all know, in overall charge of security. As well as communications and physical security, we have additional protection from the work that Simon Barrington does through the Templewood Gazette and Andrew Blund with the estate agency to ensure we keep unwanted intruders, whether by accident or design, out of Templewood. Villagers are reassured and motivated by the positive news reported regularly in the Gazette. This all helps to keep morale high and to minimise the likelihood of defectors or sabotage. The additional security issues that we have asked Lisa to examine and address will add to our overall protection.'

'Well, thank you, Peter. As requested, you have kept it brief. We now have a better understanding of the risks and the additional actions necessary to address them,' said Gygges. 'In most cases, it is obvious where the responsibility lies for action. I will consult with Arthur outside of the meeting, and we will confirm responsibilities in the minutes. I will, of course, advise and recommend to the Masters those actions that will need to be implemented within and beyond Templewood. Peter, I would like you to join us for that discussion. I think we can all agree that none of the points you have raised imposes a need for delay. Is there any other business before we close the meeting?'

Gygges looked around the table. No-one was preparing to speak. Members started to shuffle their papers and collect their few belongings together.

'I have an issue to raise. In fact, it's another risk, one that no-one appears willing to address, yet we must,' said Peter.

Gygges sighed.

'Very well. Go ahead.'

'Thank you, Mr Gygges. As you have heard, the benefits of the Visitors' arrival appear clear, even if the potential hazards are not. There is one question that nobody ever asks. The topic that Mr Gygges reminds the Council, when opening each meeting, is not for discussion and not to be named.'

Around the table, a fresh bout of paper and chair shuffling broke out. Some members searched for imaginary objects in their briefcases to avoid attracting attention. Mr Gygges pulled an expression suggesting he had sat upon something uncomfortable or unpleasant.

'We need to discuss why the Visitors are here and why they continue to provide us with these so-called gifts. The biggest risk is not knowing what they want from us. I have come to this view because we need to discuss the disappearances and what action we should take in response. This is the greatest risk we face, of inaction in the face of possible adversity.'

Peter felt an intense infusion of relief as he finished the sentence. He was confident in his position within Templewood. He knew and understood the boundaries of the esteem and respect in which the villagers held him. It was fine when everyone was in agreement, as they had been, for the most part of the past fourteen years. He had found it a struggle to gather the courage to be open about the threat that others were unable or unwilling to admit to. It was as though, inflated with anxiety as to the possible response to expressing the problem, his bubble of concerns had been burst by a pinprick. The response was silence, initially. Some members' expressions and demeanour betrayed their reactions of fear, anxiety. Some, like Richard, smiled, as did Arthur, who bore the look of a reprieved man, grateful that Peter had not named him or hinted that he was a promoter of this view.

Gygges took a deep breath before responding.

'Peter, I am sure you are aware that this represents a change of direction on your part. I must remind you that it was you who recommended that we prohibit discussion of the topic. There is some truth in what you say. We have failed to address the issue. This was not due to complacency. There is no way we could have foreseen the disappearances. It has been all too easy to accept the benefits that the Visitors have brought without questioning their intentions. Although this is an extraordinary meeting, called to present and debate one specific topic, I am prepared to accept that what you would like to discuss forms a part, perhaps the most important part, of the analysis of risks and that we should therefore discuss it. Will anyone second me?'

Almost all hands were raised. The exceptions were Sarah and Andrew Blund. Both remained calm and dispassionate. Peter leaned forward, his hands resting clasped on the table. Gygges adjourned the meeting for ten minutes to give the attendees a short period to collect their thoughts. When all had returned to the room, Gygges reconvened the meeting. He asked Peter to continue.

'I'll begin by stating the three main questions we need to consider regarding the presence of the Visitors. First of all, what's in it for us, as human beings, the indigenous occupants of planet Earth? Secondly, what's in it for the Visitors? Thirdly, what is the end game for the Visitors?

'We are all familiar with the benefits they have brought us and very welcome they are too. I see the plus points as follows. The fact that we have been presented with these gifts is comparable to the early geographic explorers who exchanged gifts with the natives of newly discovered countries. The bringing of gifts, regardless of their use and value, provides a sign that they come in peace and that we need not feel threatened. The value to the Sect is that they endow us with knowledge unavailable to the outside world. The promise and delivery of new knowledge bring influence leading, ultimately, to power, locally at first and eventually global control.

'As for the Visitors, their demonstration of friendship is rewarded by confidence and assurance that they will not be attacked. They are seen as allies who might bring more gifts to enrich our civilisation. They recognise that they are not seen by humans as a threat; they are regarded as a force for good by most people.

'So, what is their endgame? I believe there are three main possibilities. One is that they wish to live, to co-exist, with humans, peacefully. Perhaps their planet is threatened or has been destroyed. They may have run out of essential resources or are about to. Another possibility is that they have polluted it beyond the point of recovery, rather like we are doing on Earth. They may see our planet as a new home to share with us, offering the resources they have exhausted on their own. A second reason for their landing may be that we have something that they wish to extract from us and take away. As we would with, for example, the mining of trace minerals discovered on an extra-terrestrial object. By establishing an apparently friendly relationship, they may be building trust before making moves to take what they want or need. The third possibility is that they are assessing us as a race, identifying what makes us tick and our strengths and weaknesses. Once they have completed their assessment, they will take over the planet as conquerors.'

'Hmm. On what basis have you come to that conclusion,' said Arthur. 'All we have seen so far is positive, to the benefit of humankind. There doesn't seem to me to be any basis for concern.'

'Look at it this way,' said Peter. 'Over the past five to six hundred years, humankind has had a history of colonisation, the seeking of new worlds. Adventurers have often undertaken hazardous voyages with a variety of motives. Some have been looking for new trade routes, others for treasure or in the hope of discovery of new lands to colonise or exploit. Some of the invasions were undertaken in peace, intended to open up new opportunities for trade or expansion in a non-threatening way. They introduced, with good intentions, the culture and customs of the explorers to "improve" the lives of the indigenous population, including religious conversion. All too often, things turn for the worse. The explorers become invaders, bringing violence and bloodshed, plundering the natural resources of the discovered lands, and adopting unacceptable practices, such as slavery. Think of people such as Captain Cook, still thought by many to have been a brave and upstanding example of a pioneer who opened up a new world. Yet, in New Zealand, his conduct was far from exemplary; he was responsible for the unjustified killing of native people.'

'That's all very well,' said Martel. 'We haven't seen anything of the sort here. Everything's going to plan, and we have a lot to show from the Visitors.'

'What I am saying,' said Peter, 'is that we must be on our guard and not continue to accept everything at face value. We have to examine and evaluate everything that's happening, to look at the complete picture. The disappearances are a prime example.'

'There's no proof that the Visitors are responsible,' said Nightingale.

'Because there is no proof doesn't mean that we shouldn't be aware of the possibility that they are responsible. In the same way, we have to consider their motives for being here. We should consider whether they are just giving or intend to take and the effect that whatever they intend to take might have on us as a species. You may not all be aware that, only yesterday, there was a discovery of salt extraction close to their spacecraft.'

A look of puzzlement spread across the faces around the room.

'What on earth would they want salt for?' said Martel.

'They may need it to maintain their own metabolism, just as we do,' said Sarah.

'I'd have thought that they would have brought everything they need with them, given how far they must have travelled,' said Richard. 'I suppose they could just be topping up.'

'This is an example of what I am trying to get across,' said Peter. 'We should be looking at alternative explanations. After the discovery, I did some quick research on the extent of salt deposits worldwide. They are way beyond what I would have dreamed of. The total world production of salt is over 300 million tonnes a year. The biggest producers are China, the United States, India, Germany, Canada and Australia. The reserves of the largest mines are enormous; one in Pakistan is estimated to have 6.687 billion tonnes. This may be what they have come for.'

'I don't see how they could take it back to their planet,' said Hugo Payne. 'Imagine, you have come millions, perhaps billions of miles, taking goodness knows how long to get here. We've seen the size of their spacecraft... How many would they need to transport a worthwhile quantity back home?'

'You've raised several issues, Hugo,' said Dr Hadfield. 'There has to be a reason for the Visitors coming here. I suspect this vessel is on an exploratory mission, hence its small size. Who knows how many other planets they are looking at? We know or suspect that theirs is an advanced civilisation, way beyond ours. We don't know how large their planet is — they may have colonised several others. We don't know the size of their population or how long they live for, and we can only guess how advanced their technology is. They could have constructed spacecraft of a size that would astound us. They may even have unlocked the secrets of time travel, allowing them to travel enormous distances, or of teleportation, to allow them to transfer large quantities of materials.'

'It all sounds like science fiction to me,' said Nightingale.

'Nevertheless, they are here,' said Richard. 'There's no denying that. Fifteen years ago, you would have laughed if you'd been told what we know today.'

'Do you think we're making too much of this, Peter,' said

Andrew Blund. 'If, as you say, we have such enormous reserves of salt, is there any harm in letting them share it? We could offer to allow them exclusive access to some mines or help them locate new sources. Trade is what cements friendships. It would demonstrate to them how grateful we are for their gifts.'

Peter was pleased he had stimulated much discussion. He could not recall the last time that Andrew Blund had contributed to a discussion at a Council meeting.

'It depends how much they want and where they take it from,' said Peter.

'What do you mean?' said Gygges.

'Clearly, the deposits we found were extracted from the river, close to the estuary. I acknowledge that only a relatively small amount was taken. If it was the Visitors, it represents no more than a sample. There may be a reason for this, possibly some special properties of sea salt that are not found in other varieties. What if they intended to extract salt from the sea, in quantities so large that they upset the balance of the oceans?'

'I don't see a real problem with that,' said Gygges. 'The oceans are so large they could absorb the loss.'

'That's not strictly true,' said Dr Hadfield.

'I have to remind you of what I said earlier,' said Peter. 'We don't know how large their civilisation is and how much they require. All of our judgements are based on what's familiar to us: our planet, our environment. Dr Hadfield, what's your opinion of the potential damage that excessive removal of sea salt would do?'

'Ocean salinity has been stable for billions of years, most likely as a consequence of the combination of a chemical and tectonic system that removes as much salt as is deposited. For example, sodium and chloride sinks include evaporite deposits, pore-water burial, and reactions with seafloor basalts.'

'I apologise for interrupting, Dr Hadfield.' said Arthur. 'Is it possible to keep the language simple? I'm afraid I'm not a scientific person and am having difficulty understanding.'

'Sorry about that, Arthur. Don't worry. The process is irrelevant. The real issue is the need to retain the balance; to maintain a constant level of salinity. As Mr Gygges says, any threat would depend on how much they take. However, we're talking of enormous numbers here. About 97 per cent of the Earth's water is found in our oceans. Of the tiny percentage that's not in the ocean, about two per cent is frozen in glaciers and icecaps. Less than one per cent of all the water on Earth is fresh. One estimate is that there are over three hundred and thirty million cubic miles of water on the planet, of which the oceans form three hundred and twenty cubic miles. If all of the salt in the ocean could be removed and spread evenly over the Earth's land surface, it would form a layer more than 500 feet thick, roughly the height of a forty-storey office building.'

'Well, there we are,' said Gygges. 'There's more than enough to go round.'

'It's not as simple as that,' said Dr Hadfield. 'As I said, it's vital that the balance is maintained. Observations of the breakup of ice shelves and glaciers have sent alarm bells ringing through the scientific community. We've seen how an iceberg the size of a large island, with torrents of very cold fresh water emerging from it as it slowly melts, could have disastrous effects on the phytoplankton in the surrounding waters. It's akin to a gigantic ice cube floating in the ocean, cooling and freshening the water around it. This could have extremely serious repercussions, as ecosystems in these cold regions are delicately balanced. This could affect the base layer of the ocean food chain.

'Phytoplankton, the microscopic marine organisms that float in the water, could be killed off. This would affect the creatures that feed on phytoplankton such as krill. In turn, this could affect populations of seals, penguins and whales, which all eat krill.

'Ice shelves at both poles are being destabilised by

climate change. This increases the risk that more and more giant icebergs could drift to lower latitudes, disrupting the ecosystem and the food chain. It may seem small-scale, but believe me, it's a serious problem!

'I won't bore you with the details, but it should be obvious that if we allow this balance to be changed, the effects could be catastrophic. You only have to think of the consequences, not only on the ecology of marine life but on the economies of coastal communities worldwide.'

'What action do you suggest we take, Peter?' said Arthur. 'If they decide to take something, whether it's salt or anything else, we're hardly in a position to do anything about it. We can't exactly blow them to smithereens, not that that would solve anything. What, exactly, is your recommendation?'

'I can't recommend anything specific at this point in time. We have to be vigilant. By that, I mean we have to be aware that they might have different motives from what we have come to believe. We have to exercise caution and share information between us that might indicate an undesirable outcome. I recommend to the Council that we add a new regular agenda item to discuss and review our relationship with the Visitors. I hope that in time we'll be reassured that they mean no harm. Until then, we must all be on our guard.'

'I'll second that,' said Richard.

'We would need to take a vote on that, as with any change to the agenda,' said Gygges. 'It's one thing to instigate new programmes that are relevant to our brief, such as the risk analysis. It's a different matter to initiate actions that could subvert the Masters' plan and timetable. To announce your proposal to the Masters through a new agenda item would not be well received. This is a separate issue from the risk analysis which, has shown that there are no risks, real or potential, arising from the Visitors' gifts that cannot be managed. Now that it is complete, I can inform the Masters, in summary form, in advance of the scheduled meeting. No doubt they will remain eager to proceed with their plan without further delay.'

'Our relationship with the Visitors is indeed a separate issue,' said Peter. 'We must also apprise the Masters of the possible dangers when they return here in a few days.'

'Let me stop you right there,' said Martel. 'Peter. We agreed, somewhat reluctantly, at the previous meeting to your proposal for the risk analysis, subject to it being completed quickly. The whole purpose was to avoid delays with the rollout. Our time has come, after centuries of false starts, especially after what happened fourteen years ago.'

'Oh, come off it, Martel. You know full well how close to disaster we came then,' said Richard. 'If it hadn't been for Peter, we could all have been killed, along with everyone else on the planet.'

'There's no way we can start putting doubt in the minds of the Masters,' said Payne. 'They don't want to hear questions about the motives of the Visitors. The benefits they've brought us, and the probability of unlimited amounts of further knowledge and improvements are obvious. Let's have a vote on it.'

'Okay, okay,' said Peter. 'We'll keep it to ourselves and continue to discuss and review it.'

'That's probably the best course of action,' said Arthur. 'Mr Gygges, will you please add the topic to the agenda of future meetings?'

'I object,' said Nightingale. 'You are well aware that the Masters see the minutes and the agenda of the meetings.'

'True,' said Gygges. 'There are only two courses of action. Either we hold a vote, or Peter withdraws the request. It's probably best not minuted.'

'Very well, I'll withdraw the formal request. All I will ask you to do is to question everything that is happening, to ensure that we continue to act in the best interests of Templewood and the rest of the planet.'

'Good,' said Gygges. 'In that case, think we can bring matters to a close. Oh, one more thing. Sarah, at the last

Council meeting you hinted that you might have an announcement to make. Is that relevant to today's meeting?'

'No, Mr Gygges. It's something I'm still working on and is unrelated to the risk analysis.'

'Very well. We will close the meeting.'

*

A heavy silence ruled Mill Cottage that evening. Peter was annoyed that he had not canvassed support for his idea in advance of the meeting. He should have sounded out opinions and only raised the proposal once he was confident of sufficient support. He had let his friends down by not thinking the subject through. It was unusual for him to make mistakes and rare for them to be visible to others.

'Why did you back down so quickly?' said Richard. 'Some of us knew you were right. We should have debated it and forced a vote.'

'It was the wrong time and place,' said Peter.

'I disagree with you there,' said Richard. 'It was the right place to make the point with those in power here, albeit limited, and I'd say it was the right time, with the Masters due back here.'

'Sometimes, I think I've been here too long. I worry that I'm beginning to deviate from my own principles and have delusions of my own power and influence.'

'Nonsense. We wouldn't have done the risk analysis if it weren't for you. That's saved a lot of time and work in the future. We've achieved so much in Templewood over the years you've been here, so don't forget it. It's a good thing that you're able to recognise when you think you've made a mistake. It allows you to step back and reframe the situation. It's not as though nothing positive came out of it.'

'How do you mean? I don't see any positives. What I've done is to create a division in the Council.'

'The positive is that you've alerted them to the potential of a problem. They are all now aware that things aren't necessarily what they seem. There'll be thinking about the subjects raised: the disappearances, the salt… And as for dividing the Council, it's always been bubbling beneath the surface, ever since the days of the Pros and the Cons.'

'I thought that was all over, that we'd been through a healing process and come together, working towards shared objectives.'

'Your trouble is that your standards are too high,' said Richard. 'You've forgotten what conflict is like.'

'It's because I remember how things were when I arrived here in my teens that I'm keen to avoid conflict. There are so many good things about Templewood now — first-class healthcare and education, no crime or poverty…'

'No freedom,' said Richard. 'How many times do we hear people here referring to a benign dictatorship?'

'True. Sadly, I have the feeling it's all beginning to change. There's a danger that everything will begin to fall apart in adversity. That's not a good place to be at the best of times. When the Visitors first arrived, all we saw were improvements. Now they are starting to do things we don't like, things we don't understand, which might have bad outcomes.'

Richard nodded. A solemn pout confirmed his mood.

'I can see trouble ahead.'

Saturday 22nd August: The Salt Mine

Peter ambled from the kitchen of The Abbot's House, cup in hand, unsure of why he felt resentful of the interruption. He did not often work from home other than when it was necessary to focus on matters requiring detailed thought and reasoning. He preferred to be accessible and visible in the community. To be perceived as 'doing something'. He believed this stimulated and motivated other residents of Templewood. Occasionally, as was the case today, a Saturday, it was a treat to work uninterrupted, with his phone switched off and personally disconnected from the rest of Templewood.

Peter had another reason to remain at home today. He

wanted to be alone. He felt hurt by the Council's dismissal of his suggestion to alert the Masters to his concerns about the Visitors. His feelings were exacerbated by the sense that he had let Richard down. Richard had been prepared to stand up to the other Council members to support him and was annoyed that he had backed down. Peter was not used to rejection. For as long as he could remember, he had exercised confidence in his ability to assess situations and make the correct judgement. Peter liked certainty; the spectre of doubt was an unwelcome stranger.

Someone was at the front door, a clumsy, panicked rattling of keys at the lock. Emily dashed inside, red-faced and panting.

'Peter, where are you? Have you seen the news?'

Emily kicked off her shoes and pushed the door closed behind her. Peter knew that another task or responsibility was about to be added to his list.

'No, I've been here working all morning.'

'You wouldn't believe it. An incredible coincidence, after we were discussing it the other day. There's been a raid on that salt mine in Pakistan. Thousands of tons of salt stored outside and awaiting export vanished overnight. There's no trace of a break-in or any damage to the buildings or security equipment. And no evidence of what happened on the CCTV. One minute it was there, the next it had disappeared.'

'It must have been a local job. Perhaps dissatisfied employees looking to make some extra money for themselves.'

'There's no way. It would have taken hundreds of lorries weeks to remove the quantity taken. And only days after we were discussing the possibility that the Visitors could be interested in the planet for its salt.'

'What makes you think it was the Visitors?'

'It just has to be the Visitors — there's no other explanation. There's no way that such a large quantity could vanish in such a short time. There are only two routes in or out and no trace of vehicle marks. Neither of these detected anything on their CCTV recordings. No-one can provide any explanation or motive.'

Emily knew Peter well enough to tell from his expression that he was alarmed. She had always admired his talent to grasp the essentials and possibilities of cause and effect in all aspects of his daily life.

'If what you say is correct, it's worrying. They've never made their presence felt outside of the Sect's two main bases before.'

'That's what I was afraid you'd say.'

'This marks a new departure. It must be part of a plan of action. But why now?'

'Do you think it could be connected to the disappearances? They've found out what they need to know about us as a race, and they've gained enough knowledge to move to the next stage.'

'This could be a game-changer. It's one thing to be in contact with the Visitors in an enclosed society, such as Templewood; the population can be managed. If the outside world discovers that we've been invaded by an alien life form, there will be panic and chaos, with all the consequences: riots, looting, suicides…'

'You need to go back to the Council, now, Peter. The Masters have to be told. Why are you shaking your head?'

'I don't know. I tried at the Council meeting to persuade them to let the Masters listen to me and failed. I don't know what to do for the best.'

The Ascent to Power

The arrival of the Visitors was a godsend for the Sect. Their invisible, unobtrusive presence, and their gifts, provided the most promising means in world history to establish global power. Here, at last, was a way to take control of the world's countries, peoples and economies without aggression, through solving shared problems, problems they could not, or lacked the communal will to address effectively, principally those related to climate control and stewardship of the planet. Solutions are best received when sought by the beneficiaries. Those the Sect could offer were of the moment.

Throughout history, the Sect had drifted in and out of power, taking advantage, sometimes of empires and political movements, sometimes of local conditions, to exercise control by solving problems or bringing knowledge. Things were different now. The Sect would no longer reinforce the positions of established rulers and movements. Its thrust would be to empower all nations with the benefits provided by the Visitors. It would spread and share knowledge in a spirit of cooperation, providing its representatives in almost every country with its newly acquired wisdom and guidance for its use. It would introduce improvements to farming, ecology, health and education. It would liberate countries from oppression, aggression and competition to create a commonwealth of trade and friendship while respecting local culture and history. It would reduce poverty, disease, famine and planetary damage.

Now it could acquire power without force or revolution. There would be no competitive or commercial gain; all nations would be equal, with the gifts available for the convenience and benefit of all. No single gift would provide an advantage to one party to the detriment of others.

Sunday 23rd August: The Clearing

The recollection of her guarded discussion with Françoise, out of Sarah's earshot, had been troubling Emily. From her discussion of the risk analysis with Peter, she had learned that several action points had been assigned to Sarah. She decided to visit Sarah at Saracens Farm. A first-hand discussion would provide a positive message to the community to report in the Templewood Gazette. It would also conceal her real motive: to assess Sarah's mental state.

Could it be that her extensive role and responsibilities were beginning to overwhelm her? Perhaps Françoise had made the aside as a discreet call for help. The three women had always got on well. Emily felt a duty of care to watch over her friend.

Sarah welcomed Emily with a hug and a smile. She put Emily at ease instantly and showed no sign of stress. Françoise had sent her apologies for not joining them. She had errands to attend to. Sarah was unaware that Emily had asked Françoise to let her spend time alone with Sarah.

'Let's take a walk around the farm while we chat. Then we'll come back to the farmhouse, and I'll make some tea,' said Sarah. 'We'll walk through the orchards, through the woods, then back along the track that skirts the fields.'

In the orchards, the bee drones busily attended to their work.

'They're programmed to avoid colliding with people and inanimate objects in the way that other robotic machines are. It's essentially the same technology as used in cars, vacuum cleaners, lawnmowers and so on. That's the easy bit — the close-range hazards. The challenges come with teaching them about the wider environment. A simple example is control over the height at which they fly, to avoid aerial collisions. We can obviously control the area in which they operate to ensure they do the job they are intended to. Of course, they might have to travel from one place to another, such as between separated orchards. They have inbuilt navigation systems with accurate mapping information, including details of the mapped terrain and layers of information describing the in-between areas. That allows the inclusion of instructions to avoid hazards and specified land boundaries. As you can imagine, there's a fair amount of tailoring to be done in certain parts of the world. Fortunately, these days the base data from satellites is comprehensive. The majority of the tailoring is to identify land ownership and restrictions.'

'So, the configuration and training are a significant

feature in introducing the technology to new users,' said Emily.

'Yes, although the same applies to any item of farm machinery. We'll have to train a team of trainers to support new users, in the same way as you would with a combine harvester or any other piece of complex, intelligent machinery.'

They walked through the orchards towards the woodland at the far end of the farm. Sarah was keen to answer Emily's prepared list of questions. She described how she proposed to manage the risk of uncontrolled spreading of the plant species brought by the Visitors and the methods for testing and monitoring the possibility of mutations. Emily asked how her work with Dr Jay was progressing to develop the ethical code for genetic research and its application to humans.

'That's all very straightforward. It's common sense, really. You start with the moral aspects and issues and work forward from there. You could probably design most of it yourself, with no specialist knowledge. Oh, sorry — no offence intended.'

'None taken,' said Emily, laughing.

By now, they had walked a kilometre or two into the woods, oblivious to the passing of time. Emily was enjoying her work in Templewood. She had proper journalistic interviews and research to do now. Working with The Templewood Gazette was fulfilling in a way that a local paper in the outside world could never be.

'Why have you stopped, Emily? What are you staring at?'

'I'm not sure. There's something odd through those trees. I can see a bright spot. Let's take a closer look.'

Emily glanced at Sarah. For the first time that morning, she appeared uncomfortable, as if there was something she didn't want her to see. Emily responded by marching off the footpath and through the bushes. Sarah hesitated, then ran after her. The parting of the bushes revealed a freshly opened-up area. Beneath the tree canopy, contiguous with its surroundings, the woodland floor had been cleared of bushes and all other undergrowth, including grass, to leave the topsoil exposed. It was as barren as a newly cut turf meadow.

'What's happening here?' said Emily. 'Why has the ground cover been stripped? Are you planning to build something here?'

'No, there's no plan for any new building. I was hoping you wouldn't spot this area from the track. I suppose I'll have to tell you now. It's a secret project we're working on, very much work in progress. I'm waiting until I have more evidence before I present it to the Council meeting.'

'Is it connected with the military in some way?'

'No, they're not involved. We're doing research on alternative methods of communication.'

'Really? It looks nothing more than a large patch of bare earth interspersed with trees. Will you be planting it with something? Another new crop, gifted by the Visitors, perhaps?'

'It's best if you let me explain. Some of this might be familiar to you from press articles published over the past few years. Where shall I begin?' Sarah took a deep breath.

'In recent years, trees have been recognised as creatures with capabilities that in animals we would describe as learning, memory, decision-making, and even agency. Are you familiar with the discovery that plants and trees can communicate with each other? It's been known to scientists for a couple of decades. Beneath the forest floor, there are enormous underground networks called mycorrhizae. These are symbiotic unions of fungi and roots that connect trees. They allow nutrients to flow between trees in a mutually beneficial exchange. What's interesting is that they form a channel for communication signals. They can even include learning and decision-making. Within the networks, trees and plants can recognise their own kin, with larger "Mother Trees" supplying nutrients to their own offspring in preference to other seedlings. The offspring respond by growing better or developing better chemistry. A parent tree will even kill off its own offspring if it perceives they will not thrive. We've discovered that if we suppress the health of the recipient seedling, the mother tree will increase the resources it provides. Many scientists are starting to believe that this behaviour resembles neural networks, the sort responsible for intelligence in human brains. The root systems and mycorrhizal networks that link trees are designed and behave like neural networks. Neural networks are scale-free and are the basis of intelligence in our brains.'

'You're losing me — what does scale-free mean?' said Emily.

'Basically, each node in the network I connected to the same number of other nodes, regardless of how large the network is. So, if you start off with a node connected to, say, five other nodes, each of those will, in turn, be connected to another five nodes and so on through the system,' said Sarah. 'It's amazing that networks between and within trees should demonstrate similar properties to the networks in our brains.'

'Are you saying that trees possess intelligence?' said Emily.

'That's a dangerous comparison,' said Sarah. 'As a scientist, you have to be careful with language. There are two common definitions of intelligence. The first stipulates that intelligence requires a brain, requiring such qualities as reason, judgment, and abstract thought. The second category, unlinked to a brain, emphasises behaviour: intelligence as the ability to respond in optimal ways to the challenges presented by one's environment and circumstances. Plant neurobiologists fall into the latter group. Intelligence implies the ability to solve problems. Rather than a brain, what I'm seeking here is a sort of shared, distributed intelligence, the sort you find in the swarming of birds. In a flock, each bird follows a few simple rules, such as maintaining a prescribed distance from its neighbour. Yet, the collective effect of many birds performing according to a simple algorithm results in complex, well-coordinated and beautifully patterned behaviour. You find similar behaviour in insect colonies, where you can observe many mindless individuals organised in a network. I believe, and many others do, that something similar is happening in plants.'

'I'm amazed. You say all this has been known for a couple of decades?'

'The basic research goes back as far as Charles Darwin and his son. They demonstrated that plants could sense light, moisture, gravity, pressure and other environmental qualities and use this information to determine the optimal trajectory for the root's growth. Darwin discovered that the tip of the radicle — the primary root, the first organ to appear after germination — has the power to direct the movements of the adjoining parts. It acts similarly to the brain of one of the lower animals, located at the anterior end of the body. It receives impressions from the sense organs and directs movements. Darwin was asking us to think of the plant as a kind of upside-down animal. When you look at the underground networks, you find that their thousands of root tips individually play roles similar to those of the flocking birds. They gather and analyse information from the environment and respond in local, coordinated ways that benefit the entire organism.'

'Is there any evidence that plants and their networks can learn from their environment?' said Emily.

'We prefer the words "habituation" or "desensitisation" to learning. Yes, there have been studies and experiments based on protocols commonly used to test learning in animals. Habituation experiments involve teaching a subject to ignore an irrelevant stimulus, allowing it to focus on important information and filter out the noise. An important factor in the experiments is measuring how long the plant will remember what it has learned. Some plants respond to stimuli so radically that they can be observed moving, such as the Venus flytrap. One variety of mimosa has fernlike leaves that fold up immediately when touched, presumably to frighten insects. It will do the same when dropped. In one experiment, researchers dropped a plant from a height numerous times at intervals of several seconds. After a few drops, some of the mimosas started to reopen their leaves after just four, five, or six drops, as if they had decided the stimulus could be ignored.'

'What you've described is learning from external stimuli,' said Emily. 'Are there any examples of plants and trees acting intelligently in a proactive way?'

'You find everyday examples of what must originally have been acquired intelligence, passed on genetically. Take, for example, a bean plant. As it grows, it is looking for something to climb. Laboratory experiments have shown that a bean plant knows exactly where a pole or other support is, well before it makes contact with it. One theory is that it is using echolocation. There is evidence that plants make low clicking sounds as their cells elongate. One theory is that they can sense the echo of those sound waves bouncing off the support. This is another example of the plant focussing on only relevant information. It doesn't waste time or energy "looking" anywhere other than in the direction of the pole.'

'I'd never have believed that plants could detect sound,' said Emily.

'If you play a recording of a caterpillar chomping a leaf to a plant, it will respond by starting to produce defence chemicals. Plant roots can detect buried pipes through which water is flowing even if the outside of the pipe was dry, suggesting that they somehow "hear" the sound of flowing water. But it's more than just sound,' said Sarah. 'Plants have a highly developed sensory apparatus to allow them to locate food and identify threats. We have identified between fifteen and twenty distinct senses, including equivalents to our five. They can smell and taste chemicals in the air or on themselves. They react to various wavelengths of light as well as shade. I expect you know they react to touch, as in the beanpole example. Scientists are using PTR-TOF machines — a sort of advanced spectrometer — to read and analyse the chemicals produced by a range of plants. In this way, they can compile a dictionary of each species' entire chemical vocabulary. Plants typically have three thousand chemicals in their vocabulary.'

'And all this without a brain,' said Emily.

'Brains are useful for creatures that move around a lot, but they're a disadvantage for those that are rooted in place. Self-consciousness is just another tool for living, good for some jobs, unhelpful for others. Clearly, brains have been a key factor in human evolution.'

'It's all very interesting — and I sincerely mean that — but where are the benefits? What good can come of it?'

'A good question. Plants are also able to create scalable networks which are self-maintaining, self-operating, and self-repairing. One of the key opportunities is to rethink the way we design computers, robots and networks. Up until now, they have been designed in our own image. What we are starting to do is to apply plant "thought-processes" to help us to design automated solutions to problems. For example, there is a type of amoeba, which can grow in the direction of multiple food sources simultaneously while calculating and remembering the shortest distance between any two of them. This methodology assists in the design of transport networks. Robots, too: up until recently, they were based entirely on animals or insects. Now we can design them to mimic plants. In the outside world, there are already teams developing a robotic root, using plastics that can grow and then harden. This will be able to penetrate the soil, sense conditions, and alter its trajectory. This type of mechanical "nose" could help farmers identify plants under insect attack, allowing them to spray pesticides only when and where they are needed. Similar applications of the technology would be useful in space exploration.'

'So, where is your work on plant communication taking

you?' said Emily. 'Tell me more about it.'

'I mentioned the mycorrhizae and the communication between trees in the network and the Mother Trees. The Mother Trees are at the centre of communities that are in turn linked to one another. They exchange nutrients and water in a literally pulsing web that includes not only trees but all of the forest's life. It's been described as a "wood-wide web". The network allows hundreds, thousands, of trees in a forest to convey warnings of insect attacks and to deliver carbon, nitrogen, and water to trees in need. In one experiment, radioactive carbon isotopes were injected into fir trees. The spread of the isotopes was tracked through the forest community by various methods, including Geiger counters. These showed that radioactive carbon had been spread from tree to tree, to every tree within an area thirty metres square. Some of the oldest trees functioned as hubs, with as many as forty-seven connections. Other experiments demonstrated how fir trees used the fungal web to exchange nutrients with paper-bark birch trees over several seasons. The fir trees would nourish the birches when they had sugars to spare; the birches would repay the debt later in the season.

'The tips of plant roots can sense gravity, moisture, light, pressure, and hardness. They can also detect volume, nitrogen, phosphorus, salt, various toxins, microbes, and chemical signals from neighbouring plants. Growing roots that encounter an impenetrable obstacle or a toxic substance know they must change course, even before making contact with it. In one experiment, researchers found that when they put four closely related Great Lakes sea-rocket plants in the same pot, the plants abandoned their usual competitive behaviours and shared resources. Because they remain stationary, rooted in the same spot, plants have evolved a complex molecular vocabulary to signal distress, to deter or poison enemies. They even recruit animals to perform various services for them.

'Many plants produce caffeine. They use this not only as

a defence chemical but, in some cases, as a psychoactive drug transmitted in their nectar. The caffeine encourages bees to remember a particular plant and return to it. This acquired loyalty improves the efficiency of the pollination process. Since the early nineteen-eighties, we've known that when a plant's leaves are infected or attacked by insects, they emit chemicals that send a signal to other leaves, instructing them to mount a defence. In some varieties, the plant can identify the insect from the taste of its saliva and then pass the information on. This defence might involve altering the leaf's flavour or texture or producing toxins or other compounds that make the plant's flesh less digestible to the attacker. One example is when antelopes browse acacia trees. The leaves emit tannins that make them unappetising and difficult to digest. In extreme cases, acacia can produce sufficient quantities of toxins to kill the animals.

'One of the most incredible examples of communication between plants and insects is where two insect species are involved: one being a pest and the other as its exterminator. For example, corn and lima beans attacked by caterpillars emit a chemical distress call that can be detected by parasitic wasps, which respond in turn by attacking the caterpillars.'

'This is incredible,' said Emily. 'I had no idea. I'll look at plants differently from now on. Have you been able to recognise any other untapped potential use for all this knowledge?'

'If you look at everything I've described — things we were unaware of twenty years ago — trees communicating with other trees, plants with insects. We've recognised that they have senses that we had no idea they possessed. If you take this to a logical conclusion, we humans may well have senses we are unaware of.'

'That sounds a bit far-fetched,' said Emily. 'How could we possibly not be aware?'

'There could be several reasons. It could be a sense that we used to possess, that we no longer need, like the coccyx in our skeleton. Or something innate and dormant for which up until now there has been no stimulus.'

'You think it could be awakened by connecting to the root and fungus network?'

'There's no reason why we, as a species, shouldn't be able to plug ourselves into the same system. And take it further, too. I believe we can use this intelligent network as a means to communicate with the Visitors,' said Sarah.

'Surely, that's going a bit too far,' said Emily.

'I don't believe so. When you look at the parallels, plants can communicate with each other and with insects — two classes of beings so different in their biological makeup. It's just one more step for them to be able to communicate with the wider animal kingdom, to us, and to the Visitors. We would, in practice, all be speaking the same language.'

'Exactly how do you plan to achieve this?' said Emily. 'Does that mean you'll have to coax the Visitors over here to the farm?'

'I don't know exactly. That's what I'm working on. There should be no need to encourage the Visitors to come here, assuming the network runs from the farm to their spacecraft contiguously. All it would require is for us — me, perhaps — to plug myself in here and for them to do likewise to the network surrounding their ship. This could be an incredible leap forward, Emily. It could be the Rosetta Stone for our times!'

'It would certainly be a leap forward,' said Emily. 'Have you told anyone about this?'

'Not yet. I'm not ready. Emily, I'd be grateful if you'd keep it to yourself for now. Can I trust you?'

Monday 24th August: The Return

Emily was woken by a tapping sound coming from behind the curtains. She had been aware of it as she ascended through the layers of sleep, unsure whether it was a part of the dream. A dream she had already forgotten, other than a few images of bright lights and speeding trains. She often dreamed of trains and had the vague intention of looking up the significance. Life was too short to bother with such trivia. No doubt she would find references to Freud and New Age nonsense. There were more important things to be getting on with.

She stepped out of bed and walked to the window. As she drew back the curtains, she was startled by a blue tit flying off from the outside sill. The bright sun made her squint; it must be later than she thought. She checked her watch. It was nine-thirty. Why had Peter not woken her up when he left for work? She remembered that she had told him last night that she would be working from home. He needn't have assumed that meant a late start.

While she showered and dressed, she planned her now shorter day. Firstly, a walk into Temple Walden to stock up on food (it was her turn this week). Then a coffee before returning home and working straight through the day.

She walked the quarter mile into the village, concentrating on being mindful of the sights and smells of her surroundings. As she headed towards the square, she saw a small crowd, growing in numbers as she approached. At the centre was Peter, standing on what must be a stool or a chair borrowed from a shop or café. As she drew closer, he raised his hand and waved in acknowledgement while continuing to talk.

'I can't tell you any more at the moment. I'll let you know as soon as I hear anything.'

The small crowd appeared excited, agitated. The group turned to each other in lively discussion. Peter was doing his best to answer questions, many of which came from a small group close to him. Emily could not hear clearly from where she stood, other than occasional words and phrases: son, husband, safe, unharmed. Peter stepped down and politely eased his way through the group towards Emily. He led her away by the elbow.

'What's happened?' said Emily.

'They've come back. The missing ones: well, the group

of five. All returned together, at the same place and time.'

'Are they OK?' said Emily.

'They seem so. We've taken them off to the base to be examined and check for any ill effects or contamination. As you can see, it's caused a lot of excitement, particularly from the friends and relatives of those who were taken.'

'So, they were abducted. The Visitors did take them.'

'We don't really know. It's too early to say. I do know that, when they arrived back, the pentagonal objects vanished. We've had to assume the worst and take the necessary precautions. We've put them in quarantine, although they've obviously been in contact with a few people.'

'Why on earth would the Visitors take five people, knowing they would be missed and that they, the Visitors, would be suspected? And why return them a few weeks later, with no explanation?'

'It's anyone's guess. I can think of a few motives, the main one being that they want to examine human biology. And human minds. If you were from an invading race, I expect you'd want to understand the inhabitants. What makes them tick, how to get on their good side and assess them for threats and vulnerabilities.'

'At least they've come back. I hope you're right and that they've not come to any harm. It does look as though the Visitors were signalling that they had been taken, using the pentagonal objects, the placeholders, as you called them. It must be pretty traumatic being taken by an alien life form. Do you think they'll remember any of it?'

'It's too early to say. We don't; know yet whether they have any recollection or whether their memory has been erased. We'll need to test whether they've been changed in any way.'

'How do you mean?'

'We'll test for any physical and psychological changes and scan them for implants.'

'Oh God, no!'

'It's just a precaution. The Visitors obviously need us or think we might be useful to them. Otherwise, they could have wiped us all out as soon as they landed.'

'So perhaps I was right. They could well have been here before. They know enough about us to know we're not a threat. They don't need to kill us, not straight away anyway. And now they're taking things to the next stage.'

'Well, they could have taken, or borrowed, people on previous visits. We've no way of knowing. They could be looking at genetic mutations since they were last here, or just verifying their findings.'

'How long will it take to do the tests on the five and put them through quarantine?'

'A few days. A week at the most, I'd say.'

'What will the Sect have to say about all this? Do you think they're getting close to rolling out their implementation of the gifts?'

'I don't know. That's in the hands of the Masters. I've heard nothing. I don't imagine they'll do anything before the next meeting.'

'Surely, they must have given some sort of clue as to how they intend to proceed. Do you think they could be planning something large and destructive, like last time?'

'I've no idea. They come; they go. They tell us only what they want us to know. It's all very secretive.'

'Peter, the taking of these people could be a significant part of the Masters' plan. They could be in league with the Visitors. Don't you see? The Visitors could be testing humans' tolerance or resistance to various conditions, or exposure to substances.'

'I hadn't thought of that, although I have no idea of how they could be communicating at that level.'

'It could mean that the Masters are close to taking a course of action that's different from what we're expecting.'

Peter contemplated Emily's words. She thought she detected the hint of a pout. She said nothing.

'You're right. I'll talk to Amit and to the farmers and

some of the others. I'm not sure they'll know any more than we do. I'll let you know as soon as I hear anything about the tests on the returned ones.'

'Good. We need to find out as soon as possible!'

Friday 28th August: How They Have Changed

'You seem to be in better spirits today, Peter,' said Emily.

'A little. The return of the five villagers helps. It's one less thing to worry about. I might have been right all along, in which case perhaps I didn't need to alert the Council about the Visitors' intentions.'

'We've been through this. The fact that the villagers have been returned doesn't reduce the need to be wary of the Visitors' motives. You were right to question them, albeit belatedly. Have the results of their tests come back yet?'

'I believe so. Dr Jay has asked me to call in on him later at the cottage hospital. I expect he wants to talk to me about them.'

'In that case, I'd like to join you. It would make an interesting article for the Gazette, to follow up on my report about their return, assuming it's good news.'

'The fact that they've returned the people they took is a positive sign of their intentions.'

'Yes, it'll reassure the villagers. I'd also like to get Dr Jay's views on how the ageing trials are going.'

Dr Jay invited Emily and Peter into his office at the hospital. He glanced up and down the corridor before closing the door quietly. Emily was familiar with his habitual worried expression. She had wondered whether it was an affectation cultivated to give him gravitas.

'I wasn't expecting you, Emily. It's not a problem. We all know you well enough.'

'Peter told me that you were coming over to hear how the results of the tests on the returned people. I thought they might make a good leading article for the Gazette, assuming there are no problems. I hope that's the case.'

'Not necessarily,' said Dr Jay. 'That's the reason I asked Peter to call in. Superficially, they appear well, and their medical test results were normal, or at least consistent with their clinical history. It was only after a couple of days that we started to notice signs of odd behaviour. At first, we assumed it was the shock of their experience — I won't use the word "ordeal", as there is no indication of anxiety or trauma. On the one hand, you would expect them to be affected by such an unfamiliar experience. The good thing, in some ways, is that they have no recollection of their time away. They may have been drugged or hypnotised to counteract this. On the other hand, it's an opportunity missed.'

'How do you mean?' said Emily. 'What sort of opportunity?'

She was cautious, even suspicious of Dr Jay's motives, a thought she tried to suppress as unjustified, attributable to his ever-cold demeanour.

'If they could recount the experience of being taken and held, we would be able to learn more about the Visitors. As you know, no-one has ever seen them. If there had been communication, we could have learned much more.'

'I'm interested in the odd behaviour you say they are exhibiting,' said Peter. 'What can you tell us about it?'

'It seems their thinking is affected. As though there is some form of barrier that stops their minds from working in certain ways. It's as if they'd had an overdose of tranquillisers or a mild stroke — their personalities have changed in various ways ranging from apathy to neglect. Their cognitive abilities are diminished, and they lack empathy, even with loved ones. They have become uncharacteristically compliant, totally lacking in drive or aggression.'

'Is it possible that their brains have been operated upon and things inserted, or parts removed?' said Peter.

'Not that we can tell, from X-rays, scans and measured electrical responses. It's possible that strangers wouldn't notice the change in their behaviour, but their families certainly do.'

'It must make it difficult to treat them if there are no physical symptoms,' said Emily. 'Even if you do, how would you know they'd been cured if that's the right word?'

'What's the next step,' said Peter.

'Continued observation and monitoring. We're thinking of trying hypnosis to try to unlock their memories of the experience. It's not without its risks. Who knows what they might have suppressed? There could be a very bad reaction. Something which, if brought to the surface, could bring on a devastating shock. We have to decide how to manage that risk.'

The questions and answers continued. Dr Jay was at his most communicative when he knew he was regarded as an expert, in control of knowledge and able to demonstrate his competence. Eventually, Peter's and Emily's questions were exhausted. There were limits to how much they could ask when so little was known of the captives' experience.

'Thank you for being so open with us,' said Emily. 'With so little detail available, it will be challenging to write the sort of article I was hoping to produce. I'll have to focus on the positive news, that they are back and apparently have suffered no ill effects. I don't want to mention the changed behaviour. It would worry readers. Let's move on to discuss the ageing project.'

'I agree. Very wise,' said Dr Jay. 'Before we move on, I'll mention one more unexplained change in these people.'

'What's that?' said Peter.

'As you would expect, we tested all of their senses. Again, no injury or disease was found. Their vision, hearing, and everything else responded as normal. One strange thing we noticed was that, in certain lights, their eyes appear amber, like those of a cat or a large bird.'

Monday 31st August: The Masters Return

Gygges confirmed the date of the Masters' visit as firm. It had been arranged as provisional, pending the commissioning of the Risk Analysis. As always, the messenger delivered the notifications to the Council members and promptly disappeared. The notes were always received with apprehension. The Masters' control was absolute; their decisions would often transcend the normal rule of law. All were aware that the consequences of incurring their displeasure could be draconian and that there was no avenue of appeal within the confines of Templewood.

*

Top Secret – Memorise and Destroy.
International Committee for Change – Notice of
Extraordinary Meeting.
To be Held at 8 p.m. Monday 31st August, Archangel
Hall, Temple Walden.
Agenda: Global Change Programme —
Implementation.

*

Once again, the Masters' leader raised a gavel and struck three raps on the table. Once again, Gygges responded with a call of 'Order, order, order', inviting the leader to deliver the opening speech.

'We are here today to perform our duty…'

All present listened attentively, as if hearing it for the first time.

'…may we perform our obligations with diligence, compassion and humility. Let the session begin.'

Gygges duly passed copies of the agenda to a grey-hooded figure, who distributed them to the Masters and to the other councillors, together with Peter's risk analysis report.

The preliminaries were quickly completed. The leader was keen to proceed to what he clearly considered the most important issue, the reason for which the meeting was called.

'As you are aware, we have delayed the proposed initiation of our proposed plan pending the risk analysis recommended by Peter. We agreed to this delay, albeit with some reluctance. I therefore call upon Peter to present the contents of the papers we have before us.'

'Thank you. I hope you will find my recommendations clear and reasonable. I will begin with the proposals for controlling the introduced plant species.'

Peter described the precautions to be taken to confine *lignum petrum* and *purgatem arem* from spreading. Some of the Masters looked at each other and exchanged comments in whispered voices. Notwithstanding their disguises, Peter could tell from their body language that they were unlikely to raise objections to this part of his report. His recommendations for monitoring the health of those working on telecommunications projects evoked similar acquiescence. Much nodding accompanied his proposal to develop an ethical code for implementing the ageing solutions. Controls over the genetic editing of human cells and a ban on introducing non-human material were well received. He would not have expected otherwise. He had always found it strange, almost amusing, that he could sense the Masters' thoughts beneath their hoods and headwear from their silent, involuntary gestures.

Encouraged by the apparent polite acceptance, Peter decided to blast the meeting from its calm deliberation. Without notice, and in breach of his implied undertaking at the Council meeting, he decided the moment had arrived to deliver his warning of the potential dangers posed by the Visitors. The mood changed abruptly; there were gestures of surprise at his recommendation that the Council should closely monitor the relationship with the Visitors and consider their motives. He repeated his concerns to the Masters, to the anger of Council members present.

'Sit down at once! We agreed that this topic would not

be discussed,' said Nightingale, his eyes bulging, his face crimson.

'Just a moment, Mr Nightingale,' said Arthur. 'We didn't agree that it would not be discussed, only that it wouldn't appear as an agenda item. We should ask the Masters if they would agree to allow Peter to proceed with this important topic.'

'We would like to hear what he has to say,' said the leader, looking around to his colleagues, who nodded.

'Thank you, Arthur; thank you, Masters,' said Peter. 'I will continue. If the Visitors are here for the Earth's resources, be it salt, trace minerals or whatever, there are only two ways of satisfying their needs. Either they take what they want back to their own planet, or they settle on ours, whether as equals or superiors. If they decide to settle here, we've no idea how large their population is. If their planet is substantially smaller than ours, there might be little or no problem. If it's much larger, the Earth could be overwhelmed. We don't know what other Earth resources they would need that are essential to us but in short supply.'

Peter reminded the meeting of the disappearances. Although there was no proof that the Visitors were responsible, convincing evidence demonstrated that the captives had been taken for examination. The gestures of the Masters suddenly became agitated, although they remained silent. Peter continued, changing his tone of voice from matter-of-fact to emphatic, almost forceful, culminating in his imperative for all to ask what's in it for us humans? What's in it for the Visitors? What is the Visitors' endgame? Peter knew he must respond to the Masters' restlessness, to avoid them dismissing his report entirely.

'It is not my intention to convey a negative outlook, only urge that we all exercise caution and vigilance. I hope that in time we can be assured that the Visitors mean us no harm.'

The Masters looked around at each other quizzically. The leader announced an adjournment to the meeting to discuss what they had heard.

An hour passed before they filed back into the room and took their places. The leader struck his gavel and waited for silence to settle before he spoke.

'We have considered your report and accept many of your recommendations. We thank you for alerting us to the possibility that the Visitors might have negative intentions towards us as a species. You questioned the benefits to us, the human race. We believe these are self-evident and will assist us in creating a better world. In return, we believe they seek a new or additional home or intend to harvest minerals, quite possibly salt, that are abundant and superfluous to our needs. We are not concerned about the taking, or borrowing, as it appears to be, of some of our citizens. It is reasonable that, to ensure they can survive on our planet, the Visitors should be confident they will remain free of disease or other threats. They are our friends. We have a relationship of mutual trust, almost symbiotic. The overwhelming evidence is that they are a force for good and wish to live alongside us in harmony, for how long we do not know. That, we believe, is their endgame. And besides, I understand that those taken have now been returned. They are of little consequence. One is suffering from dementia and has not long to live; the others hold minor positions in the research facility at the military base and are dispensable.'

Silence hung like a damp fog. None of the councillors showed any sign of wishing to speak or interrupt. It was not that they were afraid of expressing an opinion, either of agreement or dissent. They were waiting for the remainder of the message the Masters were about to deliver.

'You are all aware that our recent initiatives to address some of the issues of climate change have proved popular. They have brought our representatives to power in many nations. At long last, ordinary people are protesting their support for changes to enforce the rapid reduction or elimination of fossil fuels. We intend to build upon this near-universal desire for change. Our intention is to achieve this through a carefully managed and internationally coordinated programme. We will synchronise the announcement of the Visitors' gifts and the associated developments we have built here in Templewood. By this means, we will deliver improvements to the lives of men, women and children across the globe. We will eliminate poverty and improve the quality of lives, starting with the poorest in society. We will spread peace and prosperity across the world. The Sect is a force for good. Now is the time for it not to seize power but to segue to power through democratic processes.

'How, you may ask, will this transition be achieved? We will begin with the countries and areas where we have already gained political power. There are another eleven countries we regard as having reached a tipping point where we need only give the word to initiate a change of government. Given what we have heard today, it is likely that this instruction will be given imminently, once we have had time to confer. Our movement is gaining traction rapidly, although it is not recognised as a global movement and will not announce itself as such. There is no need. The demonstration of shared, beneficial objectives will propel momentum organically. Change will occur naturally over a relatively short period. We estimate that, within one to two years, our organisation will ascend to power in all but the smallest and most insignificant countries. Those remaining outposts will have little alternative than to embrace our shared objectives quickly, to allow them to share the benefits of the early adopters. I will now outline what will be expected of you here, in Templewood. Before I do, are there any questions at this stage?'

Feet shuffled and bodies adjusted themselves. The councillors looked around the room at each other. All had questions; each was aware of saying anything that could be considered by the Masters as being disloyal or doubting of the chosen direction.

Martel was the first to speak.

'I can understand that our changes will be welcome in most quarters and supported by the majority of citizens of their countries. There will, nevertheless, be nations in which long-established rulers, often unelected dictators, continue to exercise power by force, threat or fear. I put it to you that there will be some, if not many, of those rulers who will resist change and do their utmost to retain their own power base at the expense of their subjects. I am interested to learn how change will be handled in those countries where the rulers resist and clamp down forcefully on their populations.'

'You need not concern yourself with such matters. They are not relevant to the Templewood operation. We will deal with these according to our plan.'

Martel sat down, embarrassed by the naivety of his question. Barrington stood up.

'In practical terms, what do you want us to do to inform the people of Templewood of the implementation of the plan?'

'We have produced a comprehensive document explaining how it will be achieved. You and Martel will be responsible for producing a press release to inform the local population through the medium of the Templewood Gazette. Undoubtedly, there will be questions. Arthur and Mr Gygges will be the focal points for questions.'

Peter clenched his fists beneath the table. He would have expected the Masters to appoint him to this role. Arthur was a good, well-meaning and respected man who adopted a cautious and conciliatory attitude to politics. His desire to see the best in everyone led him to avoid conflict. In doing so, he could be slow to react to warnings of danger. Gygges presented a different threat. His confident vanity, his obsession with duty and compliance with instructions could blinker his reasoning. He was known to be sympathetic to Martel and Nightingale, both of whom were considered to lean to the right of the democratic centre of Templewood's politics.

Peter knew he must take care not to antagonise the three, now that his influence was coming into question. The leader resumed his speech.

'Councillors, this is a momentous day that you will remember for the rest of your lives. Today is the day that we begin the implementation of our plan to change the world. It is also the first stage in saving it from the self-destruction brought on by years of political neglect by disparate systems of national governments. Today we begin the move towards unification through common goals and strong leadership. We will share a safer, greener, more harmonious planet.'

Wednesday 2nd September: The Third Group Taken

Emily, Rachel and Lisa relaxed in the sun at Mill Cottage. Richard and Alice had invited them to a midweek lunch. It was a public holiday in Templewood, to commemorate the distant day of the community's founding. Peter had sent his apologies; he needed to complete a work task. They enjoyed the women's company; it was a blessing that they had moved into the village. Alice said it made a welcome change to have guests. Richard had a reputation for being grumpy and expressing candid opinions that led their few friends to be wary of joining them.

Lisa and Rachel insisted to Emily and Alice that Richard had been maligned. He was forthright without being rude or personally aggressive. He often said that his anger and frustration was directed towards events and circumstances, not people.

'People are who they are because of their experiences,' he would sometimes say. 'If we can improve people's lives, they become better people.'

Rachel countered this view with the observation that the villagers had little to worry about. All of their needs were provided for, in return for their contribution to the work of Templewood.

'Freedom! That's what they're missing. The choice of whether to stay or leave,' he replied. 'You should have heard the tosh spouted by the Masters at the meeting. I'm sick and tired of hearing about their "benign dictatorship". You only have to look at the list of such regimes in history to realise they don't stay benign for long, with a few exceptions, like Castro.'

'If they, the villagers, really wanted to leave…'

Emily interrupted Rachel.

'Here's Peter. I thought you were working all day. What's the matter? Has something upset you?'

'I can't stay long. There's a big problem. Some more people have vanished. I thought you ought to know.'

'Oh no!' said Alice. 'How many this time?'

'We're still checking, but it looks like twenty-five. All within the space of an hour. Most were reported by their families.'

'Was anyone able to say how they disappeared?' said Lisa. 'Were they seen to be taken?'

'No. We don't know how it happened. One minute they were there, and the next minute they were gone. No-one actually saw any of them in the act of vanishing, if you understand my meaning.'

'Was anyone we know taken?' said Rachel. 'Sorry, that sounds callous. What I meant was…'

'I'm afraid so. Amit is one of them. I'm so worried for all of them.'

'How can you be sure the Visitors are responsible?' said Richard.

'Absolutely sure, this time,' said Peter. 'The same placeholders were left as with the group of five.'

'I'm worried now,' said Rachel. 'This is the third time it's happened, with even more people vanishing. It seems worse when it's someone we know.'

'Let's all try to keep calm,' said Alice. 'It won't help to get excited. Remember, the last group all came back. There's no reason to think that these won't be with us again soon.'

'I've just thought of something odd about all of this,' said Lisa.

'What's that?' said Emily.

'There are patterns,' said Lisa. 'First one person vanishes, then five, then twenty-five. Don't you see? The number taken is five times the number on the previous occasion.'

'My God, why didn't that occur to me?' said Peter.

'Does that mean they'll do it again and take one hundred and twenty-five?' said Rachel?

'And then five times that, and five times that...' said Peter.

'There's something we need to work out, urgently,' said Lisa. 'How long was the interval between each group being taken?'

'Let's work backwards,' said Richard. 'When did the five disappear?'

'It was the day after the Masters' last visit — not this week, the one before — when the Risk Analysis programme was agreed,' said Peter, counting the days on his fingers.

'I make it twenty-five days,' said Lisa.

'Me too,' said Rachel.

'What about the first one, the old man? When was he reported missing?' said Richard.

'Soon after the three of you arrived. The day you visited Whytecliffe farm,' said Peter.

'What? Do you mean we were already here when it happened? And that you didn't say anything, not even to me?' said Emily.

'It was too soon after you'd arrived. At the time, we hadn't made the connection with the Visitors. It was only later that the way he disappeared was described by someone who came forward.'

'Let's not argue. Can you remember the exact date?' said Richard.

Peter thought hard.

'Yes, it was twenty-five days before the group of five went missing.'

Rachel and Alice gasped.

'It could be a coincidence,' said Alice.

'Or there could be a reason that they are taking people at intervals of twenty-five days,' said Rachel. 'And taking five times as many people each time. I suppose it's a blessing the numbers are so small. I know each person has loved ones and they all suffer the stress as individuals.'

'But the numbers aren't small,' said Lisa. 'Or won't be if they carry on at that rate.'

'What do you mean?' said Rachel.

'Would you pass me that pen and notebook, please, Richard?'

Lisa scribbled some numbers, line by line, to the astonishment of the group.

'The rate of increase is exponential. The numbers start off small but quickly grow to enormous amounts. Think of it as like a virus spreading. One person infects five, each of whom infects another five and so on,' said Lisa. She turned the notebook around.

'If they carry on at the same rate, after fifteen such attacks the total numbers will be over seven billion: the total number of people in the world.'

'How long would it take to reach those numbers?' said Alice.

'It's here, on the right-hand side of the table I've drawn,' said Lisa. 'If we take just one location, it would be three hundred and twenty-five days. Less than eleven months from when the first person was taken.'

'Roughly nine months,' said Lisa.

'We're already fifty days into the cycle, so that leaves two hundred and seventy-five days from now,' said Peter. 'And that's not taking into account that it's happening at two locations.'

'Do we know it's only happening in two places?' said Rachel.

'I'm pretty sure,' said Peter. 'We'd have heard about it through our network by now. The Visitors know we have two enclosed, secret sites. I would guess they want to avoid panic.'

'If they intend to go global with this, it won't take long before they have to start taking people outside of Templewood. The population's little more than seven thousand. How long until that happens, Lisa,' said Richard.

'Another hundred days,' said Lisa.

'It'll be fewer than a hundred days,' said Peter.

'What makes you say that?' said Richard.

'They'll start once the Sect starts rolling out the gifts worldwide. It's the ideal time. They'll want a docile, compliant society. This must be the reason why the Sect is in such a hurry to get on with it. It's fine to start taking people in Templewood while all the research and development is going on here, the numbers taken will be within the limits of the local population.'

'There must be something we can do,' said Rachel.

'We need to keep track of everyone in the community. I'll set up a system to ensure that on each twenty-fifth day everyone in Templewood is accounted for. That way we'll be able to check the numbers of people taken from here.'

Thursday 3rd September: The Appeal

'Come in, Peter, take a seat. It's bad news, I'm afraid. No doubt you expected that.'

Gygges was not Peter's closest ally in the village. They were not enemies — Gygges was, in Peter's opinion, obsessed with self-importance. He regarded himself as having superior knowledge and intelligence to his peers. This attitude had advantages: he was not open to bribery or other forms of persuasion that went against his personal views, which, although stern, were usually in Templewood's interest.

After the Masters' visit, Peter had asked Gygges to intercede with the Visitors on his behalf. Peter asked him to request that they delay introducing the gifts in those countries where their representatives were in power and postpone bringing about regime change in the eleven countries they had claimed were at a tipping point. He was concerned that, despite the risk analysis having identified no significant threats from the Visitors' gifts, there might be unidentified consequences from their rapid adoption. Could it be that they were distributing an as yet unidentified virus through this medium? Given the captives had returned with recognisable personality changes, was this another means of implanting some form of control by an unknown means?

Gygges had initially rejected Peter's request. He explained that it would be neither politic nor expedient to propose any action that challenged a decision already taken. He knew where the power lay and the potential consequences for him if he were regarded as being less than compliant. Peter called upon him to acknowledge Dr Jay's medical judgement of the changed condition of the returned villagers as a new risk factor, one that had not been presented to the Masters. Beneath all his arrogance and bluster, Dr Jay was a medical practitioner, obliged by his training and the Hippocratic Oath to abstain from intentional wrongdoing and harm.

Peter had sowed the doubt in Gygges's mind. He followed it up by sharing the conclusions of the discussion with his friends. If the pattern of taking captives were to continue at the recorded rate, the Visitors would change the thought processes of the entire population of the world within nine months, rendering them incapable of resistance and susceptible to becoming little more than compliant workers or slaves. For the first time, Peter detected doubt in Gygges's demeanour. Peter and his friends had, until now, refrained from sharing the information. Gygges agreed it would be best not to disclose that they had identified a pattern to the abductions. The meetings of the Council and Masters had not discussed this aspect of the Visitors' presence. If the Masters were conspiring with the Visitors to enslave humanity, sharing their secret could trigger a more aggressive approach.

No-one in Templewood knew whether the Masters were communicating with the Visitors, other than by the hieroglyphics. It was assumed that they were not. They appeared to accept the gifts at face value and to plan their strategy around them. The Masters were not open to questioning and shared only the information that suited their purposes.

'How did they react? What did they say?'

'As you might expect, really. They listened politely and rejected your idea unanimously. They said that you had already set them back by proposing the risk analysis.'

'I hardly think that two weeks...'

'It's not important. They said that you had been given the chance to speak up once and that you were now inventing, as they put it, new ideas to introduce delay. Peter, I don't know quite how to put this, it will seem strange to you, but I'd like to talk to you as a friend. I've known you for many years. Your contribution to the well-being of Templewood and beyond has been immeasurable. As a friend, I must caution you that all of your good work will be put at risk if you are seen to be objecting to the Masters' plan.'

'I'm not objecting. I'm giving a warning. If the possible dangers are not recognised in advance, it could become impossible to correct the situation later. We can't keep quiet just to avoid upsetting the Masters with the truth.'

'If what you say is true, how can we stop the abductions and the changes in personality? I don't see that delaying the Masters' plan will have any effect. One thing I don't understand is whether there is any logic behind who they take. Or is it random? You would think they would start at the top of the political tree and work down, to gain control quickly. I suppose Amit is relatively important, but he's not a leader.'

'I've thought about that. There could be several reasons. It probably suits them to retain the existing infrastructure until they've worked out what to put in its place. If they wanted to start at the top, the Masters would undoubtedly be at the top of their list. If they took that route, they'd have to work out how to control and communicate with the Council and get things done. On the other hand, so far, they've only taken a single person, then five, then twenty-five. So, we can't be entirely certain whether there is any real pattern. By waiting until a fourth batch is taken, we can verify the theory. Once we have a cast-iron case, the Masters can't fail to act. Even they will realise that, once the Visitors have taken over the whole population, there will be neither the scope nor any purpose in carrying out their plan.'

'Peter, I was dubious about your request when you asked me to approach the Masters. I have to confess this new possibility does worry me. I can't see any way we can stop the abductions and, more to the point, what the Visitors are doing to the abductees? What do you think we should do?'

Peter took a deep breath, then exhaled loudly. It must be obvious to Gygges that, if he knew the answer to the question, he would have made the point already.

'We need to understand more about the process. I'm hopeful that, as all of the captives to date have been returned, the twenty-five will be. In that case, Amit will be one of them. When that happens, we need to question Amit, carefully, of course, about his experience. I'm hoping that we can learn from his recollection, to draw sensible conclusions and devise an appropriate plan of action.'

Friday 4th September: Amit's Return

Emily had spent the morning in the office of the Templewood Gazette. She had arranged to meet Alexander Martel and Simon Barrington to discuss her draft press release announcing the Masters' decision to proceed with the global implementation of their plan. In the past, during her youth here, she had found Martel intimidating. He had a superior, gloating smile, exaggerated by his strong facial bone structure and the deep furrows and heavy beard shadow, that suggested good looks in his youth. With the age difference no longer relevant, she no longer saw him as a fearsome figure. She was able to stand up to his forcefulness with rational argument. Her decision to meet both men had been justified; Barrington had proved useful by supporting her views. With the press release agreed, she could walk into Templewood to buy lunch.

Once again, Peter stood at the centre of the crowded square. Emily sidled to the front to ask him the reason.

'They're back! The Visitors have returned Amit's group. All twenty-five of them. They are at the hospital now, undergoing tests.'

'Excellent news! Have you spoken to Amit?

'No, not yet. They need to examine him first, along with the others.'

'Yes, of course. Look, can we visit him tomorrow? It's an ideal opportunity to ask someone we know whether they remember what happened.'

'I'd already thought of that. I'm going over there later. Why don't you come with me?'

*

Dr Jay greeted them in a hushed voice.

'We're not officially allowing visitors until the tests are complete. I'll make an exception in your case, given that you have a special interest in the matter.'

'I'm very grateful,' said Peter. 'I know you understand my concerns. We've known Amit for so long. It's the best opportunity to understand the reasons for what's happening. Has he said anything about it?'

'No. We've given them all a mild sedative as a precaution in case they suddenly remember anything traumatic. It's best to allow them time to get used to being back with us in stress-free surroundings — if a hospital can ever be stress-free. I'm sure I can rely on you both to be cautious in how you talk to him. I must insist you to wear full PPE, for your protection as well as his.'

Emily and Peter sanitised their hands. The nursing staff showed them how to put on their gowns, surgical masks, face shields, boots and gloves in the correct sequence. Dr Jay led them to the private room where Amit lay in bed.

'You have visitors,' said Dr Jay. 'Not the sort you've been accustomed to in recent days. I'll leave you to talk in private.'

Emily and Peter exchanged glances, in disbelief at the poor taste of Dr Jay's presumed joke. Amit had either not heard or had chosen to ignore the remark.

'Hello, Amit. Can you hear me?' said Peter.

Amit made a feeble move with his head and opened his mouth as if to speak.

'Take it easy. There's no rush,' said Emily.

'Let's take it as it goes,' said Peter. 'We'll keep it to closed questions, as far as we can, so that you can simply indicate yes or no.'

Peter bore in mind the return of the group of five. How it appeared that a barrier was impeding their thought processes. He dreaded Amit suffering the same fate. It would be cruel if his cognitive and emotional functions were to be impaired. Amit's intelligence, hard work and support over many years had allowed Peter to work at a higher level than would otherwise have been possible. Now, lightly sedated, Amit looked vulnerable, as Peter had never seen him before. Yet something was visibly stirring in his appearance. His expression suggested concentration, focussed not forced, on suppressing a barrier preventing him from communicating: a form of mindfulness.

'Slowly,' said Amit. 'I need to speak slowly. You need to know.'

'Well, only if you're sure,' said Peter. 'Take it gently and stop whenever you need to.'

'Do you remember anything about what happened, how you were taken?' said Emily.

Amit lay still, save for a faint movement of his head, not quite a nod, and long quiet breaths through his wide-open mouth.

'Warm wind, pressing all around, spinning, dissolving into me. Rising into a mist, then darkness. Onboard the vessel. Silent, bright. Golden rays.'

'Did you see them — the Visitors,' said Peter. 'Did they talk to you or try to communicate in any way?'

'Not sure. Something below, below vision and memory. An ache. Deep pulsating, pressure inside my head.'

'How did you cope with this?' said Emily. 'Were you afraid?'

'Focus. Concentrate. Keep my mind empty. Resist pressure. No fear.'

'What are you saying, Amit? Were you practising some form of mindfulness?' said Emily.

'No mind. Empty. No sleep.'

'You can sleep now, Amit. You're safe here,' said Peter. 'We can see you're exhausted. It's best if we come back tomorrow, once you're rested and the sedative has worn off. Try not to stress yourself but, if you do recall anything of significance, try to write it down or ask someone to do so for you. We'll keep in touch with the hospital to check you're OK.'

'We're so pleased to have you back,' said Emily. 'We'll talk again tomorrow.'

Amit nodded and lifted a forearm in acknowledgement, his eyes closed. Peter stood up and gestured to Emily to follow him out of the room.

'I can't tell whether it's the sedative or the stroke-like symptoms that were noticed with the other returned people,' said Peter. 'I get the feeling that he was making an enormous effort to talk to us. It was as if he was trying to overcome a mental barrier stopping him from doing so.'

'I agree,' said Emily. 'Did you notice his eyes — the amber reflections that were reported in the others, like a cat or an owl?'

'Yes, although he doesn't seem to be as badly affected as others are, so they tell me. You can see it's a struggle for him, but he still has his wits about him. Let's hope he's better tomorrow.'

Friday 4th September: Sarah's Communications

After leaving the hospital, Emily and Peter decided to go to Mill Cottage to share the news of Amit's return. Richard made a pot of tea while Alice cut some slices of cake. The many questions and responses about his condition were met with a mixture of relief and ongoing concern.

'Why are they doing it, the Visitors?' asked Rachel. 'And with increasing numbers each time. There must be a reason.'

'Who knows,' said Peter. 'We shouldn't jump to conclusions. It's possible they bear no ill-will.'

'Then why don't they communicate with us to let us know — to reassure us?' said Lisa.

'I wish I could answer that,' said Peter. He frowned, realising that he was becoming increasingly bereft of answers.

'I've got an idea,' said Emily.

'This could mean trouble,' said Peter.

'No, seriously, Peter. Rachel, you've mentioned your linguistic expertise. Would you be able to devise a way in which you, or someone, could communicate with them?

'It's not really my type of specialism — I have no experience of communicating with aliens.'

'That's a brilliant idea,' said Alice. 'Surely, the principles of communication are common to any type of language.'

'Yes, and Peter, you told us that the Visitors deliver their new gifts in a sort of large rubber ball, remember?' said Lisa. 'You said that each ball is marked with instructions in hieroglyphics describing what it contains and how to use it and that the code had been cracked. If it works one way, surely, we could use the same code to send messages back.'

'I don't think it would be as simple as that,' said Peter. 'Given the nature of the gifts, we've only seen a limited version of what you could call their vocabulary.'

'Depending on the form of the hieroglyphics, there might be a way of deconstructing the messages, to identify the building blocks, as it were, to create different concepts. It's difficult to know without having seen them for myself,' said Rachel. 'It's a two-way thing, of course. We're not just receiving; we want to send messages. We should be developing protocols for telling them about us, explaining that we are not hostile and what, if anything, we want to achieve together.'

'You've reminded me of something else,' said Emily. 'When I went to see Sarah, she described a theory she's working on. Well, it sounds nonsense — I'll tell you anyway. She believes it should be possible to communicate with the Visitors using the fungal networks that connect trees. She gave me a detailed account of how the tree root systems communicate information about nutrition and threats from insects and other sources and how they use this network to share nutrients. She described a lot of scientific research that's been built up over decades. It all sounded quite plausible. Do you think there could be anything in it?'

'I'm familiar with that research,' said Rachel. 'It's quite well-established knowledge in scientific communities.'

'She believes there could be a way of plugging into it, rather like a pair of old-fashioned telephone handsets, with her at one end and the Visitors at the other.'

'This must be what she was hinting at the Council meeting,' said Peter. 'She said she expected she would have some news to announce shortly. She didn't give any clues as to what it was she was working on. It sounds as though this could be it.'

'She was quite happy to share it with me,' said Emily. 'She was quite excited about it.'

'I can understand her not wanting to broadcast it before she's ready. It can be embarrassing to have to retract if you find you are mistaken later,' said Peter.

'This is promising,' said Richard. 'If we could communicate with the Visitors as equals, we'd get a better understanding of why they're here. I think Rachel should get together with Sarah and see if they can't work together.'

'I might be able to add some value to that discussion, too,' said Lisa. 'Remember, my experience with ICT is exactly that: Information and Communications Technology. It's not only the processing of data, it includes the means of sharing it — data, voice and images.'

'I'm up for that,' said Rachel. 'It'll take me out of my comfort zone, but hey, that's not a bad thing. And I get to work with Sarah.'

'Oh, that could give me a problem,' said Emily. 'She asked me to keep it to myself. I shouldn't have said anything, really. I don't want her to think I've betrayed her trust. I'll have another chat with her first and make the suggestion. I'm sure she'll agree once I tell her about Rachel and Lisa's skills.'

'I'm glad this subject has come up,' said Peter. 'This is one of the reasons we've invited Rachel and Lisa to Templewood. To work on the communication with the Visitors. I haven't said anything before in case things didn't work out: if either of you didn't fit in, for example, or insisted on leaving.'

'It's a shame you didn't tell us before,' said Rachel. 'We could have started weeks ago.'

Saturday 5th September: Recovery

'Ah, Peter, I'm glad you were able to come over. There's some good news. Amit is a lot better today. Would you like to see him?'

Even after knowing him for many years, and despite his recent offer to speak to Peter as a friend, Peter found it difficult not to wince at Dr Jay's manner. He maintained the same public front, regardless of the circumstances. A combination of self-importance and arrogance, with a veneer of supercilious disdain for whomever he was speaking to. Peter had learned to brace himself to deal with it. It was important, in his role, to get on with everyone in the village to allow him to perform his role effectively. He went as far as to defend Dr Jay to others by explaining that Jay's demeanour reflected his confidence in his abilities and judgements. Peter's personal opinion remained private.

'Excellent news. Is he able to communicate better?'

'Very much so. I'm amazed at the difference from yesterday. He's still weak; that's to be expected after his ordeal. We'll keep him here for a couple more days. Barring any new problems, he'll then be free to leave. Come along, I'll take you to him.'

Amit was sitting up in bed, reading some papers that he put down as soon as he saw Peter. Dr Jay left them together, closing the door without comment.

'Peter, how good of you to come back. Come in and sit down.'

'We were all worried about you, Amit. When you disappeared and yesterday too. You do indeed look much better. How are you feeling?'

'Almost back to normal, I'd say. My thinking is clear, and I can talk normally. It was such a strange feeling to be incapable of expressing myself or focus on my thoughts. It made me wonder what they had done to me.'

'Do you remember any more about being on the spacecraft? Can you recall seeing them and what they look like?'

'No, it's all vague. Dr Jay thinks my mind has suppressed the memory. He's talking about hypnosis to loosen things up. I'm not sure… If my brain wants to suppress something, there's probably a good reason.'

'So, you can't remember anything — images, sensations — nothing at all?'

'I was aware that something was happening to me. It felt as though my body and brain were being scanned in some way. It's difficult to define. It wasn't painful, just stressful, not knowing what might happen next. All I could do was to focus on my mind being blank, empty of thoughts. It must have worked.'

Peter's relief and joy that his friend appeared unharmed by his experience were tempered by disappointment. He had hoped that Amit would be able to provide information that would enlighten him and the villagers about the purpose of the Visitors' actions and intentions. He continued chatting to Amit for half an hour. Before leaving, he spoke again to Dr Jay, in the vain hope that Jay might know more, perhaps from an earlier conversation with Amit while he was under sedation. A recollection of something that had since been suppressed.

*

In the kitchen of the Abbot's House, Peter shared the news with Emily.

'I didn't spend too long with him as he was tired. Dr Jay says he should be out in a few days,' said Peter.

'It sounds as though he's making a quick recovery,' said Emily.

'It was as though he'd never been away,' said Peter, his expression changing suddenly.

'What's the matter, Peter?'

'I've only just realised. The amber eyes — they had changed back to normal. I know you could only see them in certain angles of the light. I would have noticed; his eyes had returned to their natural colour.'

Emily was startled by a loud, repeated knocking at the door. Peter strode into the hall, leaving Emily in the kitchen.

'Is something wrong? What's happened? You'd better come in.'

Peter led Dr Jay through to the kitchen.

'I thought I ought to let you know as soon as possible. The group that was taken at the same time as Amit. They've all recovered — they're speaking and behaving normally, totally alert and coherent. And their eyes too: they're no longer the golden amber.'

Dr Jay's uncharacteristic excitement was unmistakable. Was it joy for the well-being of his fellow villagers? Or was he relieved that, as the senior medical practitioner in the community, he would no longer bear the burden of diagnosing and curing the unfamiliar symptoms shown by the abductees? Peter had never seen him so joyful and garrulous and allowed him to chatter on. Emily brought the moment to a close.

'Dr Jay, do you think the same could have happened to the group of five and to the old man, the first one taken?'

'No, there's no change in their condition, unfortunately. We've been monitoring them all closely. Now, I won't keep you any longer. I need to let the other Council members know.'

'Don't worry about Richard. We were on our way over to Mill Cottage. Would you mind giving us a lift?'

'Were we?' said Emily. Peter glared.

*

Peter and Emily found Richard and Alice alone at Mill Cottage. Peter would bring Lisa and Rachel up to date with the conversation later. Richard and Alice knew many of the villagers; their opinions might prove more relevant.

'I'm so pleased to hear that Amit looks as though he's making a full recovery,' said Alice. 'It would be dreadful for such a brilliant man to be impaired like the others. It's not that they are unimportant, just that they're older and won't have to suffer for so long.'

'That's the other good news. Four of the others have made a miraculous recovery too!'

'That's amazing. Tell me more!'

'There's not much more to tell,' said Peter. 'Suddenly, according to Dr Jay and to the surprise of everyone, they were back to how they were before they were taken — completely normal.'

'Do you think there could be a connection? Between Amit and the other four?' said Emily.

'How do you mean,' said Peter.

'We know, or at least we're fairly sure, that they are taken in multiples of five. Supposing each one taken has to recruit five more, so to speak. Not knowingly, necessarily, but there is a connection. If that's the case, then Amit and the four others who've recovered could have been recruited, if that's the right word, by the same person from the previous group, if you see what I mean. When the present group came back, all of them exhibited the same symptoms. Except for Amit, who had been able to exert some form of self-control to resist the effects of whatever they were all undergoing in the spacecraft. Could it be that the Visitors found Amit to be unsuitable for their purpose, and they've rejected him? Not only him but the whole batch? Sorry, I didn't mean to put it so bluntly.'

'My God. I wonder…' said Richard. 'Do you think this could be a way of stopping them from taking people?

'There's nothing to stop them from taking another twenty-five,' said Alice.

'It depends,' said Peter. 'I think we should consider how they came to choose the twenty-five. That might give us a clue.'

'Let's look at what we know,' said Emily. 'First, one individual was taken, then five, ten twenty-five. We already know the pattern of increase. Do you think there could be some connection between those taken? If the first one knew the next five, and each of those five has a connection with five more, and so on.'

'If that's true, Amit should be able to help us,' said Peter. 'We'll ask him how he knows any of the other four and whether he has any special connection with any particular one of the group of five. If he does, then we can trace back. That could provide important information about the pattern and give us a better understanding of what's going on.'

'That's a great idea,' said Richard. 'Something I don't understand is how they selected the first one, the old man. I hate to say this, but he doesn't seem the ideal choice for aliens wishing to learn more about the inhabitants of this planet.'

'It might have been bad luck,' said Alice. 'Peter, you said that he was seen disappearing from close to the spaceship. The Visitors may have just seized an opportunity to capture someone they could tell was alone. Until they examined him, which we can reasonably assume they did, they wouldn't have known that he wasn't typical of us as a species.'

'It would also seem sensible to take a single person initially, rather than a group. An individual poses less of a threat,' said Peter.

'What about the tokens, the placeholders? I wonder whether we should be paying more attention to those,' said Emily.

'Possibly. Well, yes, we should,' said Peter. 'They could be a sort of homing device for when the people are returned. On the other hand...'

'Do you realise what all this could mean?' said Emily. 'It could be that this is the way to stop them from taking over our planet — if that's their intention.'

'How would we do that?' said Alice.

'If we were to analyse how Amit put himself into the state of mind he described, we could devise some sort of mass training that people could use if they were abducted,' said Emily.

'I doubt it would help the first ones taken. The six, I mean, and the other twenty taken with Amit who haven't recovered.' said Alice.

'It doesn't matter. If we can stop them from taking people at a geometric rate of progression, it will take them more than nine months to take over the whole world. That buys us time to find a permanent solution,' said Peter.

'So, it would be like a form of mass vaccination, except using thought processes instead of drugs,' said Richard.

'We would need to convince the Masters,' said Peter.

'That'll be fun,' said Richard. 'Explaining that we can save the world through mindfulness.'

'It's worth a try. It's all we've got at present. I'll speak to Gygges tomorrow.'

'We could be missing another thing here,' said Emily. 'If it does turn out that there's a connection between those taken, we have another means of holding them up.'

'How do you mean,' said Alice.

'You'll remember, Lisa said it would take another one hundred days until they needed to go beyond Templewood. We could completely close the community off, put Templewood in quarantine. It's pretty isolated already, of course, other than those with security clearance to come and go on essential business.'

'We've already discussed this,' said Peter. 'They're waiting for the Sect to take power in other countries, and then they'll start to spread worldwide. We're jumping ahead a bit here. We need to determine whether there are connections first. I'll discuss it with Gygges.'

'It didn't do much good last time,' said Emily. 'Wouldn't it be better to go straight to the Masters?'

'That's not the way things work here. Gygges is the only point of contact with the Masters. He's the gatekeeper.'

*

Later that evening, Peter reflected on the earlier discussion. Why hadn't he thought of it before? Why should Gygges continue to be the gatekeeper to the Masters? If he could find a way of contacting and addressing them directly, his concerns might be reviewed sympathetically. Even better, if he could arrange a meeting with one of them alone, it might be possible to make a convincing case that would be communicated to the whole group, without the need to posture in front of the councillors. At present, though, the only route remained through Gygges. How would he react to Peter's request?

Monday 7th September: Collaboration

Lisa and Rachel decided to work in the warm sunshine in the garden of The Abbot's House. They sat on a blanket, each with pens, a notebook, a Templewood-authorised laptop computer and cool drinks. The online research they might use to assist them with Visitor communication would not raise any alarms. Although Lisa was confident that she could bypass the monitoring systems, she had no need to today. There was no point in taking risks.

Rachel proposed that they began by defining the purposes of language. The categories of language used by grammarians — declarative, imperative, interrogative, and exclamatory — were less relevant than those used by logicians.

Logicians, according to Rachel, preferred five non-exclusive categories: the informative, the evocative, the expressive, the evaluative, and the performative. The purpose of the informative, naturally, was to inform or exchange information. The evocative was used to elicit a response. The expressive, to convey feelings and generate empathy. The evaluative included making ethical pronouncements and judgements. The performative use was to perform a social act and implied cultural knowledge. It was important to recognise the use of specialist language, examples of which were found in sports, religion and specialist occupations such as the law and information technology.

Lisa added another element, how language can be used inclusively or to exclude.

She said they should define their objectives and then decide on the right questions before developing answers. They agreed that they must consider the many methods of communication: verbal, paralinguistic (the use of bodily signs and gestures with words to convey emotions, either truthfully or with intent to mislead), written language, sign language, symbols, diagrams, images, video, and how style can be used to modulate the message to achieve the desired effect.

'We seem to be getting on really well — there's nothing we've disagreed on, so far,' said Lisa.

'This is the easy bit, defining the conceptual boundaries.

The challenge will be to work out the way forward.'

'We ought to consider how we would initiate the communication. The closest analogy I can think of is how you would go about making contact with a gorilla in the wild: remaining calm, avoiding eye contact and anything that could be interpreted as a threat.'

'We could tell them that we come in peace,' said Rachel, laughing.

'It depends whether they've seen the same films,' said Lisa.

'The basic principles of how we communicate with them seem clear. We must be non-confrontational, cooperative, clear... Quite how we achieve these things is another matter.'

'OK, we should move on. Let's think about what we want to get out of the conversation.'

'Yes, I've been thinking about that. Where did they come from? Why are they here? What do they want? Do they wish to harm us? Once we've made a list, we ought to confirm the questions with Peter. I'm sure he'll appreciate that we've given it some thought.'

'We'll have to prepare for the Visitors' questions too. That'll be more challenging, working out what they'd like to ask us.'

Tuesday 8th September: The Second Appeal

'Peter, it seems like only yesterday that I stuck my neck out and asked the Masters to delay their plan. You know what the answer was. Why do you think it should be any different now?'

Gygges remained calm and showed no sign of the exasperation that Peter believed he must feel at Peter's latest request.

'I can understand your reluctance to make such a request. I can see that they might blame you, as the messenger, and that this would not be in your interest. I'd like to ask something that I've never considered before. Will you arrange a meeting for me with one of the Masters? It could be any one of them that you choose. I'm assuming you know them personally.'

'Well, that's a big ask, Peter. No, I don't know them personally. To be more precise, I do know that each of them represents a group of interests and countries. You could say that I am familiar with their roles rather than their identities.'

'So, you do know how to contact each of them individually?

'Yes, although I rarely do so. The Masters prefer, indeed insist, that for regular purposes, I deal with them through a secretarial function to arrange meetings, distribute minutes and papers and so on. The rule is that I am only allowed to approach them individually in the case of an emergency. Why are you making this request, Peter? What do you think you will achieve?'

'To be honest, the position I find myself in, well, it's my fault entirely. I realise that I've been indecisive and have made a few errors of judgement. It worries me that, in my position of responsibility, I am in danger of becoming a liability to our community. I recognise that I can't absolve myself from these errors and that it's unreasonable for me to ask you to put my concerns to the Masters yet again. It has to be me alone who states the case, to avoid tainting you, and others, with the consequences of whatever conclusions the Masters come to.'

'I'll need a little more than that to gain their attention. What exactly shall I tell them you want to discuss? I'll have to convince them that something has changed since you were last before them.'

'I think you know the answer to that, at least in part. I need to warn them that the attacks, the kidnappings, are increasing at a geometric rate. We've seen from Amit that there is a ray of hope, that we might be able to train, to educate people how to resist and set back the Visitors' plans. They need to know that there is limited time in which to take action before the process becomes irreversible. They have to make a decision quickly and ratify and synchronise their plan for its rollout worldwide, just as they would in the case of a pandemic.'

Gygges stroked his chin, showing a hint of a frown as he thought through the possibilities.

'I'll see what I can do, Peter. I'm not promising, mind.'

'Thank you, I'm very grateful. This could be our last chance.'

Both men stood up to leave.

'Oh, and one more thing,' said Gygges. 'If I am to try to assist you, you are not to repeat this conversation. For security reasons, no-one, absolutely no-one, must know that there is a hint that a Master might visit Templewood alone.'

11 - RESISTANCE

Monday 14th September: The Secret Meeting

Gygges passed Peter handwritten details of the time and location of the meeting he had arranged with one of the Masters. He was instructed to memorise the contents and destroy the note. Peter suppressed his surprise that just a single Master would attend. He understood that it would be impractical to discuss his concerns with the whole group owing to the journeys necessary from their designated or home countries. It was unimportant; no doubt the topic discussed would be related to all of them immediately afterwards. Peter was a trusted member of the community and would not be regarded as presenting a physical threat.

Peter had expected the meeting to take place at Archangel Hall. The long narrow route through the maze of alleyways was ideal for ensuring security, demanding pedestrian access. The surrounding two- and three-storey buildings with their arrays of observation cameras guaranteed rapid identification of approaching visitors and potential attacks.

Peter arrived at the designated address in good time, an insignificant building hidden in a cul-de-sac close to the centre of Temple Walden. At Gygges's insistence, Peter had not declared his appointment to Emily or to anyone else. He took the key to the door from the hanging basket, smiling at the lack of originality of such an unimaginative hiding place. No doubt it had been placed there only a few minutes before. Any unexpected visitors to the cul-de-sac would have been observed from the surrounding properties. Peter let himself in and located what appeared to be a living room, decorated in old-fashioned oak and chintz. He waited patiently for his host to arrive, taking one of two opposite high-backed seats at a solid dark oak table. He had no idea of whether the Masters were male or female. They were only ever seen wearing cloaks, hoods and conical hats; their voices were always modified by electronic devices. He wondered how the person would arrive, dressed in this conspicuous fashion, so obviously one of the Masters to any passers-by in the adjacent street. His musing became irrelevant when he heard footsteps from the room above, moving slowly to descend the creaking staircase.

The two men sat opposite each other in silence. Peter had always assumed that the Masters were all men. No-one knew who inhabited the gowns, hoods and conical caps with their electronic voice boxes. Each waited for the other to speak. Peter hoped that the Master would open the discussion, arranged at his request, to allow him to assess his host's empathy and direction of thought. Peter knew this would be his final chance to be heard. Unless he made his case convincingly, all could be lost. He had to focus on the key issues; if he were to permit himself to be carried away in a fit of anger or speculation, all would be lost.

The Master broke the long mutual stare.

'Good morning, Peter. Gygges has briefed me on your account of a perceived threat and your proposal to address it. I have discussed the subject with my colleagues at length. Let me say first of all that we value your sincerity, your intentions and your loyalty. I am here to communicate our decision to you and to explain our judgement within permitted limits. You will, I am sure, appreciate that there are issues of secrecy and confidentiality that I cannot share with you. I will rely upon your trust and understanding. You should not take this to mean that we do not share some of your concerns, only that we have a broader world-view of what is happening and where it will lead.'

Peter suppressed his instinct to challenge the word 'perceived'. If the Masters as a group did not recognise it as a threat now, it was too late to change their minds. He knew that no individual member would break ranks. Peter could already tell that the meeting was doomed, confirmed by the Master's condescending remarks and his pronouncement that Peter was not privy to all relevant information. They had already passed judgement on what he was here to say. Peter's disappointment that he was about to hear confirmation that his recommendation had been rejected was tempered by his need to know more. What did the Masters know that they were keeping to themselves?

'The message I bring, Peter, with certainty and perhaps a little regret is that, while we understand the reasons behind your warning, we cannot accommodate your request. We value your idea to deal with the perceived danger but, if it were to be implemented, it would cause innumerable problems.'

'What greater problem could there be than the entire world population being turned into near-zombies?'

Peter suppressed the thought. 'I hear what you are saying, that there may well be issues I'm unaware of. Especially as we are dealing with a unique situation involving an alien life form. Are you able to give me any more information to help me understand the reasons behind the decision? If, as you say, I'm not fully aware of all the factors, it would help me to deal with it. It would also make it easier to justify and continue our work in Templewood, and to be able to explain things to the community.'

'I will say what I can. As you are aware, we are at the beginning of our journey to bring the benefits of the

Visitors' gifts to the rest of the world in a controlled rollout. Many of the gifts, imminent and planned, involve enormous leaps forward in science and technology. These can be explained as the outcome of secret, cooperative scientific developments on a scale hitherto unknown. The true source does not need to, and will not, be disclosed. The slightest hint that they come from beyond the stars and are being delivered by aliens who are already among us would bring widespread fear, panic and insurrection. This goes totally against our ethos of bringing change in the form of equality, elimination of poverty, improvements in healthcare and longevity and, above all, peace, enforced by a benign network of world government. If, in addition, we propose the population undergoes a form of brainwashing to inoculate against a threat from the Visitors, all will be lost.'

Peter struggled to defeat a sense of rising resignation. The Sect was prepared to accept any risk to accede to power, just as they had intended during the Templewood Summer. Peter could see that they were now, almost certainly, too far into the alliance to withdraw. They had taken the Visitors' gifts and a price would be paid. Would there ever have been the possibility of a different outcome? Once the Visitors had landed, what would have happened if their gifts had been declined? He could see, now, the dilemma of resistance. The cure was worse than the disease. Would there have been hope, had it been possible to realise the benefits of the gifts, before introducing the idea and reality of the Visitors' presence slowly, in a controlled fashion? By improving lives first, it would have been easier to explain a presumably kindly presence.

Peter passed the next two hours with the Master, debating what might or might not happen. There were no answers to be found.

'So, there you have it,' said the Master. 'We are where we are and must make the best of it.'

The Master, who until now had sat immobile in his seat, gave a single, slow nod. He adjusted the sleeves of his cloak, briefly allowing a hand to protrude. He immediately retracted it into the garment. In this defining moment, Peter reframed the discussion that had just taken place. It was time to bring the meeting to a close.

Monday 14th September: Peter Relates the Meeting

Peter closed the front door of The Abbot's House quietly. As Emily marched from the kitchen to greet him, he put a finger to his lips and gestured with a nod to follow him outside. They had agreed to use this signal when a confidential discussion was required, away from the house. Peter arranged for the building to be swept regularly for listening devices. Vigilance was the best policy, as Peter suspected that the house could be under surveillance. This seemed more likely now that his judgement was being called into question.

They crossed the road to the field.

'I wasn't expecting to see you home before this evening,' said Emily. 'Has something happened?'

'I've had a meeting with one of the Masters, one on one. Gygges arranged it for me. I'd previously told him that we need to find a solution to the kidnappings. The Masters don't seem to take the problem seriously. They're in denial of the predicted numbers. I'd already offered Gygges a solution. He discussed it with the Masters, but they rejected it. So, I spoke to him again and asked him to arrange today's meeting. I felt it was the last chance to persuade them to take action to resist the abductions.'

'How did it go?'

'Not well. He listened to me politely. He said that the idea of individuals resisting being taken over using mind control wouldn't make much difference. Each successful case would only delay the taking of five new people. There was no way of predicting who will be taken next. He agreed that, so far, all of the targets have been taken from Templewood and that soon they will be taken from other locations once the rollout takes place. He said that there's insufficient time left to respond.

'We talked for almost two hours. They are too far down the road with their plan. The main objection is around the Visitors. They don't want it known outside the Sect that the Visitors are here. They want to avoid panic and riots and everything that entails. I can understand their point; I just wish they'd have thought it through before.'

'A bad day at the office then?'

'Not entirely. There's more to it. Something amazing happened. I'd never have believed it.'

Peter looked away towards the ground and sighed.

'Well? Are you going to tell me?'

'This is difficult to believe…'

'Try me. Come on, you can't leave me in suspense. What happened?'

'We were getting to the end of the meeting, about to get up to leave. He must have dropped his guard. He was wearing his hooded cloak and cap, as they always do — you can't see any flesh other than a glimpse of their eyes through the gap in the hood. He briefly pulled back the sleeve of his cloak as if it had caught on something, revealing his hand. He quickly pulled it back, but it was too late. I'd seen it. I knew it was him.'

'What did you see? Who was it?'

'It was our Dad. He was wearing the ring that Mum had specially made for him. As you know, it's unique. There was no mistaking it.'

'Oh my goodness… Did you let him know you recognised him?'

'No. It happened so quickly. I couldn't challenge him as we were in a building controlled by the Sect. I'm sure the conversation would have been monitored. If I were in their position, I'd want to know where my key people were. He was taking an enormous risk meeting me. I honestly believe he was letting me know. There's no way he would make a mistake like that!'

'It reminds me of the time we went for a meal at The Compasses, during the Templewood Summer.'

'You're right. We were the only ones there apart from the group upstairs. I remember that, as we left, Mum realised she'd left her handbag behind. She went up the outside fire escape and looked through the window. She recognised him in exactly the same way, in full garb wearing the ring.'

'There's so much going on here,' said Emily. 'This could explain why we've not seen him since I've been here. I'd been wondering why he hadn't dropped in to say hello. He must know I'm in Templewood. Whose side is he on? Either he's one of them and is using us all, or he's infiltrated them and is waiting for the right time to take action.'

'We've half-known this for years. Remember that mum told us they both used to work in intelligence.'

'And now he's a double agent, a government intelligence person who's convinced the Sect that he is of value to them.'

'I wonder why he let me see the ring. I'm sure it wasn't an accident.'

'This could mean there's still hope. Do you think he's on to something? A way of either stopping the rollout or some form of pact with the Visitors?

'There's no way the rollout will stop now. Whether he's in contact with the Visitors, either alone or with others, who knows. Yes, I think you could be right. There is hope, and we need to believe in him.'

Wednesday 16th September: The Golden Record

Rachel and Lisa had spent a week working together to devise a language or medium to communicate with the Visitors. Their initial enthusiasm was beginning to wane. They had assumed that, as the Visitors' intelligence was so far in advance of the human race, the exercise would be logical and straightforward. No doubt the Visitors could translate whatever simple communications were directed towards them and had the means to decipher the simple languages of humans. After several days of dedicated work, Lisa had asked what now appeared to be the obvious question. If they wanted dialogue, why have they not taken the initiative?

'We could be wasting our time,' said Rachel. 'I'm worried that Peter said that this is one of the reasons we were invited here. We're not delivering!'

'I know what you're saying, Rachel. Yes, we could be. But we won't get anywhere unless we try. We're making an effort, doing something. That's the important thing.'

'Do you know whether Emily has spoken to Sarah about working with us?' said Rachel.

'She has. Sarah sent a message via Françoise apologising. She says it would be too much of a distraction from the work she has in progress. Françoise thought her reaction strange, as we're working towards the same objective. Emily confided that Françoise is concerned about Sarah. Her behaviour is becoming odder and odder, and she's withdrawing into herself. That might explain it.'

'That's a shame. Never mind, we'll press on without her. Let's go back to basics and think through what we know. The Visitors' gifts are delivered by powerful miniature drones inside what looks like a rubber ball. The ball is marked with descriptive information and instructions in hieroglyphic form. The communication is entirely visual. Everyone we know here accepts it as normal. I get that. What I'd like to know was how it all started — how was the first communication made? You would assume that it must have been directly with the Masters to let them know they could regard the Visitors as friends. Allies who would provide them with the means to pursue their global ambitions. That implies that there must have been more to the contact than just a few symbols on a parcel. If the Masters had regarded the Visitors as a threat, they would have taken some sort of action, and we, or Peter, would have known about it. There must have been a discussion, to use the word loosely, or at least a one-way message from the Visitors. And another thing… What makes the Masters so confident about working with them? How do they know whether the Visitors can be trusted?'

'You could be right. We ought to talk to Peter about it,' said Lisa. 'I think we can short-cut this task. What we should do is to forget about devising a language for now. That's fine for the longer term. We need answers now. What we should do is to agree with Peter and the Council a list of questions to ask the Visitors, including follow-up options for whatever responses they offer. We can then construct a multimedia script — text, image, audio, video, animation — and leave the interpretation to them.'

'I agree. It'll be obvious that we're talking to them. The problem is that they may not want to talk to us. Nothing we can do about that. Here's another topic we should consider. We should put together a presentation of what the human race is: who we are, how we live and what drives us.'

'We ought to talk to Sarah to see if we can persuade her to join us. If she's made any progress with her work on communications, it could make all the difference.'

'Dr Hadfield too. She would add a lot of value.'

*

Dr Hadfield welcomed Rachel and Lisa into her office. She gestured to them to sit on one of the sofas while she took the one opposite.

'I understand that you'd like me to review your ideas on producing a communications package to make contact with the Visitors,' said Dr Hadfield. 'I thought you might bring Emily with you as she's a communications professional of sorts.'

'I invited her, but she declined,' said Rachel. 'She said her skill set was more related to the delivery of the message than the content. She offered to critique whatever we come up with and make recommendations on the presentation.'

'That will be useful,' said Dr Hadfield. 'Have you had any thoughts on how to go about this?'

'We thought a multimedia approach would work best,' said Lisa. 'The Visitors' brains undoubtedly work differently from ours. It's likely they perceive and regard the universe in ways we would not understand. By offering information and asking questions using a variety of techniques, we believe there will be a better chance of success.'

'I agree,' said Dr Hadfield. 'As a species, we're not yet close to fully understanding intelligent creatures on our own planet, such as dolphins, even though we're closely related to them. I've been giving it some thought, too. Let's imagine we were trying to communicate with them not as new neighbours but from a distance. To do so, we would need a concise package of information, complete with instructions and clues of how to understand it.'

'Like a time capsule?' suggested Lisa.

'I read about that idea a while ago,' said Rachel. 'An American company invited people to subscribe to a project to land a collection of miniature packages on the moon. You could send anything, with a few exceptions, subject to it being incredibly small. Some people were sending a tooth or a lock of hair. A group of authors collected their works onto a microSD card.'

'You've got the right idea. I believe that project was more of a commercial venture by a private rocket-launch company to promote its capabilities. There was little scientific purpose or benefit to it, other than providing evidence to future visitors that we had managed to send something to the moon. There were a few earlier ones that sent things such as a United States flag and coins. Goodness knows what extraterrestrials would have made of those! No, what I had in mind was more akin to the Voyager Golden Record – you're too young to remember that.'

Lisa and Rachel looked at each other, pursing their lips and shaking their heads.

'OK, I'll have to step back a little. The Voyager space missions were launched in the 1970s to explore the outer planets of our solar system and then to journey on into interstellar space. Mindful that other space voyagers might encounter the two Voyager spacecraft, they each carried copies of the Golden Record. These were a kind of time capsule designed to communicate information about our world to extraterrestrials. The information is included on a 12-inch gold-plated copper phonograph record containing sounds and images representing the diversity of life and culture on Earth.'

'You mean they sent the equivalent of a vinyl LP into space – not digital?' said Lisa.

'There were no jpegs before the 1990s. I recognise that a digital message would hold far more information than a phonograph record, but it may be more difficult to decode. There was a form of user manual etched into the Golden Record, explaining how to interpret the information that was encoded on the disk in analogue form. It's complicated, although if we were sending a similar message today, a guide for deciphering a digital message could be more so. Who knows what an extraterrestrial would make of a jpeg?'

'And vinyl is coming back into fashion now,' said Rachel, as ever trying to lighten the conversation.

'What exactly was on this Golden Record?' said Lisa.

'It was the brainchild of Carl Sagan, the American astronomer and populariser of science. The record cover was aluminium and had an ultra-pure sample of uranium-238 electroplated on it. This allowed the discoverer to date when it was sent into space — I've no idea how. As I said, the record was made of gold-plated copper. The information on the cover showed how to construct pictures from the recorded signals using a similar method used to transmit the television signal standards of the day. They even had to include a picture of a circle as a reference point to allow them to verify the vertical to horizontal ratio.'

'That's amazing,' said Lisa. 'Even if it were intercepted by an intelligent life-form, they would still have to interpret an archaic form from what would effectively be the distant past. It would be like trying to decipher cuneiform writing from stone tablets but at a higher level of technological development, if you see what I mean.'

'What about the contents?' said Rachel.

'There are a hundred or so images of people and locations from many cultures, including biological images of people, animals, insects, nature in general. There are scientific images of our solar system and greetings spoken in around fifty languages. There is music: classical, popular and ethnic. These are all positive messages designed to show the diversity of our planet and its inhabitants. A decision was taken not to include negative images, such as war and conflict. It would not be a good idea to expose our flaws on a first date.'

'This was fifty years ago,' said Lisa. 'I wonder why there hasn't been an updated version put into space.'

'One of the reasons,' said Dr Hadfield, 'is the need to use the gravitational systems of the planets *en route* as a means of propulsion — to catapult the vessel onwards. This requires alignment, or near-alignment, of the planets to achieve. It only occurs infrequently, and timing is crucial.'

'I wonder what they would include on a modern-day version,' said Lisa. 'With science and technology having moved on so far, I'm sure it would be very different.'

'That's exactly the challenge we have now,' said Dr Hadfield. 'We need to get into the mindset of the Visitors, to be able to communicate our message clearly and succinctly. We have the advantage that we don't need to project a package into space – we can deliver it to them directly. All we have to do is to decide on our message and the medium.'

'Getting into their mindset won't exactly be easy,' said Lisa. 'We've no idea how their brains work if, indeed, they have a brain in the sense that we would recognise.'

'Precisely,' said Dr Hadfield. 'And we can't take it for granted that their senses are the same as ours. Here on Earth, we have creatures that are blind, deaf and presumably some that have no sense of taste or smell. You would assume that touch is a shared sense. We have no idea of the conditions where they come from. We assume that from our limited exploration and knowledge of the universe that extraterrestrials will have the same senses as us. There again, who knows? On the other hand, the Visitors may have senses we are unfamiliar with.'

'Like radar in animals,' said Lisa.

'Every creature has evolved its senses in response to its environment. There is no reason to assume the Visitors will be any different. We can only work from what we know. It's reasonable to assume that they have travelled an enormous distance to get here. if we ignore their potential knowledge and capability to exceed the speed of light, our best option would be to assume they have senses of touch and sight, or the equivalent of sight. These are the areas that I suggest we focus on.'

'I don't relish the thought of communicating by touch,' said Rachel.

'I'm not suggesting we touch them directly. We could produce tactile objects that convey ideas. If they do have senses unknown to us, that would be a bonus.'

'Let's take stock, then,' said Lisa. 'We should draw up a list of what we want to tell them to produce the best outcome.'

'I agree,' said Dr Hadfield. 'The most important thing is to let them know that we are a peaceful race and pose no threat to them.'

'I think there would be some people in the outside world who might disagree with that,' said Rachel.

'The act of bringing a package and leaving it should be seen as a peaceful exercise. It would be a gift of welcome, supplemented with helpful information. We should convey images of love, inclusion and cooperation. Many of the things included on the Golden Record would be valid, updated for today. Images of people, animals, geography, science and technology. Expressions of joy should be a prominent theme. We have a significant advantage over the

Voyager mission: unlike sending an object into space, we have fewer size constraints. Digital information is fine, as long as we provide a medium for interpreting it — to save time — but not everything has to be so. Another idea is to include video-based information to show how things work, starting with human anatomy.'

'What do you have in mind?' said Lisa.

'Several things,' said Dr Hadfield. 'Movement, blood circulation, digestion… These could be supplemented with physical samples, such as blood and hair follicles.'

'Hmm, I find that a little worrying,' said Rachel. 'We would be providing them with information that they could use to wipe us out.'

Dr Hadfield leaned back in her chair and took a deep breath.

'They have already taken many captives. While we should be grateful that they have been released, who knows what investigations they have made while the people were in their custody. Providing them with biological samples will make no difference.'

Sunday 27th September: Another Group Taken

'One hundred and twenty-five more taken. Twenty-five days after the last batch. There seems little doubt now that our conclusions were correct,' said Peter.

A solemn gloom hung over the friends in the garden of Mill Cottage, mirroring the sultry late summer weather. Several days had passed since the sun last shone. The mood of the weather had infected the mindsets of all present. Peter had always thrived on adversity. He was driven to defeat anyone or anything that threatened his well-being or sense of righteousness. He now struggled to remain positive, with so little hope of a solution.

'It looks that way. I assume they were all from Templewood,' said Richard.

'Yes, most from Temple Walden, the rest scattered

around the other villages and the countryside in between,' said Peter. 'There's been a similar happening in North Korea.'

'I can't make up my mind whether it's a good or a bad thing that they are keeping the kidnappings within the Sect's territory,' said Alice.

Peter repeated his account of the meeting with Michael and his belief that the rollout of the gifts would extend the geographical area. Peter knew that sharing his knowledge of Michael's presumed role was safe. They would not betray him.

'It's worrying that if he's spent so long among them that he doesn't have an answer,' said Alice.

'Or enough influence. It can't be easy,' said Peter. 'He has to retain their trust as a double agent. They would be suspicious if he were to argue against their plans. I can only suppose they find him useful as their appointed intermediary with the controlling influencers in Government. He must be working with secret service people who oppose the Sect and are waiting for the means and opportunity to coordinate some form of effective resistance.'

'I find it incredible that all of this is going on behind the public's back,' said Lisa.

'That's what Governments do,' said Peter. 'The primary objective of every Government is to stay in power, using whatever means is at their disposal, regardless of whether they are a dictatorship or a so-called democracy. The difference being that a dictatorship tells its citizens what to do, whereas a democracy lets its subjects think they are in control while pursuing their own agenda in secret.'

'There must be some way of breaking the mould,' said Richard.

'Telling the truth would be a start,' said Alice.

'It's a bit late for that now,' said Peter. 'The Visitors' arrival has changed everything. There's a far greater force about to control our affairs.'

'We're not going to give up, though,' said Emily.

She knew that Peter had no intention of giving up. He had come to The Mill House for more than to report the disappearances.

'How's the communications work going?' Peter directed the question to Rachel and Lisa with little expectation of an encouraging answer. Their research offered the best hope of success. Establishing a dialogue with the Visitors might provide clues to their intentions towards humankind and its future. Living in harmony with the invaders had become the most optimistic outcome.

'As well as can be expected,' said Rachel. 'It's still at the early stages. We're working as quickly as we can.'

'The ideal solution would be to find a way that we could co-exist with them,' said Peter. 'No-one wants conflict; if it came to that they could easily wipe us out.'

'They must have a weakness, a way of destroying or repelling them. There always is in films,' said Lisa.

'What, like triffids and seawater?' said Emily.

'And Martians and the common cold,' said Alice.

'Or country music?' said Rachel, in a cautious attempt to lift spirits.

'The one area where I agree with the Masters is the need to keep the knowledge of the Visitors' presence a secret,' said Peter.

'Surely, if we were to identify a way of stopping the Visitors from taking over, we'd need help from the outside,' said Richard.

'Not until we have a plan,' said Peter. 'Unless we can put forward a possible solution, there will be panic and unrest. The Masters know this.'

Monday 28th September: The Rollout Begins

The Sect was emboldened and encouraged by the successes it had already achieved in regime change. Even before delivering the Visitors' gifts, they had brought their representatives to power in many countries through their popular policies. Neighbouring countries and other allies took note. People, especially the poor, could see improvements in their lives and the potential for more once the promise of halting or reversing climate damage took effect. These were popular policies with the potential for sustainable benefits, delivered through a democratic process, unlike the short-term promises habitually made by previous rulers.

Over a little more than a week, the world witnessed changes in power in the eleven chosen countries announced at the meeting with the Templewood Council. Some were the result of scheduled elections, others from coups, all peaceful. Nothing like it had been seen since the Arab Spring and the fall of the Communist bloc. Unbeknown to the populations, the present-day changes had been orchestrated by the Sect. Either by direct control, where they were already in power or had substantial influence, or nudging key players. They had chosen not to instigate armed revolutions in countries where success looked unlikely. They had chosen instead to pick off the soft targets. It was easier to suppress minority resistance by negotiation or rational argument than to provoke civil unrest or war and fight hostile incumbents in prolonged conflict. Their hope was that these countries would recognise what was happening elsewhere and deduce that their time was nearing its end. One by one, they would lean the same way. The Sect's prognosis for organic governmental change, leading to a global tipping point, had been vindicated. Their hopes for accelerated change, once they began delivery of the gifts, were raised. No country would surely want to be left behind and risk a true revolution.

Wednesday 30th September: Contact

On the morning chosen for the package delivery, Lisa and Rachel were invited to join Dr Hadfield at an extraordinary

Council meeting to rehearse their presentation to the Visitors.

In a departure from the accepted protocol, the decision was taken not to inform the Masters of the meeting. To the surprise of most members, the farmers and Gygges had agreed not to declare their plan. Peter had reasoned that this was a 'local matter' with no bearing on the relationship between Templewood and the Masters. Privately, he believed that his message was belatedly getting through to the Council members. Could they have come round to the view that the Masters might be in communication with the Visitors? Was it possible that they had been since their arrival or before? Had they engaged in active discussion rather than passive acceptance of their gifts. But how and, if so, why had they not shared this with Templewood? Although too late to influence the rollout plan, now under way, he felt that he could finally be regaining their confidence.

Dr Hadfield, Lisa and Rachel had shared the content of their package with Peter. Peter had presented it to the Council in advance of the meeting and obtained their unanimous agreement. The objective for today was to confirm the logistics of delivery. Success was critical; there must be no risk of failure through miscommunication or a perceived threat of hostility or aggression. After an hour of focussed and constructive discussion, they decided that the women would lead the party, escorted by the farmers and a small contingent of military personnel. These would be unarmed and dressed in civilian clothing. The role of the soldiers would be to observe and maintain radio contact with their base and the other members of the Council. They would take great care to avoid any suggestion of confrontation. If the meeting were to turn out badly, there was to be no retaliation. All agreed that it would be inadvisable to start a fight that they could not win.

They arrived at the site, now surrounded by a one-mile exclusion zone installed to deter and protect the curious and to minimise any perception of threat by the spacecraft's occupants. With slow, small steps, the women approached the crater.

As on their previous visit, it appeared to be empty. After a few minutes, the faint pulsating glow began. Once again, the glow modulating through forms of an eerie light, mist, a flattened sphere and, finally, a disc.

Lisa and Rachel lifted the package together to show it more clearly and communicate that it was a gift. They placed it on the ground, took a step back, bowed deeply, and slowly walked backwards towards their companions. They waited for an hour, hoping for a response or an acknowledgement or for it to be taken inside. Before leaving, they checked the camera they had set up when they arrived to ensure it was working.

Lisa and Rachel returned to Mill Cottage, where Alice and Richard eagerly asked how the expedition had gone.

'We approached the Visitors' spacecraft — with trepidation, I have to admit. We went through the entire routine that we'd put together and rehearsed and left the package of materials on the edge of the crater. We walked back to a respectful distance and waited, hoping that we would see them take it inside. There was absolutely no response. It was so disappointing,' said Rachel.

'Just like my work emails, back in the city,' said Lisa.

As she spoke, Peter arrived. 'I have some good news. You'll be pleased to know that the package has been taken into the spacecraft. Well, we assume it has. I've heard that it, what's the best word? Dematerialised. It must have been the Visitors. We're hoping it won't take them too long to interpret the information and, with any luck, respond.'

'Even if they choose not to respond, they should recognise our peaceful intentions,' said Lisa. 'You have to wonder how much they know about us already.'

'There's nothing more we can do,' said Rachel. 'We just have to wait.'

'I'm not so sure,' said Peter. 'I believe that there's more

we can do. I have the germ of an idea; I need to work on it before sharing it with you.'

Friday 2nd October: Observations

'Peter, thanks for coming over. There's something I'd like to show you.'

During his many years in Templewood, Peter had rarely visited the Astronomy and Astrophysics Research and Monitoring Unit, located at the military base to the south of Templewood. The building design was simple, built of modern steel and glass, its form resembling a World War II mizzen hut. From here, links to telescopes worldwide tracked and monitored uncountable celestial bodies, tracking their movements, looking for patterns of interest and significance.

Carlos was proud of his little empire. His allocated budget allowed his team the freedom to pursue whatever research he could justify as necessary or useful to support the monitoring programme set up to identify threats to the planet from asteroids, space debris and alien activity. He led Peter into the conference centre, modest in size with a hundred seats and invited him to sit in the centre of the front row. Carlos sat next to him and fired up his laptop to connect to the large screen.

'We didn't spot the connection at first. New bodies are constantly appearing; they're usually in motion, which makes them more readily detectable. The ones I'm about to highlight, in order of their appearance, looked to be stationary. Obviously, all movement is relative to other objects. These appear to be static when we compare their positions to that of Earth.'

'I haven't yet spotted the connection,' said Peter. 'You'll have to enlighten me.'

'Let's join up the dots.'

Carlos leaned forward in his seat and turned to face Peter, grinning, childlike at Peter's expression of amazement.

'I assume these are the Visitors' spacecraft,' said Peter.

'I can't think that they could be anything else. And I'm sure you can recognise the significance of the pattern.'

'Pentagons. Tessellated pentagons. There's something about the number five that's important to them. The multiples of five people they've been taking at intervals divisible by five days. And now this. What could it mean?'

'Who knows? It could be something peculiar to their anatomy. On the other hand, it might not be important or relevant to us. OK, so it's a prime number that's not divisible by a smaller whole number other than one. The pentagon is a shape that fits well with identical neighbours. I could think of a few more mathematical features.'

'You're right. It's probably not the most important thing. We still don't know what they are here for. Are they friends or enemies? Are they genuinely here to give, to make our lives better, or to conquer us? Are they looking to take something from us, other than the salt, and what will be the consequences? Are they here to stay, to colonise the planet, or just to give or take things? What about their own planet? Is it thriving or in serious decline? Why on earth have they chosen to come here, to a planet in near-terminal decline, whose inhabitants have failed for years to do enough to protect it from climate change?'

'Until they give us a sign, I doubt we'll know. I find it odd that they've not tried to communicate with us. They must be capable and have enough knowledge of us by now,' said Carlos.

'It seems we're not important enough to them. Why should they feel an obligation to interact with an inferior species? They don't need to. They can bring us gifts and take what they need without explanation or justification. We should be grateful that, so far, they haven't shown any sign of aggression.'

'Nevertheless, with such a build-up in their presence, it looks as if they are preparing for something. And there's nothing we can do about it.'

Monday 5th October: The Final Chance

'They should have taken my advice,' said Peter. 'The cure is simple and not expensive to implement. All it requires is a few easily learned routines that could be taught quickly to an army of trainers across the globe. Mindfulness, adapted to the needs of the situation, isn't exactly rocket science.'

'Couldn't you still do that? Bypass the Council and the Masters and use the influence of others to achieve the same result?'

'No, Templewood is about to go into lockdown, including blocking communications with the outside world.'

'Why on earth are they doing that? It's madness!'

'They think that, by locking down the main global locations and isolating the operational groups in each country, they can stop any possibility of disruption to their plan.'

'Is there nothing you can do to stop them? Surely, in your position, you must have some influence beyond Templewood?'

'I'm not sure. You've just given me an idea. It's a very slim possibility.'

'What's that? Tell me… Anything's worth a try.'

'Leave it with me. I'll catch up with you later.'

Peter returned to The Abbot's House. He retrieved a mobile phone he had hidden in a lead-lined case to render it undetectable. It was time to call in a favour.

*

'Lisa. I need your help urgently. Where are you now?'

'I'm at work, at Solomons Farm. Why?'

'Excellent! I can't explain now. Can you meet me in half an hour, at the entrance to the driveway? It's really important. Try to make it look like you're just taking a break — going for a stroll or something. And please, be discreet. I'll wait until the coast is clear and then call you over. I'll be among the trees on the drive.'

*

'This is all very unexpected, Peter. What's it all about? How can I help?'

'I need you to authorise this phone for calls to locations outside of Templewood, without it being visible to the network and without leaving a trace of what you've done. It's critical to an idea I have to stop the Visitors. Can you do that?'

Lisa smiled. It was the sort of challenge, tinged with risk and danger, that she relished. She looked up and away from Peter as she thought through her response.

'Is this a permanent change or for a limited time? Would you need to repeat the request on other occasions?'

'I'll only need it for an hour at the most. I'm hoping I won't need to use it again. There are no guarantees.'

'Yes, I can. It might take an hour or two to set up. Single use makes it easier. Obviously, I have to check that I'm not being watched or tracked. I'll have to set up a fake ID, using a fake ID, if you see what I mean. Registering and changing the device settings is the easy part. I'll have to write and insert some code that will permanently erase part of the system logs, so the changes won't be noticed and can't be traced.'

Thursday 8th October: Sarah and the Trees

Sarah lay on the mossy grass, looking up at the open sky. Each day she took the same position, her arms raised above her head, her legs spread, to form a letter X. She loved the cool, soft texture, the smell and the give of the moss, so refreshing and relaxing on a hot day.

She had learned techniques to relax and enter into a state of mindfulness in several stages. One of her favourites was to tense her body, then allow it to relax completely. The second stage was to imagine her body as weightless, to feel as though it were an empty crustacean shell, so light that it could be blown away by a light breeze. Soon, she reached a state of calm that, until she had discovered this technique, she had only been able to attain through focussed breathing. Once she had reached this level of absorption, she began to feel connected to everything around her. Her body ceased to exist as an entity independent of the landscape on which she lay. There was no longer a boundary between her and the mossy ground: they became one and the same, with a single mind. Her cares wicked way into the green carpet. Everything would be fine.

As the minutes passed — she had lost all sense of time — she felt as if something foreign was draining from her body. Not in an unpleasant way. Something surplus to her body's needs evaporated from within her, imperceptibly: the trickling away of a melting, invisible, unnecessary organ. A small part of the newly created void began to fill with something new, something undefined, incapable of being expressed in words, yet satisfying, fulfilling. Words were now superfluous to feelings, as a superior form of communication enveloped her. A comfort blanket of shared intelligence that created a universal conversation, a sharing of thoughts and knowledge.

How had she come to discover this miracle, unknown to others, or so she assumed? She was not going to ask or to verify the uniqueness of the sensation. She had a duty to perform, regardless of any reward, although it was just possible...

The first occasion was pure chance. She had found it impossible to continue working through the heat of the early afternoon. She walked out into the clearing, immediately noticing the contrasts in the micro-environment. In the open spaces, the parched grass barely covered the solid earth. In the partial shade of the trees, the moss remained dry and green. She was sure that, only recently, it had formed small patches beneath only certain types of tree. How had she not noticed it spreading until it had formed a continuous plush carpet stretching uninterrupted, save for the trees, deep into the woods and up to the farmhouse? She had intended to trace how far it extended. She was too busy; it was unimportant. Having decided to take a short rest and rehydrate, she had made a jug of fresh fruit juice and had brought it outside to the garden. The shade of the trees and the cool moss was a more attractive option to the thinning, compacted yellow grass. She poured a glass, took a few slow sips, then eased down onto the greenery, first to sit and then stretch out completely. The feeling was strange, not at all unpleasant. Soon her mind became empty of all conscious thoughts. She savoured the relaxed feeling. She had been working long hours, which she had enjoyed, so much so that the idea of taking time out for herself in the afternoon felt indulgent. But this heat...

She became aware of a change in her state of mind. The nearest feeling she could compare it to was when she had undergone an operation to remove her appendix some years ago. She had first been given the pre-med. Then the anaesthetic was introduced through a cannula. She was asked to count slowly to ten. She remembered reaching six before passing in an instant through a pleasant state into a deep sleep. The present sensation was similar, but instead of drifting into unconsciousness, a new world of awareness opened up to her. The world had changed. She had been let into a secret. What it meant, she could not explain in words. She knew that it was something special, something to cherish and nurture.

And so, here she was again, imparting and receiving. Did anyone else experience the same process and sensations? She did not know and did not care. This was her moment to savour. One that she would not allow anyone to share.

Not even Françoise, who, unbeknown to Sarah, looked down from an upstairs window, aching with feelings both of envy and jealousy. And the fear that she, Françoise, was about to lose something. In some yet to be defined way, life would never be the same. Françoise stepped back from the window, far enough to be out of sight of the car that stopped a short distance from the front door. The person who stepped out from the front passenger seat looked familiar. She could not confirm his identity as he closed the door and walked away towards Sarah. Little of their conversation was audible. Françoise watched as Sarah's expressions changed from the surprise of recognition to puzzlement and then attentiveness through to pleasured surprise, ending with enthusiastic nods of agreement.

The conversation lasted fifteen minutes. It ended with a brief hug; the stranger stared at the ground as he strode back to the car. A glance up to the window confirmed Françoise's suspicions. Why was he here? Should she challenge Sarah? No, she would keep it to herself until Sarah was ready to discuss it with her. There was nothing to be gained from risking a confrontation. Neither would she share the news of the visit with anyone else. There could be danger in doing so.

12 - INVASION

Friday 23rd October: Another Group Is Taken

Peter's prediction was fulfilled. Twenty-five days after the group of one hundred and twenty-five people were taken from Templewood, news reached Peter of reported abductions in overseas locations. None were reported from Templewood. Minimal information was available to him, owing to the communications lockdown. What little information he received came through a secret channel opened by Lisa.

The expectation was that the number would eventually climb to six hundred and twenty-five. There were no clues as to whether those abducted were connected, whether by personal or working relationship. The only common attribute shared by those so far reported was that all were from countries where the rollout was in progress. Little significance could be attached to this information. The Sect's adherents in those countries could have been forewarned to look out for signs of abduction. It was equally possible that others were being taken from other lands. The pattern would become clear, Peter thought, as each additional twenty-five-day period elapsed and took the planet closer to... To what? And why would it matter as the

Earth reached a tipping point? There was nothing more that he could do. He resisted speculating upon the outcome of the extrapolation. It was too late. The acknowledgement did nothing to assuage his feelings of guilt and inadequacy. There now seemed little hope of meaningful action. He might as well follow Sarah's example and lie back on the grass, staring at the sky, waiting.

Friday 23rd October: Patterns

Rachel stretched out on the garden bench. She leaned back, her head resting on her interlocking fingers. It was so calming to stare at the clear night sky, to count more and more stars appearing as her eyes became accustomed to the darkness, unspoiled by light pollution. Above the far distant horizon, she picked out the navigation lights of aircraft heading to or from the six airports within a fifty-mile radius.

'It's so strange to think that they don't know we're here, not being on maps or flight paths.'

As the minutes passed, more stars and moving lights appeared. Rachel searched for patterns as their paths crossed. It was good to be home, even better to be alone. To collect her thoughts and try to make sense of all that had happened. To speculate about the ways the future might be changed by the recent past. Changed not only for her: changed for the billions of people who were unaware of what they had been spared.

So many aircraft... So many lives, developing, changing, crossing for a few hours, most never meeting again. Rachel watched as the patterns of the lights changed. The air traffic was increasing; lights glowed in all directions. She tried to guess which of the six airports the planes had taken off from or were travelling towards.

And then she noticed... Emerging from the lines drawn by the trajectories of the many journeys, a theme in the lights. Some began to appear brighter than others. She could have mistaken them for aircraft had they not been stationary, spaced at identical intervals, as if flying in formation. The lights moved at a uniform speed, travelling with a purpose, intent, yet random in direction. Until a pattern began to emerge... Rachel shivered with disbelief as those which shone the brightest — greater in number by far — arranged themselves into pentagons. For a brief moment (in her state of increasing shock, Rachel could not have said for how long, exactly), they remained still. They then slowly revolved to present themselves in three-dimensional patterns. The sky was now filled with regular dodecahedrons as if to emphasise the power of the number five.

13 - ENDINGS

Saturday 24th October: A Family Reunion

'Mum, Dad! What are you doing here? I wasn't expecting you. What a lovely surprise.'

'If only it were all good news,' said Michael.

'Emily! Mum and Dad are here!'

Emily ran from the kitchen, wiping her hands on a towel. She and Peter embraced their parents in turn.

'I expect you've heard what's going on across the world. With the gravity of the situation, we agreed we had to see you both. In case it's the last time,' said Catherine. 'For a while, at least.'

'I haven't seen any news. I decided to take a day off and have some time away from everyone and everything. You'll have to bring me up to date. I'm so pleased to see you both — come in, come in! It's been such a long while.'

'Well, it has, and it hasn't,' said Michael, holding his distinctive ring in front of Peter's face. 'Thank you for getting in touch.'

'Does this mean you were successful?' said Peter. 'Tell me all about it. I want to know everything. Don't worry, the house has been swept, and so has the garden. Let's sit outside anyway.'

Peter and Emily arranged the garden chairs and set drinks on the table.

'You won't believe how timely your call was, Peter. It was clever of you to work out how to get authorisation to contact me on my mobile without being detected. You've helped to bring years of undercover work to a climax. The least I could do was to give you an explanation. Not just for the events of recent weeks but for the past fifteen years or so. We, sorry, the Masters — forgive me, I've secretly lived the part for so long now — had no idea that Sarah had made so much progress with communication with the Visitors. As you know, she was reticent about reporting it at the Council meetings. She kept saying that she was close to a breakthrough and that there would be a further update at the next meeting. I went to see her at Saracens Farm. It gave her quite a shock at first. I explained how important it was for me to make contact with the Visitors, as it could be the final chance to make a difference to what was about to happen with the rollout of the Sect's plan. I suggested that you could be in danger unless immediate action was taken. She quickly agreed on the condition that I did a deal with her, which she asked me to keep secret. I was concerned that Françoise was watching and listening from an upstairs window and ushered Sarah further away from the house. She said she would arrange contact and asked me to come back later that day when Françoise would be out.'

'Why were you worried about Françoise,' said Emily. 'She's one of ours. She told me about her concerns for Sarah and how she had been acting strangely.'

'It was for her own safety and mine. I wasn't sure whether she recognised me and might have made a connection with the Masters. If she said something out of place to the wrong person, the plan could have been scuppered. I went back the next day to talk to Françoise, to let her know that Peter could be put at risk, given the loss of confidence in him by some of the Council members.

'What happened when you went back to see Sarah in the

afternoon?' said Peter.

'It sounds almost laughable. She took me to a clearing and told me to lie down next to her. I was to empty my mind completely. She said that once I was fully relaxed and "in tune", the Visitors would flow through me. She said they would analyse my thoughts and feelings by temporarily taking control of my mind and body. It would be safe, as it had been when they had taken other people. They would know everything about me, my knowledge and thoughts, my motives and intentions. There seemed nothing to lose. She explained that she had done it many times and had come out of it safely. I felt like an ageing hippy.'

'Do you think she had her own reasons for keeping her contact with them secret?' said Emily.

'Definitely. As I said, I promised not to tell. I do believe, though, that my presence, being regarded as one of the Masters, gave her additional credibility.'

'Is that because the Masters have been in direct contact with the Visitors?' said Peter.

'No. Like the Council, they have accepted the gifts and devised ways of using them to meet their own ends. In the same way that Lisa and Rachel's attempts failed to elicit a response, the Masters' efforts were similarly unsuccessful. That's not to say that they didn't understand what we humans were trying to talk to them about. It's just that communication was one way. They are so far ahead of us and so in control of the situation that they have no need to justify their actions.'

'Tell us about the communication — lying in the field with Sarah. Did it work? What did it feel like?' said Emily.

'It was so strange; unlike anything I've ever experienced. It took a while to properly get into it. To let go and let this "network" of vegetation and fungi integrate with my internal processes. And then, suddenly, it happened. It sounds laughable, but I was at one with the Visitors through the network of trees and plants: there were no barriers between us. We were a single entity.'

'It sounds like they were magic mushrooms,' said Catherine.

'I know, I know. That's the amazing thing. To discover that this whole intelligent framework, which we knew nothing about until a few years ago, surrounds us and that we can plug into it is a complete revelation.'

'Tell us exactly what happened,' said Peter.

'I'm coming to that. Once I felt connected, I was aware that my whole being and thought processes were being shared. It was incredible: thoughts were exchanged, not in words — that would have been far too slow — but as a sort of digital analysis. That's the closest I can describe it. I felt that information was being exchanged and analysed at the speed of light — I had no secrets. I knew instantly that they understood everything about me and that my continued existence in their universe was at their sole discretion. Not only me, the entire human race. If I had a single thought or emotion, it was one of complete submission. They knew enough to decide in an instant whether I, or anyone else, should continue to exist.'

'Did you have any control over this process?' said Peter.

'No, none at all. I felt as if a flood of data was being methodically switched through a series of gates to examine the consequences of all my thoughts and beliefs. I have to say, it appears to have worked. They have taken action on what they discovered. That is why the world is a different place today from what it was a few days ago, or would have been, had I not undergone the process.'

'How's that? I don't understand. You'll need to explain,' said Emily.

'They acted upon what they found — and quickly. As I'm sure you are aware, Thursday marked the end of another twenty-five-day period. With Peter's control process in place, you were able to verify that none had been taken from Templewood. I can tell you that six hundred and twenty-five were taken worldwide. I can also confirm that these were all senior members of the Sect, operating in many countries. Unlike the others who were abducted, these will not be returning.'

'Are you saying what I think you're saying?' said Peter. 'That from examining your mind they targeted six hundred and twenty-five people that you had identified who should be taken out of action. What makes you so sure that they won't come back?'

'Yes. It's the best thing that could have happened. It's taken me and my colleagues years to compile the list of those Sect members in a position of power who represent a danger to humanity. I'm certain we won't see them again. There was something in their communication with me, something I can't define but of which I'm sure, that confirmed they would not be seen again.'

'What happened to the benign dictatorship?' said Emily. 'All the talk about improvements to farming, ecology, health and education. All the stuff we've been hearing about the elimination of poverty, disease, famine and planetary damage, the new world order where oppression and wars would no longer exist?'

'It's true. These are the objectives and ideals that many of the top Sect members aspire to. Unfortunately, a minority with a controlling interest saw these goals as a short-term stepping stone towards implementing their own idea of power. People with little regard for human rights and equality, interested only in fulfilling their personal ambitions, at whatever cost. You will remember that, throughout history, the Sect has drifted in and out of power through various political and governing movements. Power corrupts. During every period of major influence, they eventually lost sight of their guiding principles, betrayed by individuals whose self-interest betrayed their ideals. This falling from grace is not confined to the Sect; you can find evidence of similar instances in most examples of long-term government. In the case of the Sect, their ambitions are worldwide. Hence, the greater the effect, the greater their inability or lack of control to stick to guiding principles.

You've heard the quote before, Emily, that the stream is clearest near the spring.'

'How did you and your colleagues manage to identify a network of this size?' said Peter.

'It wasn't easy. As with all forms of espionage, one of the challenges is to work out whom you can trust. That's why it took so many years. One false step could have set us back to zero. Fortunately, advances in technology came to the rescue. We developed an encrypted communications app for the sole use of the Masters. We convinced them that it was developed internally, here in Templewood, which it was. Unbeknown to them, we were able to monitor every conversation. We created a directory of all of their members and recorded their allegiances. We then read this into visualisation software — the sort used by the police and the military — to map the relationships between people, data, locations, property, events, and so on, to provide historical and predictive links connecting those individuals. It saved us years, possibly decades.'

'How did you manage to develop this app secretly in Templewood?' said Emily.

'I thought you might have guessed that. It was built by Lisa with no other help. This was one of the reasons she was invited here. She did an amazing job, developing it in secret in a few weeks. She really threw herself not the challenge.'

'I had no idea you'd met Lisa. She never said anything. How did you make contact with her?' said Emily.

'I asked Arthur to introduce us. I had to ask her to keep our discussions secret, even from you, as I'm sure you'll understand. That wasn't the end of it, though. We still had the problem of coordinating action across countries and continents to effect regime change within a secret organisation. That's where the Visitors have stepped in and provided the solution. If we'd been forced to coordinate taking these people out in a military-style operation and it failed, all hell would have been let loose. They would have stopped at nothing to get their way or their revenge. You only have to remember the Templewood Summer when they were prepared to risk the destruction of the planet to attempt a foolhardy scheme that could never have succeeded. And those people were still in place!'

'None of those taken was from Templewood, I believe,' said Catherine.

'Correct. There is no-one with any real influence in Templewood. Although Templewood is at the centre of many of the Sect's activities, no other Masters are based here. As you know, the Council has no real power. So, you can deduce that the Visitors decided to focus accurately on the key targets. Unlike those previously taken, these will almost certainly not be returning.'

'What's in it for them, the Visitors? Why should they care what happens on a small, badly run planet, unconnected with the rest of the universe?' said Emily.

'I can think of several reasons. In the short term, improved governance by removing the reckless among the Masters will provide stability. We know the Visitors are interested in salt, which we have in far greater quantities than we could ever need. I've been told that they are likely to target the Atacama Desert and the Salar de Uyuni in Bolivia. And quite possibly, they will take some trace minerals, which we can also spare. My theory is that their own planet may have been running out of salt for hundreds of years. They knew this and, centuries ago, they decided Earth was a good source. They wanted to build a relationship with its inhabitants so that they could extract it without conflict. That's why they have been giving us gifts and sorting out problems for years through the medium of the Sect. They were aware of the potential for us developing climate problems as a consequence of negligence. From early times, as far back as the Egyptians, they infiltrated the population…'

'… through the Goddess Isis, who imposed laws and helped protect nature,' said Emily.

'Precisely,' said Michael. 'Another reason they might be interested in our planet is that they are wary of our primitive forays into space. How will we act beyond our own world in the future?'

'It'll be ages before we pose a threat to other worlds. Until now, the Visitors have been the only confirmed extraterrestrial life form,' said Peter, adding, 'as far as we know.'

'The rate of exploration is likely to increase exponentially. As far as timescale, who knows whether the Visitors' perception of the passing of time is comparable to ours. For all we know, a thousand years of our time could pass in a minute of theirs. We shouldn't forget, too, that they may be acting out of altruism or as a space police force and possibly not alone.'

'Are you sure this is a good deal?' said Peter. 'We may have been complicit in the sell-out of the planet.'

'It's the best we have, the only one on the table. We've shown ourselves to be responsible as a race by not tolerating dictators. We have to hope that they respect, or at least recognise, our good intentions as well as our weaknesses. We have no hold over them other than the ability to accelerate their understanding of us and our planet. Once they have all the knowledge they need, they will make their decision. They will decide whether they wish to leave us in peace and move on, after taking what they need, or occupy the planet in harmony with us, or destroy us.'

'What do you think they will do?' said Emily.

'We know that their intelligence and maturity as a species are way beyond ours. We can now tell from the size of the Visitors' mission — the number of spaceships — that their population is far greater than ours. I think it unlikely that they will want to colonise us unless as one of many outposts. I would like to think that they would regard us as a stepping stone on their journey across the universe to find a larger, permanent home. Neither do I think they will want to destroy us. They could have done so already. Despite the many weaknesses of humankind, I believe they recognise that we collectively have good intentions. Nevertheless, they are aware that we are too slow to act together when there are signs that things are beginning to go wrong. And whatever we do or do not do, at present, our activities are limited to this planet. They don't represent a threat to the wider universe with which the Visitors are more familiar. Our best hope is to become a stage on an intergalactic Silk Road. A trading post from which we benefit on equal terms. The original Silk Road was an enormous force for peace and cooperation and a major cultural exchange for thirteen hundred years. This could be the beginning of our place on a new Silk Route, provided we act rationally and play our part responsibly, adapting to the new order. We can't justify projecting our moral code onto them. Their values may be completely different. On the positive side, we know that, at heart, the vast majority of Earth's inhabitants wants little more than to live in peace, free of hunger and disease.'

'I confess, I have reservations about the forcible removal of a large group of the Masters. If we support the Visitors eliminating people, doesn't that make us as bad as those we are replacing?' said Emily. 'Wouldn't it have been better if the Visitors had imprisoned them in some way instead?'

'There are some evils that are so bad that they have to be totally eliminated. There's no room for weakness or complacency. If these people were allowed to live, there is the possibility that they could build up support for their views and methods and get back into power. Believe me, Emily, both your mother and I have seen so many instances of this. Our whole training is based on taking firm decisions, without emotion, to achieve agreed objectives, to maintain the safety and freedom of the democratic world.'

'A laudable ideal and, don't get me wrong, one that I agree with,' said Peter. 'However, we are no longer free. In fact, we weren't before. The difference is that we didn't know it. With the arrival of the Visitors, the level of real power in the world has moved up a floor.'

'It's so different now, here in Templewood,' said Emily. 'It all seemed so glamorous when we were here in our teens. We're in a different world now. It doesn't make much difference what planet people, or other resident beings, are from. Our petty squabbles, here in Templewood and across the world, have been put into perspective.'

'Do you think that they'll stop taking people now?' said Catherine.

'That had crossed my mind,' said Michael. 'It's possible that they will see that part of their work as complete. They've experimented on the Templewood residents, and they have removed the offenders from the Sect. They have no need to continue. That's one way of looking at it. On the other hand, we've seen that there are longer term effects on those who are taken and returned.'

'I've heard that there has been some activity close to the spaceship,' said Peter. 'We think they might be preparing to leave.'

'That makes sense,' said Michael. 'They've reached the end of one phase of their plan. They've gathered knowledge and helped us make changes, both through the gifts and their intervention with the Sect.'

'Where do we go from here, now that everything has changed?' said Emily.

'I guess we learn to adapt to a new world,' said Michael. 'Not that it is new, it's changed because we now recognise that it was different from how we thought it was. Your mother and I have decided to go back to city life. I've had enough of the world of secrecy and deceit. Arguably the world will be a better place now, with less poverty and significant levelling up. Safer, too: nations will think twice before embarking on hostilities, now that they know the Visitors have such powers of intervention. We could be on the cusp of a new era of peace and equality. As for your mother and me, we plan to spend some quality time together for the first time in twenty years. We need to get to know one another again. How about you two? What are your plans?'

'I'll stay on here for a while until I'm confident things have settled down,' said Peter. 'Rather like after the Templewood Summer, really. It's a time of change and will need to be properly managed. I was hoping that you would be able to help me with the changes in the Sect, to use your inside knowledge.'

'I can certainly put you in touch with someone who can help. I know your work here is valued, especially over the past few months when you have been forced to deal with so many challenges. What are your plans, Emily?'

'Templewood is not for me. Perhaps I'll try to pick up where I left off. Not in a provincial newspaper, though. Print is the past now, and not many have fully adapted to online. The problem is how to climb out of that level. It's a world that cares more about paper qualifications and who you know, rather than what you are capable of.'

'I can help you there,' said Michael. 'The Sect will want to spread its message globally, share its good news and promote a spirit of cooperation and international friendship.'

'Thanks very kind of you, Dad. I don't think that's the right solution. I can't complain about cronyism in one breath and jump on the gravy train the next.'

'That's not what I'm suggesting. You have many under-used talents. What you don't have is contacts with influence. I can introduce you to global decision-makers. You will have unprecedented access to key players. Our family connection will give you credibility, in the same way that Lisa and Rachel were identified as suitable candidates here. Nevertheless, you will be earning your keep.'

'Hmm, I suppose that's a possibility. As a freelance journalist, I'd be in control.'

'There may be a better opportunity. How does the role of global press officer for the Sect sound? I'm sure the terms of reference could be drafted to suit you. You'd have a large team reporting to you. It won't be an easy ride; there will always be dissenters. The trick will be to emphasise the positives of the changes underway while not flinching from reporting those areas in need of attention.'

'I don't know what to say! That would be such an enormous leap. I can't demonstrate having had the experience to justify the appointment.'

'Yes, you can,' said Michael. 'Unbeknown to you, you have friends in the organisations in which you have worked. I have seen copies of some of the serious journalism you have produced that has been suppressed. Accounts of corruption and other crimes covered up to protect the circulation of those newspapers. First-class stuff that never saw the light of day, recognised by senior editors who were powerless to publish for fear of their own jobs.'

'How do you know about this? How could you know?'

'I may not have been around very much over your lifetime, but I have been watching over you. One thing you will have learned from your adventures is that the Sect has influence in many places. There was no way I could intervene at the time. It wouldn't have been right, and it would have risked blowing my cover. It's payback time, Emily — you deserve it. You don't need to make a decision now. I suggest I arrange a few informal discussions. You can then make up your own mind. I won't try to influence you — it will be entirely your choice. What I do know is that you will be fully capable of succeeding. Enough of the future, let's enjoy the present together.'

'One more thing,' said Peter. 'How was it that when I asked Gygges if he could arrange for me to meet one of the Masters that it turned out to be you?'

'I thought that was obvious,' said Michael. 'Gygges was the only person in Templewood who knew that I had infiltrated the Masters. He played the villain for all those years to avoid suspicion. He saw what a rough time you'd been having and how your credibility had been eroded. It was fortunate that you chose the moment that you did to request a meeting. When he spoke to me, he told me, quite apologetically, about your mindfulness proposal. I was sceptical of it, believing that it was a creditable but desperate attempt at a solution. Of course, he didn't know, and neither did you at the time, that Sarah's work was about to yield benefits. When you made the connection and persuaded Lisa to hack the communications network, well, everything came together at the right time. It could all have ended very differently. It's been a lesson in perseverance. It shows that when you have the conviction that you are right, you should never give up.'

The Villagers

'You've done a great job here, Lisa. We're very grateful to you. Are you sure we can't persuade you to stay on?'

'In some ways, I'd love to, Peter. The work has been satisfying, and I feel appreciated, which is always good for your self-esteem. I know that if I were to, I'd quickly become bored. The work is largely done here. I need a new challenge, possibly with a Government or cyber-security organisation in the wider world. In the short term, I'd like to spend some time with my mother, perhaps take her on holiday to give her some respite from the care home. I'll be able to afford a carer to accompany us now.'

'I can understand that, and I'm sure we can help you find a new cyber position through our worldwide contacts. You can, of course, expect glowing references.'

'Thank you. I'll miss many of the people here. I imagine there must still be plenty for you to do, now that we're living in a different world.'

'Yes, nothing can ever be the same. We can't undo our awareness of the Visitors. I can see lots of positives… People will realise that they are a small part of an ever-widening universe of which humankind is not the dominant species — far from it. I'm hoping that this will lead to a greater communal spirit and celebration of our identity. The original aims of the Sect in improving equality remain valid.

The diseased branches have been removed, encouraging the healthy parts to thrive.'

'I'm pleased Rachel wants to stay on here. She told me that she intends to. Despite everything that's happened over the past months, her real work is only just beginning. She's looking forward to focusing on communications research and learning methods; and applying her theories to the next generation to attend the school. I know she was disappointed that our work on the Golden Record came to nothing.'

'That's not true,' said Peter. 'Michael told me that it was an enormous benefit. It allowed the Visitors to understand so much more of our civilisation and outlook. He said it came through while he was communicating with them. There were things they knew and understood that could only have come from that source. I must have a chat with her to reassure her. Thank you for letting me know.'

'That's good. I'm sure she will appreciate that. How about the local people? Do you think any will want to leave, assuming they're allowed to?'

'Not really. People have a comfortable life here. Those who do move on do so typically within the Sect's network. They have personal and financial security, good health care... Most have satisfying work. Take the farmers, for example. They are the same all over the world. There's nothing a farmer likes more than to grow a successful crop or herd. They also enjoy moaning about the weather. Anything less than perfect that detracts from the ideal growing conditions is regarded almost as a failure. Like a baseball batter: once their average falls below one hundred per cent, it can never be that figure again. They'll continue to strive for the perfect crop, albeit the new hybrid species.'

'What about Carlos?'

'He's in his element. He's always been excited by new scientific opportunities. The Visitors have opened up all sorts of new possibilities. Like many here, he is in control of his own microenvironment. Dr Hadfield, too. There's a massive task to be done taking the children of Sect members worldwide and giving them the education and training to equip them to become responsible world leaders.'

'And Dr Jay? I found him scary at first.'

'Dr Jay has mellowed and become more compassionate, though he probably wouldn't thank me for saying so. Now that the problem Masters have been weeded out, he will be in a more comfortable position. He'll be able to practise his profession in the way he was trained to. As for others, you've seen what a unique community we have here. Arthur will be stepping down as mayor soon; I can't imagine him adapting to anywhere else. There's going to be a lot of change and rebuilding to adapt to the new world.'

'Will you stay here, Peter?'

'Yes, although I'm looking forward to occasional trips outside to see my family. I've been here for fourteen years and, for various reasons, mostly relating to my family's security, I've been obliged not to leave. I still have work to do, and it would be best if I stay for a while to re-establish my credibility. It took a dip for a few weeks, and I want to reassure people that I'm very much onside. I hope that everyone can now see I was right and in no way disloyal. It's a shame that I can't persuade Emily to remain longer. She doesn't feel she has added to the process other than to support me, you and Rachel. Still, she's had enough excitement, both now and fourteen years ago. Not many people can claim to have witnessed such key events at different times, one of which almost changed history, the other that did.'

'I'll miss you, Peter. Do you think we'll ever meet up again?'

'I'll miss you, too. And Rachel. Who knows whether we'll meet again? Quite possibly, if you were to take up a position that we recommend you for. Let's not be sad; we'll organise a party before you both leave.'

EPILOGUE - SPRING

A Child Is Born

'Such eyes, such beautiful eyes.'

'But why, Sarah? How could you betray us in this way? You told us that there was no risk of genetic mutation or fusion to create new species.'

'I wanted a child, more than anything else. Can you imagine what it's like to be the last person born in the village and have no hope of having a child of my own? And it's all down to the fertility problems that have plagued Templewood for years, which everyone knows are caused by the historical research work at the base. The Visitors respect me as an individual. They don't feel sorry for me like everyone else here or value me purely for my work. I learned how to communicate with them through natural means, the tree root mass and vegetation, in the way nature shares information and warns of dangers. All I have done is to speed up the process of discovery. As for betrayal, I've helped unlock the channel through which the planned excesses of the Masters have been thwarted. If I hadn't kept it secret and instead had announced my discovery at the Council meetings, I could have been killed. Where would that have left us?'

'But the child, Sarah, the child…'

'Surely you must have realised that if the Visitors can create complex plants, they can create complex sentient beings? This child will be the first of many. A new race of hybrid beings with enormous intelligence and speed of thought. The combination of the Visitors' advanced intelligence, technology, powers, combined with human empathy and the enhanced natural resources of this planet, under their protection, will ensure a better future for all. Our place on the Silk Road is assured.'

* * *

ABOUT THE AUTHOR

Owen W Knight is a writer of contemporary and speculative fiction. His works include Another Life, described as 'It's a Wonderful Life for the 21st Century' and The Invisible College Trilogy, an apocalyptic dystopian conspiracy tale for young adults, described as '1984 Meets the Book of Revelation'.

Owen was born in Southend-on-Sea at a time when children spent their days outdoors, creating imaginary worlds that formed the basis of their adventures and social interaction.

He has used this experience to create a world based on documented myths, with elements of dystopia, mystery and science fiction, highlighting the use and abuse of power and the conflicts associated with maintaining ethical values.

Owen lives in Essex, close to the countryside that inspired his trilogy.

Lightning Source UK Ltd.
Milton Keynes UK
UKHW010615140922
408843UK00006B/269

9 781739 630928